CW00471931

Heir of Doom

Heir of Doom

The Roxanne Fosch Files Book 2

Jina S. Bazzar

Special thanks to my family and everyone who supported this journey, and of course, the blogging community—for all the tips and incentives and encouragement you gave me.
To Tyler Colins—for putting up with all my shudder-worthy mistakes.
To Katja S. and Carol Winge—for your honest feedback.

The battle of will is the hardest and most brutal of all. Depending on the circumstance it might very well leave you broken and bleeding, though never a physical wound to be seen. A shell, perhaps, in the worst occasion.

I must know, since I've been fighting this battle for the better part of my life, between my human part and the Fee–or Unseelie.

The dejected, kind part and the revengeful monster.

I don't always win. Or my human side, who I like to think is the one on the driver's seat. But occasionally, that ugly raging side of me, the thing I try to keep buried deep inside wins the upper hand-and heads start rolling. Of course, the Unseelie inside is cunning and clever and when my human takes over again, it tries consoling me what I did–what *it* did–it had been for my own good.

I have killed before. Many times, though it was always a spur-of-the-moment thing without a second thought; it was never without conscience, and buckets of regret and guilt always followed toe in toe.

Now that it's been confirmed a monster slumbers in the depths of my soul, this battle of wills has taken a new importance, a new urgency.

I must always win.

Against all odds, no matter what, or how or when–I *must* win.

–Roxanne Fosch

Prologue

I should have accepted Vincent's offer to drive me home. It was painfully cold outside, with brown piles of slush heaped on every corner, keeping the sidewalks icy and slippery. Frigid gusts of wind froze my nose, my neck, my lips, even my eyeballs. Of course, I should have expected it. After all, it was the end of December in the city that never sleeps. Despite, or in spite of the angry heavy gray clouds and the freezing temperature, it was a cheerful, optimistic time. Red and green lights danced to happy Christmas tunes, fat and skinny Santa Clauses rang bells of every size and shape, along with their eternal companions, the elves and reindeers. And there were the decorated trees. Live ones, plastic ones, sagging ones, printed ones. All glowing cheerfully against windows of vehicles, shops, homes, restaurants, boutiques.

It was the season of holidays, forgiveness and optimism, of exchanging gifts, of celebrating. Of friends and family reunion.

Of *hope.*

The city seemed fuller than before, people spilling out of every gap, every doorway in herds, crowding the streets, malls, shopping centers. It seemed like all the homes in the city and surrounding suburbs were empty.

It was peaceful to my lonely soul. Or serene I guess was the word.

The day had been sweaty and tiresome under Vincent's relentless training, and although my muscles still screamed from the straight eight hours exercise I endured, I wanted to walk home. It was a six-block walk from the compound to the small ground-floor apartment the Hunters, the government-affiliated group who policed our kind, had provided me for a living, and most days I completed the track with no problem. Today, however, seemed colder than any of the other evenings.

With my hands tucked inside the pockets of my black coat and a wide ruby-red scarf covering the bottom half of my face and neck, I hurried home, seeing only the legs of people with my head lowered against the cold.

That's why I didn't spot her at first.

I was contemplating a white spot on my black boot, wondering if it was toothpaste or if I'd spilled some yogurt from this morning when I sensed eyes on me and glanced up. She stood like a statue against the current of pedestrians, a boulder in a river.

The chill racing down my spine had nothing to do with the early evening sudden decrease in temperature. Nothing to do with the vague recognition in the back of my mind I was unable to place. Nothing to do with the fact she stood waiting for me. No, it was the nervous anticipation in her eyes, black that shifted to yellow after a second of meeting, and the almost non-existent silvery shine of her blue aura.

Dhiultadh. A rejected.

An Unseelie.

A child, no older than ten, a small eleven maybe.

My steps didn't fault, my expression didn't change. My uneasiness was covered underneath an indifferent facade.

When I was but two feet away, I stopped. There was no need for pretense. I knew she was there for me; she knew I knew.

Someone bumped my shoulder and called me a filthy name I pretended not to hear.

Her eyes, now as black as mine, were keen, wise in a way no child should have the right to have. Her body was short, bearing on the side of thin, but she was dressed nicely and expensively. The brands were just another thing from my childhood I could no longer name from the top of my head. Her dark-brown coat reached beneath her knees and was twice as thick as the black one I wore.

The recognition in the back of my conscience stayed out of reach, and when I pushed, it slithered farther away, like a slimy snake.

"Hi," she said, her voice clear and pleasant.

I cocked my head to the side, as if it would make it easier for me to reach that thing in my brain eluding me. "Hi," I replied.

This time the hesitation was longer. "My name is Mwara Longlan."

I inclined my head in acknowledgment, "I'm Roxanne."

"Mwara Whitmore Longlan," she clarified, a little embarrassing blush adding more color to her already pink cheeks.

A dim bulb in my head brightened.

"You're Elizabeth's kid," I said, my tone almost accusatory.

She nodded and looked away, scanned around for a second. Maybe because she'd glimpsed the flash of suspicion in my eyes.

"Can we go somewhere to talk?" she asked.

I looked around, searching for familiar black eyes. There were thousands of people nearby. One could be hiding on Broadview and I couldn't tell if she was alone.

This wasn't good, my inner voice said, but I nodded to the café across the street, unwilling to go anywhere farther with Elizabeth's kid, even if I lived a block away. We both made our way across the clogged street amidst screeching horns and shouting drivers, the season and rush hour working in our favor.

At the glass door of the crowded café Mwara hesitated. She looked up at me, an open expression of doubt and–fear? Making her seem younger.

Despite my better judgment, I gave her a reassuring smile and held the jingling glass door open, then followed after her.

Like any other venue in the city, the café was packed with bodies of every shape, size and color. Rock music competed with shouts and laughter. Here and there a lonely figure sat, either texting on a cell phone or just browsing the time away. The smell of coffee and sweet pastries permeated the air, along with undertones of sweat, perfume, and–not so pleasantly–feet. Nonetheless, my stomach reminded me I hadn't eaten anything since that morning. I shrugged out of my coat and motioned to the line with my head. Mwara nodded, shrugged off her coat. She was wearing a nice creamy button-down shirt with lilac butterfly buttons and brown slacks. Cute.

It was loud and lousy for a conversation, but Mwara didn't seem concerned.

I stopped at the back of the order line and Mwara signaled to the rear with a finger and pointed chin, telling me where she was headed.

Because I had nothing else to do but wait for my turn, I watched her move away. Like any other predator I ever met, she moved with a fluidity I associated with jungle cats in a role.

Her hair, brushing her shoulders, was a shade darker than I remembered from the photos, a honey color, a shade darker than Elizabeth's.

By the time it was my turn to order, I gathered a few things by watching her whenever there was a clear line of sight. One, if she was sent here by someone, they didn't want to be seen. Two, whatever reason she had to approach me, it made her nervous.

She avoided direct eye contact with me, looking instead at the people around her or at her hands, lacing and unlacing on the tabletop. Sometimes she lowered them under the table; sometimes she drummed her fingernails on the vinyl top. Now and then she'd scan the room in a way that would have made a detective proud, absorbing everything. Not once did she glance in my direction. If she did, not once did I catch her.

I ordered a hot chocolate for her and plain black coffee for me, then couldn't resist the delicious looking brownie with hot chocolate sauce and yummy chocolate chunks. I got four pieces of those.

If Mwara didn't want any, I'd eat them all.

It took me a few minutes of maneuvering through the crowd to reach the table Mwara was seated, but the coffee and brownies reached intact. I handed her the hot chocolate and two brownies and placed the rest on the table before pulling the chair to the side so I'd also monitor the entrance.

We ate in silence, and while I savored the rich-flavored sweet, Mwara was clearly building up her courage to speak. I gave her room instead of prodding her, acting like I had nothing to do and nowhere to go but sit there in that crowded place and get fat.

Someone shouted an obscenity to my right and laughter followed. Mwara glanced up, scanned the room once before returning her attention to her plate.

After she finished both the brownies and hot chocolate with not a word but a few surreptitious glances when she thought I wouldn't notice, my patience began to wear thin.

"Elizabeth knows you're here?" I asked in a normal voice, glad I wouldn't need to shout.

She shook her head and focused her gaze at something above my right shoulder.

I held back a sigh and tried again. "It's a long way between Sacramento and here. She must be worried, searching for you." I added the latter casually, wondering how much trouble she'd be in–if she was telling the truth.

She shrugged and, still fascinated with something behind me, said in a clear voice, "It's a fast track through the paths."

Oh? That gave me pause. Hmmm. Should ask Vincent about that. If traveling from coast to coast was faster through the paths, it was something I wanted to learn. I'd call and ask as soon as I got home.

I mean, if Mwara ever got the nerve and said whatever it was she came here to say.

"So how's your mom?" I asked half an hour later, after I exhausted all the small talk I could think about. School, finals, grades, boys, weather, bicycles, tennis.

To my surprise, Mwara met my eyes straight on and it was bone-deep fear I saw there. She was trying to hide it, and a small tremor fluttered in my stomach. Something happened to Elizabeth. Mwara had really come alone.

And... I hardened my heart against worry. I didn't care. She could die a million deaths from here to tomorrow and it was none of my concern. *Not. My. Concern.*

Except for a part of me, deep down but not well buried, still thought of her as my mother.

I shooed away the fear, telling myself she wouldn't–and hadn't–minded whatever torture I had gone through. But what Mwara said next wasn't even in the list of things I'd expected her to say.

"Is she?" she asked, and along with the fear, defiance shone in her eyes.

"Is she *what*?"

"Is she my mother?"

For a moment my mind went blank, then understanding began to dawn.

I leaned back and studied her. Her cheeks were flushed–from the cold or emotion, I couldn't tell. And the fear, now that there was a context, could have been either worry or anger. "What makes you think she's not?"

She waved a small hand. "I, I eavesdropped in a meeting a few days ago, and I heard about you, what happened... why... what the scientists did. My mom's part in it." Her eyes lowered in shame. After a few moments, she looked up again, and panic filled her eyes. It was the oh-shit expression when you realized the building was coming down with you in it. It was so prominent, so there, I couldn't help it; I reached across the table, took her small hand in mine and gave a gentle squeeze.

"What is it?" I asked, but I already knew.

The contact seemed to have reassured her. She squeezed back, took a deep breath before blurting, "What if she's not my mom and she sends me there, and I can't run away and no one comes for me? I'd spend years and years being tortured like you, and no one would even care. What if she's not my mom and there's already a contract for me? I'll be eleven in a few weeks. What if I get my period early–like when I'm eleven instead of twelve and I can't shift either? Linda Johnson got hers when she was nine. It was all the school talked about for days.

What if the scientists don't wait for puberty like they did for you? Will they take me then?" A small sob escaped and she lowered her head, her hair concealing her face from me. Her hand shook, but she didn't let go.

Pity prickled my senses. A thousand thoughts ran through my head, reassurances and comforting words. Things I could say to ease her mind and send her home with no worries. Underlying them all was the question: what if she's not? In my wildest imagination, all the scenarios I had conceived as the reason for Elizabeth's desertion, her not being my mother had never been one of them. For one, we had the same eye color and pale complexion. There had always been a resemblance, and coming from the same species had never been the reason for it in my mind. For instance, Mwara had the same black eyes, though her complexion was darker than mine. Or Elizabeth's.

No, I had no right to give her all the reassurances she came searching for without knowing if they were true.

I could say the words, give her a pat on the back, then wash my hands of a problem not mine to begin with, but I'd been there in that place. I'd lived her fears for a decade.

Hell, I'd just begun to shirk the fear less than two months ago.

Perhaps if she had waited another few years to approach me, after the fear had faded enough to loosen the tight grip it held around my neck, dictating my every action like a general still uttering orders at the sidelines of my conscience, perhaps I could have reassured her enough and still go home with a lighter heart.

But the fear that this security wouldn't last, that I'd wake up in the morning and realize it had all been a hallucinogenic-induced dream, held back all the words.

As if sensing my thoughts, her shoulders slumped and began shaking in earnest. I kept hold of her hand, although it was a small comfort.

"If I stay with you…"

"No," I said at once, shaking my head, but she wasn't looking at me. Because my denial sounded abrupt even to my ears, I softened my response. "They'll find you. There's Diggy and there's Vincent–"

"Would you come for me?" she clenched my hand tightly in hers, strength no ten-year-old should possess. "Would you come? If they take me, would you come for me like you did for Archer?"

"I, I don't know."

She let go of my hand, and I missed the warm connection.

"I can talk to Vincent," I offered, not knowing what else to do.

"No! Uncle Vincent would only send me home. If there's a contract for me, he won't interfere."

I fell quiet, at a loss for words.

"I'll run away now. I'll jump leeways every time I sense someone,"

"No, no," I cut her off, "No, don't do that. What if there's no contract? What if whoever you sense is just someone trying to bring you home? There are other things out there, monsters with more horrific intentions than the PSS. It's too early to say." I frowned, because maybe she was right. "What about your father? Why don't you talk to him?"

"If she's not my mother, then he isn't my father. And he left for Austria yesterday. I don't know when he'll come back." She got up, wiped at her tears with the sleeve of her coat before shrugging it back on. "I have to go. If she finds out ... please don't tell anyone I came to see you."

She was afraid of Elizabeth. I had never been this afraid of her when I was growing up. Even when I did something worth being grounded for, I had never been this afraid. Maybe she wasn't her mother after all and treated her badly. I had been the first, so she was more tolerant? Maybe her disciplinary punishments were fierce with Mwara?

I followed Mwara outside, my mind spinning with questions. Before Mwara crossed the street, I stopped her with a hand to her shoulder.

"Look, Mwara, If ... if they take you, I'll vouch for you." It wasn't a small thing, considering if I vouched for her I'd be announcing we were part of a pack and she was my responsibility. I could, inadvertently, be putting myself back in the clutches of the PSS.

"And if that doesn't work?" Meaning I wouldn't have the voice of the clan behind me. They might even cast me as a rogue, just to thwart the claim.

"I don't know," I murmured, because I didn't think I had anything more to give her. I wasn't going to storm the PSS HQ and compromise my life or my freedom for her, or for anyone else.

She nodded once before she crossed the street, ignoring the honking vehicles she passed in front of. The clan might not back me up, but if the Hunters did, the PSS wouldn't be able to keep her. But she'd be my responsibility from then on, and I had no idea what I'd do shackled with a kid. I watched her until she was lost in the middle of all the chaos before I turned and made my slow way home, just a block away.

PART I – The Bait

Chapter One

"It's a trap," Vicky, my childhood best friend informed me from the kitchen, peering at me with eyebrows furrowed. "That Elizabeth is trying to set you up for some fall."

"Why'd she do that for?" I propped my legs on the coffee table. I only had enough time to place my keys on the kitchen counter before Vicky arrived for our girl's night in, which we had most nights since Tommy called her. She'd hung up with him and called the number he'd given her, and after the first awkward meeting, it was like there wasn't a ten-year gap in our friendship.

I'd relayed my encounter with Mwara while I showered and changed into my version of PJs–flannel pants and an oversized T-shirt. "She got rid of me ten years ago." I sighed with relief as I stretched.

In the kitchen, divided from the living room by a half wall, Vicky fiddled with shredded ice. She shrugged, dumped ice in the blender and emptied a can of Mountain Dew after it. "Women are evil creatures. You never know why they do the things they do." As if we both fit under a different category.

"I don't know. Her fear was real enough," I said.

She paused what she was doing to look at me. "Can you, you know," she rotated a slender, manicured finger, "tell when someone is lying?"

"I can sense strong emotions. I guess it's like sensing the truth."

Vicky frowned. "But what if she was afraid of something else? Like, Elizabeth sent her to deceive you and she was afraid she'd fail? You'd sense her fear, but not the reason for it."

I stared into her earnest blue eyes, baffled. "Where do you get all those convoluted ideas?"

She shrugged again and took out a can of condensed milk from the grocery bag she'd brought with her. "You haven't learned the deceitful ways women behave yet. That's why I'm here. To point out other women's evil plots." She gave a cheeky grin and a shallow dimple appeared in her right cheek before her expression grew serious. "Why didn't she go to that guy Vincent, or that other one, Dimple? You know the one you're hung up on his *friend*?" She gave me a pointed look.

"*Diggy*, and I'm not hung up on Logan," I said in a defensive tone.

Diggy, aka Douglas, aka Doug, was the owner of the basement apartment Logan took me to after I returned from the Low Lands five weeks earlier. He was also a rejected, a Dhiultadh from our rival clan. And a respected member of the Hunters team, one step below Vincent. It had been his position with the Hunters that kept him from accompanying us to Archer's rescue attempt. He'd been the one to mark a trail for us to follow in the woods surrounding the PSS, and to supply us with the equipment and weapons we'd used. I remember Logan explaining that Doug, or Diggy as he was known by the Hunters, wouldn't accompany us in the event we got caught and needed someone to bail us out.

Vicky gave me a pitying look, but didn't argue. Logan had become a tired topic between us ever since I told her about him, something I've regretted dearly. She thought I was pining for him, which I so was *not*.

I glanced down at my wrist, at the bracelet he gave me. Arianna's bracelet, he'd called it. I'd used it to blow up an entire building into smithereens, along with whoever stood between it and me. It was a simple trinket, with five copper wiry straps braided together, supporting a jet-black rock in the center. Once, back when he'd first given it to me, the rock had been blue and had hummed with power. Now it was nothing but a simple bobble, devoid of anything. I wasn't sure why I didn't take it off, but I was *sure* it wasn't because I was pining for him.

"Strawberries in the fridge?" Vicky turned, not waiting for a reply, her long blonde hair swishing in her ponytail. She opened the refrigerator, scanned the contents once, grabbed the strawberries and shut the door, not blinking twice at all the raw meat stuffed inside. Amazingly, she had waltzed into my life five weeks ago and accepted all the absurdity I'd dumped on her without batting one eyelash.

She added the strawberries and condensed milk into the blender, pulsed it a few times.

"Anyway, why didn't she go to them?"

"She doesn't trust them." I leaned my head back on the couch and closed my eyes.

"Exactly! See what I mean. You're the last person on earth she should trust, and you're the first one she turned to."

I frowned. "Maybe because she knows I understand her fear."

Vicky snorted, but let the topic drop when her phone rang. She glanced at the screen and scowled. "God, doesn't he understand a letdown? I'm ignoring you so I can move on!" she shouted at the screen. "Guys are so dense," she muttered, throwing the iPhone on the counter.

"David?" I guessed, David being the last guy she'd gone out with. She bared her teeth in a savage grin and turned the blender full-on, silencing the ring. Behind her, a small shadow, no bigger than a child's appeared.

I dropped my feet to the floor and sat forward. The shadow unfurled itself, gaining at least a foot in height and stalked forward. The creature itself wasn't visible. Its shadow was that of a thin child, if one overlooked the pointed, arrow-like ears and tail. The protrusions on its back were small; no one would guess they were wings without seeing them.

A few feet away, Vicky was oblivious. His approach was slow, pausing when the blender turned off and again when Vicky reached for two glasses inside the cupboard. When she reached for the next cupboard,

I held my breath, sure she would see him. She grabbed a plastic bowl and returned to the blender, the shadow unnoticed.

I exhaled, watching the shadow slip closer and closer. It was going to get her. Vicky whirled around, her eyes focused on an empty spot behind her. "Gotcha!"

Frizz blinked into existence an arm's length away.

Features softening with an affectionate smile, she said again, "Gotcha. Shouldn't have tried to get this close. You could have jumped from back there." She turned her back on him then, and he hopped on, like a small monkey.

"Are you sure you're human?" I asked, sagging back on the couch and returning my feet to the coffee table. "Frizz is supposed to be a predator. He's supposed to catch his prey unaware." I aimed a disgusted look at him. "It's embarrassing."

Vicky flashed a smile, poured the cocktail in both glasses, then poured the rest in the bowl for Frizz. He let go of her and grabbed for it.

It was amazing how the two had bonded. And to think I had kept him a secret from her for the first two weeks, afraid of what her reaction would be. I'd thought she believed me unhinged, making up a story about fairies, vampires, scientists and werewolves to account for all the years I'd been gone. Then, one evening, while I'd been giving Frizz a shower, she walked in unannounced. She admitted later she had expected to find a guy inside, and I admitted a part of me wanted to share Frizz with her but was afraid. She took to him at once, treating him like a small child, or an intelligent animal.

"How old do you think she is?" she'd asked as she'd patted him dry.

"Frizz is a *he*."

"How do you know? She doesn't have the equipment to be a he."

Both of us looked down at Frizz.

"Well, he doesn't have the equipment to be a she either," I'd argued in a reasonable tone. Frizz sat on her lap, docile as a puppy, as if he had been doing that his entire life. Vicky patted his round head and scratched his ears and rubbed his neck, cooing and lisping as if Frizz were an infant.

They have bonded ever since.

"I caught her shadow when I reached for the bowl." Vicky handed me a cocktail glass and sat beside me, propping her legs beside mine on the coffee table. "I ordered pizza from Oliver's down the block. Half cheese, half veggie."

In the kitchen, Frizz made a slurping noise, and both of us turned to watch him drink the smoothie.

"You're going to spoil him. He's a carnivorous predator, he shouldn't be slurping strawberry cocktails."

Vicky gave an unapologetic smile and reached for a bag. "I got us three movies. I figured you'd be too tired for a night out on the town. Besides," she added, "it's a circus out there. I swear, half the human population is out this weekend. I practically had to shovel people out of the way to get here."

I grunted, recalling how packed the city had been earlier.

"So, are you going to talk to Vincent about the kid on Monday?" Vicky settled back and the movie trailers began.

I took a sip of the cocktail and studied her face. Although the question had been asked in a no-nonsense tone, the concern in her eyes was obvious.

"I don't know," I replied, almost sure I wouldn't.

"Come on, Roxy, can't you see this doesn't make any sense?" Vicky implored, trying not to show the concern I was beginning to sense and see.

It did to me, but I didn't say that out loud. Vicky wouldn't understand. Not because she was dense or unsympathetic, but because she hadn't been there and known such terror.

"Look, just think about it over the weekend. If by Monday you're still unconvinced, then at least test the waters, you know, throw in some random questions and see if there is any reason for the kid to be worried. If you find there's no root for her fears, then at least you could give her some peace of mind."

I considered her words for a moment, then nodded in agreement, if not for Mwara's peace of mind, then to ease the worry from my friend's eyes. "Alright. I can do that."

Chapter Two

I didn't get to talk to Vincent on Monday, or Tuesday or Wednesday, or that entire week. Every time I saw him he was in a bad mood, though bad was a gentle word. And it wasn't as if I could ask, "Yo, Vincent, is Elizabeth Mwara's mother?" I wanted to ease into the topic–just in case the kid was right–and, he gave me no opening to broach the topic.

Most of my training happened in the gym and was crammed with muscle building, endurance building and some focus building–keeping my body occupied with exercise while Vincent explained about traditions, cultures and rules of the preternatural world.

He'd make me run for hours, bench-press, do pull-ups and push-ups until I could no longer command the muscles of my body. He'd be right there beside me, running and pressing and talking, rarely breaking up a serious sweat.

Once, I'd complained about the hard and tiresome training, and he'd informed me my complaining only emphasized how behind I was, that most preternaturals my age could endure double what I was being given, and have enough energy to go dancing half the night.

Still, as demanding as he was, if he sensed I was lagging, he'd stand by to give me a chance to catch my breath and talk about past assignments, joke about funny mishaps, or feed me information about the preternatural community I couldn't fathom needing. But for the entire week before Christmas, I exercised alone. Vincent would drop by, check on me and make sure I wasn't slacking or being bothered, instruct me on the next exercise before stomping out, his mood as foul as rotten meat. I was aware this was due to a case and the fact he wanted to lead it, but Roland wasn't letting him go. Because of me?

Despite his lack of supervision, by the time five o'clock came around, my muscles would be so sore, even sitting or lying down hurt. I dreaded when it was time for my extra-ability training, afraid Vincent wouldn't have much to work with. Or he would find more than I was supposed to have. There were times I couldn't wait to find out myself, but whenever I recalled losing control to that raging monster inside of me, goosebumps broke out all over my body. What if I lost control to my Unseelie side again? How would I be able to tell right from wrong? Would I care?

Natalia, a powerful witch and a Hunter member I had yet to meet, would be responsible for my training after I mastered hand to hand combat. Vincent reassured me he'd be present in case something unexpected happened, but the fact he'd tried to reassure me made me uneasy.

The weekend brought Christmas and the loneliest time of my life. This time last year I'd worked as a waitress in a small restaurant back west. Vicky left to Sacramento for the festivities, and it was only me and Frizz at home, listening to the laughter, the ho-ho-ho of Santa Claus through thin walls and the TV.

Early Monday morning I walked the six blocks to base, something I did most days and evenings rain or shine. I guess it was a way to prove to myself I no longer needed to hide. I paused by Maggie's Heaven–the bakery where I met Mwara–their coffee was fantastic. The order line was just as long, but the barista was steady and fast, filling up orders with efficiency. The tables were mostly empty, including the one where I sat with Mwara, and I wondered if she was still living in fear, then pushed the worry away. I'd try to talk to Vincent today, and as I'd promised Vicky, if Mwara was worried for nothing, I'd tell him about her apprehension so someone could reassure the kid. No one deserved to live in terror, not even Elizabeth's daughter.

The Hunters' base, located in upper-east Manhattan, took up the first four floors out of the ten in the Edgar Lon-Kis building. The gym, an open floor plan, took up the entire fourth floor. The first floor housed a few conference rooms, Roland's and Vincent's offices. The second floor held the offices of the NSA Intelligence Preternatural Team, where the virtual team kept tabs on preternatural cybercrimes, whatever that meant. The third floor held the offices of the field members, a lounge area and a crib area for those who needed to crash before a job or after one. A cafeteria and a lounging area were on the ground floor, but aside from the time when Vincent gave me a tour, I'd never been there.

Not finding Vincent in the gym or near the lockers, I headed to the first floor to check his office, knocked and stuck my head inside, but there was no one behind his utilitarian desk. The bathroom door was closed, and I hesitated. Was it polite to knock at the bathroom door to check on your mentor? Not knowing if I should, I moved to his desk and leaned against it to wait. The surface was as neat and uncluttered and organized as the owner. A stack of papers was pushed to one side, a yellow file was placed atop. The name Fin was written on the edge with bold red lettering, and I picked it up, the stylized handwriting familiar. I'd seen it before... in Elizabeth's office, back when she'd bring work home.

My eyes moved to the photo underneath the envelope—a teenage boy with sharp green eyes and piercings on his eyebrows and lower lip. The military buzz cut no doubt was meant to make him look older, but the mischief in his eyes and the crooked curve of his lips canceled the effect. There was nothing in the photo saying he was a preternatural, but the fact he was here, in this office, spoke volumes. There was a dark spot to the side of his chin, just under the edge of his lip, and I picked up the photo to examine it closer, discovering a heart-shaped mole. Cute, I thought, returning the photo to the stack and the file on top. I glanced at the closed bathroom door.

"Vincent?" No one responded. I straightened and knocked once, and when no answer came, I tried the handle. Empty. I left the office and strolled over to Valerie, Roland's assistant.

"Hey, is Vincent in with Roland?" I asked, but the woman just typed on her laptop, ignoring me. Had it not been for the fact I've seen her talking to other members, I'd have said she was deaf.

I glanced at Roland's closed door and hesitated before turning and making my way to the elevators. If I were into the habit of carrying my cell phone, I could have called Vincent and spared myself the chase.

The doors to the elevator parted with a ping and a swoosh as I neared, and Tony, a werewolf with yellow eyes and dark brown hair, stepped out. She gave me a warm smile and a wave as she passed, and I waved back. She was one of a few who held no grudge against my human hybrid status, and I was grateful for that.

I stepped into the car just as the doors closed, belatedly realizing it was going down instead of up. Sighing, I leaned back against the side of the car. When the doors parted, it wasn't to reveal the ground floor or the parking area, but a dim corridor, with Jeremy the Bear waiting on the other side.

I took a step forward before I could think better, and he moved aside to give me room to pass. Embarrassed to step back, I nodded and stepped onto the plush carpet, acting as if I knew where I was going. Unlike Tony, Jeremy the Bear wasn't friendly, but he wasn't hostile either.

When the doors closed and the mechanical whir sounded, I sighed and searched for the stairs.

The corridor stretched long and far, with a few dark-wood doors on both sides, all of them closed. None were parallel to the other, and the arrangement seemed somewhat odd. I paused near the closest door–the one to my left–noticing carvings of symbols in the woodwork. I traced one, recalling it from a book Vincent gave me to study. A rune? Or was it a sigil?

Curious, I pressed my ear to the door, but there was no sound on the other side. I tried the handle next. Locked. I glanced at the elevator, somewhere up on the second floor. I moved to the door on the right, and like the first, there were carvings of runes or sigils on it, but no sound of inhabitants on the other side.

What was this place?

There were nine doors on this floor, four to each side of the corridor, spaced well apart, with one more at the end, directly across from the elevator. They all had carvings on the woodwork, all shut with no sound or light coming from underneath.

I was moving back to the elevator—no stairs on this level—when a noise to the left caught my attention. I inched toward the closest door. My heart raced, and although I chastised myself, I reached for the handle nonetheless. I Listened, heard the odd noise again, but couldn't decipher it. The handle turned in my hand, and I realized with a thrilling rush it wasn't locked.

An invitation to come in. What was on the other side? An image of a bright red room with a small draped table and tarot cards came to mind. Or, a sterile room with a steel slab and men dressed in white lab coats...

I pushed the door open with a foot, and what I found on the other side was so ordinary, it took my mind a second to shift gears. A spacious well-furnished living room was not what I'd expected. Small nooks on the wall supported flickering candles, providing illumination and a soothing ambiance. Deep colored cushions were pushed against the walls in a comfortable Japanese seating arrangement. Various weapons decorated the walls, but it was the guy standing in the middle of the room my eyes focused on.

Douglas Vemourly, aka Diggy as he was called here in base—or Doug, the friend Rafael and Logan had talked about. My superior, considering he was third in command.

He was naked to the waist, chest gleaming with sweat, feet bare and eyes closed, doing a macabre combat dance, a thin plain blade in each hand.

My eyes moved to the weapons adorning the walls, modern and antique, of different sizes and shapes, all gleaming with proof of a recent oiling. Cannon guns, axes, rapiers. Even a mace, dull with age, hung below a candle. But the prize went to the swords; they were countless. Some were long and slender, some wide and small, some ornate with precious stones. Dull blades, metal blades, golden blades, sharp blades, pointed blades, serrated blades.

A single, closed door stood to the left, no doubt leading to the rest of the apartment.

My focus returned to the man, now doing an amalgamation of motions, thrusts, arcs, pirouettes, even a semi-diagonal flip, kicking an invisible opponent, blade arching down on a second. Realizing I had no right to be there and Ashamed of myself, I was about to turn and leave when Diggy half turned at the waist, the powerful muscles of his back flexing, and threw a blade at me. It passed my ear with a loud frightening whiz, embedding in the doorframe. His hazel eyes blazed with anger, his breathing harsh, his sandy hair sticking to sweat-wet temples. It made for a formidable image, and if I had my phone with me, I'd have risked taking a photo. Not wanting to give him enough reason to strangle me, I turned and beat a hasty retreat, realizing too late I should have at least apologized.

Back on the first floor–I was on Level Minus One–I tried Valerie once more, only to be stone-walled. Again. Not having the patience or will to play her games, I bared my teeth–something she ignored–and marched to Roland's office without permission, knocking once before pushing open the door. Valerie didn't even twitch.

Roland wasn't in his office, or the conference room adjacent, so I returned to the gym, expecting to find a pissed-off Diggy waiting, and feeling ashamed of myself. I had better manners than that. As I started an awkward warm-up, I heard Asra and Raji, both fire mages, talking about a threat with a vampire gang turning unwilling humans into fledglings and that Vincent had been assigned the case.

Half an hour later, I was summoned to Roland's office and was dressed down for barging into it without permission. Well, it was just an admonishment, where he pointed out Valerie was out there to inform members when and if he was available, and it was disrespectful both to the rules and to him to shrug her off. I nodded, head lowered so he wouldn't notice my clenched jaw. I could almost see Valerie gloating in the next room.

Resigned, Roland pointed at the chair across from him, laced his fingers and regarded me as if I were an unruly child he didn't know how to handle.

"Vincent gave Valerie a training schedule for you to follow in his absence," he said, and I nodded, not pointing out Valerie had ignored me when I'd asked after him earlier. "He assured me you'd have no trouble following the schedule on your own until he returned."

Another nod. "When will he return?"

Roland's lips pursed for a moment. "The situation down south is delicate. The fledglings, they are like children in need of firm guidance. Vincent will need to locate the sire, provide appropriate homes for the new fledglings and deal with the media." He grimaced at that. "If all goes well, a week tops."

Meeting over, I moved out to Valerie, half expecting her to ignore me again. But without a word, she handed me several papers clipped together, filled with instructions for the entire week. Without saying thank you, I took the stairs to the fourth floor and devoted the coming days to the notes Vincent had made.

Chapter Three

On Thursday evening while I walked home, head lowered, body braced against the wind, something happened. One step, I was planning to bake some cookies to please Frizz, the next, the hairs on my neck stood at attention and goosebumps broke out over my body.

Night had fallen, but you wouldn't know that for all the lights illuminating the streets and surrounding shops. I raised my head, searched the people ahead, checked the reflection of those behind me on the windows of passing cars and shops. There was nothing I could pinpoint, no reason I could find for the alarm.

A nervous ball rolled inside my stomach, a feeling of prey being stalked, and my gut had never led me askew.

There were eyes on me. Predatory, hunting eyes. It wasn't rush hour, but there were enough cars on the street, enough people on the sidewalks for an attack to be noticed.

Someone bumped my shoulder, and I glanced sideways, expecting to see someone brushing by. Instead, I found a woman, long hair bound in a high ponytail, keeping pace with me. She was shorter by a few inches, dressed in a nice short burgundy jacket that looked expensive and not suitable for the frigid temperature. Her neck and hands were bare, the cold not affecting her. My heart skipped a beat, not for the fact a prickly memory told me I'd seen her somewhere before, or the strange thick air about her. No, it was the dark red, almost purple aura surrounding her that kicked my fear awake. That and the horrific fact her face flickered between a corpse-like mummy and a beautiful brunette.

A vampire. An ancient one if the dark purple color mixed with the red in her aura was any indicator.

"There is an alleyway ahead," she said without preamble, her accent one I couldn't place. "We will turn into it together."

"No, we're not," I replied calmly, despite my churning anxiety. Maybe I didn't know how the preternatural community worked, but I was no fool either.

A knowing secretive smile lifted the corners of her lips, the kind that said the other shoe would drop soon and she was very pleased. The guy coming from the opposite direction must have sensed the menace oozing from her, because he gave her a wide berth, his complexion draining of color.

"I have your friend. If you don't come, I'll just have fun with her alone." She looked at me and the empty, total lack of humanity in her blue eyes was like an icy splash to the face. "She's young and fragile. I'm afraid she won't last long."

She pressed something in my pocket, against the palm of my hand, picked up her pace and moved away, tucking her hands in her pockets.

Angelina Hawthorn of Bond Street, was the thought that came to mind. Like an unexpected bolt of electricity, I jolted, recalling where I'd seen her before: in the mind of the mercenary vampire who had attacked me in Marian's B& B all those many weeks ago. He'd been the reason I'd ran from that small town, even before I'd met Logan. The starting point to the domino fall that brought me here to New York.

And I'd killed him with a psychic ability I still couldn't fathom.

I watched her go, my mind whirling with thoughts. When she turned into the alleyway, I snapped out of it.

My first thought was Vicky was in Sacramento. Relief was an acute pang that left me weak.

But when I glanced down at what Angelina pressed into my hand, a honey-colored lock of hair that looked so familiar, relief turned into grave fear.

Vicky!

I didn't think twice. I followed Angelina. If she had Vicky with her… if she had Vicky with her… God, I couldn't even finish the thought. Now would be another brilliant time to be carrying my phone.

Damn you, Roxanne, damn you. So what if Roland could track you through your phone?

I cursed myself into the alleyway, knowing I couldn't risk Angelina torturing my friend because she thought I didn't follow fast enough.

A few feet in and it was as if I entered another dimension. The noise of traffic was still loud, the burning smell of exhaust still thick, but there was a muffled quality, as if I had entered a room and shut the door. Or maybe it was all the blood roaring in my ears.

The acrid smell of piss and decay got stronger the farther I got, my footsteps echoing in the confined space. I didn't slow or tried being silent, I was sure Angelina was aware of my presence.

In any other situation, I'd have stopped to consider where I was going, figured any possibility of escape, and tried to form a plan. Hell, if this was any other situation I wouldn't have been so foolish as to follow a vampire whose lover I killed a few months earlier. This had trap written all over it. I clenched the lock of hair and hurried after the vampire.

I could barely see ahead and was aware the light from the mouth of the alley marked my presence to anyone in front. I was attuned to every noise, every pair of scurrying feet, trying to pick any nuance with my other senses. That's what saved me–the air displacement behind me. I ducked, rolled, and squished something rotten and disgusting beneath my weight. What was with me and stinky alleyways? I finished the roll, jumped up and pushed Angelina as hard as I could. There was a grunt and a hiss, but instead of hitting the wall like I'd intended her to, she pulled on her brakes and did a one-eighty, barely losing momentum.

She rushed me fast, grabbing me by the throat. I garbled out a choked sound, slashed her wrists with my talons and kicked her hard. She let go with a grunt and I backed away, talons ready.

She came at me, a whirlwind of shadow and teeth, and I dodged too late. Nails and teeth dug deep into my bicep, ripping muscle when I pulled away. I punched her, catching her in the shoulder, and although my well-formed muscles were strong, she didn't budge or twist with the impact. I kicked and hit only air.

I backpedaled to the wall, keeping it behind me as I searched and listened to the darkness. "Vicky?" I called. "If you're here, grunt. Make a–"

I rolled to the right, atop more disgusting things, and jumped up. I searched the darkness, left, right, back. Where did she go...? And then I caught the shadow of a figure ahead. I rushed forward, not sure what I was doing. One thing Vincent taught me early on was to discern when it was better to stand and fight, when it was better to run. I'd have rather run, but I couldn't leave Vicky behind.

Angelina dodged the punch I aimed at her face. I aimed next at the moving shadows, and my fist found empty air. Damn, she was fast.

"Look, I never meant to"—kill—"hurt your friend. He came after me. I was just trying to live my life when—ooof." Something heavy and hard hit me from behind and I head-butted the wall. Stars appeared in my vision, along with vultures and crossed bones. Warm blood started trickling down my face.

"He was my first," A low voice said from somewhere to my right.

I straightened and turned in that direction, head pounding. Just on the other side of the alleyway, life went on as usual.

Talking was good. I pressed a hand to my head, tried to put some pressure on the wound. Talking was good. It meant she wasn't trying to kill me, right?

"I'm sorry. He wanted to enslave me. He wanted to take me somewhere and be my master." Silence met my words and I cursed. Wrong thing to say. "He sounded like he was a great guy. Had a sense of humor too," I babbled on.

"Did he talk about me?" she asked, this time from my left.

I spun in that direction and there were two of her. Maybe I had a concussion.

"Yes, yes. He couldn't stop talking about you." Angelina snarled at the lie, and I hurried to add, "He called you Angelina Hawthorn of Bond Street." She hesitated then, and I sensed her indecision.

"Liar." The shadows split. There was another person beside her. I moved back, trying to find the wall again. Instead, I hit a body. I whirled and slashed, but it seemed like their night vision was way better than mine. A strong hand caught my wrist and pulled, bringing me flush with a man's broad torso. I think I smelled gardenias, but WTF, there was nothing but urine and garbage here.

"Vicky!" Strong hands pinned down my arms and I tried to buckle free, wiggling and stomping my foot on the guy's foot. I may have been a fly, so easy was my struggle thwarted. Angelina stalked forward.

"Tell me what happened to my Jacob," she demanded.

"He ran away when I refused to become his slave. He was afraid of you." A sharp punch to my stomach had me wheezing and pulling myself forward, trying to double over and ease the pain.

"Try again."

"I'm telling the truth," I began, but was cut off with another punch. I think she broke my lower rib. Or maybe ruptured an internal organ. The pain was unbelievable. Gasping, I stomped my heel at the foot of the guy behind me, high on the arch, putting all my pain behind the stomp. I heard the crunch of bones, a grunt and the arms pinning me loosened. I wiggled free, but Angelina caught me by the neck and pushed me back with so much strength, my throat closed and I gagged.

"Hold her," she growled at the guy behind me. She moved closer and murmured, "I'll just *drink* the truth out of you."

I was still processing her words when she bit me hard on the side of my neck. Atop the scarf and all. A stabbing, piercing pain moved through my body, making my knees weak, my weight supported by the guy behind me.

The pain, however, was nothing compared to the sensation of someone violating my private thoughts like so many discarded postcards. I could tell what she was seeing, and I tried to reverse the process, like I'd done to her Jacob. The moment the thought crossed my mind, Angelina latched on to it like a burr, sucking in all that horrible memory, "drinking" the truth of what happened.

She hesitated at the part where I pushed Jacob out of my mind and followed him into his, but she could also see the horror and confusion of what I'd done.

The alarm I should've felt at how weak I was warred for first place with relief when her fangs released my neck. My knees buckled with my heavy weight. The guy let go and I crumpled to the ground, a mess of limbs and weakness.

Angelina crouched, her eyes heavy on me. "It is interesting. So many people want you, but it was so easy to subdue you." She shifted and I cringed away. Everything hurt. I was so weak. My heart beat too fast, faster than it had ever before.

Gently, she touched a lock of my hair, the gesture belying the threat of her next words. "Killing you would anger so many, but I suppose a little fun won't hurt." She chuckled. "I can't speak for you, though. I do want you to hurt, agonizingly so." She tugged hard at my hair and the bite on my neck twinged. Blood oozed from the puncture, warm and sluggish. My hands morphed into talons–I had no clue when talons shifted back to fingers–and I prayed for an opening. I remembered how fast Jacob had been and knew Angelina would be faster, smarter.

"I will keep you somewhat whole, I promise, for I don't want to lug you throughout our journey."

"I'd rather die than be taken to your master," I croaked. God, it hurt to speak.

Angelina laughed. "Oh, but I have no master. I have business associates, many of them. No one owns me. I'm the one who owns people. Maybe I can make you one of mine. Hmm-mm. Maybe I should turn you."

The thought was terrifying, and I knew I was running out of time. I had to move, *now*.

"Where's Vicky?" Though I already knew. Either she wasn't here or she was already dead. I refused to believe the latter, not without proof.

She tsked, amused. "You're in no position to make demands, my dear."

"Just tell me where she is. Is she alive?"

Angelina leaned forward and lowered her voice. "I'll tell you this. You'll find out if your friend is dead or alive soon enough."

She stood and the other guy stepped forward, picked me up and slung me over a broad shoulder. I dangled for an instant upside down, blood flowing along my neck and ear before plopping to the floor.

The guy inhaled, and I mustered strength, heaved up, braced a hand on his back. His hold tightened on my leg, anchoring me. Teeth gritted against the coming pain, I twisted to the left and dug my talons deep into his neck, and pulled in one swift movement. I put a lot into this motion and felt, even as I fell, unconsciousness dragging me under. How much did Angelina drink?

I dropped with a wet splat, my arms too weak to prevent my face from making acquaintance with concrete, and I think I blacked out for a moment because the next thing I knew I was upright, with Angelina's fists clenching the lapel of my coat, her face inches away. I could sense her rage, a hot wave of buzzing electrical wires.

"I'll kill you," she hissed and pushed me away, hard enough that I was airborne for a whole second or two. I hit the wall hard, cracking my head and elbow. My teeth clacked, and a piece broke loose.

Incredibly, I fell upright, but the effect was lost when my knees buckled and I went down. God must have loved me because I didn't black out again. Or maybe he hated me. Angelina rushed at me in a blur of fury and punches, and I tried to fight back, to slash at her. She batted my hand away with her fist and I felt–and heard–the bones of my hand break on impact, and couldn't help but scream at the sensation of things no longer in their proper place.

With a roar loud enough to be heard above screeching horns, she picked me up again like a wrestler and threw me against the next wall. I tried to brace myself against the impact, but I never hit it, never fell to the ground.

I opened my eyes, unsure when they'd closed. I was in someone's arms. Feminine and fragrant, the sweet, citrusy scent something I recognized.

"This is not your fight, Fee," Angelina spat from a few feet away.

I tried to stand, and was placed on my feet. I braced a hand on the filthy wall beside me, the other pulsating with pain, glanced sideways, already knowing what I'd find.

Leon Ora Maiche, aka Lee, the enforcer of the Seelie court. She was just a shadow, but the tall, proud Fee warrior was unmistakable, the silvery glow of her aura one I'd hoped never to see again.

"This Dhiultadh owes me a favor," Lee said, her voice cold and unfeeling. "Until the bargain is met, she belongs to me."

I sensed Angelina's eyes on me, an odd heavy sting of speculation. "She killed two of my scions, she owes me a blood debt."

"Ay, she did." Lee shifted her body in my direction, though her face stayed turned toward Angelina. "Did you kill her scions unprovoked, Daughter of Fosch?"

"No. I was attacked first." It hurt to speak.

"It is settled, then. This Dhiultadh owes you not," Lee concluded.

Angelina said nothing.

Lee shifted. "She owes you nothing. Leave now, before I decide mercy is not worthy of you."

Angelina hesitated for a second before she turned and fled into the night.

Lee's eyes fell on me. I shivered. Aches that had been muted awakened with vengeance, but my mind was clear of any fog. "I don't owe you for saving me today," I croaked in lue of thanks.

"You should go before she returns. Stay away from the dead." With that said, she disappeared.

It took me forever to take off the dead vampire's jacket and replace it with my bloodied, ripped coat. It was huge on me, but it was better than walking into the street looking like I'd been attacked by a pack of rabid wolves. There was nothing I could do about my battered face save for wiping the blood with a linen handkerchief I found in the pocket of the big jacket. I zipped it closed all the way, the scent of gardenias overwhelming. At least he had good hygiene.

I weaved out of the alleyway, flipping the collar up to cover my neck and ears. I got some dubious looks from a few passersby, but most ignored me.

The moment I stepped into my apartment I headed for my cell phone, lying on the counter where I'd left it. I dialed Vicky's number from memory and waited. It rang once, twice, three times. "Come on, come on, come on." It went to voicemail.

I closed my eyes and lowered my head, a prickling sensation burning the corner of my eyes, clogging my aching throat. I sank to the tiled floor and braced my aching head over my knees. Frizz appeared and leaned against my side just as the cell phone started ringing. I jumped to my feet with a boost of energy I didn't know I still had and grabbed for the phone. The display read V, with an image of her profile smiling at something to the side.

"Hey."

"Roxy! You won't believe what happened today."

I sank back to the tiles, hugging Frizz as I listened to my friend's voice.

I didn't go to base the following day. Instead, I extended the weekend and drank lots of orange juice, trying to build up strength as fast as possible. No one called to inquire about my absence, and although I was relieved I wouldn't have to explain myself, I was also hurt no one noticed I was missing.

Later that evening found me locked in an internal argument on whether I should call Roland or not. On one side, how could I explain Lee to him? On the other, Angelina had known where to ambush me, had known about Vicky–enough to use her against me. Could she have gathered information about me on her own? She mentioned business associates. I didn't put past a few of the Hunters to hire someone to get rid of me. In the end, it was the possibility of a Hunter hiring after me that prompted me to make the call. I knew Roland wouldn't put up with someone offing me after he went through the trouble of releasing me from the PSS.

Within thirty minutes of my call, he was knocking at my door.

He took one look at my grayish complexion and ushered me to the sofa. Without a word, he sat to listen to my story.

There was no impatience or annoyance as I took my time explaining what happened, starting on that rainy evening in Marian's B&B, leaving nothing out. I'm sure he'd seen the PSS's report of the vampire's attack–Jacob. Well, I left out a few details of Angelina's attack, like the fact Lee saved me. Because the Fee would have never saved me if not for our bargain, and I wasn't telling him *that*.

I admit I hadn't been prepared for all the detailed questions Roland threw at me, and could read the what-a-fool look he quickly concealed when I told him I followed her into the alleyway of my own freewill.

Once all the questions were asked and answered, Roland made a few calls, dispatched Hunter members to search for Angelina and to pick up a dead vampire from the alleyway–if there was still a body. It made me guilty, because what if someone else, a human, stumbled upon the scene?

Once that part was dealt with, He called Harry, a member of the Cyber team and asked all information available on Angelina Hawthorn be ready on his desk by Monday morning. I felt guilty here too, because Harry would spend the turn of the year stuck on desk duty.

"Would you like assistance healing?" Roland asked before leaving.

I almost said yes, before I thought better of it. I knew from previous conversations with Vincent that being able to shift to an alternative form meant instant healing. Only Vincent and Roland were aware of my inability to shift, though Vincent was hopeful I'd be able to one day soon, considering that Dratcha–the alternative beast with four arms and glowing yellow eyes–was a dominant trait, and I already had the talons.

If I accepted the help of a member to heal me now, I'd never be able to gain their respect.

"No, thank you," I said. "The worst was a broken hand, which healed when I shifted my hand a few times,"—and hurt so much I passed out—"and the loss of blood. Nothing some rest and orange juice can't heal." And a dentist, I thought, poking my tongue at the chipped molar. "I'll be back for training on Monday morning."

I must have sounded convincing because Roland nodded and left.

The weekend brought the end of the year and the beginning of a new one, and again I spent it watching TV beside Frizz and listening to countdowns and fireworks. In a few hours, Vicky would be cheering with friends on the other side of the country. I wished I had asked for the week off and gone down with her.

Awake and with nothing else to do, I checked e-mails and Facebook, finding that Vicky had posted tons of photos of herself, Tommy, and a lot of people I recognized but hadn't seen in years. I also found an e-mail from Vincent from last Sunday, detailing the same instructions Valerie had handed me on Monday. There wasn't another one for this coming week, and I presumed it meant he'd be there to pick up the training again.

Chapter Four

The following Monday arrived with Vincent still down south. That's what I assumed his absence meant. Not wanting to repeat last Monday's mishaps, I headed straight for the schedule I'd stored in my locker and memorized the entire session for the day. I changed into yoga pants, hesitated between a tank top and the turtleneck I had on. After a moment, I left on the turtleneck, deciding I didn't want to flaunt the bite marks on my neck. If someone from the Hunters sent Angelina after me, my presence here today was enough of a rub.

The moment I stepped onto the mats, I regretted it. Out of the twenty-six field members, only a handful took advantage of the fully-equipped gym. Since the day I'd arrived two months ago, I've only had the misfortune of sharing the gym with two or three other members at a time, but today was no such day. There were at least ten in attendance, not including me. With dismay, I realized all my not-so-favorite people were present.

The air inside the gym felt stifling, thick with challenge, the predatory pheromones like a live current in the atmosphere. It was loud, with shouted conversations from all directions, the sounds of weights hitting the floor and punching bags being jabbed, the combat rink in full use, all layered with the pungent odor of sweat and blood, old and new. I hesitated at the door, wanting desperately to turn and leave, knowing I wasn't tolerated, much less welcomed, especially with Vincent gone. But it would make me look weak, and weak was not the image I wanted to portray. I surveyed the room once, noticing with an inner groan all the machines were occupied and I wouldn't be able to follow the schedule in order. Apparently, crime in the preternatural world was slow at the beginning of the year.

I straightened my shoulders, ignored everyone and the snickering flowing my way, and marched stiffly, head high, to the edge of the mats and as far as I could be from everyone. Aside from their names–I had been introduced the first week to most–I knew what they were from the color of their auras. Nothing else.

So there I was, an outcast, even among the monsters.

And to think I'd tried to befriend some. It wasn't only the dislike filling the air with cold and disdain, no; some members were abrupt and rude, others downright hostile. Like Barbara, a were-hyena who had the misfortune of calling me a weakling and a human hybrid during my first week on base. Vincent had heard and dressed her down in front of other members, unknowingly making things worse with the intervention, indicating I needed protection. And now Vincent wasn't here to keep the Hunters at bay, and I was subject to their sneers and whispers. Was the fact Angelina's attack happened when Vincent was away from the base a coincidence?

I eyed the treadmills and the ellipticals. My training was supposed to start on either today, but all four machines were occupied. Jack Belle-meir was there, another were-hyena and Barbara's counterpart, the same guy I'd first seen in the MGM Casino the night I was caught and trapped by Remo in his penthouse. I was so beneath Jack; he didn't even notice when I entered or left a room.

I searched the people present, trying to spot a friendly face, found none. Figures. The urge to turn and leave got stronger, almost compulsive, and I gritted my teeth and started my warm-up.

Only a few of the Hunters had nothing against me, or didn't act like I'd killed their puppies and bathed in their blood, but most were from the Cyber team on the second level and they seldom interacted with us, the field members.

I once asked Tony what the Hunters had against me, and she'd explained it wasn't so much my human hybrid status, but the fact Vincent had exposed an eighteen-month operation to draw Remo away from the penthouse that day in Vegas to give me a chance to escape.

Seeing the guy was dead now, killed by yours truly, I didn't see why they were so wound up about it.

There was nothing I could do about my human hybrid status. However, if I could prove to them I wasn't the weakling they called me, and prove I didn't need Vincent or anyone else to look after me, maybe I could gain their respect, if not their friendship. And maybe I'd grow wings and fly.

* * *

One hour into training, Diggy walked into the gym.

I could tell, even from where I stood, his posture was stiff, his jaws clenched. He scanned the room once, his eyes settling on me before he began making his way to where I stood, his steps long, precise. I straightened, realizing his destination before anyone else did. Truly, I'd expected this confrontation to come earlier. I had no real excuse for being at his front door besides the fact I'd been curious.

I watched his powerful legs crush the distance, his air of indifference reminding me of Rafael, Logan's other friend. Although I didn't get to meet Diggy before arriving at base, Diggy's dislike of me, according to Rafael, had already been established. Still, I'd never been subject to any unfriendliness from him, or anything at all. That day in his apartment was the first time he'd acknowledged my presence.

As Roland's third, he was a well-respected and well-feared member of the Hunters. His entrance into the gym brought everyone's head up, including Bellemeir's, gaining respectful nods of acknowledgment. When everyone realized his destination, everyone stopped what they were doing and turned to watch, anticipating a confrontation.

I assumed, because of his stiff posture and the hard set of his jaw, he was still pissed. So it was no surprise I assumed he was here to give me the earful I should've gotten last week.

I was wrong.

He explained in a short and clipped tone the situation south with the gang was more complicated than Vincent and Roland had predicted, and given Vincent would have to infiltrate the legion, he'd be gone for an indefinite period. I heard what he said, but couldn't focus on his words. I'm not sure if the "message boy" role was as awkward to him as it was to me, so I just nodded politely, thanked him for keeping me updated. If the tightening of his eyes meant anything, I'd insulted him. I ignored the snickering that followed my gratitude, not knowing if there was a protocol I was supposed to follow, or if it was proper for me to turn and leave in the presence of a superior without dismissal. And it didn't help everyone's attention was focused on us.

Or the fact he was assuming the lowly role of a messenger.

And in my head, manners nagged me to apologize for spying on him last week.

I cleared my throat when the silence stretched, "Umm," I began, cheeks flaming with embarrassment, "I, I apologize for intruding on your privacy last week?" it came out as a question, and only made my cheeks grow hotter.

Diggy eyed me up and down, assessing me, and by the look in his hazel eyes and tightening lips, I wasn't measuring up.

For what, I didn't know and didn't care. He was a rejected from the other line, prone to hate me from the moment he was conceived. I said my piece, he said his. I told myself I shouldn't be offended by his disapproval. And yet I stood and waited for him to say something else.

Unlike Vincent's silvery-blue aura, Diggy's aura was as green as a were's, and although I could sense some kind of animal lurking under the surface, I couldn't tell what kind. No doubt it was some deformed beast like the Dratcha.

Still, I didn't like the way he was looking at me, as if he were measuring me for what I was worth, and was coming up lacking. I clenched my teeth, aware of the not so subtly muffled chuckles coming from the other side. Vincent may not be here to keep everyone else at bay, but this didn't mean I should tuck tail and lower my head to insults.

I raised my eyebrows, a suggestive gesture that said "go on", but he didn't get it. Instead, his brows furrowed, no doubt puzzled I wasn't groveling at his feet.

I crossed my arms, tamping the urge to check if the vampire's bite mark was visible. "If you're done ogling, I'd like to train now." My tone sounded bitchy, and although I mentally cringed, I didn't apologize. I didn't sign anywhere I was supposed to accept ridicule and humiliation well.

Someone guffawed by the machines, the sound cutting off when Diggy twisted his upper body to glare at the group.

Shit, this would get bad soon. Should I walk out and go home? Or should I take a page from Bellemeir's book and act like Diggy wasn't here? The former would be like signing my weakling papers, the latter a definite dress-down from Roland. In the end, it wasn't a choice. Stomach twisting, I turned my back on Diggy and moved away. Tai chi was next on the schedule; then, if the treadmills and elliptical were still occupied, I'd bench-press.

I moved to the corner of the mats and began the slow tai-chi motions, aware Diggy still stood, arms crossed, watching. Conscious of all eyes focused on us, waiting to see what transpired next, my motions were stiff and rusty, so I closed my eyes and concentrated on breathing.

Perhaps part of me was trying to show off, trying to impress, to prove I was good at something. I had become so familiar with this martial art, I could do it without thinking, the moves embedded in my muscle memory. Even Vincent praised me on my achievement, telling me it usually took people a lot longer to move so fluidly.

When I'd gone through all the motions Vincent taught me, I repeated them, aware the gym was way too packed. Besides, Vincent's schedule had said to do the tai-chi twice, though it hadn't been typed back-to-back.

"Is that all Vincent taught you?" Diggy spoke behind me, startling me. I hadn't forgotten about him, far from it. I hadn't expected him to come so near, to invade my private space. Stepping away, I turned and glared. He had about half a foot over me and at least a hundred pounds of pure, hard muscle.

He smirked, and I scowled in return.

"If you're done playing, let's go."

"Go where?" I asked, trying to remember if he'd said anything about us going anywhere while I'd been caught up in the tai chi.

"Train somewhere else." The muscle ticking in his temple told me he was out of patience, though his eyes remained calm, perhaps a little flat.

"No, thank you. I'd rather train alone."

Someone coughed in the group, and I wondered if it was real or mocked.

"Too bad," he replied and angled his head toward the lockers. "Now, unless you want to go barefoot, I suggest you change. You have two minutes."

By now, the entire gym stopped pretending they weren't watching.

A ball of nerves knotted in my stomach. "Train? With you, somewhere else?" An image of him downstairs doing a macabre dance flashed in my mind.

Diggy cocked his head, his eyes studying me. "Yes. I just said so."

"No, thank you. I'll train alone," I repeated, shaking my head for emphasis. The dawning realization he hadn't come to update me crossed my mind then. Diggy was third in command, which meant he took his orders from Roland or Vincent. And it was stupid and shortsighted of me to assume he came here to give me an update. No, he'd been ordered to fill in for Vincent as my trainer.

"I'm afraid that's not an option."

I glared. "Actually, it is." Short of dragging me and causing a scene, I wouldn't follow him out of here. And I couldn't see Diggy deliberately causing a scene. I should talk to Roland and see what else I could do until Vincent returned. He'd mentioned desk duty once.

I was already turning, trying to avoid more embarrassment and save face when Diggy moved. Fast enough to be considered a blur, giving me just enough time to dodge the punch. But not the kick square to my sternum that followed, flinging me backward and face down on the mat, unable to catch a decent breath.

All around the room turned quiet, save for my wheezing, panting breaths.

"Get up," he ordered, "We will train somewhere with no audience." With that said, he bent, grabbed my forearm and pulled me upright. There were green flecks in his hazel eyes, now blazing with anger.

The gym was so quiet, you could have heard a pin drop.

No whirring treadmills, no clinking metals, no moving feet, no punching bags, no labored breathing. Nothing to show there were people who'd been exercising hard just a second ago. I flushed with embarrassment. Slowly, the stabbing pain in my gut made way to anger.

Diggy's hand, still clamped around my biceps, squeezed hard enough to hurt as his eyes narrowed. He turned his head, glaring at no one in particular, but no one glanced away, the excitement of a superior kicking my ass worth the scolding. "Your meeting will start in fifteen minutes sharp. Anyone who isn't in the conference room within ten will be banned." He bared his teeth in a ferocious snarl and added, "Anyone still stinking of sweat will also be banned." Then his eyes returned to me and the room flashed white, and I was lifted and hurtled away. There was no ground, no ceiling, no walls, no sky, no earth. No air to breathe.

I reached for Diggy, the only solid thing in the universe, and clung to him as the world spun out of axis.

Chapter Five

I stood, afraid of what I'd find and turned, searching. Indeed, for as far as I could see, about a fifty-yard radius of dim lighting, the ground was nothing but packed, hard and cracked soil that hadn't seen water in centuries, the trees blackened husks and dead twigs of a life long gone, and in the dark sky, a dreadful and beautiful cluster of planets still stood, imperious and indifferent rocks that marked the universe with color and mocked my existence.

The Low Lands.

Exactly the way it had been when I'd been dragged here by Dr. Dean two months ago.

"Why?" I asked, my voice soft and low–to keep him from hearing my fear.

"To train," was his flat reply. He stood straight, unperturbed. There wasn't a single strand of sandy hair out of place on his head.

In contrast, my sweat ran despite the frigid temperature, my hair was in disarray, some sticking to my temples and wet neck. I clenched my hand into tight fists to stop their uncontrollable shake.

"No," I whispered. "No, you will take me back now," I said louder, straightening, ignoring the sharp rocks digging into my bare feet.

"No."

Was he the business partner Angelina had mentioned?

I narrowed my eyes. "There will be *no* training in this place."

"Oh? Who said you have a choice?" he asked, eyebrows raised.

I took a step forward, tightening my fists hard enough to feel my short nails digging into flesh. "I refuse," No sooner had I begun speaking when I was flung back with another kick to the stomach. This time the pain was intense, like tidal waves spreading from my midsection and outward.

"Then I will just keep beating you until you fall unconscious." Diggy circled me like the vulture he was, keeping some distance so I couldn't grab him. My breathing was short, shallow gasps of air that seemed to elude me. "Then when you wake, I will do it again. And again. And again until you have had enough and start learning." He stopped by my head and eyed me with disapproval.

"Go to hell," I wheezed between pangs of agony. There was blood in my mouth.

He chuckled, a grating sound with no humor, and crouched in front of me, his eyes cold. "Let me make something clear to you, love." He gave me a once-over, his eyes saying he wasn't impressed. "I like having to stick with you and endure your presence as much as I like to do paperwork, stuck inside a box-sized office in a crowded building. But I got my orders, and unlike you, I respect my chain of command." He threw a napkin at my face and surveyed me once more. "Now, you have two choices. You get up and learn, or you keep stubbornly refusing." He bared his teeth in a savage smile. "And I assure you, I will enjoy beating the crap out of you." He stood and said under his breath, "a human hybrid, no less."

I spat a wad of blood on the napkin and balled it into my fist. Soon the metallic taste was filling my mouth again, and I probed the shallow cut on my cheek with my tongue before spitting the next ball of blood at the ground between us.

I swallowed the next mouthful of blood, not sure I could afford to lose it again so soon after Angelina's attack, and ignored the rocks digging into my feet when I stood. The land was nothing but a vast emptiness of cold darkness, and I was way underdressed in a soft turtleneck and yoga pants. Still, my sweat ran, as if I were a slab of fat above an open fire pit.

"You," I began, stepping forward, fists clenched, trying not to step on needle-sharp rocks without looking down. "You are a despicable excuse of... of... shit," I finished lamely, unable to find a filthy enough name to call him.

His lips twitched. "Good enough." He motioned me forward. "Show me what you got."

I flew at him, talons out, wanting to scratch that smirk from his face.

He evaded me without effort, dodging my kicks, blocking my punches, always staying ahead, anticipating my every move, every step, every thought. His moves flowed as fluid as water, while mine were clumsy and uncoordinated.

I feinted right, kicked air, and went for his exposed arm. But Diggy had either seen it coming or he was that fast, grabbing my wrist and twisting hard, making me fall onto my knees with a painful gasp. I bent to diffuse the pain as he pulled my arm toward the nape of my neck, my nose hitting the hard ground.

He mimed stabbing me in the back with a finger, poking hard enough to bruise. "You're dead," he said before letting go and retreating a step.

"Lesson number one," he went on, circling me again, "Never leave your back defenseless, unless you want to be attacked from behind."

I waited for him to pass, jumped up, wanting to fight dirty, but again, he had seen that coming. He whirled, blocked my kick and punched me in the chest, the blow so effective, I had a hard time breathing. Even my heartbeat grew erratic.

A few feet away, he patiently waited.

An hour later, I was panting from my lame efforts, and Diggy still smirked, every hair on his head in place. My feet throbbed, skinned like fine fillets. I was aware of every single bloody footprint I was leaving behind. I eyed his sturdy, combat boot, the one he'd just slammed on my abdomen, hugged an arm around my middle and waited for his next attack. My stomach muscles were all bruised and tender. At that point I was not only in pain, but having a hard time standing up, staying conscious. My vision was splotchy, my head reeling. Diggy hadn't even broken a decent sweat. He was probably used to walking on burning coals or sleeping on a bed of needles. He probably didn't even have a nervous system.

When he took a step forward, I moved back a step. "You arrogant prick," I hissed when a needle-sharp rock dug into a previous cut.

Diggy chuckled, amused.

I saw red.

With a mad scream I lunged for him, and this time he didn't step away, but met me head-on, caught my wrists—mindful of the sharp talons—and twisted them outward and down. Then he pulled me forward until our faces were inches apart, his gaze going flat at the hatred in mine. He shoved me back, flinging me away like an annoying bug.

I skidded on the hard ground, teeth clacking on impact, needle-sharp pebbles shredding my backside.

I stayed down, my breathing heavy. How was I supposed to sit down when my backside was all cut up? Diggy's combat-clad feet paused beside my head, and I looked away, defeated beyond belief.

"Lesson number two," he said, his tone mild, "anger is a weapon. Unless you can control it, it will only be used against you."

He bent, took hold of my forearm and the world flashed white, and I was falling, falling, spinning out of control, thudding to a breathless stop on the blue mats of the training room, Diggy's face above mine, his eyes wild with exhilaration. The smell of my blood and sweat filled the room, mixed with the scent of the old and the new. The gym was so silent, I thought we were alone, then someone chuckled, and I closed my eyes, my humiliation complete.

When I opened them again, Diggy's face was still above mine, the exhilaration having been replaced by a calm facade. "You be here tomorrow at seven-thirty sharp for our training." He turned and left.

"Go to hell," I murmured loud enough to be heard across the gym. There was a collective intake of breath, and Diggy paused at the edge of the mat. For a horrible moment I thought he'd come back and flash us back to the Low Lands, but then he kept going, not once glancing back.

Chapter Six

I didn't go back to base the next day. Fortunately, no one came to drag me as I'd feared. It didn't matter if Diggy was the third in command and a superior; he was not in my contract and I refused to be subject to scorn and derision. Instead, I soaked my ribboned feet in warm water and bandaged the deeper wounds on my backside and the backs of my thighs, though the bleeding had long stopped.

I missed Vicky a lot. Her non-stop chatter, her laughter, her witty remarks. Her companionship. I hadn't realized how attached I'd gotten until she'd left. She was all the normal I had.

Grimacing in pain, I stretched my bandaged legs atop the coffee table and turned the TV on low for Frizz. He hopped beside me and settled down in his usual crouch, his wings limp. He smelled of the strawberry shampoo Vicky bought, his pelt softer than any animal had the right to have. I watched him for a moment, wondering if he was capable to miss someone. His ears flicked back and forth, sensing my attention.

With a deep groan I couldn't help, I leaned on the sofa and picked up the *Guidebook of the Preternatural*, flipping to an earmarked page about types of bonds, still trying to free Frizz. There was the bond of the clan, the bond of soul mates, the bond of motherhood, the bond of familiars, the bond of a pack, the bond between master and slave, the bond of bargaining, among many others that sounded so strange, even the titles had no meaning. Like the Chimera bond, or the one between a Volech and a subject. What was a *Volech*? I read them all, paying special attention to the bargaining bond and the master and slave bond, figuring our bond would fall under either.

There was nothing there to help, however. In the bond of a bargain, formed when a bargain was struck, the connection between the two would dissolve once the bargain was fulfilled. This was not the case between me and Frizz; I'd already asked him for a few things and he was still around. The master and slave bond was another dead end, considering this bond was formed once a dominant subjugated the other to his will. I subjected Frizz to nothing, and he certainly wasn't fighting the bond. What kind of bond did we share?

I sighed, closed the book, and put it aside. Maybe there wasn't a bond between us and Frizz was here because he wanted to be. I scratched his head, admitting I liked to have him around. Maybe he liked to stay around, too.

When hunger turned difficult to ignore, I limped to the kitchen and prepared a box of macaroni and cheese and warmed a bowl of ground meat for Frizz.

No one came—or called—on Wednesday, either.

On Thursday, around 7:00 a.m., I woke up to the sound of my cell phone ringing. The hazy recollection of a bad dream lingered on my tongue, coating my mouth with a bad taste. I sat, picked up the small device, and read the display.

"Hello?" I asked, still groggy.

"Get up, get dressed and go to base," Vincent said.

"Are you back?" I asked. But Vincent had already hung up.

I dressed slowly, putting on thick socks and running shoes, mindful of the way the soles of my feet stretched and pulled at the newly-closed wounds. I went against tradition and hailed a cab.

I took the elevator to the fourth floor and searched the gym first—Barbara, Jeremy, George and Raji, no Vincent. I checked the locker room next; it wasn't uncommon of him to wait for me there.

It was Diggy I found, lounging on the bench with legs stretched long and muscular, typing on a touchscreen cell phone with his thumbs. He had on a plain white tight T-shirt and dark jeans, plus the same boots that kicked the stars out of me the other day. He'd gotten a haircut, the sides shorter than the top, giving him a bad-boy look I was sure had women tossing themselves at his feet, begging to be noticed.

"Don't even think about walking out of here," he said to my retreating back.

I stiffened at the commanding tone and turned. "Look, I know you said you were following orders, but you're not part of my contract," I said, nervous about returning to the Low Lands, especially with him. What if he left me there and claimed he had no idea where I was? Who would challenge his word? No one would care. No one would accuse him of foul play, no one would even consider the possibility.

"Does it say on your contract you'd be only training with Vincent Vagner?"

I opened my mouth, snapped it shut again, saying nothing. Because there was no exclusivity clause anywhere in my contract.

Damn him all the way to Hell and back again. Roland told me Vincent would oversee my training, and I took him up on that. Perhaps I should take a trip down to his office and explain I could follow Vincent's last training schedule until he returned. If that would keep Diggy away, it might even be worth the verbal–or silent–war with Valerie.

"No? I thought so." Diggy stood, stuffed his phone in his back pocket, and shrugged on a black suede jacket before approaching.

I took an instinctive step away.

"Do you know what happens if I lose hold of you in the leeway?"

He stepped forward, I stepped back.

"No." The dangerous gleam in his eyes made me nervous.

Another step brought me flush with the closed door. He reached a broad hand to my shoulder and leaned close to my face. His eyes today were darker, more honey-brown than gold. He smelled of soap, of the woods, of the outdoors. There was a small tear on the lobe of his ear I hadn't noticed before. As if someone had grabbed hold of an earring and pulled it off, tearing the flesh with it. A fresh injury, one that happened after the last time he'd shifted, otherwise it would have healed already.

Diggy squeezed my shoulder, his grip firm, though not painful, and lowered his voice as if afraid he'd be overheard. I glanced behind him at the shower stalls, but all were empty. There was no one in here but us. This close, his breath smelled of coffee and chocolate. "You could be dropped anywhere, in any of the worlds, or be let wandering the leeway until your energy is gone, or if you're lucky, a guardian may find you."

The world flashed white, and his hand slipped from my shoulder. I grabbed for him, desperate when I found nothing but air. When my hands found his jacket, I held on for dear life. I clung to him as I fell, back to that cursed land. I think I heard his laughter above the roaring in my ears, as my heart tried to beat its way out of my throat.

"Or you can fall into one of those inhospitable planets," he continued after I landed, sprawled on a cluster of particularly sharp rocks, "where fire rules or non-breathable gas exists, or in space where you would die in the vacuum and free us all of the abomination that you are."

I watched his face, feeling blood already trickling out of fresh wounds, on my back, my hands, the back of my thighs.

He stood tall beside me, his lips lifting with that condescending smirk, and I couldn't contain the anger that surged and engulfed me. I lunged for his legs, tackling him to the ground and breaking his cool. Before I could gain some hold on him, he'd kicked himself free and was rolling up to his feet. I jumped up and attacked, talons out, anger ruling.

My talons scraped his shoulder before he could escape, leaving a red ribbon of blood and cloth. I'd have bitten him if I could have gotten nearer. In fact, the urge was so strong, I wanted to jump him, tear flesh with my bare teeth. I rushed him, clasping a fistful of cloth, ripping it to shreds when he pulled away, my teeth inches from his exposed neck. I growled in frustration and rage–the sound rattling from my chest, while anger wrestled common sense for control.

There was no sign of anger or satisfaction in his expression, or any sign of the familiar smirk. He retaliated, punching back, catching my shoulder when I didn't dodge fast enough. He parried my kicks, blocked every punch, disappeared whenever my talons got too close to his skin, only to reappear behind me again and kick me to my knees. Jumping up, I whirled, teeth bared in a ferocious snarl. Somewhere inside, common sense was losing the battle.

"Control that anger. Make it your weapon." He feinted left and swept a foot under me.

I jumped at the last second and avoided the leg sweep, but the punch to the solar plexus that followed was unavoidable.

I doubled over, panting, wheezing, trying to catch a breath. I didn't know if this punch was more potent than the others, or if it was because I'd recently been punched and kicked in the same spot multiple times. Whichever was true, I had a hard time sucking in a breath, my vision gray at the edges. Tears of anger gathered in the corners of my eyes, that red-hot rage recoiling inside me, its tentacles still gripping my senses.

"Get up. Your enemy won't wait for you to catch a breath. Ignore the pain." He circled as he spoke, keeping a respectful eight feet away. "Work around it, behind it, in front of it. Use it as a fuel. Whatever you do, don't stop."

"Go to hell," I managed between raging breaths.

"Someday, perhaps. Straighten up."

I looked at him, just a few feet away, so close, yet far enough I wouldn't be able to catch him by surprise. Hate filled my being, anger boiled inside. There wasn't a drop of satisfaction in the fact there was blood on the torn sleeve of his jacket, or the lapels were shredded. The wound wasn't even deep enough to impair his movements.

But if I hit that side again...

"No, don't telegraph. Never let your opponent read your next move. Don't tense up, avoid looking where you want to hit. Keep your opponent guessing," he kept instructing, not fazed by my reaction. My pain, my feelings, my needs were nothing to him. He'd been given an assignment and it mattered not if he liked or disliked it; he'd see it through until someone higher up said otherwise.

I straightened, anger deflating, and inclined my head. "Show me."

Chapter Seven

We fought for the next five hours, stopping twice for water and a power-bar break, only to return to the locker room twelve minutes after he'd dragged me to the Low Lands.

At 8:10 in the morning, I was thoroughly beaten, hardly able to stand, and the day had just begun.

Without so much as a snarky remark, Diggy opened the door to the locker room and stepped out; no doubt glad he was rid of me. He paused at the threshold, half turned and said in that mild tone, "If you're not here tomorrow morning at seven-thirty sharp, I will only come and drag you from home. And I won't be in a good mood."

* * *

The following two weeks went by with a routine of bruises and injuries. It wasn't boring, exactly, but within a few sessions, the days started blending together. I'd arrive in the gym on time, Diggy would flash us to that horrible frigid land, where he'd kick and punch the stars out of me, and I'd do a poor job defending myself.

Two times I slept through the alarm, and as he'd promised, he'd arrive at my doorstep, pick my lock when I refused to open the door, barge in and flash us to the Low Lands with whatever clothes I had on.

He was a punctual prick, but I had to admit I was learning a lot.

He didn't talk as we trained except to critique or tell me what to do, how to move, how to stand, how much distance to keep from my opponent. Didn't pause except for water or an energy bar–both of which he'd bring with him. Within the first few sessions, I learned he was relentless, merciless, thorough, and brutal with his instructions.

On the Thursday of our second week, the routine broke. I was dodging his attack, trying to find an opening to take the offensive when he stopped mid-motion, his head rising, his nostrils flaring. My punch connected with his jaw with such force that his head snapped back with a loud crack. He was so intent in whatever had caught his attention, he didn't even flinch. My shock at the fact I'd landed him a square-on faded fast at the ferocious glint in his eyes. His head turned away, sniffing the air. I sniffed too, but smelled nothing, except for our sweat and my blood. Maybe his olfactory sense was better than mine. But whether he could smell better than me wasn't the issue. Something had caught his attention.

A chill slipped down my spine, and I rubbed my palms on my arms, trying to work some warmth into them. I glanced around and sniffed again, opened my mouth to ask him what was it, but his hazel eyes flashed with warning before he shifted eastward. Or what I thought was east in a land without a sun.

Sensing danger, I turned, searching the illuminated circle around us, trying to see into the darkness beyond. I wanted to whisper a question, but my words were held back by his savage expression.

Diggy shifted and took a step forward. I followed, and he raised a fist in the air, a silent command for me to stay still, and I froze. He glanced back over his shoulder, placed a finger on his lips, which I thought was ridiculously funny, considering.

And he disappeared. There once, then gone. Not moved in a blur or too fast I couldn't follow.

Just disappeared into thin air.

He left me. Alone, in the Low Lands.

I whirled around so fast, I lost balance and went down hard on one knee, not feeling the needle-sharp rocks digging into my skin.

He'd done the unthinkable.

He left me.

Alone in a land where no one would search for me.

With his absence, the lighted circle plunged into darkness, nothing to be seen and nothing to be heard.

Diggy! I barely contained my need to scream for him. *Diggy!*

Was this it? Was *he* Angelina's business partner?

Was this the part where he'd say "I only left her for a moment and when I returned I found her like this"–dead and dismembered?

In a land where even buzzards didn't exist, what would happen to my body?

A nearby sound had me scrambling up, not breathing, my frantic eyes roaming left to right, searching the impenetrable darkness. Another sound, this time to my left. Then another and another, and I knew I was surrounded. My hands covered my mouth, trying to hold back the scream pushing to escape. Suddenly I was back to that day two months ago with Dr. Dean and Remo Drammen. The agonizing screams, the tearing of flesh, the blood, the frenzied feeding. All rushed back to the forth front of my memory, a recurring nightmare reborn anew, breathing down my neck. Pumping my heart with fire, making my blood roar through my veins.

I could see them ahead, two bodies torn apart bite by bite, bloodied piranha-like teeth everywhere, Dr. Dean's screams of agony, Remo's roars of outrage. They came for me, their bloody, missing limbs reaching forward. Something touched my back and I gasped, blinded with fear, blood roaring like a raging river in my ears. I whirled with talons extended, but my knees buckled and I fell, a talon scraping my thigh. Something large clamped down on my shoulder and I brought talons down on it, opening a few gashes in my shoulder when it wrenched away. Fear made me careless, made my moves clumsy, my thoughts sluggish.

I was grabbed, encircled from behind, my biceps pressed tight to my sides. All the air from my lungs was squeezed out. I thrashed, a choked scream of terror escaping through my lips as my talons dug deep into flesh.

A snarl sounded in my ears, and the vice tightened, confining me. Suffocating me. I screamed, bucked, kicked backward, threw back my head. Hit something hard. I gained an inch, threw myself sideways. I pulled myself forward, rocks digging into my flesh before I had enough sense to lift my body off the ground. I was about to run blindly into the darkness when something heavy fell on top of me, grabbed my wrists and wrenched my arms above my head.

"Easy, easy, easy."

I threw back my head again, hit something that crunched. My neck spasmed with a twinge, an ache that pulled from the back of my skull to my shoulder. I bucked, up, down, sideways. But I wasn't able to dislodge the weight off my back. If it bit me... I would die in the Low Lands, like Remo and Dr. Michael Dean.

"Roxanne, easy, easy there," the voice kept saying, and through the terror, I recognized it, realized I could see again. I raised my head an inch, my neck smarting, my breathing short, ragged pants, and glanced to the left and right. There was nothing there.

"Diggy?" I choked.

"I'm letting go now. Ok?" He let go of my wrists, then rolled off, taking all the warmth with him. I glanced at him, jolted when I saw blood running down his face, the slashes on his forearms and hand. He rose and took a few steps away, expression unreadable.

I let my head drop to the ground and took in a few calming, shallow breaths. Every small atom in my body shook. When I was sure my legs would support me, I stood, turned to face him. My breathing was still rapid, my heart shoving hard against my ribcage, but the panic attack was more or less under control.

I drew in a long, shuddering breath that smelled strongly metallic, of his blood and mine. There was no satisfaction to the fact I'd hurt him at last. I rubbed both palms over my face, trying to gather some composure back. Diggy stayed put, not moving, perhaps afraid he'd trigger another panic attack if he did. His eyes were wary, uncertain.

You left me in the dark, I wanted to accuse. "Are we done here?" I asked instead, hating the fact my voice shook.

He nodded and reached for me, hesitated a fraction of a second before his fingers closed around my wrist. The world flashed white and no sooner I began falling then I was standing in the locker room, Diggy already at the door.

A glance at the far wall told me it was 7:48 in the morning. I'd been gone for less than ten minutes. I washed, covered my torn clothes with an ugly beige coat I kept at base for emergencies and took a cab home, dropping keys and coat on the counter the moment I stepped inside. I sensed Frizz before he appeared, a soothing wave wafting from him.

"You call, Master, I come to you," he said in that odd hissing tone. I could tell he was hurt I hadn't asked him to come help. Again.

I rubbed my hand over my face, weary and tired–emotionally and physically. "I'm sorry. It didn't cross my mind."

If I didn't order him to stay home while I was out, he'd have been there. He'd have been there when Angelina had attacked too. But people could sense his presence, even when he was in a higher dimension, and Vincent had told me to keep him a secret.

I sensed his need to be near, his need to comfort, to make sure I was alright, so I crouched and patted him some, scratched behind his ear before I shuffled to the bathroom. I wanted to reach out to him, to give him a tight hug, to soak in that soothing presence, but I was too filthy for that.

I stripped off my bloodied, torn clothes and threw them away, like most articles of clothing I'd worn to train in the Low Lands. My wardrobe was disappearing away like toilet paper down the hole. At this rate, I'd go naked before the end of the month.

I reached for the light switch and it hissed with static before the bulb blew in a shower of light and glass. As if that had been a signal, tears rushed unbidden to my eyes. I swallowed them, refusing to give in. I rubbed my hands over my face, pressed palms hard against my eyes until a burst of color bloomed behind my lids. I slipped into the shower, sidestepping the glass, and let scalding-hot water wash and burn away my fatigue, my memories, my sore muscles.

The next day Diggy waited for me to answer the door before coming in. He told me to get ready and dress warmly, waited for me in the kitchen. A glance at the time told me he was fifteen minutes early. Maybe he was feeling guilty for yesterday. I dressed into warm, worn sweat pants and a bulky sweater I used to wear when I had nowhere to sleep but the cab of my car, Old Thunder.

When I returned to the living room, I found Diggy standing in front of the window, hands tucked in his pockets, his back to me. There was a pile of snow at the corner of the window, the world a white blanket on the other side. It was still snowing, the flakes small like miniature white butterflies. He turned when he sensed me, his eyes wary.

"You ready?" he asked and I nodded.

He took a step forward, inhaled a deep breath. "About yesterday..." He frowned, trailed off. "Look, about yesterday. I'm not sure what really happened..." He trailed off again, raked a hand through his hair, frustration clear in his eyes as he searched for the right words.

I waited, knowing I'd overreacted big time, but still wanting his explanation.

"Yesterday, after I left ... *yesterday*," he said forcefully, "I only restricted you because you were hurting yourself. I'm sorry if I was rough, if I added to the panic attack, or hurt you in any way." He must have seen my incredulity, because his brows furrowed, and I could almost see him shifting gears. "Our training sessions are not the result of superior strength, of a dominant subduing a weaker subject," he said, insulted. "When you refuse to learn, I discipline you the way I would any other underling. When you're injured fighting back, they're like taxes paid for learned knowledge. Yesterday I overpowered you, used my strength against your weakness, and it's *not* acceptable. I apologize for doing so. I didn't know what was wrong, and I couldn't think of any other way to prevent you from hurting yourself more. It's not an appropriate excuse because I should know better. Your terror caught me off guard, had me on alert, and when you attacked me I drew on instinct, which I later realized was what drove you on the offensive in the first."

He wasn't apologizing for leaving me there alone; he was apologizing for how he handled me after he returned. I studied his frustrated expression, aware the apology sounded rustic because it wasn't something given often. Yet here he was, his nose somewhat discolored, though the swelling was gone, offering an apology.

"I can give you the day off and resume the sessions Monday," he offered, flustered I hadn't reassured him it was ok.

None of the usual hostility he'd harbored the last few weeks was present today, so I asked a question of my own. "Why do you hate me?" My tone was curious, a little intrigued.

The corners of his eyes tightened a fraction, something I wouldn't have noticed if I didn't spend so much time with him. Yet I couldn't decipher what it meant.

"Who said I do?"

"The hostility kinda gave it away." I meant to pose it as a question, but it came as a sarcastic comeback.

Annoyance flashed in his eyes, along with something else–guilt? He glanced out the window. When he glanced back, the calm mask he wore at base was back on. "I don't hate you. It's just..." He paused a second before sighing, long and hard, resigned. When he continued, his expression seemed sincere. "I don't hate you as a person. But I don't like the fact I was given the task of training you from ground zero. I'm not a patient man, and, in truth, I'd have rather been in the field solving hard cases than being stuck here, attending to bar brawls because I have to stick around base." He fell quiet, and I had no idea what to say to that.

He raked a hand through his hair. "Look, I know none of this is your fault, but it doesn't negate the fact you keep surfacing at inconvenient times and I have to put things aside for you."

"I didn't ask you to put *anything* aside for me," I said with annoyance.

Diggy nodded once. "But I keep getting dragged into the mess anyway. Vincent botched the operation in Vegas because of you. I had to get involved in Logan's plan because Rafael sniffed a trap. And now I'm stuck at base because you need a mentor. And you're being difficult... And you were at my apartment, peeping."

"I was not!" I burst out, mortification warming my cheeks. "And Rafael is a nosy asshole with a chip up his ass. It was not my fault Logan kept the truth from you guys. And I certainly didn't ask for Vincent to botch your plans of grandeur!"

Diggy angled his head sideways. "I know that. As I said, you kept surfacing at inconvenient times. I have nothing against you, Roxanne. I just rather be somewhere else, doing something else."

I studied his face, not sensing any malice or anger. Suspicion started nagging at me. "Were you the one supposed to go down south instead of Vincent?" I recalled Vincent's foul mood the week before he left because Roland refused to let him lead the case.

"No. But I was supposed to have gone *with* him. Only a handful of preternaturals know I work for the Hunters, so there's less of a chance I'd have been recognized. I was supposed to be the mole while Vincent worked on other angles."

"So why not assign someone else to take up my training? I know most members would relish the idea of beating the crap out of me."

"Because Vincent and I are the only two Dhiultadh in the group."

An unwelcome kernel of guilt took root inside me. What if something happened to Vincent because he was working this case alone?

"What if he's recognized?"

"He's using a spelled charm to look different."

"But—"

"It's an excellent spell. *Exceptionally* hard to detect."

I nodded, but the uneasy feeling didn't go away. An awkward silence fell then, and I wasn't sure what to say.

Diggy gave a resigned sigh. "Look, I know it's not your fault and I've been harsh with you," Uncomfortable, he trailed off.

I waited a moment, then took pity, recognizing how hard it was for him to admit he was in the wrong. "How about a truce?" I asked, offering a tentative smile.

In the end we resumed our training, Diggy relentless with his instructions, no traces of the apologetic, flustered man from my living room. If he held back on the strength of his punches or kicks, neither of us mentioned it.

Chapter Eight

January came and went with no sign of Vincent. I was learning to defend myself, to block attacks, to break holds, to punch or kick in the right places to cause maximum damage: acute pain, bone-breaking, internal hemorrhaging, death. I improved defense on my left side, which Diggy pointed was my weak spot, and learned to punch with the left as good as the right.

I listened to every word he said, taking his clipped and rare advice to heart, wanting nothing more than to step up my next level of training, the one where I'd explore my preternatural abilities. This time my mentor would be Natalia, the witch who had known my father. I had yet to meet her, but it wasn't the possibility of another instant enemy that made my heart beat faster at the approaching day. No, it was the alien excitement from deep within, of the knowledge my Unseelie would finally come out to play. It was that excitement, coupled with the knowledge I could never let the monster within me gain the upper hand, that squeezed my heart with the urgent need to run and never look back.

By the end of that first month, Mwara was so far from my thoughts I no longer thought about her. True, my training in real time took less than twenty minutes, but the long hours in the Low Lands were as real as the bruises and abrasions I brought home. Not to forget it took me the rest of the morning soaking and bandaging wounds, then sleeping most afternoons, an unconscious restorative dream-like state that took me so deep under, I slept through Vicky's dinner preparations a few times.

Aside from her two-week vacation out west, I saw her most nights, except for those times when she had a date. She realized life as a preternatural wasn't all candy and chocolate, having sometimes come early enough to see my deeper wounds not yet healed. Although we never talked about it, I knew she was excited about the knowledge of preternatural existence, the ability to heal, the strengths and near-immortality, having sometimes sensed the vague envy she felt when talking about my job, my life, even if guilt always followed the envy. Now she was seeing one of the nastier sides with her own two eyes, she understood being extraordinary wasn't all roses and fun. At least, that's what I assumed the worry I sensed from her meant.

I was wrong.

* * *

It was early February; the temperatures had dropped both on Earth and in the Low Lands, and of Vincent there was no word.

Diggy and I paused for water and an apple, the latter earning me a scowl. I bit into the sweet fruit, shifting from foot to foot, trying to retain some warmth from our training. Beside me, Diggy stood motionless, munching on his energy bar, his eyes scanning the edge of the dead forest. Ever since the day he'd left me behind, we'd trained in this same spot, the foot of a sloping mountain full of giant dead trees. Diggy said the mountain was the highest point in the land, and high at the peak time ran in a different, chaotic manner.

I studied the black edge of the forest, or what I could see from Diggy's circle of illumination. Did it used to have a name, once this land had been green? A million years ago? A billion? While I contemplated the possibility, I stuffed the apple core in a pocket and extracted one of two Snickers I'd brought along, earning another scowl. I flashed him an innocent look and bit into peanut and chocolate and caramel. Although I'd learned to block most of his attacks and started hitting back, forcing him to maneuver and work harder to hit me, he still beat the stars out of me every session. I guess it was easier to teach someone the art of hand-to-hand when you enjoyed giving a thorough beating as an effective stress reliever. Still, ever since our heart-to-heart in my living room, I began to see a friendly side to him, even if he tried to hide it.

Less than half an hour ago, I landed a hard kick to his middle and sent him skidding a few inches on the hard ground. I'd cheered at his grimace, and even if he'd scowled at my glee-filled laughter, his eyes had glinted with amusement.

I returned my attention back to the empty land; like always, we were alone. It was quiet, our breathing the only sound. It was so strange to be in one place and not hear or smell anything but the person next to you. Whatever happened here, I wondered for the millionth time. If I lowered my nose close enough to the ground—something that, sadly, happened all too often—I could smell the faint scent of dry earth, a whiff of dust. But aside from that, there was nothing else. No breeze, no humidity, no buzzing of insects or scurrying animals. The land was dead, utterly and completely so. It was a chilling, creepy sensation, but Diggy seemed comfortable here, more so than he did in base.

It made me wonder what kind of man he was, aside from an aloof, ruthless, brutally honest, and no non-sense merciless instructor. I shifted my gaze to his green aura and puzzled over it. He gave me a sideways glance, brow rising in question.

"How come Vincent is second in command and not you?" I asked, because if I got it right, Diggy had been a Hunter longer than Vincent had been alive.

"You think He isn't worthy of his position?"

"I didn't say that. I'm just curious about how it happened. I mean, you've been a Hunter for a long time, longer than Vincent. I don't think you're weaker than him, and you obviously have plenty of experience with the job."

Diggy grunted, looked away. "I used to be an undercover agent. When my cover was blown a few years back, Vincent was already second to Roland. He offered to step down, I suppose as respect for an elder, but he didn't get up there because he's a sweet talker or because of his good looks. If he holds second in command, it's because he earned it the hard way."

Ah, it made sense. "I'd like to learn how to fight with a weapon," I said next, recalling the day I'd spied on him training in his quarters.

Diggy raised a brow, looked away. "No."

"No?" I huffed with disbelief. "Not 'I'll think about it', or' I'll see what I can do' or maybe a dubious 'maybe'? Just plain 'no'?"

Diggy shrugged a massive shoulder. "No need for delusion. You want to learn to use weapons, you take that up with Roland. Maybe he'll assign you someone else. If you have a problem with my technique, also take it up with Roland. Maybe he'll relieve me of my duties."

A hopeful tone escaped his voice and I stiffened.

Diggy glanced at me, saw my rigid posture, sighed once and added, "My job is to see that you can defend yourself when there's nothing," he motioned at the barren land, "but your wits and body to do it with."

"Yeah, well maybe I will strip down and distract my opponent to death," I said sarcastically.

Diggy gave me a considering look, his eyes cold. "That will only get you killed faster. Maybe raped during the process."

Unbidden, an image of Dr. Dean came to mind, a letter opener sticking from his cheek, his face red with rage and pain. I lowered my head and bit off a chunk of protein and chocolate, not wanting Diggy to see the quick flash of memory in my eyes. When I glanced up, Diggy was studying me with an unreadable expression. Had he seen?

"How come your aura is green like a were's?"

"Hmmm." He watched me for a moment more before turning away. "How come you're asking me that?"

Brows furrowing, I played back the question, said nothing more.

"It's innate, an inherent trait we're born with, to recognize what's within," he said, his focus somewhere in the distance.

But if Vincent hadn't told me you were a Dhiultadh from the other line, I'd have never guessed otherwise. "I guess sometimes though there's more to it, huh?" I said instead, fishing.

When his eyes met mine again, I shrugged, suddenly unsure under his scrutiny. "I mean, like when Vincent's aura just turns simple blue and no one can tell the difference. Like you're disguising your aura right now to make it look like you're an ordinary were."

Diggy frowned, chewing slowly on the power bar as if I'd said nothing. "I guess it's not inherent with you," he muttered a moment later. It wasn't meant to insult, I told myself, trying to shrug the sting. "Hasn't Vincent *explained* things to you?"

"The subject never popped up."

Diggy's lips pressed together, expression irritated.

"I'll ask him when he returns," I added, dismissing the subject so he wouldn't feel obliged.

Diggy turned to face me. "Some of us disguise our auras to make it harder for people to sense what we are."

I nodded. I figured that out for myself.

"Not every green aura you see is a were, just as not every blue aura you see makes that person human. *You*, of all people, should know that."

I flushed with embarrassment and lowered my head. It was a jab at my mixed-breed status. Or, maybe he didn't know this was how my aura appeared at all times. Maybe he thought I was disguising it, like the way he and Vincent did theirs.

Diggy sighed, the sound long-suffering. "The rejected, no matter the line, can still read auras and see through the disguise. Apparently though, *you* can't. Which is something Vincent shouldn't have missed, should have known and addressed sooner."

"Because there's one other human hybrid," I guessed.

Apparently I guessed right, because Diggy's eyes narrowed at that. "Who told you about that?"

Cool, a secret I shouldn't have known. Score one for me. I shrugged. "I heard it mentioned once."

Diggy looked down at his half-eaten bar, his expression pensive. "Have you met this human hybrid before?" He shifted to look at me, searching for the truth even before I replied.

"I don't think so," I said with a frown. "Unless he or she is a Hunter member." Silence fell then, and I finished my candy, stuffed the wrapper in my pocket, crouched and started picking off small sharp rocks stuck to my clothes, embedded on my legs and knees.

Diggy stuffed the wrapper of his candy in his pocket and ripped open a second one. When he spoke again, he didn't look at me.

"There are very few people out there who can both see and read auras. But a lot of people, like weres, oracles and even shifters, can get a general sense of someone's true nature by the vibes they leave behind or by their smell."

Again I nodded. Logan had once told me he trusted his senses more.

"We Dhiultadh inherited this ability through our Fee blood. No matter which line we hail from, we can sense whatever is hidden underneath the aura, even when disguised. Some people use charmed bracelets to see auras, but they don't know how to interpret it. Some people take lessons to learn to read others by the way they move and react, the way they smell." He crouched, and I was thankful I didn't have to crane my neck to look up.

"Like pheromones of strong emotions," I said, "I can tell what a person is feeling even if they have no expression. If it's strong enough, I mean." Usually I avoided the topic but, damn it, I wanted to know. If the price of learning was letting Diggy in on this secret, then maybe I should pay it.

Diggy paused for a second, a hesitation I wasn't supposed to see. "You can sense that?"

"Can't you?" I countered. Maybe this was a trait only the rejected from my line possessed. Maybe the other human hybrid was so weak, even this trait was beyond him or her.

"That's called empathy. It isn't reading auras per se, but I suppose one can attach it as a subtext."

I nodded, aware he hadn't answered my question. "I can sense the animals from the aura, if that person is a were. The element he can control, if the person is a mage. Sometimes I get a general feeling, sometimes I can pinpoint it. With you, I can sense there's an animal.

But you're not a were, which is what I would have pegged you for if Vincent hadn't told me about you."

Diggy nodded once. "That's the intent. The Dhiultadh, from both sides, like to stay anonymous, even among the predators. What else can you sense?" he asked, fully interested now.

"I can tell magic wielders from humans. I can see a vampire without the glamor." I gestured with an open palm before my face when he stared blankly. "You know, this corpse-like thing. And there was this once, with Rafael–before I knew what he was–I could sense the jungle in him."

Diggy looked down, thoughtful. "You can sense all that, yet you can't tell when an aura is being disguised?" he asked, baffled.

"Your aura confounds me. And Vincent's. If I hadn't seen it shine that silvery blue the first time, I'd never have been able to tell he wasn't human."

He nodded again. "Ok, I suppose Vincent and I are different. His is not a normal animal, and you can't sense mine because I can shift into more than one. Now, for the colors… Vincent's aura, when disguised, becomes blue because of Madoc. But there isn't any of Madoc's blood in my line, though a variety of others. Because of our diversity and willingness for interspecies breeding, our aura, when disguised, feels and looks like that of a were, sometimes even a shifter, depending on how many alternative forms that person can take."

I mulled over his words, recalling Elizabeth had told me that Madoc, the first ruler of the Unseelie Sidhe, had a bluish complexion. He'd fallen for Verenastra, the daughter of the Seelie Queen, and produced an offspring, Oonag. My line of rejected started with Oonag, who had mated Finvara–also an Unseelie Fee.

On the other hand, after Verenastra fled the Sidhe land to protect herself and her daughter from the Seelie queen, she mated Elvila-chious, a being from the Tristan star. Diggy's line came from this bond. Both lines were Sidhe rejected, though each carried a different title. Mine was the Unseelie Dhiultadh Clan, and Diggy's the Seelie Dhi-ultadh Clan. Aside from the title, the biggest difference between the two clans was the capability to reproduce. While Diggy's clan mated and bred outside their clan and had no trouble reproducing, my clan forbade interspecies marriages, afraid to dilute their Fee blood, and so developed the Sidhe difficulty to conceive.

I'd learned from one of Vincent's lectures the Unseelie Dhiultadh felt superior to Diggy's line because Diggy's line had diluted their Fee heritage. Which, according to Vincent, wasn't true since Fee genes were dominant genes. It was this reasoning that made Vincent confident if I could shift hands into talons, I'd one day shift into my beast form, the Dratcha.

In silence, Diggy finished the rest of his power bar, crumbled the wrapper and stuffed it with the other. He glanced at me, still thoughtful, and stood.

I got up too, assuming conversation time was over. Honestly, I was surprised he'd talked that much.

Diggy motioned me back. "Watch this." His aura shimmered, acquiring a silvery shine to the previous forest green.

"Wow," I said, awed. The color shone like–a beautiful, metallic forest green, a vibrant color filled with power. It flashed again and returned to plain green, and although the green was still vivid, it somehow seemed dull without the silvery sheen. He retreated a few steps. "Keep watching and let me know when you can no longer see it."

A few steps later I told him to stop.

"Pay attention," he instructed, taking a tiny step forward, his aura flickering into range.

Then he took a step back, his aura disappearing, then another forward, his aura reappearing.

I shook my head when he raised his eyebrows.

"Pay attention," he said again before repeating the process. Back one step, forward another. Then again.

And again.

And again.

Half an hour later, I slumped in defeat. "Forget it."

"It takes a while for a person to tell the difference. Plus, I'm good at disguises," he said without a hint of conceit.

"So the silvery color, that's the Fee part. Can you hide the green and keep the silver, I mean, can you pass for a Fee?"

Diggy paused, eyebrows furrowed. "Have you ever seen a silver aura before?"

"Yeah, Lee's. Her aura was a pure, shining silver."

His pause this time wasn't so brief. "Lee...?"

"Leon Ora Maiche."

Pursing his lips, his gaze grew serious. "When–where did you meet her?"

I scanned the dead land, the cracked soil, the blackened husk of the forest ahead. "Here, I met her about three months ago. *Here*."

Diggy followed my gaze around the planet as if he expected Lee to appear out of nowhere. The way she'd appeared not so long ago, when she'd tricked me into making that bargain. The one she had yet to collect. I shivered, wondering if she was watching us.

"I guess she would take an interest in you," Diggy murmured, no doubt thinking about my father and the broken bargain. "Do yourself a favor. Whatever you do, wherever you go, stay away from her and her kind."

Yeah, bro, too late for that.

Chapter Nine

It took me a few days, watching his aura every time it flickered in and out of range, at other people in the streets, at work, in the market, but I finally saw what Diggy had wanted me to. Whenever his aura flickered into range, I focused on it. It had me eating a few punches I could have blocked, but the result was worth it.

It wasn't much, barely something at all, just a faint shimmer, or more a tiny silvery sheen in the inner line of the aura that appeared and disappeared in a blink. As if the light hit at a certain angle and reflected in a particular way. Later I'd be told for that tiny reflection to show in the aura of a rejected, that person had either to be under extreme stress or do it on purpose. Since Diggy's wealth of energy seemed bottomless, I assumed he'd taken pity on me. The notion was reinforced by the fact I never saw it again.

Those who had to procure charms to disguise their auras and scents, Diggy explained, couldn't hide that fleeting shimmer. A fact that was proved with Roland. I'd known he wasn't human; no one ordinary had the power and authority to command twenty-six preternatural top predators without having a lot of oomph. But viewing that reflection, a transient golden sheen, something I'd no doubt seen before but attributed to the effect of the light; it had me hurrying to the locker room, locking the door behind me, and doing a victory dance, all elbows jabbing, feet moving, butt wiggling, hips bumping.

The next day, during our power-bar break in the Low Lands, I told Diggy about my discovery. The fact he'd been the one to point where to look only meant my discovery wasn't news to him, but the pleased look I caught in his eyes before he masked it told me he was glad.

I could talk to Vicky–and I did–but the discovery wasn't as important to her as it was to me. For Vicky, important these days was what to wear for a hot new date, which restaurant to go to, and the fact the friend of a friend was a hottie without a date, and I should go out with them on a double date. And, oh yeah, the fact Valentine's Day was just around the corner didn't help at all.

She'd been dropping subtle hints about this guy for a while, and when I refused to bite the bait, she'd outright thrown it in my face.

"You need a man to put some spice in your boring life, my friend," she'd said, the concern in her baby blues real enough. My life had enough spice and was too hot even for me, but I didn't reply and she let the topic drop, to be continued another day.

* * *

That evening I awoke to the sound of Vicky rummaging in my kitchen, the smell of melting cheese making my mouth water. A glance at my watch told me I'd overslept again. Not that the extra hour brought extra rest, not at all; if anything, my body hurt as if I'd been run over by a speeding bull.

I threw the covers away and stood, groaning when my stiff muscles stretched and throbbed. Grabbing a rubber tie I'd thrown atop the nightstand before I'd crawled into bed a few hours earlier, I tied up the mess of hair. Disentangling locks would be a bitch, considering it was wet and uncombed when I crawled into bed. A job for another time, I told myself as I padded barefoot to the kitchen, where the aroma of melting cheese and coffee originated.

I was still on my second bite when Vicky began bombarding me with suggestions about blind dating and that friend of a friend. I let her talk, hmmming whenever there was a lull in the conversation, finishing the sandwich before she noticed I wasn't listening.

Narrowing her eyes, she dropped whatever she was doing in the kitchen and came around the divider, pausing a few feet away, the coffee table between us, Frizz ignored by her side. Ah, shit.

"You need to date, Roxy," she said firmly.

Licking grease off my fingertips, I stretched my legs on the coffee table and braced myself for the conversation ahead. "No, I *don't.*"

"You can't live your life like this, alone, no friends, no life beyond work. You have no hobby, no habits, no social media interactions. It's not healthy." The concern in her eyes was genuine, but not strong enough for me to sense.

"I have hobbies. I watch movies with Frizz every night when you're not around. And I thought you were my friend."

"No, that's not what I meant."

I clicked thumb and forefinger together and said, "You can say watching movies with Frizz every night is also a habit. See, a hobby, a habit and a friend. I enjoy cooking and baking too–it's both a pastime and a relaxation therapy." I gave her an innocent smile.

"Yet you live on sandwiches and takeout food." Vicky frowned at me. "You used to enjoy reading. You enjoyed shopping and dancing. You don't even listen to music anymore."

"I still like to read," I waved a hand at the guidebook of the preternatural catching dust atop the coffee table. "And I don't have time to go shopping or dancing anymore."

"You have time," She glared at me. "We all hold a nine to five like you. And before you start with all that nonsense about Dimple working you hard, you still have weekends to get out and have fun. Why can't you? You were always the first in line in the theater or the first to arrive at the mall or at a party."

"That girl died when she was twelve," I snapped, her words getting under my nerves.

Vicky was quiet for a long moment. "Why are you afraid to live?"

I stiffened. "I'm not afraid to live. I am alive, aren't I?"

"Is it because you're afraid the scientists will come again? Are you afraid to get accustomed to things, to enjoy life, only to have it snatched away again?" She crouched in front of me, took my hand in hers, her eyes direct and passionate. "I don't know how to ease your fear, Roxy, I can't do that," She inhaled a long breath, "But this isn't the answer. Look around at your life, at your own apartment. It's a place where you take care of necessities. You sleep, you eat, you bathe. But you have yet to make it a home."

"It is my home," I said softly, heart tight.

Vicky shook her head. "There are no personal touches here, no decorations, no pillows." She took a cursory look around, "Where's the music, the smell of home-cooked food, that figurine you saw and couldn't help but buy? A photo of your friends framed here or there? A misplaced shoe, a vase of flowers?"

I didn't say anything. Couldn't, for the ball of emotion lodged in my throat. "It's a bleak existence, Roxy. You might as well put back that blocking bracelet."

We both cringed at her words, and Vicky's face went pale. I bared my teeth in a savage smile. "If you think my life now is the same as it was before, then you're just like any other clueless human out there."

Vicky blanched, her guilt wafting like a spray of rancid gas. She stood, eyes stricken. "I'm sorry," she whispered. "I'm so sorry."

A kernel of guilt took root in my belly and I waved a hand in dismissal. If I were honest, I'd admit she wasn't entirely off the mark. "I'm doing fine enough, Vicky. Believe me when I tell you I'm content with this life, and that I have zero interest to go out with some random guy just because."

"You don't have to date him, Rox, just come out with us and have some fun. Meet him. Brandon can be your friend if at the end you guys don't feel the spark."

"It's not about dating. I'm just not in the mood for loud talk, big crowds, deafening music. And before you tell me about quiet restaurants, the answer is still no."

Vicky was quiet for so long, I'd have thought she'd let the subject drop. That is, if it wasn't for the calculating glint in her eyes.

"Is it because of Logan, then?" she asked, and I almost said yes. But the fact was, I wasn't sure. It wasn't like I was pining for him; no, I'd figured from the start I would never see him again. And I was fine with that.

"Is it?" she prompted when my answer didn't readily pop out.

I chewed my lip, brows furrowed. "If I tell you I'm not sure, but I'm fine knowing I'll never see him again, would that make any sense?"

Her eyes softened. She came around the coffee table and sat beside me, picking up Frizz and settling him on her lap, the subtle scent of her perfume surrounding us.

"Oh, Roxy. It *makes* sense. Because you are so hung up on him, no one else matters to you."

I groaned. I should've known she wouldn't understand. Yes, there had been an attraction between Logan and me, and I wasn't denying it, but even then, I wasn't searching for a relationship. So much of his life was unknown, and a lot of what I'd seen made me uneasy. How could I pine for someone I didn't even know? Attraction, yes, but nothing more than a crush. I didn't even trust him. For God's sake, I didn't even think about him that much, or fantasize about us meeting again.

Sure, I've done all the above, but only a few times, and mostly to wonder about his whereabouts, what position he held in the clan, and the fact he'd failed to tell me he and I were part of the same clan.

"That's why you should date," Vicky was saying. "You should search for alternative options. You can't wait for him forever." She placed a manicured hand over my knee and squeezed once. I could feel the warmth of her hand through the denim, and the faint concern vibes she was broadcasting increased with the touch. "You might think you have all eternity to figure this out, Roxanne," she chuckled at this and shook her head, "maybe even literally, but don't you see? It might take you that long if you don't start *somewhere*. Why not now, here?"

"Maybe," I said, to appease her and so she'd drop the subject.

Thankfully, "maybe" was a step up from an outright "no", and she let the topic drop.

On Saturday evening, two weeks after Diggy and I had "the talk" and three days before Valentine's Day, Diggy dropped by.

Vicky was preparing popcorn to go with the chosen movie of this weekend–*The Lord of the Rings*, one of Frizz's favorites–talking nonstop about Brandon this and Brandon that, and the fact they were all going to meet in a downtown pub tomorrow night. I was preparing Frizz dinner before Vicky could stuff him with junk food, trying my best to come up with some reasonable ploy to avoid the blind date by convincing my friend I couldn't go without having to lie.

"I'll get that," Vicky said when the doorbell rang. "It's probably the neighbor's kid again, on a dare from his friends."

"Teenage hormones," I snorted in agreement.

But then Frizz disappeared, and Vicky's breath hitched. I dropped the bowl of ground meat on the counter and hurried to the door, and there he was, a handsome devil, dressed in black tailored pants, a dark-gray button-down shirt, and shining Italian shoes, hazel eyes twinkling with knowing amusement, lips cocked in a smirk.

"What the hell are you doing here?" I snapped.

Vicky whirled at the sound of my voice, her baby blues shocked.

Diggy glanced at me, then down at Vicky, then up again.

"Who?" Vicky breathed.

Diggy's eyes shifted back to her, checked her out. *Really?*

I crossed my arms, scowling at the interested gleam in his eyes. "Vicky, this is Douglas Vemourly. Diggy, this is my friend," I emphasized the last word, "*Vicky.*"

He extended a broad hand, and Vicky, fool that she was, took it, a dumbstruck spark in her eyes.

"It's a pleasure to meet you, Vicky." He kissed the knuckles of her hand.

"Ew, Vicky! My God, Diggy," I snapped, but neither paid me any attention.

She gave him a full-wattage smile and I gritted my teeth to keep myself from snatching her away from him.

"What do you want?"

Diggy broke the gaze lock to look at me, eyebrows raised. "Aren't you going to invite me in?"

"No," I snapped at the same time Vicky said, "of course." And opened the door wider for him to pass. My scowl deepened as I caught her checking his backside as he moved by with a charming smile.

Diggy took in my place as if he'd never been there before, his eyes lingering on the bowls of ground meat and popcorn, both untouched. I cursed my stupidity, aware there was nothing I could do about that. At least Frizz had enough sense to disappear.

"What do you want?" I asked again, unable to mask the biting tone. My private life was off limits, and damn it, Diggy knew better.

"Roxy!" Vicky chastised. "Don't pay attention to her. Please have a seat." She ushered him into the living room, a propriety hand on his elbow. "She's moody like that on weekends." Lowering her voice, she added, "It's the lack of a date, I keep telling her." She looked back at my surprised face and winked with a wicked, mischievous glint.

Diggy followed, and I noticed the long hanger, encased in a soft pale-yellow cloth draped over his forearm.

He turned when he reached the sofa, but didn't sit. "You're not dressed." He gave me a once-over.

I looked down at the denim pants, yellow tank top, my bare feet, then at the object dangling over his forearm and up to his face. "For what?" I asked warily.

"The charity ball I told you about." He gave a meaningful look at Vicky, standing beside him like a midget, smiling adoringly up at him.

When his words registered, she whirled toward me, a genuine hurt look in her eyes. "You never told me about a date."

Because there wasn't one.

"Because I'm not going." I glared at Diggy.

"Why not? Of course you are," Vicky huffed, forgetting about the gorgeous guy beside her.

"You know it isn't optional," Diggy played along. "The boss said all employees should attend."

He said nothing to me. "I'm not going," I scowled, almost growled the words.

"Nonsense." Vicky dismissed my denial with a wave of a hand. "Is that for her?" She reached for the garment bag before Diggy could answer, her excitement filling the room.

"I can switch with Bellemeir," Diggy offered with an earnest expression.

"No, no. She'll go with you." Vicky grabbed my forearm, squeezing hard enough to bruise.

I yelped in protest and glared at her, but she only glared back, unfazed. She led me away, her excited words tumbling over one another.

I glanced back at Diggy, wanting to send him one last withering look, but his eyes were on the *Guide Book of the Preternatural* sitting in plain view atop the low table, before he shifted his gaze to the ground meat, to Vicky's back, and finally to me. A chill ran down my spine, and I had the sudden urge to pull Vicky behind me, to protect her from the dangerous gleam in his eyes.

Chapter Ten

It took Vicky the better part of an hour to do what I could in less than ten minutes. What was it about shrugging on a dress, putting on shoes and adding some make-up?

Vicky pinned up my hair, leaving a few strands hanging around my face and neck. The make-up was minimum, a soft-pink lipstick and gloss, an almost imperceptible darkening of the eyes, and the faintest of blush on my cheeks. All against my protest, of course.

When I stood to survey the result, I had to admit, I looked good.

Damn good.

The dress, Christian Dior–according to Vicky–was long-sleeved, done in a lilac color made of a soft fabric that stopped below my knees and fit me like a glove. It made me wonder how Diggy got a measuring tape around me without my knowing.

Four inches, also lilac stilettos looped twice around my ankles. Vicky lamented I had no precious jewelry, then unpinned the teardrop earrings from her ears and handed them to me. There was no necklace to go with the occasion, but since the neckline of the dress was high enough, Vicky claimed the lack was no faux pas. I took off the bracelet Logan gave me and left my wrist unadorned.

She clapped twice with exhilaration, her face glowing as she announced, "You look stunning."

Unable to help myself, I smiled, posing in front of the mirror.

"I know." A hint of that conceited, twelve-year-old peeked through.

"It's like the prom you didn't attend," she said in a low, conspiratorial tone I was sure Diggy heard. I shook my head for her to be quiet, but she went on. "And this Douglas Vemourly, oh my God, he's so much better than Tommy."

I chuckled, because I'd probably have gone with Tommy to the prom, if I had been there instead of at the PSS.

In the living room, Diggy cleared his throat. By the way Vicky continued gushing about "Douglas's firm, muscular ass and beautiful eyes", I was sure she hadn't heard him.

* * *

"So... About Vicky," I began the moment Diggy drove away under a heavy sheet of rain. "Stay away from her."

When Diggy said nothing, I gritted my teeth and added, "She's human, certainly not your type."

"How do you know my type?"

"Fine, then. *You're* not her type."

"Hmmm. She seemed interested to me. I must be losing my mojo."

"I'm warning you, Diggy, leave her alone. I'm not letting her get tangled up with you."

Diggy's eyebrows rose high on his forehead, but he kept his gaze focused forward. "She seemed able-minded to me. I didn't know you made her choices for her."

I inhaled a long breath, tried to calm my rising anger. "Look, Vicky is my best friend. The only one I have. I don't want her hurt, and I don't peg you as the type of guy who'd want a long-term relationship."

A long silence followed before Diggy grunted. "I'm not the type to get tangled in relationships." He paused for a second before adding, "I won't promise you anything, but I'll let her know what she's in for before I make a move." I opened my mouth to protest, but Diggy cut me off. "Your friend is an adult, isn't she? If I ever make a move, then let her make her own choice."

I snapped my mouth shut. He was right. And Vicky would hang me by my toes if she found out I warned Diggy to stay away. I sighed.

"Fine. But if you hurt her, I'll kick your ass so hard, you'll sport a pair of boobs for years."

Diggy's lips twitched, and then he chuckled, unable to help himself.

"So," I asked, "why are you shanghaiing me to this so-called charity ball?"

"You'll see," was the mysterious reply.

We drove to the Marriott Marquis Hotel near Times Square in relative silence, save for the sound of the pounding rain on the roof of the car and the low murmur of a talk show through hidden speakers. I wondered if Diggy could make out the words when I couldn't. How sharper was his hearing? His eyesight? Through the heavy curtain of rain, I watched the outside. The traffic didn't bow to nature; if at all possible, the streets seemed more clogged, moving at the usual snail's pace, bumper to bumper. Screeching horns muffled curses hurled from driver to driver, closed windows providing one more sound barrier. White clouds of exhaust pumped out of vehicles, the smell distinct even with the windows up and the heat on. Still, the sidewalks were packed, colorful umbrellas dotting both sides of the street. People hurried to their destinations, uncaring it was raining, much less freezing.

A valet came and took the keys from Diggy; two others opened our doors, huge umbrellas shielding us from the rain. We crossed the lobby in silence, the clap of my heels muffled by the heavy carpet. We received a lot of stares from guests, men and women alike, stopped by a closed double door. Diggy presented an invitation and his ID to a stiff-backed doorman, both of which were scanned before we were allowed to pass through.

We entered a large rectangular room decorated in vivid reds and bright whites, balloons and plastic hearts and cute little Cupids dangling from the ceiling. Already there was a small crowd inside, most following the theme of reds and whites, all sparkling like the crystals on the chandeliers. People grouped together in threes and fours, an undertone of string music playing in the background. The room smelled of the roses adorning the tables, mixed with men's and women's expensive perfumes, and although the scents were strong, they weren't overwhelming.

The tables were set in parallel rows, three columns deep on each side, with a ten feet aisle between. Red velvet carpet ran to the edge of an empty floor space, where most guests mingled. The silverware and crystal on the tables gleamed under three bright chandeliers. White and red expensive linen covered the tables, the colors alternating in red and white patterns throughout the ballroom. Red roses in tall Baccarat vases for white tables, white roses in tall Baccarat vases for red tables. There were eight chairs around each table, each covered in reds or whites and tied on the back with fat, velvet laces.

Waiters were also dressed for the occasion, either in white or red vests, all carrying heavy trays with gleaming crystals. Most couples were dressed to the theme, women in varying shades of red dresses or suits, the men in white tuxedos or pastels. The room was far from filled to capacity, but for a five-thousand-dollars-a-plate, there were a lot of people present.

Greek gods and goddesses sat atop red-and-white velvet-covered pedestals, placed between intervals against walls. A bar was tucked at the far edge of the room, where a few other guests gathered. A large stage dominated half the back wall, empty save for a few musical instruments.

It was a Valentine's Day charity ball. So much for avoiding Vicky's schemes.

I scanned people's faces once, twice. Nope, there wasn't a single Hunter member in sight. Uncomfortable, I gave Diggy a sideways glance and wondered what kind of game he was playing.

"So now we've arrived, are you going to tell me why I'm here?"

Diggy motioned ahead, a silent command for me to follow, but I stayed put, eyes slit at his back.

A few feet away he paused to chat with a guy in a white tuxedo and red cravat, not once looking back to make sure I had followed. A couple passed by and I stepped aside to make room, jolting when I noted the thin dark-red auras. They strolled to the back, greeting guests as they went, their paces easy, their conversation light. As if they had all the right to be enjoying a charity ball with a Valentine's Day theme.

I shifted toward Diggy, still talking to the same guy, not paying attention to the vampires scoping out the place. I watched the vampire couple until they paused by the bar and the bartender handed them two dark glasses. Now, I can't assume that the dark glasses hid blood, but what else could it be?

Curiosity piqued, I moved toward Diggy. Even before I reached him, I noticed the blonde guy had a green aura, a were-cat of some sort, perhaps a minx.

Diggy nodded to the guy and moved away, not once glancing my way. I scanned the crowd again, seeing them with new eyes. We passed a couple with a pale-blue aura, magic wielders, another with yellow auras. I gave Diggy furtive glances, jaws clenched, knowing whatever I said, somebody was bound to hear. It was obvious this wasn't a normal gathering, and though admission was couples only, I didn't think all these people were lovers, or even friends.

Most people we passed gave Diggy a nod, a smile, a glare. Halfway to the back, we passed a woman with a teal-colored aura. Startled, I stared, surprised and a little awed at the novelty. Diggy bumped my arm and I realized the woman was staring back, her brown eyes hostile. I looked away, uneasy, her eyes boring into my back as we moved away. My shoulder blades itched with a need to turn.

Diggy placed a warm hand on my back, urging me forward. "Don't stare," he murmured.

Ahead, we passed an Asian man with a teal aura, no doubt the woman's partner, even if this one stood with a brunette ringed with a yellow line. The man chuckled at something she said, holding two filled flutes in his hands.

I didn't dare look twice his way, my nerves taut. What *was* this gathering? Why had Diggy brought me here? Damn him and his secrecy to Hell. He should have explained what I was getting into.

Almost at the bar, we passed the couple with the dark-red aura, each holding that tall dark glass. It was covered with some metal top, but I caught a whiff of blood nonetheless.

Both the man and woman smiled at Diggy from emaciated corpse-like faces—fangs hidden—and raised their glasses to him. He nodded once, kept moving. I followed close, hating I was in the dark. I had this strong urge to turn around and leave.

Damn Diggy and his mysterious schemes to Hell. My heart raced, my stomach churned. And damn these high heels too, I thought as I fought to keep my balance and control my emotion.

Diggy glanced at me, not stopping, no hint he could sense my anxiety. He didn't have to tell me to get a grip. In a room full of predators, displaying any grain of fear was *not* a good idea.

By the time we reached the bar manned by a bald guy with a pale blue aura, I'd gotten hold of my emotions, locked down my nerves. No one looking at me would see anything but a composed woman with flat, emotionless eyes.

Diggy motioned to the bartender, pointed two fingers at the tall glasses and turned to the crowd. I mimicked his moves. A woman barked out a loud, hearty laugh and I turned, spotted the middle-aged couple nearby. Everything about them screamed predator, even if they had on a relaxed, pleasant smile. They were dressed modestly; the woman in a dark-navy pantsuit, the man in a tailored black one. Both had dark skin, a few laugh lines in the corners of those near-black eyes. The man had a bald spot on the crown of his head, covered with wavy gray strands. The woman's salt-and-pepper hair was arranged in an elaborate bun. Just the fact neither looked a day younger than sixty had chills running down my spine. I'd never seen a preternatural being who looked older than forty-some years, and I wasn't sure if the image they presented was glamored or real. Still, the harmless, innocent auntie/uncle image did nothing to quell the other-worldly vibes they radiated.

And there were the bobbles both sported: colored, beaded bracelets of different sizes and shapes, rings on every finger, and dime-sized earrings on each ear. It brought to mind the stories I'd read about New Orleans voodoo priests and priestesses.

Diggy handed me a tall glass of sparkling water and waited until I'd taken a few sips before asking in a low tone, "What are they?"

I sipped again, studying both purplish auras. It wasn't blue interrupted with red, or any hints of black. It was simply purple and, as far as I could tell, undisguised.

"I don't know. Something that doesn't give them longevity."

"What else?"

"Something dark. Dangerous."

"Yes. Go on."

"I'm not sure."

Suddenly the woman turned, no doubt sensing eyes on her. Dark eyes stared at me without blinking, seeing all the way through. Goosebumps broke all over my body. I tried, but couldn't break the connection. It was as if the woman's eyes ensnared me, commanded me not to look away.

Diggy took a casual step forward, blocking the woman's line of sight, breaking the contact. Body fraught with tension, I looked away. He touched my back again and motioned us forward, saying, "They sure as Hell overdid themselves with this one."

"Hmmm."

We moved forward into the throng of people, and only Diggy's hand on my back kept me taking those steps. I wanted nothing more than to leave, go home to Frizz and a book, and a cup of warm chocolate.

The ballroom was full of preternatural creatures, the equivalent of a nuclear bomb ready to go off at the slightest provocation. I've never seen so many other-worldlies gathered in one place at a time, not even in the PSS. With that thought, I couldn't help but wonder what the Scientists would do if they stumbled upon this gathering.

Probably die a horrible death, my inner voice said with glee.

Diggy moved us forward, towards the biggest cluster, a gathering of about a dozen, and that's when I spotted him, headed like a raging bull toward us.

Chapter Eleven

I stiffened, and Diggy turned, his posture stiffening as well. It wasn't something I would have noticed before, but all those hours with him gave me an insight into his tells, his masked expressions. His hand clenched the glass as he took a sip. We both watched the man approach. Even some guests paused to look and murmur.

Archer.

Would Diggy have come in this direction if he knew we'd be intercepted? It was something to mull over later. Archer's aura wasn't yet in range, but the menacing vibes he oozed had already reached us. Or me at least. I wasn't sure if Diggy was empathic, he'd never answered that question. Some people around us sure were, because the moment I sensed it, a few of the guests retreated, putting space between them and the vibes emanating from Archer.

He looked angry. His eyes moved around us, scanning the people present, met mine. They were still the same pitiless black holes, as cold as a winter's night in a place that never saw daylight once. His steps were feline, stalkish-like. He oozed danger, a wave of predatory pheromones emanating from him like angry waves, battering at my nerves. More guests stepped away, pulling others with them, whispering behind palm-covered lips. I recalled the day I'd met Remo, the way his power had battered my senses, making me recoil.

Was this how Archer acted in public, or did he want to make sure he was the biggest, meanest, baddest and most powerful being in the room? Gone was the fragile man I helped escape from the PSS. The changes were subtle, but the result was drastic. The dark circles under the eyes, the sagging shoulders, even the white hair—the ravages of the PSS's treatments—were gone. His hair was a pale yellow, glossy and shiny. He stood tall, shoulders straight, whereas back then, Archer had been incapable of even standing on his own. His eyes were the same, ancient orbs that saw into the soul.

Whatever the PSS had done to him, he'd suffered horribly. The kernel of pity I felt for him was unexpected. Even if today, here, he looked like a powerful forty-some-year-old tycoon. Restored to his full power, he felt, though didn't resemble, Remo Drammen down to a pat, *sans* the dark vibes.

I glanced sideways at Diggy and wondered if he'd ever compared Archer to Remo Drammen. It made me wonder *what* Remo Drammen had been.

I shifted my gaze to the woman beside him—it was a couples ball after all, and surprise, surprise, his companion was none other than Elizabeth, my fake mother. The thought brought Mwara to mind, the first time in over a month, but the couple behind Archer and Elizabeth sucked every clear thought out of my head like a vacuum.

Because, shit, that was Logan Graham. With a pretty redhead dressed in a slinky, slutty blood-red low-cut dress that barely covered the essentials. My dislike of the woman was instantaneous.

Logan's eyes met mine, his head inclined in acknowledgment, shifted to Diggy, did the same before returning his attention back to the woman beside him.

And that was that. With a hand hooked around his arm, the woman led him away. Elizabeth glanced at them long enough to shoot daggers at their backs.

When their auras flickered into range, the tiny shimmer I caught in Elizabeth's aura could have been imagined, or the effect of the strong lighting. Archer's, in contrast, morphed into that shiny silvery-blue, undisguised.

I supposed now that he'd been outed by the humans, there was no need to disguise himself.

Elizabeth was dressed in a nice pale-blue cocktail dress with sparkles around the wrists and neck, and an air of disdain like a mantle around her. She looked as elegant and sophisticated as ever, except for the tightness to her eyes and lips, a hardness that hadn't been there before. Was there trouble at home? Was Mwara acting up?

Archer spared me a glance before shifting his gaze to Diggy. This close, the menacing vibe scraping at my senses seemed forced, unnecessarily brutal. Staged, though I couldn't say why I got that impression.

"Douglas," he said curtly, pausing five feet away.

Nearby, people watched from a safe distance. A couple with brown auras I'd passed by earlier came closer, eyes focused on Diggy and Archer.

"Gerome," Diggy replied, raising his glass in salute. The tension in Diggy's shoulders was visible only because I knew where to look. His posture seemed relaxed, his tone nonchalant.

I took a sip of water and tried to block Archer away. Shifting my attention to Elizabeth, I was caught off-guard by the hostile glare she was shooting me. True, we hadn't parted amiably, but if someone should hold a grudge, it was me, not her.

"It's good of you to have joined the cause," Diggy was saying. "Though I must admit, I didn't think you'd be attending this ball."

"We were already in town. Might as well get it over with," Archer replied. "Where is Vincent?"

Oh, but he looked pissed. Lucky Vincent wasn't here, because it looked like Archer had a bone to pick with him.

Diggy shrugged a shoulder. "He's around, I suppose. Haven't seen him yet."

Archer's eyes shifted to me, black, pitiless, depthless.

"Why aren't you with him?"

I stiffened at his biting tone, a rebellious streak sparking to life. No matter what or who he was, there was only one thing I cared about when it came to Archer: *he* was the one who gave the scientists the green light.

"I don't see how that's your concern," I said coolly.

Diggy's brow furrowed, but he said nothing.

Archer's jaw tightened, his eyes flaring with anger. He turned to Diggy and demanded the same, his tone stiff and cold. "Why isn't she with Vincent? She's supposed to spend time with her own to learn our ways."

"Everyone's got their assignments. We take them as they come."

Archer's eyes narrowed, anger rippling from him in hammering blows. "Assignments? Is Vincent her instructor, or are *you*?"

Diggy tilted his head sideways before replying, "Him, me, whoever's available."

Archer's lips thinned. "What, is Roland's second going about aimlessly whoring for the guild then?"

Diggy paused, took a sip. "If and who Vagner whores around with is none of my concern. That's something you should take up with him."

People were watching us, murmuring, keeping a relative distance away. As if he sensed things would go to Hell if he didn't throttle back, Archer relaxed, though his anger was still there, stronger perhaps.

"I understood from Mackenzie Vincent would be overseeing to her entire discipline," Archer said in a more diplomatic tone. He clenched his jaw, as if he had to hold back what he wanted to say. "She's supposed to follow an approved, strict schedule, one to bring out her basic strengths to be polished. She's supposed to be educated on the clan's rules and hierarchy. Something I can see she's lacking in knowledge."

"That certainly falls under Vagner's responsibilities," Diggy agreed. "Meanwhile, for the first part, when Vagner isn't available, Roxanne will be following my instructions and guidelines, per my superior's approval." His tone was pleasant enough, and I gave him points for that, but I could tell Archer was wearing on his nerves.

"Your superiors ran and approved my proposal," Archer spat, anger boiling in his eyes. What was wrong with him? For the leader of the clan, he sure lacked control.

"I wouldn't know. Profile assessment is not part of my duty."

"The approval and exercise of that proposal were required for the clan to lend this subject to the guild. This is a breech in contract."

I stiffened. *Lent me?* What was I, a toy, a car, some possession they could move around at will? Diggy sent me a warning glance, his eyes glittering with banked anger. He turned his attention back to Archer and spoke politely, but now that I'd seen the anger, I could also hear it in his voice, the way the vowels were clipped instead of measured.

"She's being primed to become a Hunter member. Her discipline will be in accordance. Any problem you have with that, you take up with Mackenzie. Meanwhile, I'm doing what I'm told, by my own superiors."

I gritted my teeth and kept my silence. I didn't like Archer, didn't like the fact he was the head of the clan I supposedly belonged to, didn't like the fact I was a lowly subject required to follow rules I didn't agree with, or had knowledge about. But I remained silent.

Archer's eyes didn't narrow, but the menace he oozed took focus, beat at my core. Was Diggy experiencing the same? Elizabeth placed a hand over Archer's arm and the dangerous vibes lessened a few degrees.

"I will certainly take this breach of trust up to Mackenzie, along with the insolence you exhibit."

Diggy inclined his head in acknowledgment, and at that Archer turned and began marching in the opposite direction, the couple with the brown aura and Elizabeth trailing behind.

"Wow," I said after people dispersed, "that was intense."

Diggy shrugged, scanning the room. "It isn't smart to antagonize the head of your clan. Especially when that person is Gerome Archer."

I stiffened at the reproach, even though I'd seen it coming. "He's not the boss of me."

"Technically, he is—"

"And is he always like that? It seemed like he was itching for a fight," I commented, cutting off what no doubt was to be a lesson on respectability.

Diggy frowned. "He seemed a little out of character."

"Maybe he shouldn't be here."

Diggy grunted. "I don't think he'll break any rules tonight. And Logan is around, so..."

He gestured and we moved toward the other side of the room, away from Archer and Elizabeth. I didn't see where Logan went, but if he was here to keep trouble from brewing, he should have stuck around when Archer had approached us. He sure looked like he had murder in mind.

"Why are they here anyway?" From what I understood from Vincent, Archer's estate and the clan's base was in Wyoming. Elizabeth lived down in California and Logan ... we hadn't talked about him.

Diggy shrugged again, placing his empty glass on a tray. "I heard they're looking for a missing scion."

Achill skipped down my spine. "What? Who?" Was it Mwara? *God, don't say Mwara. Please, don't let it be Mwara.*

"Not sure. But it's a young scion, a child from what I've been told. Rumor says she disappeared without a trace."

Something must have shown on my face because Diggy frowned, his eyes searching mine.

"Is it true what he said?" I asked, not sure what my expression looked like. "That I was following a schedule approved by him, that I was lent to the Hunters like an inanimate object?"

"Every member of a clan requires the approval of their superiors before they can join other preternatural groups. It's a rule implemented by every clan, every species."

"I don't remember asking Archer for that approval."

"No, and whatever problem you have with that, you take up with Roland." His tone was mild, a sign he was edging close to the end of his patience.

A glance toward the other end of the room revealed Elizabeth's gaze on me. From this distance I couldn't read the expression in her eyes, but I suspected it wasn't a friendly one.

On Archer's other side stood Logan, his head cocked to the side, eyes fixed on me as he listened to what Archer was saying. The redhead stood beside him, her arms looped around his.

"Who's Cara?" I asked, tearing my eyes away from the group.

Diggy paused, surprise registering for a second before disappearing. With the added four inches of heels, I was almost eye-to-eye with him.

"Where did you hear that name?"

"Rafael mentioned it once." Back then, in the basement apartment that belonged to Diggy, I hadn't given it a second thought. It was seeing the redhead draped over Logan like a Christmas ornament that brought Rafael and Logan's hushed conversation to mind.

He looked away, his eyes distant, a small furrow creasing his forehead. "She was Archer's daughter."

"Oh?" I said, surprised. "*Was?*"

"Yes. She was killed a long time ago."

"By who?"

"Remo Drammen."

Chapter Twelve

"Two o'clock. White man, blonde hair, dressed in a white tuxedo, talking with a black-haired short guy," Diggy murmured into a punch glass.

We moved forward, pausing when the aura in question flickered into range.

Blue. A touch paler than when it first appeared, now sky blue. A human aura.

Regardless of the fact only a handful of preternaturals were able to see auras, Diggy explained during large gatherings, some people felt paranoid enough to pay absurd sums of money on little charms to keep their identities anonymous.

"Roland swears by them," he'd said.

"And you?"

"Can't tell for sure, but George once mistook a vamp for ordinary, so it could be true."

As I searched the blue aura for a sign of what it was, I wondered if Roland was right.

"Not human," I murmured, stating the obvious.

"Hmmm. What else?" he asked, glancing over at the crowd.

I took in the guy, trying to sense more. About my height *sans* the heels, 180 pounds of dense, solid build. He stood a few feet away, hands moving as he talked, eyes crinkling with humor at whatever the other guy replied. Suddenly, the guy looked up, found me watching, gave a winning smile.

I nodded in acknowledgment and looked away. I counted, one, two... ten... fifteen and looked back. The guy had resumed his conversation with the shorter man, oblivious to my scrutiny.

I directed my awareness ahead, in the general direction of the guy. I included a few bystanders within that range, the way Diggy instructed, and concentrated on the center part, where the guy with the white tuxedo stood.

I took a tiny step back, another forward, feeling out his aura, tasting it with my other senses. Damn those heels, I thought, when I had to fight to stay balanced.

There was a sense of... of... damn, that was a strong charm. I tilted my head to the side, concentrating harder, trying to grasp that brief flicker. Something to do with nature, maybe an element. Could be a mage.

The guy was still talking, oblivious of my senses engulfing him. Throwing his head back, he barked out a loud laugh, the shorter man gesturing animatedly, a crooked smile on his round face. I shifted again, back and forth, sensing something like a current ... water? No, nothing so dense. Again I shifted and wondered what people would think if they were watching. Probably that I had to pee, and they wouldn't be far off the mark.

The shimmer appeared again in the inner line of the aura, disappearing faster than I could make sense of the color. White? A glowing pale blue? Eyes narrowed, I focused harder.

"Easy," Diggy murmured, half shifting in front of me, ready to block the path should the guy sense my probe.

And there it was, a swirling current, a twisting sensation. I'd have never noticed it, never have thought to focus so hard to sense something I didn't know was there if Diggy hadn't indicated otherwise.

"Try not to project. Tell me what you feel, what you sense. Trust your gut."

I shifted, back and forth.

The aura flashed. Light blue. There came that current again, something strong. Air, but more.

"Air?" I guessed. "Tornados," I added, feeling silly.

"Hmmm. More like a hurricane, but that's close enough," Diggy approved. He motioned forward, towards the tables.

More people had arrived, a couple hundred now, but there was still room for many more. My stomach rumbled, reminding me I hadn't eaten since lunch, and my bladder screamed for a break.

"Vemourly, you son of a bitch!" someone bellowed from behind us.

We both tensed, ready for a confrontation. When we turned, Diggy was enveloped in a bear-hug by a giant of a man. There was a lot of back clapping and exchange of filthy names. I relaxed, realizing no confrontation was about to take place, and stepped back, giving both men room.

The guy was taller than Diggy, maybe seven feet tall. His aura was the green of a were. Some sort of hunting bird, but I couldn't decipher which exactly, a hawk, an eagle, or something of that variety. Could he fly, I wondered, awed at the possibility.

I shifted my gaze to his companion, and in contrast to the hulking man, she was short and delicate, a petite woman with dark auburn hair. It fell in delicate waves down her lower back, accentuating a creamy, porcelain complexion. If she wore make-up, it didn't show. She stood about five foot two, and despite being short, she was wearing strappy sandals with flat soles. Her deep-green eyes matched both the color of her aura and long sleeveless dress. She was smiling affectionately up at Diggy, a were-cat of sorts, a jungle one.

And she reminded me of Lee.

I retreated a few more steps, not sure if I was giving them privacy or putting distance between me and the woman, or what, and *who*, she reminded me of.

"Boris. What are you doing here?" Diggy asked, his hazel eyes gleaming with delight.

"The same as you. The food is incredible," Boris replied with a booming voice that suited his size.

Diggy snorted. "You're too cheap for that. You'd rather eat mice than pay for a meal."

"True enough. But you also know I don't pass up invitations, especially when fancy dinners and beautiful women are included."

Diggy shifted to the woman beside him, his smile widening. "Xandra. What a wonderful surprise."

Xandra stepped forward, throwing thin but firm arms around Diggy's shoulders, forcing him to bend to accommodate her. There was a golden bracelet around her right wrist, a big green rock I was sure was the real deal sparkling in the center. She brushed her lips against Diggy's cheek, first one, then the other before stepping back and looping one arm around his forearm. It was an intimate gesture, but not a romantic one.

I took a few more steps away, fading into the background. Whoever these people were, they were dear to Diggy, part of his personal life. Something I was not. I gave him space, knowing he wouldn't want me to intrude.

I looked around, searching for familiar faces, telling myself I wasn't searching for Logan. There were a lot of people in the room, and although Diggy found some disguised auras, most weren't.

A guy a few feet ahead and to the right stood alone, hands tucked inside his pockets, observing the crowd. His shoulders were broad underneath the suit, his hair, a mop of black gloss, curled around his ears and neck. His aura was sky-blue and human. I registered this, and continued surveying the crowd, then returned. Fixed on him. The aura was the blue of a clear sky, yet different, too thin to be normal. Less than half the usual size. Disguised? Must be.

With care, I shot my awareness in his direction, careful to include a few bystanders so as not to be target-specific. I waited, but the guy didn't tense, didn't seem to sense me. I shifted. Once, twice ... four times. Kept my balance.

To my surprise, there was nothing there. Nothing extraordinary. The guy felt human, completely so. A human amidst preternaturals.

What do you see, what do you sense? Trust your instincts.

To the eye, he was human–except his aura was too thin, just a line.

I was about to shift back and forth again when I sensed something. It wasn't a feeling, exactly, or an emotion, something my empathic sense caught. No, it was something more, a presence, something more tangible.

I closed my eyes and reached out, focused on it.

A tiny touch like the whisper of a thrumming sound. Like static, something that, embarrassingly, I wouldn't have noticed if my bladder wasn't so full.

Thrum thrum thrum thrum thrum.

What was that, I wondered, just as something warm and gentle brushed across my awareness, a soft caress.

Jerking, I opened my eyes and found the guy facing me. Still in his previous spot. Just a few feet away, hands deep inside his pockets, watching with deep, dark blue eyes set in a masculine, appealing face. He had a strong jaw, a patrician nose, a golden complexion. His posture suggested he was both relaxed and confident. With a body and face like that, anyone would be.

He was handsome. His hair was almost long enough to be tied back, curling in whatever direction it chose. His eyebrows were thick, arching above those eyes, a shade of blue so dark, they seemed more violet than anything else.

He wasn't so much handsome as beautiful, if a man could be called so. So beautiful, I thought, embarrassed with the thought. The guy's eyebrows raised slowly, suggestively, a sensual smile tugging at his lips.

There was something familiar about him. Had we met before?

He cocked his head, puzzling me, and again that warm, gentle thrum brushed against my awareness. I jerked back, as if the touch had been as much physical as psychic, and glanced away, face heating with embarrassment.

That's when I noticed the faint shimmer in Xandra's aura, a barely perceptible silvery sheen that marked her as something else. My eyes shifted to Boris's aura, but his lacked the shimmer. So did Diggy's.

How much could I bet that both Xandra and Boris were from the Seelie Dhiultadh clan? A lot, because I'd win the bet.

Diggy glanced up, a small smile tugging at his lips. It was genuine, and I realized I'd never seen it before. He motioned me forward. I shook my head, and the woman turned, smiling, her eyes warm and sincere.

"Is that her?" she asked, hands outstretched.

Unsure, I glanced away, caught the guy's knowing smirk, looked back at the woman. Uncomfortable with all the attention, I took a step forward, then another.

Her hands were soft and warm, and she didn't just take my hand and shake it in introduction, but pulled me forward for a close, fragrant hug before letting go and stepping back. "It's always good to meet Doug's friends. We barely get to see him with all that work and traveling he does; he's like a stranger these days." She pulled me into the group, her arm, slender but firm, still gripping mine. "Douglas says you two work together? I've always wanted to be a member, but Boris would have none of that and Douglas vetoed it."

I glanced at the big guy, who feigned a shudder at the idea. "And a favor to the world that is," he said, winking. "I'm Boris, Xandra's mate." He took my hand before I could extend it, pumped it twice, his hold firm and dry.

"Doug says you're Roland's new recruit."

"That I am. I'm still learning the ropes." I glanced at Diggy, watching Xandra with a warm smile.

It was something new, to see this tough guy with a genuine and open smile.

"So how's being apprenticed by Doug feel like?" Boris asked, leaning down to eye me better.

"Feels like I'm his punching bag," I replied, to Xandra's and Boris' delight.

Diggy scowled, but I only shrugged. "It is true."

"That's because you refuse to learn."

"No, it's because you take out all your frustrations on me."

"Tell you what, sweetheart," Boris said with a wink, "why don't you come over and let me teach you whatever Doug here is teaching you? I promise you I can teach you better, faster, even more."

I looked him up and down, his tree-trunk limbs, his thick neck, making a show of it, and shook my head. "Nah-uh, I'll take the devil I know." Xandra burst out laughing.

She hooked both arms around my forearm and smiled. "I like you already. Why don't you come over with Doug next weekend? We're getting together for dinner and a movie." Sensing a refusal coming, she added, "I'd love to get to know you. Being around those brutes with no girl company gets tedious."

I hesitated, not wanting to seem rude, but getting inside Diggy's personal life was something I was sure he wouldn't appreciate. Meeting his friends and being introduced by chance was one thing; agreeing to meet with them later was something else.

"I'll think about it," I said in a non-committal tone.

"Please do." She gave Diggy a stern look. "You bring her with you when you come. And *do* come. I hate to keep making excuses for you. It's like your job has taken up your entire life."

It was Diggy's turn to shrug, but he didn't say anything.

* * *

As the ballroom filled with preternaturals, Diggy's lesson continued.

Four o'clock, bald guy with a mustache. Nine o'clock, brunette in an egg-white dress. To the left, sable-black hair, jet-black eyes, ruby-red shirt. On and on we went, pausing on occasion to talk to someone else or be introduced. Whenever I caught glimpses of Elizabeth, worry for Mwara would rush back. Then Diggy would demand I pay attention, and I'd put thoughts of the child on the backburner.

The next time we crossed Xandra and Boris's path, I pointed with my chin and said, "They're like you."

Diggy paused, glanced at me, eyebrows furrowed. "What?"

"I didn't see anything in Boris's aura, but with Xandra, there was the telltale silvery sheen. It wasn't something I was looking for."

Diggy's gaze moved to the couple a few feet away, talking with a group of women and men, expression pensive.

"I suppose she should have stayed home," he said with a frown. "She's expecting, and it seems it's more stressful than she's letting on." He sighed, and without another word, turned and steered us toward the stage where band members were testing musical instruments. Most preternaturals were gathered there, watching and throwing funny or flirtatious remarks at them.

Halfway there, I spotted a familiar face. Two, if the woman dressed in an elegant garnet-red ankle-length dress was Tony, the quiet werewolf from the Hunters.

I grabbed Diggy's arm and pointed. "Look, that's Vincent and Tony," I said and broke away to intercept them, happy to see my mentor after all these weeks.

Tony spotted me first and smiled. When Vincent turned to me, my smile froze, half formed.

This wasn't Vincent at all. Not because his aura didn't shine silvery-blue, or because the tiny greenish shimmer in the disguised blue gave it away. No, it was the hostile glare, so out of character, that gave him away.

Tony touched the sleeve of Vincent's white suit and the glare switched to a pleasant smile, as if he'd just remembered this wasn't the right expression to display. But the disdain was still there, in the depths of those black eyes.

I recoiled a step, half turning before Diggy's hand grabbed mine and squeezed. I looked at him, ready to voice the obvious, but the warning glint in those hazel eyes had me swallowing back my words.

"Vagner," Diggy said with the respect given to a superior. "Lopez," he addressed Tony next.

"Vemourly." They shook hands.

Vincent inclined his head to me in brief acknowledgment before shifting to the crowd cheering the band. "The gathering today sure went for the theme. The enclave should make more of these, hmm, romantic atmospheres. Seems to me even the old ones are into it."

We followed Vincent's gaze to where a few vampires stood talking to Archer and Elizabeth.

"Mmm-mm." Diggy turned back to Vincent and Tony. "Will you be lingering after dinner?"

"Certainly. With the Garage playing and the crowd so primed, I wouldn't miss it," Vincent's doppelganger replied.

"Not a wise thing, given all those new cases," Diggy commented with a shrug, his gaze holding that warning glint. "Me, I'd stay long enough to meet requirement and leave, but that's just what I'd do."

Vincent inclined his head in an exact replica of the real Vincent. "Your opinion is so noted."

"And," Diggy added, expression amused, "I'd give Gerome a wide berth, seeing he's steamed that Roxanne is spending time with me."

I got it then. If I recognized this wasn't Vincent, someone else would too. Like Archer, the head of his clan.

Vincent's doppelganger glanced to where Archer stood, nodded once to Diggy and me and moved away without another word.

* * *

"Why are all those people gathered here, Diggy? What's this charity ball for?" Because it was obvious I was missing the big picture. We were standing at the back wall beside the stage, people-watching. Or rather *I* was people-watching. Diggy was searching for our next target, leaning against the wall with one shoulder, hands tucked in his trouser pockets.

One of the band members tapped on the microphone and people started cheering. The guy smiled to the crowd and announced dinner would be served in twenty minutes.

"As a front? Some mumbo-jumbo nonsense about ecology, preserving nature, historic sites, stuff like that."

"But?"

"But it's payment. For the government, to let us be. For our kids to attend any school or college of their choosing, get normal jobs, live freely. Something like taxpaying." He straightened and motioned with his head toward a group.

"You do this every year?" I stepped beside him.

"Twice a year, sometimes. There are other balls, too. This one covers the north-east region. At the last trimester of the year there will be another one, for those who couldn't attend tonight."

"So many," I murmured. "What if someone can't pay?"

"Some don't. Some won't." He paused near a group, his hazel eyes serious. "Those who won't, if discovered, have no rights. They're fair bait for the Scientists, for other rival clans who pay. Mostly, they live in isolated areas, or in fear of discovery. Their children are educated at home, their jobs nothing fancy. For those who can't afford the payment and still want the benefits, they volunteer for the war, go into law enforcement, become firefighters."

"So much money."

He nodded once. "For some of us who have lived a long while and accumulated enough wealth, these gatherings are pesky, necessary and unavoidable. Still, some would rather not attend, yet still want the benefits should the unfortunate event of discovery fall upon them. Those send clan representatives to the gatherings, pay the required attendance rate and still stay anonymous." Diggy nodded to a couple chatting with a guy with a yellow aura, falling silent as we passed. "Like Archer, for example, and most of your clan. Vincent was the go-guy for that, representing all the members who wanted to stay anonymous. And before that, I guess it was your father."

"But they took him anyway. Tortured him to an inch of his life," I added, remembering the way Archer had looked then, fragile and weak. "But if they're kept anonymous, how can the PSS tell if they pay or not?"

"Good question." Diggy nodded in approval. "Their names and prints are in the system. When they took Archer, all they had to do was run his prints. They knew who he was from day one. And because they did, they couldn't charge or ask for justice for all the carnage and damage you guys left behind."

"So now that I'm a Hunter member and am here, attending?" Diggy's flat expression softened a bit, something that I wouldn't have been able to tell a few months ago.

"Yes, this was why Roland wanted you to attend. To let people know that not only are you paying your share, but that you're a member of the Hunters too. You'd have come with Vincent if he could have made it," he added quietly, his gaze following Vincent's doppelganger across the room. "Come on. Let's do one more round before it's time to eat."

Chapter Thirteen

"Well, well," said a deep voice beside me.

I turned, only to find myself face-to-face with violet-blue eyes and an aura so thin I could hardly discern the color right.

Diggy turned, his eyes going icy cold. It was a wonder that the temperature didn't drop. "Well, well," Diggy drawled in return, eyeing the man up and down. "Look what the storm dragged in."

"Storm, no. But I did catch sight of Iris around," he responded with a fake smile, so thin and brittle, it should have cracked like ice.

Diggy took a casual step forward, half-covering me, disguising the gesture with a mock bow. "If it isn't Akinzo, finally back from a long vacation from wherever. It's so good of you to join us," he scoffed.

"It was a wonderful vacation. I saw so much, learned so much. There's so much unknown out there, it amazes me." There was a glint of excitement in his deep-blue eyes, a gleam that said the vacation was indeed amazing. "Maybe you should take one, Vemourly. You know, get that stick out."

I coughed to hide a startled laugh and the guy looked at me. We were eye level with each other, putting the man about six foot four, an inch or two shorter than Diggy, though no less formidable in presence. This close, I could see his eyes weren't really violet, but an improbable shade of dark blue.

That's when I recognized him. My mirth died, my expression blanked.

Violet eyes. Eyes I'd once seen clouded with pain. Eyes that had wanted me to end it for him.

I knew him. I remembered him.

He had been emaciated then, the bones of his ribs and back pronounced. He'd changed, gained some much needed weight. Gotten some color into his complexion. He'd looked like a ghost the last time I'd seen him. Hooked to a number of strange machines with weird symbols, connected by a slender stream of blue laser light.

He had not been on vacation. Unless the PSS could be considered an extension of Disneyland.

Ladies and gentlemen, our newest attraction! The house of horrors!

"Who's this lovely lady?" he asked, eyes piercing.

"No one," Diggy said, his voice tight.

Akinzo barely spared him a glance. Though the expression on his face was friendly, the intensity of his gaze felt probing.

He remembered me. Despite all the pain, the glazed look in his eyes, he recognized me too.

"I'm Zantry Akinzo," he said, not extending a hand.

"Hello. I'm Roxanne," I replied, ignoring Diggy's scowl.

"What a lovely name." He offered a charming smile, the corners of his eyes crinkling with pleasure.

"She's off-limits to you, so beat it."

"So, Roxanne." Akinzo tucked his hands into his pockets as he rocked back on his heels. "Are you from around here?"

He was fishing. It meant he hadn't yet found anything about me. About the person who freed him from infinite torture.

If I were in his shoes I'd have liked to know more about someone who saved my life, so I cut him some slack.

"I am now."

"Ah, new to the city. How do you like it?"

"It's alright." I shrugged, aware of Diggy's glare.

"Back off, Zantry," Diggy said ominously.

Akinzo turned to him. "Why, my friend, are you being so rude?" he asked, then straightened with realization, his searching eyes moving between Diggy and me. "Unless she's your lover?"

Diggy's scowl darkened.

I swallowed a chuckle, but I was so going to rub this in his face.

"A slave?" Akinzo asked next, and the ominous vibration I sensed from him caught me by surprise.

Diggy's rumbling growl was low, but carried enough resonance to call the attention of the nearest passersby. The brown-aura couple appeared out of nowhere, moved nearer, their intense brown eyes fixed on us with displeasure.

"No, I'm a Hunter member," I replied before Diggy could start a fight.

Akinzo paused, his head cocking aside. The information surprised him, even if it didn't show, and he relaxed. "You must be new to the guild then. I don't remember meeting you before."

"I am," I said, then added, "I became a member about Three months ago."

Something flickered in Akinzo's eyes, so fast gone that I couldn't decipher.

"Take a hike, Akinzo. She's my responsibility," Diggy snapped.

Akinzo spared Diggy a brief glance. "Are you underage?"

"No."

"Then I don't see why you're so wound up about me exchanging harmless words with this lovely lady." He gave me a charming smile, his eyes twinkling with mischief. He was baiting Diggy and loving every moment of it. "You should reserve me a dance later. I hear the band is popular."

Diggy stepped closer, speaking through clenched teeth. "Back off, Akinzo. I mean it. She's off-limits. Believe me, you don't want to go there."

"That a threat?" Akinzo asked with interest.

"If you don't back off, damn right."

Akinzo angled his head, his eyes level and not the least intimidated. "You willing to risk the enclave?" He looked at the brown-aura couple, now watching and near enough to hear, then back to Diggy, ready to accept whatever reply he was given.

The tension between the two men was tangible, and escalating with every breath. Why were they fighting over me? Diggy was my instructor, Akinzo a stranger I helped once.

I stepped forward. "I don't dance. And I think you should go," I said firmly.

The smile returned to Akinzo's eyes. He bowed once, took my hand and kissed the knuckles. A frisson of static passed from him to me, though I couldn't really say the sensation was unpleasant. "Then, lovely Roxanne, I'll see you next time." Tucking hands back into his pockets, he turned and strolled away.

I gave Diggy a sideways glance as the crowd started to disperse. Again. "Why did you do that?" I asked as we moved away.

His jaw tightened. "That man is dangerous, a traitor, and a manipulative bastard. Stay away from him."

"I imagine a lot of people here fall under that description. Even some of those you introduced me to."

His expression was icy-cold. "This one is different. You are *my* responsibility. If you tangle with Zantry Akinzo on my watch, Roland will have my ass. Until Vincent returns, I forbid you to go near that man."

I raised my eyebrows, not liking the ultimatum one bit. "If I do?"

He didn't miss a beat. "I won't stop you. But I'll report it to Roland and wash my hands of the problem."

I nodded. *The problem.* How could I forget that was exactly how Diggy saw me?

I left Diggy stewing and excused myself to go to the bathroom. It was while I was washing my hands, going over my encounter with Zantry Akinzo that the middle-aged woman I'd seen earlier walked in.

I glanced over, met her dark eyes and hurried to look down, recalling the feeling of being unable to look away.

"Hello," she said politely, coming beside me to wash her hands. Every finger had a bawdy ring on it, some matching the many necklace hoops around her neck.

"Hello." I replied, in a hurry to get the hell out of there.

"My name is Matilda. My friends call me Mattie."

I gave her a weak smile. "I'm Roxanne." I took a step towards the door.

"I know. You look like your father."

I paused, my inner voice warning me she'd said this to get my attention. "You knew him?"

"Not really," she replied. "But I'd like to talk to you. There are things you need to know. About how you–" The door of the bathroom opened, "are wearing a beautiful dress." She finished. It wasn't what she was going to say, but the woman who entered–the redhead who'd been with Logan, obviously was not supposed to hear.

The redhead's aura was blue, plain and human, but the dangerous glint in her black eyes was enough to tell me she was more than what her aura said. No doubt a Dhiultadh. A good one, because there was no silvery shimmer in the inner line.

She inclined her head at me and Matilda before heading toward a stall.

"It was nice to meet you, Roxanne," Matilda said, extending her hand.

Automatically I took it, feeling the crisp fold of the paper she passed me. Without another word, Matilda turned and left the bathroom, and I tucked the note into my tiny purse.

The stall door opened, and the redhead stepped out. No toilet flushed, no clothes rustled. She glanced at the closed bathroom door before advancing to the sinks.

"Did Logan send you?" I asked, because it was clear she hadn't come in to pee.

"Yes. He saw Matilda follow you. I was sent to make sure you were fine."

"Why?"

The redhead shrugged, dried her hands and left without a word.

When I returned, Diggy was seated, engaged in conversation with the woman of the brown-aura. Neither paid attention when I sat beside him, relieved to finally remove some pressure from my tortured feet.

Chapter Fourteen

The food was excellent, the conversation light. The band, once the food was served, began playing slow, classic music. Two vampire couples sat with us, along with the brown-aura woman, Cora, and the guy with the teal aura, David Lee.

Both Cora and David Lee were members of the enclave, a group of powerful beings that formed the Grand Council of the preternaturals.

The Hunters, Diggy said, answered to them first and foremost, even before they answered to Uncle Sam.

Aside from being one of the twelve members of the enclave, Cora was also the leader of the earth witch coven, and she was powerful and dangerous, one of a few left from her line.

On the other hand, David Lee was a basilisk, the one and only king of snakes. I'd correctly sensed something reptilian in him, but wrongly undermined his danger meter. At the moment, the man with the brown aura, Cora's counterpart, and Avaran, David Lee's mate, were seated on the table with Archer and Elizabeth. I wondered if the arrangement was intentional, a warning of sorts?

As the meal progressed, laughter could be heard from every direction, along with good-natured curses and shouts. Beneath the soft strings of the band, clinking glasses and chiming silverware echoed around the vast room.

It was the general mood of a fancy restaurant, spiked with the menacing pheromones of savage, dominant predators. I had been introduced around the table, and after everyone determined I was just a lowly mixed breed, I was cast aside without a second glance. No one talked to me, and I took the opportunity to study those present. I did, of course, search for Angelina, but she wasn't present.

A serious-looking waiter placed a huge chunk of roasted herb-infused meat and roasted vegetables in front of me, and I dug in, finding it delicious. Now and then I stole glances at Logan, talking and smiling at the redhead a few tables away. Behind them sat Archer and Elizabeth, their eyes searching the room, their expressions as if they'd tasted something sour, their food untouched.

Mwara came back to mind, her fear, her defiance. "I'll run," she'd told me. It had been the week before Christmas. Could she have been missing ever since?

My mouth went dry with worry I didn't want to feel, and the food I'd swallowed turned into led. I pushed my plate away, my appetite completely gone.

Diggy raised a brow, but I ignored him and picked up my water.

Where did you go, Mwara?

After dessert was served, vanilla-bean Crème brûlée, which I ate with gusto, the band began playing in earnest. The vocalist, who'd been playing the guitar to that point, put the instrument down and stood, to the delight and encouraging cheers of the crowd. His voice was strong and pleasing, the song one I'd never heard, but it seemed to be popular among this particular group. A lot of the guests started singing along. A few grabbed their partners and pulled them to the dance floor, to the claps and cheers of others.

Even Diggy grabbed his drink and leaned back to enjoy the song, a faint smile playing on his lips when Xandra dragged an uncomfortable Boris to the center.

It was a new side of a community I'd learned were nothing but barbarians with penchants for violence and blood.

How long would it take to become part of this community? Would I ever belong, or would I stay an outcast forever?

* * *

I'd expected to leave soon after the meal, but Diggy still wasn't satisfied with our lesson, so we mingled. My teacher was nothing but a thorough pain in my ass. And feet. God, my feet. How could people be willing to put on such mockery of footwear and march to their jobs from eight to five, five days a week? What was wrong with the women of the world? If my feet could scream, they'd be raising the dead by now.

Diggy dragged me across the room, back and forth like a serial killer searching for the best mark. The crowd loosened up after the meal and music, so it was easier for me to stare and send my awareness without being sensed.

And then my mentor decided I should find and identify disguised auras. It wasn't an easy task, given most of the time the aura was exactly what I thought it was, no disguises. Born vampires, made ones, shifters–there were only three in the entire crowd that I could find–mages, magic wielders–also called sorcerers–witches, a lot of weres, charmers, and the basilisk couple. And an elemental called Iris. Diggy explained Iris was a human who had been raised in the Seelie court–a promised child–and who now carried the element form of a banished Fee, a Seelie warrior who once defied Queen Titania. It was a symbiotic bond between both souls, giving Iris youth and immortality while allowing the banished Fee, Storm, to manifest.

It was after midnight when we'd had enough and Diggy called it a night.

By then I'd developed an annoying low-grade headache and my feet... oh God, my feet were killing me! My arches were stretched thin, ready to snap at the next step; my little toes were numb and the balls of my feet were a mess of painful agony.

We drove in silence, both lost in our thoughts. My mind played over the entire evening, snagging over and over on Mwara, taunting me with horrible scenarios where she was being tortured by the PSS, or taken by some other monster. I had to tell myself she was fine and safe, just "running" whenever she sensed someone from the clan closing in. But a part of me, a more logical one, pointed out she was just a kid, and no matter how clever she was, if she was running, someone from the clan should have found her by now.

By the time Diggy parked in front of my building, I decided to call Roland in the morning and tell him about Mwara and ask for advice.

* * *

I awoke to the insistent sound of the doorbell ringing. Groaning, I glanced at the bright-green digits on the bedside clock.

"Go away, for God's sake," I called out. Burying my head under the pillow, I imagined myself ripping the ringing box off the wall and hammering it into tiny little pieces.

Ding-dong, ding-dong.

Smash-boom, smash-boom.

Ding-dong, ding-dong. Ding-dong, ding-dong. On and on and on it went.

"For fuck's sake!" Outraged, I threw away the covers and got out of bed, promising myself if it was a salesperson I would punch him, then sick the police on them for disturbing the peace at 7:30 on a freaking Sunday morning.

Driven with the urge to do violence, I moved with purpose down the hall, my arches still smarting from the previous night. I wrenched open the door, only to hiss in shock when a gust of freezing wind hit me square on. It slipped through my thin oversized shirt and flannel pants and seeped deep into my bones.

"Good morning to you too," Logan said, his gray eyes twinkling with amusement. "You should put on a robe before opening the door in such freezing temperatures. It's bound to be uncomfortable."

"Logan," I said, surprised.

"Hello. I see your night attire hasn't changed."

"What are you doing here?"

The smile around his eyes faded and he glanced behind me. "I thought I'd come and see how you're doing since I was already in town. I didn't get to talk to you last night."

No, you were too busy with that redhead.

"Come in," I said, opening the door wider.

"I don't want to interrupt."

I snorted. "You already did. Might as well come in."

He hesitated. "Are you alone?"

I frowned. "It's too early for company. I was asleep."

"So what did I interrupt?" he asked, following me into the kitchen.

"My dreams," I replied, glancing back in time to see the glint of humor in his eyes.

He was dressed in black jeans, a leather jacket zipped up and worn, sturdy boots. His hair was tousled, either by the wind or design, his cheeks shadowed with stubble.

Unsure about what to say or what to do next, I moved to the coffee machine, deciding coffee could never be wrong. I measured the beans, filled the boiler with water, then filled Frizz's dish with ground meat, sure Vicky had returned the bowl I prepared last night and fed him plenty of grease and sweet junk. I sighed. She'd have taken him home with her if she could.

"Have your carnivore tendencies grown in these past months?" Logan asked with a bewildered smile.

I chuckled, shook my head, delayed doubt creeping in. But if I left the bowl on the counter, it would be more awkward. The same if I returned it to the fridge. After warming it some in the microwave, I placed the bowl on the island where Frizz usually sat. For a second Frizz didn't show himself, no doubt picking on my hesitation, but when I sent him an encouraging thought, he blinked into existence, not even twitching when Logan swore and jumped back. "You have a mother-fucking gargoyle!"

"A what?" I asked, startled. I glanced at Frizz, at the small wings, the clawed hands and feet, the pointed ears.

A gargoyle?

"Gargoyle, huh?" I repeated, amused.

"When did you–" His eyes narrowed and I caught the second he realized when, and how, I'd acquired a gargoyle. "Why don't you just ask him for something and let him go back to whatever hole he crawled out from?"

I stiffened at his callous words, but he didn't notice. "I thought you used him to help you back that night in the Society?"

"You knew about him?"

He shrugged. "It was kind of obvious."

He'd known that day going into the PSS I had a shadow. That reminded me. I skipped to my room, picked up the bracelet and handed it back to him.

Logan took it, expression unreadable. His finger traced the dark rock, devoid of the magic it had once contained.

"I didn't know how strong it would be," he said, glancing up.

"It was..." I trailed off, unsure what to say. The bracelet hadn't been strong enough to shatter building B alone, but I wasn't sure what happened that night. What had awakened within.

"You should keep it." He placed the bracelet on the counter.

I frowned down at it, said nothing, turned and opened the cupboard.

I poured black coffee for him and another with sugar for me, and thought about all the chaos I'd left behind that day in the PSS, all the lives I had no right taking.

Handing him a mug, I leaned back at the counter. "So why are you here?"

His eyes searched mine. "I wanted to check on you. See how you were fairing."

You could have asked yesterday. "I'm doing fine."

He placed the mug aside without taking a sip. "You weren't supposed to sign an agreement with the Hunters. They'd have gotten us out of there with or without it."

There it was: guilt.

"You and Archer, maybe Rafael. But not me."

"You included," he insisted. Frizz's ears flicked, but he didn't raise his head or pause eating.

"Archer was caught because he was searching for you."

"No. He knew about me all along. When he went to investigate the rumor about a scion captured by the PSS, he hadn't expected it to be me." I was the scapegoat because my father fucked up, something Elizabeth admitted when I'd gone to confront her.

"When I was born, I–" I swallowed and looked down at my hands, the words still hard to speak. I was the reason my mother died. "I was born with talons. The Scientists had their eyes on my parents by then, and my birth only spotlighted me as dangerous. There was some legal issue as to who would raise me after my father died. It was decided a member of the clan would raise me and determine how much of my father I'd inherited. Once it was concluded all I had was talons, strength and endurance, the clan gave the PSS their blessings." I finished with, "Elizabeth told me so herself when I confronted her."

Logan clenched his jaw, but didn't voice whatever thought churned in his head. He picked up his coffee and blew on it before taking a sip.

I went on, the resentment I'd tried to suppress bubbling to the surface. "When you took me to Elizabeth, you knew who she was, what she was to me."

"That's not true. I mean, I knew about her, what she was, her position in the clan. But I've been out of the game for a long time, long enough I was surprised to find Fosch's daughter–someone I'd vaguely heard about–running from the society, and that no one was trying to protect her" He drew a deep breath. "I was surprised when you told me the society had been waiting in Elizabeth's home for you, that she watched them take you and did nothing about it, and surprised when you told me you'd been a captive in the PSS for nine years."

"I wasn't a captive. They had guardianship over me."

He clenched his jaw again, his eyes cold, his anger wafting like cold waves, a refreshing tang I'd once tasted.

I angled my head. "Wouldn't you know if Elizabeth and Fosch had a daughter together?"

Logan nodded. "I knew she wasn't your mother, yes." He raised a hand before I could cut him off. "But when I first heard about Fosch and his bargain with the Seelie, some years had already passed, and honestly, back then, I didn't care. I was told the daughter had been hidden away, and I knew a clan member would be taking care of you. So when you said you were looking for your mother, I presumed it was the person who'd raised you. There are only a few clan members in that general vicinity, and all go by different names among the humans, so I snuck out and brought you some photos."

"You once said Archer was your mentor. Shouldn't you be better informed about clan affairs?" I asked, my suspicion not appeased.

"Yes, but at the time I wasn't in the right frame of mind to question anything. Someone mentioned to me the daughter would be sent away, told me about the bargain and Fosch. That's it. Maybe I was told about who'd be responsible for your upbringing, but if I was, I can't remember. I never asked about details, never questioned the reason, how or why."

"Yeah, no one cared to know," I murmured, regretting my words the moment pity entered his eyes. He stepped forward; I stepped back, not wanting anyone's pity, much less his.

"I'm sorry about that. I'm sorry you went through all you did. Believe me when I tell you Elizabeth took a lot of heat from Archer because of you."

I recalled the way Elizabeth had looked last night, the tension in her expression. Maybe that hardness had nothing to do with Mwara and everything to do with the heat she'd taken from Archer. Maybe Mwara was home, and the missing scion was someone else.

A hope so awful and selfish filled my being and I prayed the missing scion was someone else's kid. I was a terrible person for feeling this way, but I couldn't help it. I needed to know, though, to be sure, to banish the worry and guilt. I'd planned to talk to Roland this morning, but I knew Logan would be better informed.

I took in a deep breath. "I need to ask you something, Logan." The slight quiver in my voice didn't go unnoticed, and Logan straightened, eyes concerned. "What is it?"

"It's not anything. I mean, it's something, but it's another topic. It doesn't have to do with me and Elizabeth." I frowned at my word choices. "No, it has all to do with Elizabeth, and probably me." I fell quiet, trying to predict the way Logan would take the news.

"Did Elizabeth do something?"

I shook my head. "Well, maybe." I didn't need to interpret his furrowing brow to know I wasn't making any sense. I sighed. There wasn't a good way to go about this. "It's got to do with the reason you're here in New York."

Logan tilted his head. "What do you know about the reason I'm here?"

"I heard you were looking for a missing scion?" When Logan neither denied nor affirmed, I plowed on, "Is it—is it Mwara?"

Logan stiffened, his eyes chilled. "How do you know?"

All the warmth left my body at the ferocity in his eyes. He looked like a lion about to pounce on prey. The person standing in front of me was no one I had met before.

"I don't know anything, I didn't know she was missing. I only found out yesterday."

Logan didn't relax, but the frost in his eyes thawed a bit, his forehead creased.

"But I did see her a while back. About a week before Christmas." I hoped beyond hope that she went missing last week.

"Where did you see her?" he demanded.

"When did she go missing?" I asked instead.

"Was she alone?" he asked next, not giving an inch.

I clenched my jaw. "Yes, she was alone. She came to see me and intercepted me one evening when I was walking home from base."

"Where?"

"About a block away. Tell me, when did she go missing?"

"I want you to take me to where you saw her last. Relate everything she told you, anything you remember, and leave nothing out."

"Ok, but tell me, when did she go missing?"

"Around Christmas."

Something akin to grief prickled deep within.

"What did she want? Did you talk to her? How did she get here?" Logan fired one question after the other, either indifferent or not seeing the stricken look in my eyes. Could she be in the PSS, suffering through Dr. Maxwell's ministrations? And if she wasn't, how could she be missing all this time and still be safe, alone?

Chapter Fifteen

I told Logan everything. From that moment I sensed eyes on me to the moment I watched Mwara walk away.

When I fell silent, Logan's gaze grew distant, his expression troubled.

The guilt that began yesterday intensified ten-fold. "I didn't think she would run. I told her not to," I said, aware my remorse meant nothing.

Logan placed a comforting hand on my shoulder. "We'll find her. We have the best trackers searching for her." But if they were going to find her, they would have done that already.

"Are you part of the search team?"

"Yes."

"Let me change and take you to where I met her," I said after an awkward pause.

Logan straightened. "In a moment. We need to talk about some things first." There was an intense, serious look in his eyes that told me the important part had yet to come.

I halted, then cleared Frizz's bowl from the table and sat.

"I heard Doug took up your training."

"He did." I studied the polite expression, trying to figure him out. What *are you gearing up to say?*

"He's a good instructor."

I grunted, took a sip of my warm coffee and waited.

"He said Zantry Akinzo approached you yesterday."

I paused, my eyes scanning his calm expression, leaned back on my chair and frowned at him. "He gives you an update about everyone who approaches me?"

"No, just Akinzo."

I picked up my coffee, my eyes fixed on his, put it back down without taking a sip. "I don't see how that's any of your concern."

He exhaled. "Actually, it is, and that's another thing we should talk about, after I explain the clan hierarchy."

Unsettled, I remained silent. I didn't think what he was about to say would make me feel any better. There was a thick, tense air in the room, as if doom was on the horizon and we expected it to arrive any moment.

Logan took a sip of coffee as he scrutinized my face. "Look, Zantry Akinzo is dangerous. Take this advice from a friend, Roxanne." His gray eyes were earnest. "Stay away from him. He's not someone you want to tangle with."

"Oh, what is he?"

Instead of answering, he frowned down at his mug, got up and poured himself the last of the coffee from the carafe. "I think it'd be smarter if we talked about Remo Drammen first."

Chapter Sixteen

My heart skipped a beat at the mention of the sorcerer. "Diggy told me he killed Cara, Archer's daughter." Even as I said it, I regretted it. The pain that flashed in his eyes was so intense, so unexpected, I wanted to kick myself to next Sunday and back again. I got up, but didn't go to him. There was a distant air about him, a driving vibe that seemed to push things–people–away, that wanted no shape of comfort. "I'm sorry, that was insensitive of me."

Logan took a deep breath, composing himself, clearing the pain from his eyes. "No," he waved a hand in the air, "that's alright. I suppose you'd want to know. It's your right as a clan member."

"You–you two were close?" I asked. Of course they were. Didn't he tell me Archer raised him? However, nothing he could have said would have shocked me more than his next words.

"She was my mate," he said, expression calm.

"Oh," Was all I could think to say. I wanted to go to him, to give him a hug, any comfort at all, but I was rooted to the spot. I felt as distant from him as the sun was from earth. Wouldn't the death of a mate have debilitated him?

In the *Guide Book of the Preternatural*, there was a paragraph saying the death of a mate could cause the other to insanity, or to commit suicide. At the very least, the death would impair the survivor. I glanced at the end table where the book sat catching dust, then back at Logan.

For him to be here, functioning a hundred percent meant her death occurred a long time ago, or he confused love for the mate bond—also mentioned in the guidebook. I took a sip of coffee to conceal my face, and the confused expression I was afraid I couldn't mask. Love or mate, why did it matter? "I'm sorry I asked."

"No, you should know," he insisted. He took in a deep breath, let it out through his nose.

Wanting to give him time to compose, I excused myself and headed to the bathroom, to wash my pale face with cold water. I stared at my expression, my too-wide eyes, and wanted to slap myself. A *mate*. No wonder Diggy had been surprised when I'd dropped her name so casually.

What are you feeling, Roxanne? I asked my reflection, wide eyes staring back with no hint of emotion.

Hurt, disappointment, dejection? Surprised no one ever told you this before? Relief that you never gave in to the attraction, knowing that it'd have never gone beyond a casual fling? They were all there plus more, spinning within, with relief and hurt fighting to lead.

There was so much going on inside me, things I didn't care to examine, at least not with Logan in the next room.

Toweling my face dry, I left the bathroom, padding back to the living room where Logan sat, only to be slapped on the face with another startling, disturbing reality the moment Logan's green and yellow aura came into range and the inner line shimmered. A silvery shimmer that I wasn't supposed to see.

I stopped in my tracks and Logan gave me a reassuring smile. "It's ok, Roxanne. No need to tiptoe around me. I was going to tell you anyway..." He trailed off, his eyes distant. "I already told you I was still a baby when Archer found me in the backstreets of this city."

I nodded when he paused to peer into his empty mug, a distant look in his eyes. "He took me in and provided for me. Because I wasn't a member, I wasn't discussed with the clan right away. It was Alleena who first saw me, when I was still a toddler, and confronted Archer with it. But Archer was head of the clan and the position gave him power. If he wanted to raise me, then raise me he would."

Logan fixed his gaze on me, his expression beyond serious. "He was never a father in the way you think a father should be. Had it not been for Arianna, the woman Archer loved, he'd never have taken me home. He provided shelter, food, education. He kept me off the streets and a possible trip to the dungeons of the Scientists. But he was never a *father* to me. There was never that bond between us, though I looked up to him and tried to live up to his expectations." He frowned, his eyes searching mine. "I don't mean that to sound ungrateful. I say that so you'll understand what I'll tell you next."

I nodded again, not sure if I would understand. How could Archer have raised him and never act the part of a father? Because whatever Elizabeth's fault, she'd played her part well.

"When I was old enough to read," Logan went on, "he deemed me grown enough to be left alone, and sometimes he and Arianna would leave me for long periods, sometimes months, making sure I had enough provisions and a skeletal staff to help get me by. Then when I was about eight, they left for a long time. When Archer came back, Arianna wasn't with him, but the baby was. He called her Cara. She looked like him. When Alleena arrived for their annual meeting that year, Archer announced Cara was his daughter. No one said who the mother was; no one dared ask, even if everyone knew. They all doted on her. It was obvious she was one of them."

My heart ached for the boy he must have been, alone and afraid, waiting for his hero to return, only to be replaced by something new, something better.

"I helped them take care of her. I helped him train her. Then one day, out of the blue, I looked at her, the moon on her hair, the stars in her eyes, and something happened." Logan fell quiet for a long time, and I gave him space, waiting for the turmoil churning in his eyes to clear away.

"She'd known it for a while, but was afraid if I didn't see it on my own, if I didn't acknowledge it on my own, her telling me too soon would drive me away. So she waited for me to feel it. We were young, she was still in her teens. Giddy with our discovery, we took it to Archer, even if I'd had doubts. Turned out my hesitation had been warranted. At first, he was enraged. He wanted to kill me. Would have," he corrected, "had I been trained by anyone else. But Cara was strong-willed, as stubborn as her father. She pointed out killing me would only drive her to suicide, she wouldn't hesitate to do so. That even if he locked her away in a padded room, she would find a way to end it. That at the very least my death would impair her. We were mated, we'd acknowledged the bond." Logan took in a lungful of air, his breathing shaky. Stress, Diggy had told me, was one of the reasons a Dhiultadh could lose enough control for the shimmer to appear in the inner line of the aura.

"You don't have to talk about it," I said, my voice soft. What must it have been like, losing her?

He drew in more air and looked at me, his eyes clear of the pain I was afraid I would see. "No, you should know. Let me finish." He stood, paced to the sink, said nothing. His shoulders bowed as he gripped the edge and leaned forward, his back to me.

Such pain. How could he endure it? I waited, my heart aching for his loss.

"Arianna supported our bond, and when Archer realized there was nothing he could do to reverse what happened, he sent me away. Said if I wanted to be worthy of his daughter, I needed to prove it, that I needed more discipline. So I joined the Hunters."

I almost choked with surprise.

A small smile tugged at his lips, his eyes distant and cold. "I wanted to prove myself to Archer, to be worthy of his daughter. I excelled at my assignments. Soon I was Roland's right hand. Whenever I had a chance, I'd run home to see her. But we were only a handful, and each assignment was longer and more challenging than the previous. I'd get home one night, only to leave the next. Then, we finally locked onto Mr. Drammen's trail, a hot one."

This time my surprise was intense, bordering on shock. "Remo Drammen?"

"The one and only."

"That was how many years ago?"

"Twenty-six," he said with a thin smile.

"My God, no one has been able to catch him for that long?" No wonder everyone got mad when Vincent wasted an entire op to get me out of Remo's Vegas penthouse.

"Catching him isn't the problem. Catching him in his lair is. But we'll come to that," he said when he read the question in my eyes. "As I said, I was good in my assignments, and I got a good sniff on the whereabouts of Mr. Drammen's lair. I assembled a team. Doug and three other members were the covert operators, Akinzo and I the distraction. We would circle around, meet with Arianna and Archer, and deal with Remo. Then we'd bring in Cara. But Remo found out—who we were, how close. What we were going to do. He was faster, smarter, merciless. He knew Cara was our weak link, not in strength, but because of her connection to me, to Archer and Arianna. She was our blind side."

Logan closed his eyes, steadied his nerves before speaking again. "I got home minutes before the guardians did. Cara barely registered my presence when they arrived, one with a sword, the other with an axe." His lips drew taut.

The pain emanating from him was heart-wrenching. How could someone live with so much heartache for so long and still function?

I clenched my hands on my lap, fighting the desire to reach for him, to comfort him, aware it wouldn't be welcome.

"I got a few broken bones and gashes, just by standing in their way," Logan spoke to his empty coffee mug. "They were in and out in less than three minutes. Two days later, Archer found me unconscious, still bleeding. It took a lot of willpower I didn't have to shift, and hasten the healing I didn't want. I quit the Hunters, hid in Archer's estate. For years, decades, I didn't step out of the house. If no one bought groceries, I didn't eat. And with Arianna gone, there weren't many who cared.

"Then about two years ago, Archer made me snap out of it. The entire clan was in upheaval. I was Cara's mate, and Cara was dead. By default, I became Archer's only heir. I was being challenged left and right for the right of power, and Archer held them long enough. I was either to answer, fight like a warrior, or shame Cara with my defeat." Logan glanced at his hands. "I fought like a man with nothing to lose. I took my revenge on whoever challenged me. Everyone I confronted took on Mr. Drammen's face. By the end of the year, I'd cut down the clan's numbers considerably. The only person who didn't hate me was Archer, and even he resented me and my presence."

Unsure of what to say, I remained quiet. Two years ago, he said. He'd secluded himself for what, twenty-four years? He didn't exaggerate when he said he'd been out of the game for a long time.

"I don't know what to say, except I'm extremely sorry for all that happened, and even that means nothing," I said into the long silence that followed.

Logan straightened and looked up. His eyes were cool and level, and not a hint of the grief I still sensed showed. "I came here today because I figured I owe you this much courtesy. Telling you about Cara and my mate bond is necessary for you to understand the clan's hierarchy and how it came to be," he said, his voice stronger now that the grievous had been told. "You already know Archer is the head of the clan and the head of the council." He waited for my hesitant nod before continuing. "I'm Archer's second as an heir for clan leadership. I'm also the clan enforcer. Any problems within it come to my notice. Lesser problems are dealt without my need to consult Archer, unless a formal request is put forth that the council be involved. Then," he said, lacing his fingers together in front of him, "comes Alleena as vice-council, and Vincent as Archer's heir for clan leadership."

I nodded, lowering my eyes at the ominous look in his.

"I gather the high council you're talking about pertains only to the clan?"

"Yes, every clan or coven or group of preternaturals have their own, usually made up of three to seven members."

I nodded again. "But you aren't a council member?"

"No, I'm not. Only pure-bloods are allowed to become members, and I'm a mix-breed."

"And who comes after Vincent?" I asked, because I didn't know what else to say.

"Arabella, the redhead who accompanied me last night."

That reminded me. "Why'd you send her after me to the restroom?"

"I didn't like the way Matilda kept eyeing you all night long. And when she followed you to the washroom, it kind of looked suspicious."

"Suspicious how?"

"She was a powerful charmer once, respected and revered by many. And then one day she appeared, her aura reeking of corruption, the result of a dark ritual. It was rumored she killed other preternaturals and absorbed their power." Logan shrugged. "Again, this happened at a time I wasn't around and I don't know many of the details. But whether or not it's true, she was banned from her coven and labeled rogue ever since."

He waited for me to say something more and when I didn't, he continued, "As a Hunter member, you have some leeway with Vincent, even if he is your superior on both counts. Any disrespect you exhibit will be up to him to be called upon or ignored. However," his eyes became twin pools of icy storms, "in public, you *will* show respect to your elders, no matter how much you despise doing so. I'm your clan enforcer, Roxanne, and I will enforce order when and if necessary by *whatever* means I deem appropriate."

I swallowed and ignored the hurt in my heart. He hadn't come to see me but to warn me about consequences. Seeing my expression, his gaze softened and his voice became less frigid. "I don't want to be the one disciplining you for any wrongdoings, Roxanne, however deliberate. Neither do I want to pass the duty to Bebbette, my second."

I didn't say anything. After a moment, he sighed and took the seat next to mine. "I know this is hard on you, being that you didn't grow up with the same rules or this complex chain of command as a norm. I wouldn't be surprised if you thought of it as a barbaric way of living, and I suppose this is why Vincent didn't explain this part to you. But please understand these are necessary conduct and behavior requirements for a large group of predators who wouldn't bat an eyelash at trampling the rules if they thought they wouldn't be held accountable. This way we keep predators under control, and stay civilized with one another. Otherwise, we're no different than the animals we represent."

Again I said nothing, and Logan's resigned sigh carried more weight. "This wasn't how I wanted our meeting to go." He pinched the bridge of his nose as if he had an annoying headache, then reached inside a hidden pocket in his jacket and extracted a small worn booklet. "Stipulations and Rules" was on the cover in bold tar-black lettering.

"This will give you more insight into how the clan works. Anything you don't understand or have questions about, just call or ask Vincent."

I accepted the booklet—still warm from Logan's body heat.

"Let me tell you about Remo Drammen," he said, glancing at a silver-band watch around his wrist.

I placed the booklet on top of the *Guidebook of the Preternatural* and moved back to the kitchen to prepare more coffee, aware Logan watched in silence. I filled myself another mug, my empty stomach balking at the idea of more caffeine.

When I turned back, my emotions were under control. "Why explain about Remo? I mean, Remo is dead. What's so important about him that I should know?"

"That's what I'm here to explain." He motioned for me to sit.

Chapter Seventeen

Remo Drammen wasn't dead. Worse, Remo Drammen *couldn't die.*

He was a being made of energy from a place far off in space called the Quasar Stellar, a world of energy, billions and billions of light-years away. A world where energy was sentient, without definite form or any shape.

"Aliens?" I repeated, not sure if I was dumbstruck or just too numb to feel, to understand.

Logan's smile held no humor. "In a way, I guess, but then who isn't?" He raised both palms, let them drop back on his lap. "There used to be two others like Remo: Arianna Lennerd and Zantry Akinzo." Another thin smile at my shocked expression. "No one knows how the trio came to be, only that one day, they appeared wandering the Low Lands. Because the trio had never been part of a land of forms and shapes, it was said they had to manifest. And to manifest, they absorbed the life of that entire planet, killing it in the process."

"The *entire* planet," I whispered, but Logan didn't seem to hear.

He went on, "Everyone assumed there was a portal somewhere on the planet, and for a long time the trio searched for it. Then, one day, Arianna met Archer, and learned about the Dhiultadh, the Sidhe, the humans.

"Zantry Akinzo was the observer, Remo Drammen the planner, Arianna Lennerd the dreamer. What Arianna learned, she reported to her kin. Akinzo liked what he heard and soon he, too, met Archer. Remo

Drammen, on the other hand, was jealous. He wanted Arianna, the knowledge, and the other worlds Archer talked about."

"When did that happen?" I asked when he fell quiet, feeling I should say something.

"I'm not sure about the dates, but over five centuries ago."

Half a millennium. Five hundred years ago. My God, how old was Archer?

"Once the trio learned to control their urge not to kill," Logan continued, "Archer took them exploring through the worlds. The Sidhe land, where they met with Queen Maeve and Titania, Oberon and all the Sidhe royalty. To the Tristan star, where they met Verenastra and Elvilachious and their clan. To Earth, where Arianna and Zantry liked best. Everywhere they went, they were welcomed; they were liked. The prospect of another galaxy full of other beings intrigued everyone.

"Though Remo Drammen had gone along, showing as much enthusiasm as his kin, it was later said he was already planning how he'd open the portal to his world, to bring more of his kin to these 'lands of wonder', where he planned to rule them all." Logan took a sip of coffee, brows furrowed. "Arianna was the first to learn about it, when Remo Drammen proposed a joint partnership, where they would rule together. At first, she went along, either because she wanted what he wanted, or because she wanted to know what he planned." He waved a hand. "Whichever is true, she went along with the idea at first. But she'd seen the problem right away. If the trio killed an entire planet to manifest, what would happen if they brought an entire planet to these worlds?

"When the idea started to turn into fact, Arianna tried reasoning. Then she threatened him. But Remo Drammen would have none of it, claiming he could control them, keep them from manifesting too soon, too fast, from ending life and energy from other worlds.

"Because they were close, Arianna went to Archer, explained the problem and the disaster they were all facing. Archer enlisted the aid of his clan, the Sidhe royalties, even the other clan of rejected. For he understood Remo Drammen was an unknown, a powerful being, and to underestimate him and face him alone was to doom the entire universe.

"They ambushed Remo Drammen. It was a vicious fight. No." He shook his head. "It was a slaughterhouse. There was no equal to any member of the trio but each other. Everyone who perished then was considered a hero and is still talked about as such. In the end, either the sheer number did it, or the combination of numbers with Zantry and Arianna. But they were able to decapitate Mr. Drammen and chop him up into small pieces, as a guarantee. Then they burned his remains."

An image of Remo Drammen being eaten alive came to mind, and I closed my eyes and tried to push away the horror. He'd screamed back then, but I'd recognized the outrage for what it was.

"For a long time everyone believed they won, that they got rid of him. But one day, when Arianna and Zantry were unaware, Remo ambushed them and took them by surprise. Of course, if Remo Drammen couldn't die, neither could his kin. For a time, while everyone wondered what happened to Zantry and Arianna, Remo Drammen worked on the portal unperturbed."

"Where do they go when they die?"

Logan shrugged. "Don't know. It was after Arianna and Zantry returned we learned they were tethered to the Low Lands. Every time they die, they reappear someplace on the planet. Only they come back with the same amount of power–the same amount of energy–they possessed when they first manifested, after they'd drained the land. Whatever they'd gathered, whatever energy they'd accumulated that didn't come from that first draw, they lose once they die."

"Does that mean that Remo, if he's back, is weaker than before?"

Logan's lips pulled into a mock smile, his gaze flat. "He won't be back until he's gathered enough energy, accumulated enough power to satisfy his ego. He has no morals, no qualms to harness whatever life is available to fulfill his needs. If he's back, it's because he deems himself strong enough."

"Isn't there another way to stop him?"

Logan placed both palms around the empty mug of coffee and rolled it gently. "Once, twenty-six years ago my team, a handful of the most trusted Hunter members, plus Zantry and Arianna, came close enough. Because killing him without locating the portal was out of the question, the deal would be to immobilize him, bring in the Sidhe to help locate the portal, and then, once found, *work* on the portal. Arianna had this theory where she believed Cara would be able to destroy the portal, or at least, permanently freeze it. But everything went to Hell."

And now Cara was dead, and possibly Arianna too. The more Logan talked, the worse the situation became. I almost covered my ears when he started speaking again. I *didn't* want to know.

"There was a meeting between Akinzo and Arianna, bait to draw out Remo. They both disappeared. Through our bond, I sensed Cara was in danger and went after her. Archer left to search for Arianna and Zantry. While I lay dying, Mr. Drammen was picking the rest of the team one by one. By the end of the first month, there was only Archer, Doug and I left. To sum it up, everyone assumed Arianna and Zantry were truly dead, that Remo Drammen had somehow found a way to kill them, or maybe pushed them back through the portal. Then a few months ago, bam, Zantry's back, claiming he'd been on vacation, exploring the worlds and reminiscing over the early years."

"But you don't believe that."

Logan snorted. "No. We think he flipped sides, joined hands with the enemy."

"But why wait this long to come back? Maybe Remo trapped them and Zantry escaped?" I thought about a half-dead Zantry Akinzo, hooked to a myriad of machines back in the PSS.

Logan shook his head, though I could tell he was considering it. Then he shook his head again. "If Akinzo and Arianna were trapped all these years and Akinzo escaped, he'd have been gathering forces to go after her, not strolling around, attending parties and connecting with old acquaintances. At the very least, he'd have told us something. We've all met with the Enclave and have tried speculating as to what he'd been doing this entire time, and the only plausible scenario we were able to come up with was that it took them this long to be able to kill Arianna."

At my silence, Logan sighed. "I know he didn't look like he was a dangerous person with plans to end the world, but looks are deceiving. Zantry Akinzo is a dangerous man, a powerful one. He and Remo Drammen are the same species, come from the same planet. If you feared Remo Drammen before, it's wise to extend Zantry Akinzo this same courtesy."

Chapter Eighteen

When Vicky arrived that afternoon bubbling with excited questions about my "date" with the "hunky chunky", I was curled on the sofa and staring at nothing.

Shocking thoughts rampaged within my head, jumbled facts that jolted every time one registered. Betrayal. Love. Loyalty. The power struggle of the preternatural world. The obliteration of life. On every single planet.

And Remo Drammen was at the center of it all, still alive. Somewhere out there, he was planning the extinction of everything we knew.

No wonder all the Hunters resented me when Vincent ruined their chance to catch Remo that night in Vegas.

I'd killed Remo in the Low Lands, setting him back in his plans.

But now, according to Logan, he was back, a shifting current in the air they couldn't pinpoint.

And he would come for me. Because, for some reason I couldn't fathom, I fit right into his plans.

My worry and guilt for Mwara were overshadowed by the certainty something horrible was about to happen. It clenched my stomach, tightened my muscles, filled me with dread.

I'd taken Logan to Maggie's Heaven–the bakery where I'd met with Mwara, retraced our steps to where she'd been waiting for me, then walked back home in a hazy state, my thoughts and emotions at war with each other.

Where did you go, Mwara? Are you alive?

Curling my feet, I placed my chin on my knees and hugged myself.

Atop all the shocking news I'd received that morning stood one more: Logan had lied to me about being a were. He was a wolf, the way Xandra was some sort of cat, or Boris a hunting bird. I could sense his wolf, yes, and maybe he even had some vampire, too.

Well, mixed breed he was, but he was also disguising his aura. A rejected from Diggy's line. I wondered if Rafael was a rejected too. Hadn't Diggy said some rejected from his line could make their auras look and feel like a shifter's, depending on how many shapes they could take? It made sense for Logan and Diggy and Rafael to be alike, given they were all friends.

But why would Archer raise Logan and not the other clan? Maybe there was something more to his mixed-breed status that I couldn't sense.

Ha! What a joke I must be to everyone, trying to figure out something as simple as an aura. Inherent, my ass; this was as hard as trying to fly without wings.

Dhiultadh, General Parkinson had murmured that night on the bus. Vincent had distracted Remo Drammen to give me time to escape—either aware, or unaware, that Logan was getting ready to break me out from the other end.

Two rejected—from different lines, the same clan. I should have known, what with him being buddies with Diggy. If anything, last night's lesson should have shed light on it. Maybe I'd have figured it out, given time. And then... Mwara. I wondered if Logan already told Elizabeth her daughter had come to see me, terrified her mother was about to send her to the PSS. How would she react to this news?

"What goes around comes around," Elizabeth used to say to me when I was a kid.

"Hello? Are you even listening to what I'm saying?"

"Huh?" I scanned Vicky's frustrated expression.

She sighed, then sat beside me. "Was it that bad?"

"What? The ball? It was another lesson. It wasn't a date."

"No shit, he dragged you dressed like that to *work*?" Again she sighed, this time louder. "Men are such weird creatures." As she got up to answer her ringing phone, I lapsed back to my misery.

When she sat beside me again, concern radiated from her in gentle waves. "What is it?" she asked for the fourth or fifth time.

"It's nothing, really."

"There's something bothering you. Why don't you tell me? It helps to talk." When her phone rang again, she snatched it, disconnected without even glancing at the display. Her worry increased, wafting off of her in little waves.

I motioned to her phone. "Who was that?"

"No one."

I caught the quick flash of fear in her eyes and, frowning, I picked up her phone, only to have it snatched from my hands.

"It's nothing." Her smile was brittle and nervous as she got up and ambled to the kitchen. Picking up Frizz, she buried her face in his neck and inhaled a shaky breath.

"Vicky, what is it?" I asked, rising. "And don't tell me it's nothing. Remember, I can *sense* it."

Her shoulders slumped and she turned to face me. Now that I was looking, I noted the shadows under her eyes, the grim lines around her tight lips. How long had they been there? How come I hadn't noticed them before? What kind of friend was I? A bad one, I realized with a pang of regret.

"It's that old asshole. You know, David."

"Who?" I raked my mental files, trying to remember which one had been David. "The old boyfriend? Is he bothering you?"

She shook her head. "No, no. It's just that he keeps calling. Coming over. It's nothing, I guess, but it has me spooked. He leaves small love cards at the door. Likes all my tweets, my posts, my photos. Changes his account when I block him, finds whatever new account I create for myself. Leaves love songs on my voice mail. Sends me chocolate and flowers."

I frowned, not liking the sound of that.

"It's disconcerting. I feel suffocated, like I'm being stalked, you know? I've told him no so many times, I've lost count." She shrugged, causing Frizz to bounce. "It's just a foolish feeling. I bet it doesn't even come close to what have you all wound-up and brooding." Her tone was light, but I sensed there was something more. There was a deeper worry there, something like fear, and a touch of anxiety.

I narrowed my eyes, walked up to her. Her shoulders tightened, her gaze lowered for a few blinks. This close, I could sense the fear, a deep worry, and–a sort of joy, a faint happiness, both overshadowed by the darker emotions.

"It's nothing, really," she met my gaze for a second before glancing away, unable to look me in the eyes and lie.

"Vicky, aren't we friends? If he's bothering you, tell me. I can help." By God, I would. This, I could do. Even if I had to threaten him myself.

Vicky's shoulders slumped, giving her a vulnerable appearance I'd never seen before. Not even when we were children. She'd always been wild and confident. The more courageous of the bunch. The more daring, even comparing to Tommy.

"I'm pregnant," she whispered.

The news gave me a jolt. Of all the possibilities, all the things I'd have considered, all the cases, all the scenarios, her being pregnant would have never been among them.

I searched her downcast eyes, unsure of what to say. I'd tell from her words, her behavior, it was a bad thing. But there was that buried joy, that happy feeling underlying all those emotions.

I trod carefully. "That bothers you."

Her worried gaze met mine, and the fear was back.

"Is David the father?" I asked, beginning to see the bigger picture now.

She nodded with a jerk, burrowing her face in Frizz's neck. The gargoyle burrowed closer, soaking in the warmth Vicky offered. His shell-shaped eyes closed, a deep rumble of pleasure escaping when Vicky caressed his back, between his small wings.

"Vicky, is the baby the reason David is–" I almost said stalking "–trying to get the two of you back together?"

"No, no," she spoke into Frizz's neck and shook her head before looking at me. "He doesn't know. I don't think I want him to know. I don't know what he'll do if he finds out."

"Are you considering an abortion, then?"

"No!" A fierce spark entered her eyes. "The baby is mine. But," A tear trickled down her cheek, followed by another, and another.

My eyes widened with horror, and I took Frizz and placed him down, grabbed her hand. "Come sit." I guided her back to the sofa and let her cry for a moment, feeling useless. I patted her shoulder a few times, passed her a tissue. Some time later she finally got herself under control and looked at me, her misty blue eyes tinged with red. And she burst into laughter.

Oh my God.

She laughed harder, and I froze, a little panicked. I considered calling Tommy. He knew her better, had probably dealt with a hysterical Vicky often.

Stiff and wide-eyed, I was afraid to do something to provoke another bolt of tears. Or more laughter.

When she was able to control herself, she spoke. "You're so funny." And burst out laughing again, fat tears tracking down her face.

"I'm glad you think so."

When the bout of tears and laughter finally passed and I deemed the moment safe, I spoke. "Are you sure you're carrying? You guys haven't been together for a while."

"I'm about eleven weeks. I saw a doctor on Friday. I was getting ready to drop the news yesterday when dimple arrived."

"Eleven weeks!"

She chuckled at my astonishment. "I know. I was afraid to go to the doctor, afraid of what I would find. At first I was worried the test would come out positive, and I kept thinking what my life would be like with a baby, how I'd need to change. I gave it so much thought, the idea grew on me. And then I was afraid the blood test would return negative. So I kept procrastinating." She placed a hand over her flat belly, her lips forming a soft smile. "I heard its heart beating. The doctor said that soon I'd start feeling it move around."

I leaned back, studying the wonder in her puffy eyes. "How did it happen?" Her eyes turned mischievous, a little sly.

"You know what I mean. You didn't tell me you were planning to get pregnant."

She sobered. "I think he tampered with... you know?"

A soft blush suffused her cheeks, and I frowned. "Tampered with what?"

"We used protection. All the time. But he talked about family, about getting married a lot. I told him I was too young for that. He knew I wasn't taking any pills."

I frowned. "Do you think he knows?"

"No. I was no more than a few days pregnant when I left him."

But he maybe wonders, I thought.

"What are you going to do?"

"I'll have my baby. If I think it's necessary, I'll go back to Sacramento and start over again."

"But you aren't going to tell him?"

"No." The panic returned to her eyes. "If he finds out, I'll never get rid of him. He'll fight, and when he realizes I'm not going back to him, he'll fight for custody. He's influential, he knows people who know people. I'm afraid he'll take my baby away from me."

"Vicky, what are you saying? He's the father. He deserves to know he's got a kid out there in the world. You two can share custody. He could–"

Vicky grabbed my hand in both of hers and squeezed hard. "No, he'll never settle for shared custody. He's old-fashioned, the kind who thinks women should stay at home popping out babies while the man provides for them. He'll want marriage. And when I say no, he'll go to court. And he'll take my baby away."

"It's not up to him to decide what'll happen. I can talk to Roland. He knows people, too."

She shook her head again. "What if I win, but he takes the baby all the same and runs away?"

I could tell she'd considered all those angles already. "We can try to get a restricting order."

"Already talked to a cop. I filed a complaint." She rose and scooped up Frizz. "I feel better. Thanks for letting me dump all this on you."

I waved a hand. "Dump away whenever you feel like. Just try not to put on the waterworks again."

Chuckling, she sat again, Frizz curling like a lazy cat on her lap. "Now it's your turn. Tell me what happened. What's bothering *you?*"

I told her everything. About what happened last night, the encounter with Archer, Logan and his date, fake Vincent and Akinzo. And when I got to the part about Mwara, she expressed sorrow, but didn't point out I could have saved the kid if I'd only listened to her and talked to Vincent. I finished with a summarized version of Logan's visit this morning to explain the clan's hierarchy, the rules, and where I stood.

When I was done, I felt lighter, as if I'd pushed off some weight. It was easier knowing Vicky shared my outrage, if not the hurt and the resentment.

"I know just what you need," she said, snapping her fingers.

"Oh yeah? What's that?"

"Watch and see." Placing Frizz on the floor, she jumped off the sofa and hurried to the kitchen.

After she called off the double date–I'd forgotten all about it–we spent the night watching classic movies and snacking on Doritos and Ben & Jerry's. By the time I went to bed, Logan and Remo and Diggy and Akinzo were all far, far from my mind, but not the guilt for Mwara.

Chapter Nineteen

Despite the freezing temperature and the dreary brown slush on the sidewalks, I walked to work the next morning. The sky was heavy with imminent rain, the smell of damp air mixed with vehicle exhaust. On the opposite sidewalk, a vendor screamed something indistinct. A man shouted obscenities at a pickpocket who ran away, but no one tried to stop the thief. It was a lousy place to live, yet I was beginning to make a place for it in my heart.

Two blocks away, Zantry Akinzo fell into step beside me.

I gave him a sideways glance. The man was dressed in black slacks and a heavy wool coat, hands tucked inside the pockets, two inches of black hair sticking out from a watch cap, brushing the coat collar.

He gazed up at the tall buildings, eyes clear and vivid, and inhaled a lungful of New York air.

"Those urban canyons haven't changed much. More buildings, more people, but they're still the same. It amazes me," he said conversationally.

I glanced up at the concrete and iron bracketing a narrow passageway, forming a manmade corridor of wind.

"Your hair grows really fast," I observed. He'd been bald just a few months back; now it was almost long enough to be tied.

As if wanting to make sure it was there, he pulled off his cap and raked a hand through the thick glossy mass.

"So you did recognize me," he said, his eyes gauging. "I'd wondered."

"Why don't you tell them where you've been?" I asked, because that fact puzzled me a lot.

We walked a few paces in silence before he answered my question. "If you hadn't created all that racket when rescuing Archer, I believe he'd have claimed a vacation or something. As it is, you ruined his status of the biggest, baddest threat out there. Now he's going around, strutting like a wild rooster, trying to provoke fights so he can restore his ruthless reputation."

Startled to hear a similar assessment I'd made last night spoken by someone else, I glanced at him with a frown. "What are you saying?"

"That being captured by mere humans made him lose some of his authority. I heard there's dissension amidst his clan."

"So you rather be labeled a traitor than let them think the Scientists got the best of you?"

He gave a thin smile, his eyes cold. "It's a weird world we live in, sweetheart. You show weakness, you get trampled."

I recalled the charity ball, the way I'd sensed the vibes Archer was sending had been staged, the way people had murmured when he passed by. I shook my head in bewilderment. "So you're saying Archer was better off without the rescue?"

"In a twisted way, yes. Don't get me wrong. It's not he'd rather have stayed behind; I certainly wouldn't have. But he'd have rather you guys extricated him quietly, like *pro* thieves."

With a frown, I considered all the destruction we'd left behind. Of all the people we'd helped save—only for them to be captured again. Or killed.

"Is Arianna there too?" I wondered aloud. Had she been one of the people we'd helped escape? No, or Logan would have recognized her. Unless she'd been weak like Zantry and beyond recognition. I frowned, trying to figure which it was.

"I'm not sure. I didn't even know she was missing until the day I was confronted a few months ago."

We moved on in silence, following the flow of pedestrians, then waited for a green light to cross the next intersection before I spoke again. "They think you killed her. They think you flipped sides. I was warned away from you."

He faltered in surprise and looked at me, his eyes so intense, so blue, they were startling in their beauty. "But you didn't tell them otherwise even if you recognized me. Why?"

My reply was simple. "Not my story to tell."

"No, but a lot of people would have already spread the news. I heard it's hard to resist good gossip."

"Not everyone is that shallow."

"Apparently not," he said before sidestepping a guy with green and yellow spiked hair who kept coming straight at him, daring him not to move.

"You know, Logan was the one who broke down the door that day."

He studied me and waited.

"If you tell him it was you, he would remember," I offered.

Zantry shook his head. "Finding me there was the farthest thing from his mind. Because the notion was so ridiculous, so farfetched, he didn't see me. He saw someone, helpless and dying, and moved on."

It was true. Logan had glanced inside the room, not seen Archer, and moved on to the next door.

"What about Rafael Sanchez?"

"Who?"

"The guy who came in while I was trying to help you."

"The one who offered the mercy kill?"

"Yeah." Zantry had looked so weak Rafael had offered to kill him to end his misery.

He shrugged. "Don't think I ever met him."

"Do you think she could be dead? *Truly* dead?"

He didn't answer for a long while. "I don't know. But I need to find out. Someone let Remo know about our ambush. People think it was me, but since I know it wasn't, there's someone out there helping Remo." He gave a nonchalant shrug, but the promise of retribution was there in his eyes. There was grief there too, faint but present.

"Maybe she's in the PSS. Did you try checking there?"

"I've done some probing–both to find about what happened the night I was set free, and to see if I sensed her there. But I found nothing, except that the Hunters got involved with Archer's break-out, so I came here to see what else happened." He glanced at me again, his lips forming that sensual smile. "And I wanted to know who the beautiful woman with the mysterious black eyes was."

I blushed and he chuckled, the sound wicked.

"You guys can sense anyone, or is there something unique about the three of you?"

"Both, depending on how strong one resonates in the ether. But the three of us, we resonate in a unique way and, within a limited distance, we can tell where the other is. Still, Remo's machinations made us hide our presence from the ether.

Arianna and I were close friends, but we had different tastes and interests, and sometimes years would go by without us seeing each other. Because it was absurd to go around the world searching for the other, we developed a code, a signature we leave in the ether for the other to find and follow. I can't find one from her, and so far she hasn't tugged on the one I left." He shrugged, "I've been gone for a long time. Arianna may not know to look for it. I don't know. I don't know where she is, why she disappeared when I did. She could be with the PSS, maybe in some other location. I don't know." He spoke the latter in a soft, quiet tone.

His grief peaked, along with his sense of loss, but there was determination there too, a sense of purpose. He wouldn't give up, and I admired that. "Can you tell where Remo is?"

"Maybe. I've sensed him once about six, seven weeks ago, but not since."

"Are you searching for him?"

"Not really."

"Are you going to stop him?"

"Don't know. I'm not at full strength yet. In many ways, I'm weaker than when I first arrived all these many centuries ago."

"I killed Remo a few months ago," I said, and an African American guy coming from the opposite direction widened his eyes and gave me a wide berth.

"I heard." I raised my eyebrows and he smirked. "I'm not all out on resources. Back when I worked for the Hunters, my job was to gather information."

Akinzo was the observer, Logan had said.

"Tell me what you want for saving my life and to keep your silence." After a pause he added, "Anything."

"Nothing. I'd have done it for anyone, no payment owed." I didn't want him to feel obliged.

His smile didn't reach his eyes; it was cool and dispassionate. "I'd owe that way and I don't like owing, much less when it's my life."

I looked ahead at the car-clogged streets, the clouds of exhaust. I understood the need not to feel obliged. But I really didn't want anything from him. "There's no debt to pay. You owe me nothing."

"That's not a smart reply," he said tightly, and I recalled I'd bound Frizz to me through a similar act. I couldn't literally bind Zantry to me—I was almost sure of that—but he'd feel bound regardless, because of the debt.

I inclined my head. "Then I'll think of something later. At the moment, let's just leave it at that."

"Good enough. Until then, I'd appreciate if you keep what you know to yourself."

"I don't intend to gossip," I said, and he smiled. I thought now that he said what he'd wanted, he'd turn and leave, instead he kept pace, escorting me through the tangle of people.

At the next intersection, I stopped, turned to face him. "You should go from here. The Hunters will recognize you if you get any closer."

Zantry looked at me, trying to figure me out. "How about we have dinner tonight, get to know each other?"

I hesitated. "I don't think that's a good idea." The small pang of regret that followed my rebuff surprised me. I'd like to know him better, I realized.

"*I'll* go," the woman beside me said. "I'll even pay."

Zantry flashed her a dazzling smile, and I caught my breath.

"Oh my," she said under her breath.

He was really beautiful. In this light his eyes were an intense dark blue, his eyebrows thick in an elegant arch. His face was shaved clean, his nose straight and aristocratic above sculpted, sultry lips. Eyes twinkling, he looked back at me, bowed once, and kissed my hand. A pleasant hum traveled up my arm, but before I could pull back, he let go. "If you ever change your mind, Roxanne Fosch, I'll be around."

With that said, he made his way onto a side street.

I watched him go, the woman beside me doing the same.

"I hope you have a good reason for turning down such a fine specimen."

I shrugged and made my way across the street, toward the base.

Chapter Twenty

The moment I stepped foot into the locker-room, Diggy whisked us to that dreadful land and resumed the routine of critiquing my moves, telling me to do better, faster, higher, only to return us to base, no more than fifteen minutes after we'd left. We'd arrive dirty and sweaty, bloody from the long session in the Low Lands. On base, other members would just be arriving, or leaving home from a graveyard shift. While I'd go straight home to soak and soothe my aching body, Diggy would shower and change, then do whatever it was his job demanded of him. I wondered where he found all the energy to work all those hours straight, if this was normal for all preternaturals, or if this was just one of Diggy's many quirks. But I never asked, no matter how curious I got. I never talked during our training, except to ask for clarification, and sometimes after Vincent and his case during a break. Except today there was a bunch of questions rotating inside my head, things that woke me in the middle of the night and plagued me until morning.

I parried a kick, blocked a punch, crouched and swept Diggy's feet from under him in one swift motion.

"Logan came to see me yesterday," I said as Diggy fell and flipped backward, his feet aiming with a point-kick to my chin. I pulled back, dodged a round-kick, advanced again.

"He told me about Remo, Zantry and Arianna." I punched left, right, upward, forcing him to take the defensive. He grunted when a punch hit his shoulder, and I think he muttered, "About time" under his breath.

"What?" I asked, pirouetting when he tried a hand-slice for my throat, aimed an elbow at his kidney when I found his back to me. He avoided the blow and backpedaled.

"If you thought I should have known about them, why didn't you tell me?" I demanded when he didn't reply. We circled each other, both trying to find an opening in the other's defense. Sweat pooled under my armpits, my lower back. Diggy's shirt was also wet with sweat, his jacket long discarded.

"Because it's not my place." He advanced with a kick I deflected, jumped away from the leg sweep. "I'm not sure why Vincent didn't explain it to you, but I believe he was trying to protect you." His punch hit my forearm hard, the pain traveling up to my shoulder. Ouch.

"From what?" I asked, putting distance between us and jerking my arm up and down to help blood circulation.

He motioned me forward. "I don't know. Maybe he wanted to give you some peace of mind."

We fought in silence for the next half hour, Diggy's attack coming so fast and swift, he kept me on my toes, my movements instinctive, my brain blissfully blank.

"I caught the silvery sheen in Logan's aura," I blurted, though I hadn't intended to tell him I knew.

Diggy stopped mid-kick, expression surprised. I gave him a thin smile. "He doesn't know I saw it. He was talking about Cara, explaining the clan's hierarchy and where I fit."

Expression unreadable, Diggy glanced away, either thinking about what to say, or because he didn't want to comment. So I plowed on, "He's a Dhiultadh from your line, one Arianna found after he was abandoned."

I waited, and after a long silence, Diggy said, "Logan's situation is kind of unique. His father was a rogue from my clan, his mother from yours. I don't know the specifics about their affair, but when his mother was pregnant, his father was killed by an unknown faction.

Because his mother left the clan to be with a rogue, she was no longer welcome back, and had no one to turn to."

"What happened to her?"

"I don't know. It was assumed she was killed while fending for herself, but her body was never found."

"He believes she left him in the cold because she didn't love him," I said, recalling the hard glint in his eyes when he told me about his mother. "Maybe she just thought he'd be better off away from her."

Diggy studied me for a moment before looking at the edge of the hill. "Logan is convinced Arianna finding him was just a draw of luck. But maybe you're right. There are some who believe his mother left him in that specific alleyway because she knew Arianna would never have left him behind." His lips twitched in a mock smile, "This speculation, of course, was always brought up to point out that Archer wasn't fit to lead the clan, that his judgment was addled by his love for Arianna, and how he'd do anything she'd ask of him, even bring home the son of two rogues to raise as his own. And if you want to know more," he said, eyes flashing with finality, "you should ask Logan." Without waiting for my next words he attacked, and soon we were back to our rhythmic dance of punch and kick, deflate, retreat and attack.

As soon as I announced defeat—after Diggy caught me with a sneaky round-kick that had me wheezing for breath—we returned to base. At 7:56. After having trained more than five hours.

Barbara was in the locker room, half naked, and after a small bow from Diggy in apology, her frosty gaze turned to me. She sneered at my dirty clothes, the small patches of blood where the rocks of the Low Lands had cut me, and gave me her back as she continued changing either for a new day or after a long night.

Thirty minutes after I'd walked with Akinzo to base, I was walking back home. Sending my awareness around, I tried to pick him—or another preternatural—out of the crowd.

A block from home, I took an impulsive detour and hurried across the street. The bells on the door to Maggie's Heaven jingled when I opened it, and the sweet aroma of freshly-baked goods assaulted my senses, making my mouth water.

The place was emptier than I'd ever seen before, the line shorter, and soon it was my turn. I ordered a cup of black coffee with a shot of espresso and four chunky brownies—two for me and two for Frizz—then asked the barrister for his manager.

He startled at my question, brow furrowing with confusion. "Why? Is there anything wrong with the food?"

"The food is excellent," I assured him. "And you're efficient. I just wanted to ask your manager a question."

The barista's frown remained. "I'm not to disturb her unless it's important."

"It is. I need to check something in your surveillance records."

His eyebrows arched so high on his forehead, they disappeared under floppy bangs. The woman behind me cleared her throat. The barrister signaled down the counter to a teenage boy stocking doughnuts for display. "Tony? Please attend the register."

With a nod, Tony took his place and the barista took me aside. "Look, I can't just walk into Maggie's office and tell her a stranger is asking about our surveillance without giving her logical justification. Why are you asking for the manager and our surveillance?"

I hesitated a second, then did something I'd never done before. I pulled out my ID from my back pocket and handed it to him.

He flipped it open and arched an eyebrow. "NSA?"

"That's my ID and vocation. The reason I'm asking after your surveillance and your manager is personal."

He waited, and I went on, "I met a kid near here around Christmas. I brought her in, bought her a snack. We ate, we talked, I went my way, she went hers. A few days ago I discovered she's been missing since that evening. I wanted to take a look, to see if there's anything that can help me find out what happened to her."

"A homeless kid?" he asked, his eyes sad.

"In a way," I replied.

The barista looked down at the ID again before handing it back. "Maggie won't give you access to our surveillance without a warrant."

I must've looked as discouraged as I felt because the guy's brown eyes softened. "But I'll let you know our feed deletes itself on the last day of the month. You won't find anything recorded that far back."

* * *

Later in the morning, I was drawing Frizz a bath when the doorbell rang. The talk with Maggie hadn't done any good. She hadn't asked for a warrant, but she let me know that even if I got one, the earliest feed she'd show me started on February first.

I told Frizz I'd send whoever it was away and be back to give him the promised bath, padded barefoot to the door and peered through the peephole. A guy stood there, his back turned, and he didn't look familiar. I was contemplating the merits of leaving him there when he turned to ring the doorbell again.

Eyes narrowing, I opened the door, glad the temperatures had risen enough that I only felt mild discomfort.

"Hello. It's Roxy, isn't it?" the man asked with a charming smile, a dimple appearing on his right cheek.

"Roxanne. Only my friends call me Roxy."

His smile dimmed a fraction at my cool tone, his moss-green eyes lost some warmth.

"We've met before. *Le Parisien*? I'm David, Vicky's boyfriend."

"No, you're not. I remember well she gave you the boot." His expression darkened as I leaned forward. "You guys are over, pal. Go find someone else and leave Vicky alone."

"She just needs some time to get over her mad. We were good together, she'll see her error and realize she still wants me." I didn't like the gleam of obsession in his eyes.

"No, she won't. She's moved on, David, she's not getting back with you."

"Is she here? She didn't go to work today."

"Leave her alone."

"No. If she sees how much I still care, she'll remember how good we were together. She keeps the gifts I send her. That means she enjoys the attention I give her"

"Do you go through her garbage bin? Because I'm sure that's where the gifts end up. Let her be." I hesitated, then added, "You're scaring her with all the attention. Give her space. Stop stalking her."

David's expression grew thoughtful. "You think she'll consider coming back if I give her some room?"

I hesitated again, then decided on honesty, "I don't think she will. But you're suffocating her now, and I know you're only pushing her away."

* * *

Later in the evening, after Frizz and I had a long restorative nap, the bell rang again. Ding-dong, ding-dong.

"God, can't you just use the key I gave you?" I muttered, thinking it was Vicky, too lazy to dig in her purse for the spare key. But when I opened the door, it was Diggy who stood there. And I should've known. After David left, I'd called her and was told that she'd been sick that morning, and after all the vomiting she'd been too weak to go to work. I decided not to tell her about David's visit, promising myself I'd deal with him myself if things got stickier.

Diggy glanced back inside the apartment before asking to come in. I stepped aside for him to pass. "What is it?"

"There's something I need you to check for me. Get dressed. Please," he added after a pause.

"Put on your warm coat. It's freezing out there," he called.

I put away the short jacket I'd picked and went for a long gray wool coat.

"You expecting your friend tonight?" he asked once I'd joined him in the living room.

Wary, I asked, "Maybe, why?"

Diggy hesitated. "Maybe you should call her and tell her you have some work tonight. I don't know how long we'll be gone."

Alarm bells rang inside my head. "Where are we going?"

"To the Low Lands."

"But hours there pass in minutes here."

Diggy's lips thinned. "Not in the mountains. Time there is known to be erratic, depending on which planet's path you're on."

I paused, an anxious pang traveling through my body. "Why there? What's in there?"

"That's what I need *you* to find out."

Chapter Twenty-One

"I want you to tell me if you sense anything, anything at all out of place."

Diggy flashed us to the same mountain where we trained every day, the only difference was he'd flashed us halfway to the top instead of the valley. Flashing any higher could get us caught on a time loop even before we hit the ground, so we'd hike the rest of the way and adjust course as needed.

"Anything strange, a smell, a sound or whatever you sense or feel that you haven't before; I need to know. Alright?"

"But isn't your sense of smell better than mine?"

"Maybe. And I'm just cautioning. I want you to keep your senses open, don't dismiss anything."

I nodded, my stomach contents souring.

Diggy paused before saying, "We might not find anything, and that's fine too. I just need a different perspective of things, a new eye." He waited for my nod before he turned and began hiking up the mountain.

We moved through a cemetery of dead trees. Some lay broken on the ground, some no more than twigs. Some lay horizontal, others were uprooted. Some stood tall, as if waiting for life to return as abruptly as it left. Sometimes the brambles were so thick; we had to hack our way through. Everything was a blackened husk of a life long gone, as if fire had consumed it, though not enough to bring it down to ashes. Some horizontal trunks were wider than Diggy and I combined, others taller than a two-story building, even uprooted. All gave testimonial to the devastation Remo Drammen could cause if he brought other beings from his world. If three caused all this, I wondered with increasing dread, what would happen to life in general when an entire planet trespassed through? How close was Remo Drammen to opening this portal?

I imagined the land and undergrowth full of life, full of scurrying and foraging animals. The image my brain conjured was startling in its beauty, especially when I pictured myself lying on the damp ground in a lush clearing surrounded by rustling leaves, those colorful planets in the night sky swirling and dancing, the grass green and soft, the musical sounds of a small stream flowing downhill.

What other kind of creatures inhabited this land, besides gargoyles? Had there ever been any warmth? Or snow? I'd dressed warmly, with a wool sweater that had seen better days, black jeans and combat boots, and a silky olive-green scarf tucked inside the gray coat. Thick gloves completed the ensemble. Despite all this, the cold cut through, provoking goosebumps to break all over my body. I eyed Diggy's half-open leather jacket, the V-neck charcoal-gray sweater peeking through, his bare neck and hands, and wondered if he felt the chill at all.

We trekked in silence, up into the dead forest, each of us lost in our own thoughts, until we reached a small clearing. Rocks of every size and shape lay strewn haphazardly, needle points that could tear flesh as easily as a fine scalpel.

Diggy paused at the edge, his back to me, and waited until I reached him.

"There's a small cave up ahead," he began, pointing at the darkness. "There's a ward at the entrance. Could have been there for a long time, could be new." He paused, considering his next words. "This ward is complex, meant to keep things out, not to be seen or felt. It's a working I haven't seen before, with a signature I don't recognize. But this ward isn't warding against humans." He fell quiet, waiting for me to catch on.

"You want me to go inside and scout out the place?"

Diggy's lips thinned. I could tell he hated to ask this of me. Why? Because it endangered me? Because I could do something he couldn't?

"Yes. I can't get any read past the ward. It's like a wall, hard and impenetrable. I want you to walk a few paces, send your awareness ahead; tell me what you sense and what you see."

I hesitated. If he couldn't get in, and there was something inside I couldn't fight?

"I'll be at the entrance," he said as if reading my mind "One minute, no more. If you don't sense anything at the one minute mark, you come back. If you sense anything, you come back." He searched my face before continuing. "I can break the ward if necessary, but I don't want to alert whoever placed it there for no reason." He dug inside his pocket and came up with a thin bracelet, took my hand and hooked it around my wrist. "We use this to form a bond between agents, to tell when the other is in trouble, to know where they are. If you feel any sort of alarm or are in danger, I'll know." He raised his wrist and showed the twin to the one around mine.

I examined the metal band, didn't find any button to press. "It's magic?"

"Yeah, kind of like a charm."

I glanced at the darkness ahead. "You think this cave is something important?"

"People don't lay wards on a cave entrance to conceal nothing. Either it's hiding something important, or it was, when there had been habitants on this land."

"And if I don't want to go in?"

He considered my question, his gaze on the dark peak. "I've been staking out this place for the better part of a month. There hasn't been any disturbance, any visitors, anyone going in or coming out in that entire time. I've studied the surrounding area, the ward and all its intricacies, found nothing alarming. If I thought there was danger, I wouldn't ask this of you."

My gaze dropped to the bracelet.

"Precaution will never do you harm," he said quietly, "but it may save you from unpredictable situations. I don't sense any danger. I don't believe there's any harm, but I don't want to take any chances. I've been known to be wrong at times." He took a deep breath and added, "If you don't want to go in, then you don't have to. I'll take you home and that's that."

I glanced from the bracelet up to the darkness ahead, still unable to tell how far up the peak stood, despite all the distance we'd climbed.

"Alright."

"Thank you." He searched my face. "I'll have to let the light die from now on. The higher we get, the lighter it gets. Just grab on to me until your eyes adjust."

He waited for my nod before complete darkness engulfed us. I reached for him, grabbing blindly for his arm, hating myself for the weakness, unable to help it. Blood rushed through my ears as my heart pounded hard.

"Ok?"

I caught the faint glow from his eyes, like that of a nocturnal animal. He could see me, could see in the dark; all this time the light had been for my benefit.

I nodded, loosening the death grip I had on him, and after a hesitant moment he turned and we resumed our hiking through the forest. I stumbled a few times, then Diggy began murmuring the layout of the obstacles in my path, whenever he couldn't maneuver us around. The entire time my heart tripped with adrenaline, and I couldn't help but resent he could hear it, though he made no comments. No creatures followed our progress, the way Frizz and his band had followed Dr. Dean and me.

Because Diggy was a stronger predator, the thought crossed through my mind.

Soon I could see the silhouettes of the dead trees, obscure shadows that inclined sideways or horizontally, or even upside-down. I let go of his arm and he stopped at once, waiting for me to grab on again.

"It's ok. I can see some now." My voice came out louder than I'd intended.

As he'd promised, the moment we broke free of the forest, I was able to see with more clarity. Not as well as when Diggy illuminated the land, but clear enough I could make out the peak of the mountain, bare of any trees, stretching far above, a darker shadow against the black sky.

It was to our left Diggy motioned, and there, against the face of the mountain stood a cluster of huge onyx-black rocks. Unlike the jagged little rocks I was accustomed seeing, the cluster ahead had no points, seeming smooth and unmarked. At first, I couldn't make out the darker shadow in the mountain-face, concealed behind all the rocks.

We approached slowly; the only sounds were our breathing and gentle tap of shoes. The mouth of the cave became clearer the closer we got, and smaller than I'd guessed. It seemed unnatural, even to my untrained eyes, as much as something could be unnatural in a land that went against all I knew and was.

We maneuvered around the big rocks, some almost my height, others reaching up to my waist; all at least four or five feet in diameter. The slash in the mountain-face was narrow, wide enough for a person to enter sideways.

We paused a few feet away. Diggy glanced over. "Can you sense the ward?" His voice was just a whisper.

I frowned, shook my head.

"Try harder."

I closed my eyes, sent my awareness ahead. And sensed nothing. I concentrated harder, my forehead creasing with effort.

"No, nothing," I murmured.

Diggy nodded. "It's not an offensive work, just something to keep predators out. There's nothing against humans either."

I glanced around the land, at the planets orbiting far in the obsidian sky. Why should it ward against humans?

"No more than a minute. Don't linger. Remember, just take a look inside and send your awareness in. I'll be right by the entrance, ready to break the ward if you need me."

"But what am I searching for?"

"Don't know. I want to know what's in there. See if you can sense anything out of the ordinary." He fumbled inside a jacket pocket and removed a penlight, similar to the one Dr. Dean had used, and handed it to me.

I turned to the entrance and studied it, took a long calming breath and, focusing hard, sent my awareness toward it one more time. But again, I sensed nothing, saw nothing.

Diggy waited. The fact he wasn't pressuring me, that he would accept my refusal without a word, had me clenching my teeth and stepping forward. Sliding sideways, I entered the cave, Diggy's penlight barely making a dent in the dark. My phobia of enclosed spaces threatened to return the chicken sandwich I'd eaten earlier, and I almost didn't notice the ripple when I passed through. A weird ripple that I red-flagged as something I should tell Diggy about.

A few feet ahead, the ceiling vaulted, the sides opened up, giving me breathing room. Glancing back outside, I found Diggy's glowing eyes on me. Reassured, I took a few cautious steps inside.

I shone the light around, down and up, left and right. It was a big chamber, the light not reaching the ceiling. The walls, made of smooth gray stone, stood a fair distance apart.

I moved in a few more steps, panicking when I looked back and didn't find the slash in the rock. But when I returned, I found it, just a mere slash, a thin gap in the rock. I shone the light out, realizing with an icy chill the light refracted, bouncing back from the entrance, never going through. Diggy was still there, unmoving, his eyes lit with that feral glow. If I'd stood longer, watched him a little closer, I may have seen how unnaturally slow the slight motion of his chest was, how the up and down motion of his eyelashes took an eternity to complete one blink. But I assured myself he was still there, standing guard, and

I turned and moved away, in a hurry to scope the place and get the hell out of there.

I shone the light around, but the place was so big, the thin stream died without finding the end wall. The ceiling, just a vague shadow, was bare of stalactites, or stalagmites, or nocturnal animals. It was a huge chamber, the ground little more than pebble-covered rock. There were no footprints, human or animal. My steps echoed, giving me the sense of a vast, empty place. I slowed down, not wanting to get lost in the dark, inched sideways to the wall, where I could retrace steps to the entrance. The back of my hand brushed the dry porousy surface of the rock, telling me the walls weren't so smooth after all.

The penlight split the darkness ahead in two, leaving everything else pitch-black. Behind me stood an impenetrable mass of darkness. I shivered, unable to help but feel as if the world was closing behind me. The ground sloped down and I followed, careful to avoid slippery pebbles as best as possible and trying, unsuccessfully, to keep my approach silent.

Ahead, the chamber divided into three narrow tunnels, each more sinister than the next.

Alrighty, this is it. I aimed the light into each tunnel. *This is it; this is far enough.*

This is as far as I'll go. My light was a weak, feeble thing against the massive black, the darkness a giant stretching within each tunnel.

My heart beat an erratic drum, like the music of death.

Thump bump thump thump bump bump thump.

I closed my eyes, quickly opened them again. *No no no, I'll do this with my eyes open.*

I inhaled through my nose, exhaled through my mouth, concentrated on evening my breathing, my heartbeat. Then I opened my senses, let them spread to the sides before sending them into the caves ahead.

Nothing.

Nothing moved ahead, nothing scurried inside. No wings of nocturnal birds fluttered, no lungs, small or big, moved inside. There was nothing there, as far as my senses could tell.

Relief, so acute it ached, spread through me. Unwilling to step inside any of the three tunnels, I made my way back, afraid the one minute was almost up.

If a small part of me told me to make sure, I suppressed it by reminding myself Diggy warned me not to go far, not to linger. I hurried so Diggy wouldn't worry and break the ward for no reason. Forty, no more than fifty seconds had passed. I was making a lot of noise, my breathing coming fast. But there was nothing hiding in the darkness.

Nothing I could sense, anyway.

I made the way back quicker than when I'd entered, eager to get the Hell out. Stones and pebbles crunched under my boots, sounding like thunder.

Maybe it was an old, forgotten ward. From a time when this land still carried life. Maybe someone once dwelled deep inside one of the three caves, warding the entrance against whatever predators lived outside. Perhaps its remains were still here, deep in the bowels of the cave, untouched by the wilderness that had existed out there. Maybe that was why the ward still stood, because no one knew to break it. Because there was *no one to break it.* Maybe, like Diggy, someone crossed here before, sensed the ward, and hurried away, afraid to be caught or burned to ashes.

I flexed my hand, recalling how Remo's ward had burned it to charcoal, and brushed aside a cobweb from my face, understanding why Diggy wouldn't risk the ward without reason...

I froze mid-step.

What was that?

Spiders?

I moved the light across the ground, searching.

Breath held, I cast my senses out, listened hard. Where was it?

I aimed the penlight up, traced the ceiling rock for small, long-legged insects, trying to catch a darker shadow against the rock. Found nothing. Doing a 180, I searched around and listened.

How did cobwebs get here if there were no spiders?

Not my concern, I told myself, shaking my head. I'd just flag that fact and tell Diggy. I frowned. Something about red flags... narrowing my eyes, I tried reaching that vague thought, that something trying to cross to the forefront, but it skidded and evaded, and with another head shake, I let it go. Turning back to where the entrance should be, I left my senses open and continued forward.

Had I moved this far into the cave? Diggy must be getting ready to break the ward. Maybe I should hurry up and jog.

There! I froze, right foot in mid-air, penlight arcing left and right.

What was that sound? Where did it come from? I listened, but only silence answered back.

Just projecting, Rox, just projecting.

Still, my heart drummed fast and hard, my breathing faster still. I needed a break.

I promised myself I'd let Vicky drag me on one of her shopping sprees. Maybe we'd even go for dinner and a movie; let her invite that friend of a friend. I'd call her the moment I got home. How much time had already passed earth-side? Ah well, Vicky would understand. She'd gotten a kick out of the fact I trained four to five hours every day, only to be gone less than fifteen minutes standard time. She'd be delighted to know I was away for a few hours, only to realize I'd been gone for a couple days standard time.

She'd go all OhmyGod excited, wanting to hear all about it.

And where the hell was that cave entrance? She'd laugh at how silly I was being, at my fear of the dark, like a small child afraid of the monsters under the bed.

Whirling at a sound behind me, I flashed the light everywhere. The ceiling, the ground, the rock wall beside me.

I *heard* that. I wasn't projecting. I was sure. Someone was in there. *Something* was in there.

Diggy, come on, *now's* the time to break the ward.

Chapter Twenty-Two

I didn't know how long I stood, barely breathing, waiting, before I heard it again.

The cry of a child, quickly cut off as if someone covered its mouth with a hand.

Goosebumps erupted all over my body.

A child. There was a child in there!

Forgetting Diggy's warnings, aware he'd be behind me soon, I moved back down, my steps as quiet as I could make them. When I reached the entrances of the three tunnels, I paused, listening. What if the sound didn't come again? Did I dare wait for Diggy? He was the better tracker, the Hunter.

The sound came again, fainter, farther in. From the center tunnel. I hesitated, glancing back at the wall of darkness. If I waited for a while longer, Diggy would come. He'd track me via the bracelet; follow me to wherever I was. But if I waited, I might lose the child. Already the sound was fainter, farther.

I slipped in, not giving myself time to consider any further, aware there would be danger facing me. If someone was taking the child deeper inside, away from me, it was because that someone knew I was there. Yes, I was aware, though I didn't let myself debate my actions. Or the consequences of following an unknown into the unknown. My next step faltered, but when the cry came again, nearer this time, I hurried. If I was afraid of whatever hid in the absolute dark, how could a child not be?

I stumbled out of the small cave into a big open area. Or was I back outside? Maybe the cave was just a passage to another side of the land.

I beamed the small light around, at the ground, at the walls of the cave I'd emerged from.

Where to now? Where are you?

I silently begged the child to keep struggling, not to give up. Would it answer me if I called her? Or was it a boy? Or would whoever had brought the kid here answer instead?

Maybe it didn't know I was here. Maybe it hadn't heard me yet. Maybe it was deaf.

There was nothing ahead but a dark so deep, it seemed tangible. Afraid to get lost, I followed the wall to the right, switching the penlight to that side to keep my left hand ready for attack. The wall stretched as far as the thin stream of light went, making me wonder if I was inside an enormous cavern, so huge my light could find no end, no ceiling above.

There were no sounds but that of my shallow breathing and the thunderous beat of my heart. Shining the light through a cavity in the wall, I peered inside. It was about ten feet deep, though no more than three feet wide.

Inside laid a bunch of brown, jagged sticks, a few smooth rocks roughly the size of my closed fist. I sent the light far at the dozens of similar niches pockmarking the surface of the rock wall. The dark and eerie silence gave me the creeps, but I moved on, shining the light inside each hole, but found no child. Some niches were too high for me to see inside, and I reasoned if I couldn't reach them, neither could a child. Some weren't even big enough to accommodate one, though every hole contained twigs. It was as if someone had been hoarding the wood from outside, anticipating a long stay.

I reached inside a shallow hole for a particularly sharp, jagged stick and examined it, testing its toughness by beating it against my thigh. I brought it up, closer to the light, noticing the Small, tiny holes dotting the surface, some bigger than others.

Turning the jagged end up, my heart began pounding like hooves inside my ribcage, the rhythm vibrating inside my throat. A scream bubbled inside my chest and I dropped the stick. It was hollow. It clattered to the ground, rolling a few inches away. The sound was so loud, I almost screamed in terror.

Bones. Every niche was filled with bones.

Tremors ran down my body, and I clamped it down. *No, don't panic. Don't panic.* The bones are old. *They've been here for a long time.*

The child cried again, the sound creepy without the echo. It came from ahead, from inside the wall.

Oh God, the child was the next meal for the monster who lived here.

Don't think about it, don't think about it. I raced to where I'd heard the cry come from, but must have passed it because the next cry came from behind. I whirled, backtracking, frantically shining the penlight at every small opening, every gap.

Then the cry was right beside me, not in the hole, but on the other side. I turned, the light arcing with the motion, searching the darkness ahead. My breaths came in small pants as I moved the light left, right, left, right. Nothing. Nothing but a dark void ahead.

"Where are you?" I whispered, my voice breathy but loud.

As if in answer, the cry came, somewhere ahead and to the left.

I hesitated, already disoriented. If I moved into the darkness, I might not be able to find the wall again.

The cries of the child, however, urged me forward. There was such despair, such agony. Loud once, then abruptly cut off. A struggling child, not giving up hope.

I stepped forward, away from the wall. And froze when cries sounded from multiple directions. I backed up, all the blood draining from my face as I broke into a cold sweat. I hit the rock behind me, the uneven lip of a whole digging into my back.

Three cries, three long wails emanated from three different directions.

My stomach heaved. I shone the light around, but there was nothing there. Reaching into a hole with my free hand, I searched among the bones, grabbing the longest, not taking my eyes off from the darkness ahead.

When the next cry sounded on the right, all I caught was the shadow of a small hunched figure scurrying away on all fours.

Not a child at all. Not even human-like. *Come on, Diggy, come and save the day. Tell me what a fool I am, come yell at me.*

Come on, Diggy, where are you?

The cry came again, two sounds from opposite directions. No longer sounding like the cry of a child, but the sound of a triumphant predator ready to pounce on a cornered prey.

I was wrong. I made a mistake. A colossal mistake. The long wails came again, the sound all wrong, too many to count. My heart stopped beating, but the tremor that shook my body more than made up for the lack of a pulse. A second, two seconds, and my heart kick-started, a fast, chaotic drum. The beats tripled, quadrupled.

Time to hoof it, Roxanne. Now.

Inching sideways along the wall, I cursed my stupidity. How long had I been gone? Surely long enough for Diggy to come looking?

Feel my panic, damn you and your bracelet, Diggy. Come on, feel my panic.

And where the hell was the entrance? Had I passed it already, thinking it was a niche or hole?

Back or forward, I asked myself, fear clouding my ability to think clearly.

God, help me.

My hesitation cost me. Claws grabbed me on my right side, sinking deep beneath my right arm and shoulder. I dropped the light, a scream of pain and terror tearing from my throat.

The claws dug deep, through cloth and skin and into muscle, tearing with long, downward swipes.

Survival mode took over and I jerked my hand and brought talons across my body, against something furry and hard. A shriek sounded near my ear, repeated a dozen, a hundred, a thousand times. The creature on my side jumped off and scurried away, its screeching cry of pain distinguishable from the others. I picked up the light and the bone I dropped and ran, searching for that damned entrance.

Something cannon-balled on my back, and I went sprawling onto my face, my nose and lips smacking the pebbled ground. Again, the light flew from my grasp, breaking with a sickening crash.

Complete darkness fell. There was a silent pause as the creatures assessed the new situation.

Then a creature jumped on my back and dug its claws deep into flesh. I screamed in pain. As if it was a signal, the creatures echoed my cry, their claws clicking the ground, their approach the countdown to my heartbeats.

Frizz!

I reached for the creature on my back, realizing with horror it was gnawing on my coat. I hooked my talons around its neck and flung the shrieking creature away.

Slowly I stood, my back bleeding from multiple wounds, my fear and the smell of my blood thick in the air. I sensed them now, the creatures surrounding me on all sides, closing in. I sensed their hunger, their anticipation, their malevolence.

Something brushed against my leg and I kicked. It cried, that horrible child-like shriek, the sound echoed by its companions.

The cries disoriented me enough that when they next attacked, I was caught off guard. I went down on one knee, overwhelmed by their numbers.

Frizz!

With a roar of pain and a tremendous desire to survive, I stood, shaking loose a few of the creatures. I fought with all I had, clawing, punching, kicking, and even biting when a furry limb came close to my face. Their blood was bitter, acidic.

Claws dug in all over, ripping my clothes, biting over them, through them. They were caught in a frenzied feeding and I was the succulent meal. Was this how Dr. Dean and Remo felt when they were dying? This much pain, this much terror?

How fitting I died the same death I'd dealt my enemies.

I didn't notice when one of the creatures was pulled off me. Or the second or the third. I was in so much pain, I couldn't tell the difference. Except when there was nothing else clawing for my bones, reaching for my soul.

"Diggy?" I croaked, but I already knew it wasn't him. Instead, Frizz's thin body pressed against mine, and I finally noticed the ferocious beating of small wings.

"Can't see," I gasped. Slowly, things began appearing, as if dawn were approaching, though the sky remained a dark void above.

Frizz crouched, his wings still, watching me with those dusky, shell-shaped eyes. Behind him, fanning out in a familiar semi-circle, squatted eleven other gargoyles, dripping with dark fluid. All around us, like a scene in a horror movie, pieces of the creatures that attacked me lay scattered. A caved-in head of what looked like a cross between a monkey and a dog lay a few feet away, the place where its eyes should be nothing but a shadowy patch of fur. The mouth, however, or crushed muzzle, was full of long razor-sharp teeth, covered with blood–my blood.

"Don't suppose you know how to take me home?"

"No, Master," Frizz hissed, wings opening and closing in agitation.

Bit by bit, consciousness slipped, trying to drag me under.

Aware I was running out of time, I gave Frizz one last command.

* * *

Our progress through the cave was slow. Frizz and another shadow supported me on each side, practically carrying my entire weight as weakness crept in, bowed my head and made my legs shake. The remaining shadows made sure the path was clear, ready to attack anything that came near me.

Sooner than I'd expected, or maybe because I lost track of time, we were leaving the cave.

Frizz stopped by the entrance the way I'd instructed and waited for me to catch my breath and gather myself.

We slid sideways out of the cave, with Frizz leading. The shock in Diggy's eyes had some of my anxiety escaping with a loud, rasping hiss.

When he came near, Frizz growled in warning, the sound so foreign and so new, it took a second for me to understand he was warning Diggy off. He'd picked up on my confusion, my sense of betrayal. No doubt, it was the fact Frizz smelled Diggy on me every day, saw him around my place more than once, that kept him from attacking Diggy right away.

I murmured to Frizz to relax and Diggy pounced, relieving the gargoyles of my weight, laying me down and kneeling by my head. The moment the rocky terrain touched my opened wounds, I blacked out.

"What happened? Talk to me, damn you!" he repeated over and over, his hands moving up and down, not touching anywhere, the sight of all the blood confusing him as to where to look first. "How bad is it? What attacked you?" he kept asking, but I didn't answer.

Too much effort. My eyes fluttered open and closed, his face going from and coming into focus.

"Shift, damn you," Diggy snapped, not for the first time.

Can't.

But Diggy was no longer above me, but a pair of violet-blue eyes. Then they also disappeared, and the sound of scuffling ensued.

I stared at the dark sky above, wishing I was facing the orbiting planets. I could feel my life essence leaking from my wounds as something else killed me from within.

Soon, violet eyes appeared again. Zantry Akinzo. What was he doing here?

His eyes weren't glowing like Diggy's, they were dark, shadowed, guarded.

He looked savage with that silky gloss of hair tumbling around his face, his shadowed strong jaw ... those beautiful eyes. He was easily the most beautiful man I'd ever seen.

A warm hand brushed my forehead, fiddled with my torn clothes, touched my bare stomach. Warmth permeated my cold skin, sipped into me.

Diggy said something no one acknowledged. I wanted to move my head, but my head was too heavy and the effort was too much.

"Shift," Akinzo demanded with a deep voice, deeper than I remembered. A frisson of energy ran through me. My hands shifted, answering the command.

Somewhere near, Diggy swore.

"Shift," he repeated, the command ringing with power. The frisson of energy came again, passing from his warm hand above my abdomen, coursing up into my chest, my neck, my head, down to my belly, my legs.

"Shift. *Now.*"

I focused on the movement of his lips, aware the energy coursed through me whenever he spoke.

"Shit, man." Diggy stumbled behind him, but Akinzo didn't turn. "If she doesn't shift..."

Zantry's lips pursed, his eyes narrowed. The energy turned into a torrent. His eyes shifted to blue, glowing like Diggy's, and the smell of ozone filled the air.

Soothing. The current moving through my body was soothing, dulling–if not numbing–some of the sharper edges of the agonizing pain. Like the hum of a mother to a child, a lulling music only I could hear.

My eyes closed and the darkness began closing in.

"Fuck me. It's not working, man. Move!" Diggy snapped.

There came a pressure above my chest, just beneath my collar bone, a prickling sensation spreading through before everything disappeared. The warm hand over my abdomen, the frisson of energy coursing through, the soothing sensation, all vanished away. But darkness didn't take me to oblivion and let me rest. No, I was still aware.

Still slipping away. For the first time, my need to just let go, to stop fighting, was stronger than my need to survive.

"Look at me, damn it. Shift," Diggy snapped from my other side, his voice urgent and angry.

It was better being numb, where I couldn't feel.

Diggy cursed.

That frisson of energy streamed through me again, soothing and familiar, but Zantry's command changed: he was telling me to breathe.

Wasn't I? No, I didn't want to die. With great effort, my eyes fluttered open.

"Breathe," he murmured again. "Breathe. Breathe. Breathe." Hypnotically, I watched his eyes, electric-blue now, draw nearer and nearer.

"Breathe for me," he urged over and over, his face blotting out the darkness from above.

Diggy said something I didn't understand.

"Breathe, Roxanne. You *have* to breathe," Zantry whispered against my lips.

I closed my eyes, felt him breathing into me, forcing my lungs to expand. I swear, the air he forced swelled throughout my body and entwined around the thing killing me. It was a quieting, calming sensation and I sighed, or thought I did, before the prickling sensation in my chest increased, a pressure that intensified so much I wanted to cry out from the pain.

Breathe! Zantry's command sounded inside my head. And although I wanted to, it was too much effort. There was too much pain.

With a kind of dreadful relief, I let myself go.

Chapter Twenty-Three

I awoke in fits and bursts, lying on my stomach, aching all over and unable to remember what, or where, I was. The pain of waking this way, disoriented and cold sent me back to the past, to the PSS, waking inside a cage. Because I was chilled and uncomfortable, I had the impression of lying on a cold metal slab, the way I usually did after stressful testing.

But the sensation wasn't right. A little confusing.

Opening my eyes, I noticed the familiar dark-hued wood of my nightstand. A glass filled with water sat beside my clock. The green numbers read 9:17. I was in bed, in my apartment. The PSS faded into the background, like the memory of a bad dream.

Something shifted at the foot of the bed, and seeing Diggy there, sitting in the high- chair from the kitchen, legs stretched and crossed at the ankles, still dressed in the gray V-neck and black jeans, brought back all that happened, crashing into my thoughts with startling clarity.

I was still alive, I realized with wonder.

I shouldn't be, was the thought that followed.

With one arm dangling to the side and the other lying across his stomach, Diggy's posture suggested relaxed, but tension rolled from him in angry waves. His eyes were guarded and wary.

"How do you feel?" he asked, voice gravelly.

"Like shit."

"You look like it."

I shifted and regretted the movement when every muscle in my body protested. Gritting my teeth against the pain, I turned slowly, dropping my legs to the floor–*ouch ouch ouch*–trying to look more dignified.

Diggy helped me into a sitting position. I hissed long and hard when still open wounds pulled and stretched. The world turned around once and righted again.

Diggy picked the glass of water and handed it over without a word. Parched, I accepted it, surprised at how heavy it felt. I took a few sips and, with trembling hands, returned the glass back to the stand.

Diggy sat again, placing one booted foot atop his knee, and I could tell he struggled, impatient, yet didn't rush me.

"What day is it?"

"Thursday. We've been back for about two hours."

Thursday! Three days. We lost three days in the Low Lands.

"What happened?" Diggy asked in the silence that followed.

You never came, I thought, covering my legs with the duvet, before I glanced up. *You left me there to die.* "I'm not really sure."

My poker face must not have worked because he dropped to one knee in front of me and surprised me by taking my hand in his warm one. His eyes were earnest, searching mine. "Roxanne, you were gone exactly forty-three seconds. Not a second more."

I gaped, then shook my head–regretting the motion when the world shook with it. "I was gone for a long time." At least half an hour.

"No. Not where I stood. I would have broken the ward if you stayed more than a minute. I was counting the seconds when your shadow brought you out."

I looked down, trying to make sense of what he was saying, noticed the bracelet still on my wrist, touched it with a finger. Diggy picked up my hand, examined the band, a match to the one still around his wrist.

"I didn't sense anything alarming from your side until you were out of the cave. I've never seen a ward tampering with the bond before tonight. It's never failed before, not even with worlds between the bearers."

Unsure what to say, I glanced around the room. "Zantry?"

Diggy's lips pursed, his eyes chilled. He raked a hand through his hair, tousling it more. "He's gone." He hesitated, leaned back on his haunches before he added, albeit grudgingly, "He saved your life. He told me to tell you his life debt was paid." He waited for an explanation, but when I said nothing, his eyebrows furrowed. "Why does Akinzo owe you a life debt?"

I didn't answer.

Expelling a long breath, Diggy returned to the chair. He looked puzzled, baffled even. "Was the charity ball the first time the two of you met?"

"Yes."

He paused, head tilting to the side. "Never saw him before that night?"

I didn't answer.

Frustrated, Diggy hissed through his teeth. "He wasn't on vacation, and you know where he'd been, don't you?"

I met his eyes and said, "Ask him."

Diggy nodded, but I could tell he was far from satisfied. "Why didn't you shift?"

Again, I didn't answer.

He took a long breath, exhaled slowly. "Alright, what happened there? Can you tell me that? Do you remember?"

"I do, though I wish I didn't."

I told him all, from the moment I entered the slash in the rock wall, the layout, the way it sloped and branched, how I was coming back when I heard the cry, how I moved back, wanting to be sure, counting on him to break the ward and come after me.

I told him all I saw–or didn't. The way I followed the child's cries, the way it kept getting cut off, as if someone had placed a palm over the child's mouth to muffle the sound. The feel of the open space on the other side. The attack, how swift it had been, how it happened, the acidic bitterness of the creature's blood.

Diggy listened to it all, his gaze intent, not showing one bit of emotion, going distant the second I finished talking.

"Poison. Akinzo said you were full of poison. Maybe that's why you weren't able to shift. Because of the poison."

I recalled the bitter taste of the creature's blood, the way I bit more than a few. I murmured my agreement. It could have been poison, the way I sensed myself dying from within, but I didn't shift simply because my talons were as far as my shifting went.

There was nothing more to say, and soon Diggy left, promising he'd be back to check on me, advising me to shift and accelerate the healing.

The moment the front door closed, I stood, swaying as I made my way to the bathroom, dressed in nothing but an oversized T-shirt. After I relieved a full bladder, I headed to the kitchen. I found leftover lasagna Vicky made sometime in the past three days, and I shuffled to the microwave, saliva pooling at the scent of home-cooked food and the prospect of filling an empty, growling belly.

The doorbell rang just as I pressed start. There was a boom of a small explosion, followed by the microwave door blowing open and lasagna flying everywhere. Thick smoke spiraled from small ventilation gaps behind the appliance. Ding-dong. Startled into motion, I rushed forward, pulling out the plug, swearing when a few wounds on my back opened and started bleeding anew. My blood, warm and metallic, soaked the bandages, plastering my T-shirt to my back.

Tears threatened to spill, but I swallowed them, mentally slapped myself for being a ninny. Meanwhile, the doorbell rang, ding-dong, ding-dong, ding-dong.

I ignored it; there was no one I wanted to see. Vicky had a key and Diggy just picked my lock whenever he wanted in. Plus, he hadn't left that long ago.

"Frizz," I murmured, knowing I'd need him to help me change the bandages.

Ding-dong, ding-dong, and a determined hand pounded the door.

"Roxanne," Zantry's voice came through the door, low and urgent, "I can smell you. I know you're hurting. If you don't open, I'll assume something is preventing you and I'm coming in." He paused. "I'll count to three."

I moved to the front door just as he started counting. One, two–I opened the door.

My eyes zeroed in on a bag of Chinese takeout he held in one hand, then at his face. Worry radiated from him in soft waves as he scanned my face, down my body and bare legs. I knew what he was seeing, knew he hid the horror of all the bite marks, all my injuries from his face as he completed his clinical checkout.

"You're bleeding."

"I know."

"You shouldn't be exercising." His attempt at humor didn't work, but I gave him a faint smile. He peered into the house. "Why isn't Vemourly taking care of you?"

"He had things to do."

Zantry nodded. "Can I come in?" It was his concern, along with the takeout bag that had me stepping aside for him to pass.

I closed and locked the door behind him, only to turn and find his eyes on me.

"We better take care of the bleeding first. I can help you with that," he offered.

"I thought you told Diggy your debt was paid."

Zantry studied me for a moment before nodding. "It is, but my efforts would go to waste if you die of blood loss, or infection, or the consequences of the same wound I should've healed properly."

My eyebrows arched. "*Should've* healed properly?"

"Well, you were too weak to be moved through the leeway. The drain alone could have killed you, but we didn't know what attacked you, so we couldn't stay there. The moment you were stable, Vemourly flashed you back."

I grunted. "I'm not owing you any favors."

"No favors owed," he agreed, motioning at my soaked shirt. "Let me see."

I hesitated. The bleeding was already weaker, but any sudden moves from me would only cause the wounds to re-open.

"Can you stitch?" I asked, aware Diggy left to give me privacy to shift, assuming I wouldn't need any.

Zantry cocked his head to the side, studying me, and I braced for the next question—why I wasn't shifting and hastening the healing process myself, now that the poison was gone. Instead, he said in a somber tone, "As a matter of fact, I can. I once joined a group for sewing-and-needle crafts for elderly women."

I started to explain it wasn't what I meant when I caught the gleam of humor in his eyes.

Zantry's method of stitching consisted of him covering the length of the wounds with his palms, and doing something that made my skin itch and tingle like crazy. By the time he was done, my wounds were nothing but angry, puckered scars, and not just the ones on my back, but all those on my arms and legs too. I was grateful for that, but as I watched him cleaning off the lasagna, I wondered why he had come. Because if he had intended to come, he wouldn't have given Diggy that message to pass on.

He turned once he finished washing the tea towel from remnants of cheese and tomato sauce and faced me.

"Why did you come? Not that I'm not grateful for the help," I quickly added, "but you didn't have to and you didn't know I needed it."

His reply didn't come right away, but when it did, it was simple and sincere. "I was walking to my hotel when I realized I wanted to see you, so I turned around." Our eyes held for a significant moment, and uncomfortable, I looked away first. When I looked back, he was drying his hands on paper towel. "Are you hungry?" he asked, picking up the bag of takeout food he'd placed on the counter earlier.

"Starving."

"Me too." His smile was beautiful, the kind that lit up a room, as he took out cartons and sauce containers from the bag. He'd brought some for Diggy too, so I supposed he hadn't expected to find me alone.

* * *

Zantry Akinzo was a pleasant surprise. He answered my questions without evasion, without any hesitation, telling me things about himself other people would have tried to hide. He explained the process of energy manipulation, something I found fascinating, going as far as talking about how some processes worked–something that I could understand, but not explain. For one, his immortality came from the fact energy couldn't be destroyed, something humans had discovered a few centuries ago, and was taught in high schools nowadays. When he realized this was a topic I hadn't studied, he explained the process, but when he added the preternatural angle, my eyes glazed and he changed the subject.

When I asked about what the PSS had been doing to him, he didn't falter, he just explained. The contraptions he'd been hooked to drained him of energy and gathered it into a spelled box they later used to power their concoctions, and to boost the abilities of their elite guards.

It was then I recalled every spell I'd been given had a bluish tinge, similar to the blue laser light emitted by the machines he'd been hooked to. The stronger the spell, the darker the concoction. The obedience spell, the hallucinogenic, the amplifying spell, all came in a shade of blue, all powered by Zantry's energy. What must it have been like for him, being drained of power for twenty- six years?

Seeing the horror in my eyes, Zantry clasped my hand and squeezed gently, that buzzing static warm and pleasant. He didn't reassure me it was alright, or it was all over now, or give any bull to make me feel better. Instead, he changed the topic altogether.

He did most of the talking, and although I could read curiosity in his gaze, not once did he push me to talk about myself, though I would have answered his questions if he'd asked any. Maybe it was foolish to feel comfortable with someone I just met, but that was exactly how

I felt. There was a certain connection between us I didn't have with anyone else, a feeling of kinship, a level of understanding I shared with no one.

Here was a guy who talked to me as an equal, someone who didn't see me as inferior, or balk at my mixed-breed status.

When my eyes drooped, Zantry stood and cleaned up the empty cartons and containers, stuffing them back into the takeout bag.

I stood also, and he motioned me back to the couch. "Stay. I can see myself out. You need to rest so your body can finish healing."

I walked him to the door.

"Can I come back again?" he asked at the entrance, his eyes searching mine.

"Why?"

He smiled, those eyes such a beautiful shade of deep blue. "Has anyone ever told you have a suspicious mind?" He flicked a finger across my nose. "I just want to get to know you better."

"We'll see."

"Can I kiss you goodbye then?"

My eyebrows arched high. It was polite of him to ask, but did people really do that? It was kind of embarrassing too. I blushed, and the amused glint in his eyes didn't help. "Umm, I-I'm not sure."

"It's a simple question. Yes or no?"

"Yes?" I asked. He chuckled and brushed his lips against my cheek, a warm frisson of static accompanying the touch before he turned and walked away, hands tucked inside his pockets.

PART II – The Setup

Chapter Twenty-Four

I stayed home recovering for three days, but was strong enough on the fourth to return to base. Surprisingly, my training with Diggy was over; Vincent had returned the day after Diggy and I left for the Low Lands. Although we were gone for three days standard, we'd spent less than four hours there, including our hike and the time I spent inside the cave.

During my short convalescence, Diggy–because he felt obliged–dropped by every day. When he saw the closed wounds, he'd assumed I'd shifted, and he urged me to keep shifting until I was completely healed. Despite the fact Zantry had closed the wounds, what was left was taking longer to heal than injuries caused by ordinary means. They looked grotesque, the edges puckered and angry, crisscrossing my entire body, with my back being the worst. But at least I could move without them opening and bleeding anew, despite my stiff muscles and the skin pulling and stretching when I raised my arms or bent double. I wondered if those scars were here to stay, like the vampire bite marks at the crook of my neck, courtesy of Angelina Hawthorn, and the ones on my left leg, courtesy of her scion, Jacob.

The moment Diggy would leave, Zantry would arrive with takeout food, stay for an hour or so, and always ask permission to kiss me goodbye. He'd offered to heal the puckered marks, but I declined, not knowing the toll my healing took on him. Later in the evenings Vicky would drop by and prepare dinner, and fuss over me like a mother hen. She'd have slept over too if I let her, but I was afraid Diggy already suspected she knew too much, and I didn't want anything confirmed.

Before I'd joined the Hunters, I'd had no problem revealing the reality about the preternatural community, but now was a whole different matter. For one, exposure was punishable by death, not mine but the human who'd been exposed–Vicky in this case. And two, now that I was a Hunter in training, I was, by default, a protector of the law. So I made her leave every night, not wanting to risk anyone wondering how much this human knew.

By the end of the third evening, I was strong enough to return to base in the morning, though I didn't tell anyone.

I walked the six blocks to base, half expecting Zantry to fall into step beside me. But I reached the Edgar Lon-Kis building without any sign of my blue-eyed hero.

To my delight, I found Vincent by the lockers getting ready for his morning work-out. He smiled at me, warm and welcoming, scanned me from head to bottom, no doubt searching for proof of injuries.

"If you're feeling well enough," he said, "we could do warm-ups together."

I hurried into a stall, changed into yoga pants and a loose T-shirt. For the first time since I'd arrived the gym was empty, save for Vincent and me. He wasted no time. We went through the slow motions of tai chi, and even if he scowled when I fumbled with some moves, he didn't comment or criticize–the way I'd come to expect from Diggy.

Each flowing movement tightened, stretched, and relaxed my wounds, helping restore flexibility. I realized with some amusement Vincent had been soft on me, even when I'd complained about him being too strict. I guess it was true the saying it took one evil to recognize another.

After the energizing tai-chi session, Vincent motioned me to sit. I complied, sensing he had something important to tell me. Or a lecture to impart. I waited as he strolled to a small metal cart tucked near a large water cooler and fetched two steaming cups of coffee. I'd never tried the coffee here before, and was surprised it tasted this good.

"How're the injuries?"

I shrugged. "They no longer feel like they'll tear open with every move I make."

His eyes tightened with concern and I waved him off. "They're healing fine, Vince. I'm fine."

He hesitated as if he wanted to argue, but he only nodded once, his eyes warm. "Alright. Tell me, Roxanne, what have you been up to since I left?"

"I trained. Then I trained some more. Then I'd go home to soak my sore muscles. Then I trained again. And again." I chuckled. "What else was there for me to do?" My mind flashed back to my conversation with Vicky.... It's a bleak existence, Roxy. You might as well put back that blocking bracelet.

Vincent grinned, the corners of his black eyes crinkling. "Then I guess it's time for you to step up. How about you start going on assignments?" The surprise and delight in my eyes must have been comical because he gave a hearty chuckle.

"I thought the trial stage was six months?"

"It is," Vincent confirmed, bursting my bubble. "But the remaining time will be in assignments, before you become a full member. For the next two months you'll be accompanying me, observing and learning the ropes. Twice a week you'll train with Natalya, so we can determine how much of your father you've inherited. After that you'll be teamed with a partner, and... " Vincent trailed off and turned to the door before scrambling upright.

I turned, alarmed. And there he was, standing like a Viking warrior, his gaze fixed on me.

Archer.

My heart skipped a beat before I could contain it. He came forward into the gym, stepping on the matt with his shoes, marching up to us as if he owned the room. He held himself straight, arrogantly proud and self-assured. My resentment for him was strong, an ugly feeling I wasn't proud of but couldn't help.

Archer took in the entire training room with one swift glance before focusing on us. Beside me, Vincent snapped to attention like a good soldier. I stood slowly, not caring if it was viewed as disrespectful.

"Sir," Vincent said with deference.

Archer gave him a small nod, glanced at me–and a reluctant "Sir" passed through my lips.

"I have come to collect due payment," he announced without any preamble.

Beside me, Vincent stiffened. "For what?"

"Ruben's child hasn't been found."

There was a small silence where my heart paused, holding its breath. It didn't help I could feel the tension emanating from Vincent, or the total indifference coming from Archer.

"That's not true. Roxanne would never do that."

"How would you know? You've been too busy with guild politics to properly guide her," Archer snapped, his anger at Vincent surfacing.

"With all due respect, sir, my position with the guild was your suggestion."

"Yes, but not at the cost of your clan. I gave you a directive and you shifted that responsibility to your subordinate, a Seelie Dhiultadh no less, just so you could play hero for the guild."

"I was given permission by my alpha to serve this guild to my utmost capacity."

Archer waved a hand in dismissal, "This is not the reason I am here today."

Vincent paused, shifting gears before he repeated, "And on what grounds do you claim due payment here?"

"She has threatened the child. She lured the child here. She–"

"I did not!" I snapped, cutting Archer off.

"Sir, those accusations are ludicrous. They're all lies."

"Alleena says otherwise," Archer challenged.

Vincent gritted his teeth. "Sir, she lies."

A muscle ticked spasmodically on Archer's temple.

"She has sworn by our father." His eyes dared Vincent to deny. "And this scion has admitted being the last person to see the child." He reached inside his jacket and extricated a folder from his pocket, handed it to Vincent.

Vincent spared me a glance before extracting the contents of the folder. A picture of me and Mwara, as I held the door of the café open for the child, stared back at us.

Shocked, I stared at the photo, my mind blank. Mwara's face looked up at me with that gaze no child her age should possess. I snapped out of the haze when Vincent flipped to the second image. Another photo showed me standing with a hand on Mwara's shoulder, her eyes brimming with fear as she looked back at me. Blood began roaring like a current in my ears.

"This is her last trace," Archer said in a quiet tone, or maybe the roaring in my ears muffled his voice.

Vincent turned to me, his eyes stricken.

"Fosch's daughter has confessed meeting the child, but only when she realized she had been cornered," Archer added, and my jaws dropped open with the realization Logan had betrayed me.

Vicky had been right after all.

It had indeed been an ugly trap–with all the snares and barbed wires attached. "Do you deny the evidence, Daughter of Fosch?"

"She came to see me one evening while I–"

"And do you admit threatening the child to her mother?" Archer cut me off, not wanting any explanations. I could see it in his eyes, for him, I was guilty of the crime.

"I did not," I replied hotly. "Whoever this Alleena is, she is lying."

Archer's hand clenched beside him. Anger pulsed from him once, a biting, red wave. "Have you not," he took a step forward, his dark eyes hard, daring me to deny, "Escaped your duties to this guild to question Elizabeth's rightful deeds and threaten her child with exposure to the scientists in her own home?"

I opened my mouth to protest, then snapped it shut again, narrowing my eyes when comprehension dawned. "Rightful deeds? You mean sending a twelve-year-old to the mercy of the scientists? You've been there before, sir," I said with a touch of derision, "you tell me, do you think it was a rightful deed to leave a twelve-year-old there for years when you, older by centuries, couldn't bear a few weeks?"

I ignored when Archer's lips thinned in anger and Vincent made a warning sound low in his throat. "You think it was right, a great decision when you all donned your important robes and decided Fosch's daughter would be a great diversion to keep the scientists from looking too hard at you? After all, she's just a human hybrid."

Archer's eyes grew harder, and the same menace from that night in the charity ball filled the entire room. Flecks of yellow appeared in his black eyes, his jaws clenching.

"It was the deed agreed upon by the council," Archer growled with a thick voice. "You are not to question the decision of your elders. Now answer the accusation. Have you not threatened Mwara, Ruben's child, with exposure to the scientists?"

I huffed out a laugh. "How ironic."

"You dare mock this grave accusation?"

"Roxanne," Vincent warned. I could tell Archer was furious, but damn it, so was I. In his eyes, I was already condemned, and he hadn't even given me a chance. This was just an inconvenient formality he had to check out before I was dealt my judgment. What would my punishment this time be? Another trip to the PSS? Solitary confinement somewhere remote and cold? A few years in a dark dungeon cell while the clan led on their lives, unconcerned? With all the possibilities that crossed my mind, indignation and outrage grew and took root on my resentment towards this clan.

"Answer the accusation, scion. Did you threaten to set the scientists upon Mwara, Ruben's child?"

I ignored Vincent's warning glance and said to Archer in a voice that shook with anger, "No, sir, with all due respect, I believe that's your specialty."

The slap that sent my face rotating ninety degrees was so loud, I was sure it could be heard down in the streets. My ears roared with blood, my cheek burned with the aftershock. My lips bled from a wide cut, and I'd bitten the inside of my cheek.

In front of me, Archer's jaws were clenched so hard, his teeth should have cracked. "You will show respect, scion!" he thundered in a voice that didn't belong to him.

Seeing the blazing anger in my eyes, Vincent took a step forward, bravely coming between Archer and me. He raised both hands in a placating gesture before reaching for me.

I sidestepped, avoiding his grasping hand.

"Why did she come to you? Why ask for help from you?" Vincent asked, trying to diffuse the explosive atmosphere.

I inclined my chin at Archer. "Ask the all-knowing."

Archer growled and Vincent's eyes turned pleading. "I want to hear it from you. Please."

I was silent for a second, and only the plea in his eyes had me saying, "Because she's afraid the clan would send her to the PSS. Because she wasn't sure Elizabeth was her mother."

"Nonsense," Archer scoffed.

Vincent shook his head. "Elizabeth would never do such a thing to her own daughter."

I raised my eyebrows high and ignored the need to cover my throbbing cheek with my cold hand. "No? That's weird. I thought that was exactly what she did to me."

Vincent's mouth opened and closed twice before he said, "Mwara is her child. She loves her."

"I thought I was too."

"You lie," Archer spat, his voice as cold as frost. "Ruben's daughter has no knowledge of you. She has no reason to mistrust or fear her own family. She is loved by everyone." his eyes narrowed, "Have you been meeting with her in secret, telling her wild fables?"

"I had never met the child before that day." I pointed at the photos clutched in Vincent's hand. "And she was the one who approached me. She was here in New York, not the other way around. Plus, she told me she eavesdropped in on a council meeting when you were discussing me."

"Roxanne, why didn't you come to me?" Vincent asked.

I leveled my eyes at him. "Because she's afraid of you too. She's afraid of all of you." I turned to Archer. "The people who let the scientists torture a twelve-year-old with the blessing of the council." I held Archer's angry eyes, not flinching when he took a step forward.

There was a heavy pause before Vincent spoke again. "Sir, I believe her. The annual meeting was held in Ruben's home. I can see Mwara sneaking around in the corners, trying to eavesdrop. Roxanne didn't do it. I'll talk to Roland; put some of our men in the hunt. We'll find her."

Archer's angry eyes dragged from me to Vincent. He spoke each word with care, as if he was having trouble putting the sentence together. "She has disappeared from the ether."

This time, Vincent's pause was heavy with denial. "Alleena didn't tell me."

"You were unreachable. And she has reasons to mistrust you. Apparently, they're good ones." Archer glanced at me when he spoke his last words. "She has been missing for over two months. We have searched all over for her."

"She ran. She told me she would," I said.

"She is but a child," Archer snapped. "She is naïve and inexperienced. She would never be able to hide from trained trackers unless someone was covering her."

I didn't point out I didn't have any experience either.

"Maybe someone took her for ransom?" Vincent suggested, grasping for straws.

"We have waited this long for any demands. None has come forth."

"She could be inside a heavy ward."

"For what purpose?" Archer asked. "No one has made any demands. We have given up on the hunt. It is obvious someone has disposed of the child."

"And you think that person is me?" I huffed out a laugh. The joke was on me.

"Maybe someone helped you." Archer's eyes gleamed with suspicion.

My hysterical moment died without a trace. What? Who were they trying to accuse of helping me? My thoughts went to Diggy, but he wasn't from the clan. Vincent? He just came back after a long assignment. Who else?

Swallowing back his grief, Vincent took a step forward. "Roxanne didn't do it," he paused a fraction of a second before adding, "I swear on our father her innocence." I knew this was some sacred vow. He was defending me, and he didn't even know me that well.

When Archer didn't say anything, he added in a decisive tone, "I promise you we will find out what happened to her." Couldn't he see his leader was so angry he was beyond words? His eyes alone could've frozen us to the spot. The anger that had pulsed from him before now battered at me like a hammer as his eyes flashed that yellow, alien color.

"Do you know what you pledge, fool one?" Archer demanded. The fury in his voice was like a double-edged whip, it sliced through my senses, making me grit my teeth against the onslaught.

Vincent didn't cower or back down. "She didn't do it."

Archer was silent for a long time. Neither Vincent nor I spoke, waiting for his verdict. At last, Archer inclined his head, and Vincent exhaled a quiet breath of relief.

"She has a fortnight to bring back the child," he raised a hand to cut off Vincent's protest, "or approved evidence by the council she's innocent of the alleged accusations." He glanced at me, and not knowing if I should protest or if I was expected to thank him, I stayed quiet. Focusing back on Vincent, he laced his hands and took a step forward, his eyes coldly assessing him. "You will go to Salzburg, where Fin has committed some travesty against the human authorities and is wanted once more." Vincent opened his mouth, but shut them again when Archer's eyes blazed, his patience at an end. "Ruben is here searching for his daughter. So you will go in his stead and find where Fin is hiding. You will bring him back within the fortnight."

"Sir, Roxanne's training isn't yet complete. She has no skills in tracking yet"

"It is decided. This is the only concession I'm willing to make for her." His dark eyes met mine and they were livid. "In a fortnight and a day, we will meet again by the stone circle." He turned to leave, but paused when I called out.

"Wait."

Vincent took a step toward me, his eyes begging me to stay quiet.

I took a deep breath, summoning the courage to speak my next words. "If I can prove I had nothing to do with Mwara's disappearance, I want something in return."

Archer didn't snort, exactly, but I sensed his disdain when he turned to glare at me. "You are in no position to make any demands, child." The last was an insult, not an endearment, and I gritted my teeth against it.

"According to the rules, Sir, I am in the position to make this one," I said with forced politeness.

Archer's head inclined once, indicating for me to go on.

"Once I have proven that I have been wrongly accused, I want to go through the abjuration ritual."

"No!" Vincent whirled, his shock so strong, for a moment I wondered if I just signed my death warrant. Then my resolve strengthened, and I clenched my fists. "I am tired of being accused for every wrong that happens within this clan I have never met. If casting myself as clanless is the price to be free, then so be it."

"Do you know what you are saying, Roxanne?" Archer demanded. It was the first time he called me by my name.

I swallowed once, then nodded. "Yes. I have read the rules." And although it had been a possibility for the far future, I hadn't planned to make this request.

"No, sir, she doesn't know what she's saying," Vincent protested at the same time, turning to me, his eyes frantic. "Don't do this. Let me first tell you what will happen to a rogue. You have no clan, no family, no one who can officially step in for you."

I shook my head, knowing Vincent really wanted me to belong. "I've read the book. I'm a Hunter member, will be for the next ten years. Until then, I belong here."

"Ten years will pass in a blink. What then? What will you do after that?"

"I'll think about that time when it arrives. For now, I want these ten years of freedom, free of all the strings this clan has around my neck." I waved in Archer's general direction. I took a step toward Vincent, took his callused, broad hand in mine and squeezed, wanting him to understand. "What has it given me? Look at me. I'm the first person they go to when something goes wrong. I've been that person since I was born. If I make through this time, I want to make sure I am no longer bound to all the rules and none of the privileges."

"Well?" Archer interrupted.

"Wait," Vincent said with an urgent tone, clearly casting for a solution. "Give her some time to think. Don't officialize it yet."

"I'm firm on it," I said, my stomach fluttering with anxiety.

Archer studied me for a moment longer before nodding once, just an incline of his arrogant head. "Then so be it, Roxanne, Daughter of Fosch. When and if you return in a fortnight with proof of your innocence, then we will, in front of the clan you so renounce freely, go through the abjuration ritual as you wish." With that said, he pivoted and left without another word, and after one desperate glance at me, Vincent followed, not bothering to change or put on his shoes.

Chapter Twenty-Five

I stayed in that same position–back straight, head held high–for a few minutes until the full weight of my situation brought me down to my knees, head bowed, fighting back useless tears.

My hands shook out of control, my insides quivered from a sundry of emotions: anger, resentment, bitterness, fear, grief… fury. I pressed my clenched fists to my eyes until I saw red, the color of my raging emotion. A scream built inside my chest, a pressure that grew and grew until I could no longer contain it.

"They did it again!" The words burst out, and I pounded a fist hard on the mat.

I pounded again, then again with both fists, but it wasn't enough. I jumped and whirled at the punching bag, taking my fury out on it with punches and kicks. Once I kicked so hard, it slapped the ceiling with a resounding boom. *They had done it again.*

My breaths came in panting gasps, the injuries on my back and shoulders stretching and spasming. Just when I thought I was getting my life on track, they came back to ruin everything.

"Just leave me be!" With a roar of fury, I slashed the bag with my talons and fell on my knees, covering my aching face with the palms of my hands. Sand fell through the slashes of the bag and formed a small dune in front of me. Like the sands of time in an hourglass, marking the near ending of my life.

They did it again.

A hesitant throat clearing had me jumping to my feet and whirling around, talons bared, a savage snarl escaping my lips.

Diggy, dressed in his usual attire of jeans and leather, stood at the edge of the mat. A small frown creased his forehead. Concern or disapproval?

I bared my teeth. "What? Come to gloat? You're finally getting rid of the abomination."

Diggy's eyes hardened, his lips thinned. "I came to inform you that Roland is giving you the next two weeks off so you can focus all your time and strength on the search."

I scoffed, my tears threatening to break free. "I won't come back. I won't find her." Opening my arms wide, I raised my voice, "Everyone! In two weeks the world will finally be free of this abomination! It's time to celebrate!"

"Simmer down, Roxanne," Diggy snapped, stomping onto the mat with his boots on.

"Or what? Are you going to punch and kick me until I go home unable to walk or sit without crying out? Because, oh yeah, been there, done that already." Diggy's eyes went flat, but I didn't care. "I'm no longer your punching bag. And in two weeks, I won't be anyone's."

"You'll never win if you believe you already lost before you start."

"Bravo!" I clapped twice. "A philosopher. Was that lesson number five million?"

Diggy pursed his lips, pausing just a few feet away from me.

"News flash for you, pal. If I believe I lost so early in the game, it's because I have nothing, no clue, no hint, no experience whatsoever to help me find her. It means I'm realistic and am facing the truth."

Diggy cocked his head. "What's this," he mocked, "pitying yourself for the tragic life you have? Or is it a bid for sympathy? Because you'll get none here."

I slashed at him, but he'd seen it coming, dodging the attack and closing in, punching me in the abdomen and not holding anything back. I doubled over in pain, my vision dimming, my back injuries stretching as if they were tearing open.

"Get up. Fight back." He jerked his arms, motioned me forward.

I straightened, ignoring pain, feinted right, then kicked Diggy so hard he skidded back. He jumped up, but I didn't give him time to recover. I went for his back, opening three long gashes in the buttery leather of his jacket. I was fighting dirty, the way Logan once told me to. With a crazed chuckle, I soaked in the satisfaction of ruining his favorite jacket. "How does that feel, Instructor?"

Diggy unzipped the jacket and let it fall to the ground, his eyes narrowed. Then he attacked. A left jab that would have put out the lights if he'd hit home, then a right one, then a left, and another left. I parried, blocked, jumped back. He was forcing me on the defensive, but I learned my moves from him. So I parried, fainted left, which he knew I would follow with a right, but I didn't. Instead, I followed with another left, catching him square on his side, letting some of that otherness inside me out with the punch for better effect. When he stumbled, I followed with a kick to his kneecap. I was fighting an enemy, not a colleague, not my trainer, certainly not a friend. We punched and kicked, blocked and parried, parted and returned. On and on we went.

Finally, with a growl Diggy stepped forward, entering my private space when I thought he'd pull back, and with an upper jab, punched me on my solar plexus with such force, he lifted me off my feet. I fell on my back with a strangled cry, some fragile gashes on my back tearing open with the impact. The ceiling dimmed, then cleared again.

Diggy's face appeared above mine, a trickle of blood coming from the corner of his lips, a bruise following the line of his jaw, but I didn't remember punching him on the face.

He gave me a once over, I guess to make sure I was still alive and in one piece, before turning and limping his way out of the gym.

* * *

After peeling off my bloody tank top, I slipped on a smelly shirt I found stuffed in the bottom of my locker, threw on a short wool jacket, and left to go home. I guess word was out about my impending doom, because even Barbara didn't make any snarky comments or offer any of her condescending smiles. Chris, a shifter I saw around but never talked to, nodded curtly as he made room for me in the elevator. I heard him sniff once; no doubt smelling fresh blood, but he didn't say anything. I considered going down to Roland's office, telling him what happened, maybe ask for assistance or advice, but remembered Diggy had come on Roland's behalf to give me my two weeks off.

So I went home, soaked in warm sudsy water until it was no longer pink, and asked Frizz to help bandage the wounds. After a hot meal and a tall glass of orange juice, I sat down with my laptop and booked a trip to Seattle. This time, I'd be taking Frizz with me. As a matter of fact, from here on in, I would take Frizz with me everywhere.

Chapter Twenty-Six

The cab stopped in front of the PSS front gates at 11:35 a.m. It was one of those days where clouds covered the sun and rain drizzled with annoying frequency. A light wind blew leaves back and forth, and snow covered patches of smooth ground here and there, slowly melting onto drab brown puddles.

It was a gloomy and forlorn morning, the kind where people huddled by fireplaces with hot cups of chocolate. And watched horror movies.

The fortress walls of the PSS loomed above, guardhouses full of guards. To the outside world, this was a penitentiary, a place for monsters, though not the kind they imagined.

Melancholic thoughts circled inside my head, things I had no answers for. Was Mwara in there, getting ready for "experiment day"? Why did I keep ending up here? Was this a twisted joke of fate? Would this be the last time?

"Would you like me to wait here, ma'am?" the cabby asked.

I glanced back at the man, a forty-some-year-old balding black guy with square glasses and a goatee. "Yes, please. I won't be long." I stepped out into the perpetual rain of the northwest, into the annoying, frigid drizzle of deep winter, even though we were weeks away from spring.

I approached the heavily-gated entrance, realizing this was the first time I'd ever come in through the main entrance, even though I'd lived here for nine years.

A guard stepped out of a small cabin beside the gate and intercepted me when I was about ten feet away.

"That's close enough, miss," he said. A beefy hand rested on the butt of his weapon, a point thirty-eight. Not what I was used to seeing, but I supposed tranquilizer guns would call attention. The man's aura was blue, the smudge faint. Elite. His name tag read Carson, E.

"I'm here to see Dr. Maxwell."

The guard was too well-trained to show any surprise. "This is a penitentiary, miss. We have no doctors here but the one who resides in the infirmary. His name is *not* Dr. Maxwell."

"I know what kind of facility this is. Tell him Roxanne Fosch is here to see him on official Hunter business." I hated to use the Hunters' name like this, not knowing what Roland would do when he heard. I was too much a coward, however, to walk into the PSS of my own free will with no guarantee of backup to ensure my walking out.

The guard narrowed his eyes, no doubt recognizing my name. He pressed a hand over his ear, listening to whoever was on the other side, his head lowering a fraction, his eyes fixed on me. The other hand stayed closed around the butt of his gun.

I stood with arms to both sides, hands opened and relaxed–a non-threatening gesture.

After a moment, the hand over his ear dropped, and he inclined his head for me to come forward.

My stomach tightened with nerves, but my face remained calm, my eyes cold. My steps were measured, evenly so.

The gates behind Carson opened enough for us to pass through, a tight fit for the guard's broad shoulders. Inside, we were met by three other elites, something I hadn't expected, though I should have. One stepped forward and politely asked me to enter the cabin, where he efficiently and thoroughly frisked for weapons before announcing I was clear.

The courtyard looked familiar, a sterile place where I'd spent a lot of hours roaming, some alone, some with Dr. Maxwell, all being watched. I glanced to the right, at the wall beside the garage where we'd blown a path to escape through when we'd come for Archer all those months ago. The wall stood erect, the new construction outlined in lighter tones. Ahead, between Building A and Building C was a gaping hole, a destruction of my own making. I glanced down at my wrist, at the place Logan's bracelet had been until the night of the charity ball.

It was to Building C I was taken, a fact that caused my nerves to bundle and knot.

We found Dr. Maxwell on the second level, one floor down. It was a level I was seldom taken to. I could tell right away security was less strict on this floor, doors swishing open at our approach, with nothing but a hiss of air, instead of keypads and thumb or retina scans. We stopped at the first doors to the right—wooden swinging doors with two glass windows and a plaque that read Laboratory 1, and Carson knocked twice before pushing them open. Here the similarities with the lower levels were stronger: a sterile room with two metal examination tables, a long desk, locked cabins, telescopes of varying sizes and shapes and, of course, the standard cage—two in this case. The familiar smell of disinfectant was strong here, one that brought back a terrible feeling of helplessness.

Dr. Maxwell sat by the desk, scribbling with a Bick pen in a small leather-bound notebook. It brought to mind the journal I'd stolen from him, one I'd burned before storming the facility with Logan and Rafael.

Against the far wall, both cages were occupied. The one closest held a white wolf with clear blue eyes. A thin green aura surrounded the animal, but the intelligence in his eyes alone would have told me this wasn't just an ordinary wolf. In the second cage was another wolf, a gray one. Where the white wolf sat patiently watching, the gray one stood on all fours, hackles raised, a feral snarl displaying its sharp upper canines. No aura surrounded this one, and the savage gleam in his yellow eyes was unnerving.

I stood, both guards flanking me, and waited for Dr. Maxwell to acknowledge our presence, acting like I had all the time of the world by studying the room, though I'd already taken in all I would.

"Blink twice if you're here against your will," I said to the white wolf. It blinked once, but I wasn't sure if it was in surprise or a no. Dr. Maxwell's shoulder tightened, but he kept scribbling for a few seconds more before he looked up.

"Roxanne. What a delightful surprise," he said, as if he hadn't known I was there.

"Is it?" I countered, forcing myself to keep my hands from fisting.

"Of course it is," Dr. Maxwell said with a fake smile, "You were always one of my best subjects."

Yeah, I bet so had been Zantry.

"Let's not bullshit each other. I cost you; you hate me for that, blah-blah-blah." I waved a hand. "I'm here for the child. Give her back."

Dr. Maxwell's left eyebrow arched high. "*Child*? Is this official Hunter business, then?"

"Yes."

Dr. Maxwell's lips pursed and his head shook. "I must be getting addled. No one mentioned there was a request." He scratched a balding spot at the front of his head, his eyes lowering in thought. When he looked at me again, there was a chilling gleam of madness I'd never notice before. "Do you know I can hold you here until I can confirm your official claim?"

My heart skipped a beat, but I knew nothing showed in my eyes.

"Of course," he went on, "I've already sent an assistant to check on your claim. And while we wait, why don't we talk about this child you mentioned?" He leaned forward, feigning interest. "Is she like you? How old is she?"

I smirked. "You know I have an excellent olfactory sense. If I so much as sniff her in here—"

"You will do nothing about it," he interrupted, his eyes hard. "There is no child here, believe it or not. It's up to you. Your... colleagues already came sniffing around, though I admit they weren't as bold as you."

My *colleagues*? Did he mean the clan already came searching for Mwara? "I don't think you understand, Dr. Maxwell. It's in your best interest to give me back the child without a fuss. I'll walk out of here with her and you'll never hear or see me again." A cell phone on the desk began buzzing and, without glancing over, Dr. Maxwell picked it up and grunted his hello. He listened a moment, then smiled coldly. At the same time he hung up my cell phone began ringing.

A chill skipped down my spine at the expectant look in his eyes. Removing my phone from my pocket, I read the Hunters' base name on the display. "Hello?"

"Miss Fosch," began Valerie, Roland's assistant. "Per Mr. Mackenzie's order, you are to remove yourself from the premises of the Scientists' base this very instance. You've been ordered outside the walls and to refrain from assuming any authoritative role on behalf of the Hunters in the future. In exactly five minutes, you'll call me from outside the facility's wall, and will be transferred to Mr. Mackenzie. In the event you fail to do so, Mr. Mackenzie will be informed you willingly volunteered to be subjected to the Scientists."

The connection clicked off, and I took the moment I pocketed my phone to compose myself.

"I see you still have a hard time obeying orders," Dr. Maxwell commented wryly.

I gave him a mocking smile, portraying a nonchalant air, but inside my stomach was hollow. "I'm claiming this child as mine. If I so much as sense her anywhere near this facility, Dr. Maxwell, I will burn this place to the ground, Hunter or no." I let him see the truth in my eyes.

"Is that a threat?" Dr. Maxwell asked with interest.

"Of course not. I wouldn't dare threaten *you*, Dr. Maxwell. It's a hypothetical consequence only, the end result if I ever discover this child here. I'm walking out now, per my superior's order." I turned to leave and both guards stepped beside me.

We paused to wait for the elevator. The moment the doors parted, I nudged Frizz and stepped inside. The doors had already closed when unseen Frizz let loose the feral wolf and helped break things inside the lab.

The guards kept pace with me, postures stiff and tense, listening to the shouted orders in their earpiece.

I was back in the cab within the five minutes. With shaking fingers I called Roland and was informed he was on an important call with Johnson, head of PSS security.

At Sea-tac airport, a call came from a pissed-off Roland, ordering me to base at nine tomorrow morning, promising disciplinary actions when I returned to work. Seeing that the chance of me returning was slim to none, Roland's threats didn't scare me at all.

And I had accomplished *nothing*.

Mwara probably wasn't there, and there were no more leads for me to follow.

Chapter Twenty-Seven

When I arrived home late that evening, I found Logan waiting for me. He was the last person I wanted to see.

He watched me approach, eyes guarded, posture rigid.

"Hello," he said, his tone cautious.

"Hello." I fished my keys from my pocket, unlocked the door and stepped inside. I didn't invite him in, but he followed anyway. I dropped the keys on the counter and began the process of preparing coffee, aware I hadn't eaten anything since yesterday evening, save for a doughnut at the airport early dawn today.

"I didn't know," Logan said, breaking the heavy silence.

"You're his second-in-command, his enforcer," I tossed his words back at him.

Logan clenched his jaw. "I swear I didn't know. We talked about it, yes, but I know you didn't do it, and blaming you means whoever did it is still free out there. I'm sorry he won't see reason."

"Sorry won't help me find her." Catching guilt in his eyes, part of the hurt of his betrayal dissipated, but not all. I clenched my teeth, wanting to hold onto the blame. "It doesn't matter," I said, not because I forgave him, but because I was tired and didn't want to argue.

His jaw tightened even more. "It does. Archer should have talked to me before he came to you."

"Apparently *he* didn't think so."

There was a heavy pause before he spoke again. "Mwara's been missing for more than two months. I was part of the team assembled to search for her. Believe me when I tell you, Roxanne, I put the best trackers on the hunt; I handpicked them myself. Alleena could feel Mwara in the ether when she was traveling the leeway, but about five weeks ago, her daughter stopped registering."

"Alleena is Elizabeth?" I asked with surprise. Of course she was. They don't use their real names, he'd told me once.

Logan waved a hand. "That's not the point. The *point* is we were at a dead-end until you told me about your encounter with Mwara and showed me where to look. We went over that part of the city with a fine-toothed comb. We found a faint imprint in an alleyway close by and thought we'd found her, but we were only able to follow the trace to the Low Lands. It just wasn't strong enough to show us where she went after that."

"But if she disappeared in the Low Lands, won't that make the accusation moot? I can't travel the paths."

"That's why you weren't accused before, even with all the evidence pointing your way. But," Logan hesitated before adding, "It's recently been said that you've been training in the Low Lands for that entire time."

"*What*?" I stiffened with shock. "I was training with Diggy. He can testify." I recalled the way we'd parted earlier and pursed my lips. Was he that petty that he'd refuse to tell the truth to save my life? "Wait, what do you mean about all evidence pointing my way? What evidence?"

Logan looked uncomfortable when he said, "Well, the Longlans are a valued and well-respected family. You're the only person with a grudge against them. Then there's the threat, the photos and the fact you were the last person to see her." Logan shook his head when I opened my mouth to protest. "Alone, none of it is substantial evidence, or enough to build a case against you, but together they carry weight."

"I didn't kill her."

"I know," he murmured. "I'm sorry." And he looked like he was.

But sorry or not, Mwara was still missing, or dead somewhere out there.

"I have two weeks to find her and I've already exhausted the only lead I had. I have nothing to help, nowhere to start." My words carried my despair, so I turned away, stared at the now full carafe.

"Where have you looked?"

My shoulders slumped. "The PSS."

A heavy pause followed. "Why–You went there *alone*?"

"She told me she was afraid Elizabeth would send her there, too. It was the only place I could think of."

Logan exhaled through his mouth. He was frustrated, that much was clear. "Look, once a person has been given a second chance to prove her innocence, she has to prove it on her own." I scoffed, but he ignored and went on. "I'll have to step back from the search, but there's no rule that prevents me from guiding you from the sidelines. I brought you every note I've made during these past ten weeks, every place we've checked, every spot we've sensed Mwara in. I know it isn't much, but it'll keep you from following a dead-end."

When I didn't comment, he reached into a pocket and took out his cell phone. It was a big shiny thing with a long screen and no keypad, a big leap from the museum-quality device I'd last seen him carry. "Give me your number."

I rattled it off and a moment later my phone pinged. I didn't reach for it.

"That's my number. Whatever information you need, call me and it's yours."

I nodded, poured myself a mug of coffee. After an awkward pause, I grabbed another mug and poured him one, sensing he had more to say.

Logan accepted it, eyes searching mine as he took a sip. "About the request for the abjuration ritual," he began, pausing when I frowned. "I'll talk to Archer, tell him you changed your mind–"

"Oh no, you won't."

"Look, Roxanne, don't be so mule-headed. Abjuring yourself from the clan isn't going to solve anything. It's ridiculous."

"Is it? I don't see how that can be." My voice was cold, my fear converting to ire in a heartbeat.

Seeing my expression, he throttled down whatever hot comeback he was about to make, took a step back and raked a hand through his hair before trying again. "Look, once you abjure from the clan there's no going back. Once you abjure, you no longer can turn to it for protection. You're a rogue and that means you'll have no one to back you up if an occasion arises, and believe it or not, Roxanne, that time will come."

"What protection?" I asked, showing my empty palms.

Logan rubbed a hand over his face, clearly upset. Like Vincent, he wanted me to belong, I could understand that. But I didn't belong, and I wasn't going to just because they wanted it to be. "Becoming a rogue also means the clan has no hold over me. If I make it past these next two weeks, abjuration will be a reward, not punishment."

Insulted, Logan pursed his lips, his eyes chilling a few degrees. "I know that right now it feels like the clan is against you, but give them time to adjust; they'll come around."

"This clan has been against me ever since my father gave up his life for mine. They resent that fact, and the fact I'm a mixed breed even more. I've seen the disgust, the hatred, the resentment. I've made up my mind, Logan. Don't try to change it." When he opened his mouth to argue again, I added, "This is my choice to make."

Logan nodded once. "In any case, I'll talk to Archer. If after these two weeks you come to your senses, the option will be open."

I murmured an agreement, but we both knew I wouldn't change my mind. If I made it past the two weeks, that is.

"Can I ask you something?" I asked, eyes fixed on the countertop.

"Anything."

"There's a part in the *Guidebook of the Preternatural* that says an eye for an eye, an ear for an ear, a life for a life..." I let the sentence die. When the silence stretched on, I had my answer but asked anyway. "If I can't prove I had nothing to do with Mwara's disappearance, if her body isn't found, what happens?"

"It's not going to come to that," he said, but his voice lacked conviction.

"Will my punishment be death?" I looked at him, saw the answer in his eyes.

"Roxanne."

"It is, isn't it?" I pressed, wanting to hear him say it. "I won't be locked up or dealt any other judgment. Execution is the punishment. For a crime I *didn't* do."

Logan didn't say anything, but I knew he wanted to.

Turning away, I picked up my coffee. I didn't need to point out that *he* was the executioner. My stomach churned, but I forced myself to drink the coffee as if I craved it.

After a moment, Logan stepped forward. My shoulders tensed, and he stopped. "I'll go now. You call me whenever you need anything. I'm staying in town. If you find a clue, remember anything at all, just call."

I sipped again and said nothing.

He left and I went after him to lock up. And found him standing at the front door, Vicky in front of him, grocery bags hanging from one hand, takeout food from the other.

"Who are you?" he asked, frustration clear in every word.

"Who are you?" she countered.

"Logan Graham. Who *are* you?" he asked again, and I caught the recognition in her eyes. Unfortunately, so did Logan.

"Vicky."

Logan glanced at me, his expression unreadable. "The friend from Sacramento?"

Vicky glanced at me too, eyes uncertain.

I narrowed my gaze, trying to recall if I'd talked about her to him, *almost* sure I hadn't. But Tommy had, and Logan had been standing there, watching. And listening.

Logan returned inside, stopping when he was inches from me. He took my chin between thumb and forefinger, forcing my head up so he could stare into my eyes. "You know the rules, don't you?" he murmured, his eyes searching mine for any sign of guilt.

I nodded, kept my expression neutral, unsure about him.

"Don't break it."

Anger bubbled to the surface, but I contained it.

Logan glanced at Vicky, still standing at the doorway gawking, and he grabbed my arm and pulled me back into the kitchen. "I'm the enforcer, Roxanne. Don't make me have to discipline you." His eyes softened and he added, *"Please.* I don't want to cause you any pain. But if you break this law, I won't be able to avoid it." He studied my expression and eyes, trying to read my thoughts.

When I said nothing, he stepped back, turned and left, nodding to Vicky as he passed.

She closed the door, blocking my view of Logan climbing into a rental.

"That's him?" she asked, her voice bubbling with excitement. "My God, I'd give my left pinkie to work with men that look like that." She rushed into the kitchen and dropped the grocery and takeout bags on the counter before doing the boogie dance. "My. God. No wonder you're..."

She noticed my panicked expression and froze, her wide smile fading. "What is it?"

I took a deep breath, trying to clear the panic from my head. Had Logan just threatened me? Threatened Vicky?

With shaky legs, I moved into the living room and lowered myself onto the sofa.

"Rox, you're frightening me. What is it?" She took my cold hands in hers and sat beside me. "My God, you're shaking. What happened?"

I swallowed hard, closed my eyes. The tears that had been threatening to erupt ever since Archer had appeared in the gym yesterday became overwhelming. "I think it's best if you stayed away for the next two weeks," I said, my voice thick.

"I certainly will not."

The conviction in her voice had my tears backtracking, giving way to a churning fear. I gripped her hands hard, trying to squeeze sense into her. "No, Vicky, you *have* to. You don't understand."

Her pretty blue eyes, which just a moment ago had been filled with excitement, were now brimming with concern and tension. "Tell me so I can. Does this have to do with the out-of-town trip you took today?"

I nodded and told her about Archer's visit, his decision and my request, about the trip to the PSS, Roland's phone call, and Logan's words.

She listened, and the fear I'd expected never came. But anger and indignation did.

"How dare they do this to you? After all they put you through, and it isn't enough?" She got up to pace, picking up Frizz and placing him on her hip like a toddler.

If Logan could see her now... a chill slithered down my spine at the thought. "You *have* to stay away from me," I said hoarsely.

She whirled around, her eyes blazing. "No, I don't. They are *not* going to separate us again. Do you hear me? They aren't going to win this time."

I shook my head, unable to speak past the lump in my throat. "You don't understand. There are rules. I broke the most important one. I let you know."

Vicky's expression fell, her eyes stricken. "They deny you even your friends?" She sat beside me again. "Will they punish you for letting me know?"

I closed my eyes and nodded. They would kill her and consider it my punishment.

"Oh, Rox. What a mess." She hugged me with one arm and leaned her head against my shoulder.

When her phone rang she tensed, but she didn't answer.

"Are you going to get that?"

"No."

"It's David, isn't it?"

She sighed. "Yeah. He isn't calling as much as before, and I think he's losing interest. But then he calls or sends me something, a card or box of flowers, and I think I'm like an addiction he's trying to shake and is failing miserably."

I grunted, thinking about his visit the other day. "I can deal with him if you want."

"No, you have enough to worry about. But if he doesn't let up soon, I'll let you know."

Chapter Twenty-Eight

I took a cab to base the next morning. I was sick to my stomach, tired of everything.

Easy. Fragile. This hold I held on my life, this fragile, tenuous hold; it was easily taken away, an illusion that what I held belonged to me.

I took the stairs to the first floor, crossing the foyer of Roland's office to what seemed like my last visit. Vincent's door was open, his office empty.

Valerie sat behind her semi-circular desk, typing on a laptop.

I waited for her to acknowledge me, even if we both knew she was aware of my presence. Not wanting to give her the satisfaction of asking for permission to see Roland, or wait for her goodwill to buzz me through, I picked up a magazine from a corner table and sat, legs crossed.

I had nothing to lose, nowhere to go. Nothing to do. I flipped a page, smirking when I caught her brief glance my way.

It was an opulent space, meant to impress as much as for comfort, one that welcomed important meetings with high officials, law-enforcement representatives and key political figures. The chief of police, the mayor, the governor. If the president himself stepped out of the elevator, I wouldn't be surprised. On the wall across from me was the NSA emblem, behind me an enormous American flag. A vase of fresh pale-yellow flowers sat on an end table to the side. An elaborate gold-and-silver cart stood in a corner, offering fresh beverages and delicate baked goods. The carpet under my feet was thick, of flowery, pastel colors. The double doors at the end had a brass plate the size of my arm with Roland Mackenzie etched in bold, dark letters.

There was a potted fig tree to the other side, verdant and vivid, but the lack of scent told me it wasn't real.

I got up, picked a fat muffin from the cart and resumed my seat, flipping another page, looking for all intents and purposes like I was enjoying myself.

"He will see you now," Valerie announced without looking at me or stopping her typing.

Creepy, but I had been expecting that. It made me wonder, not for the first time, if she and Roland were telepathic. Or, did Roland tell her to send me through the moment I arrived, and she was yanking my chain, trying to get a rise out of me by making me wait? Or did he tell her to make me wait... an intimidation tactic? If so, they were wasted on me. On a person slated to die in twelve days.

I pushed open the heavy double doors and stepped inside Roland's office. If the lobby was opulent, his office was understated, to say the least.

His desk was made of glass and gleaming iron, a monstrosity that took a third of the room, with Tall windows overlooking Central Park. There was an arched doorway to my right that led to a conference room, the edge of an oval, wooden table and a high backed chair peeking through. Another golden cart was set to the side, also holding beverages and baked goods and a tall see-through glass brimming with colorful, fresh flowers. There were no medals of honors, no framed certificates on the walls, but a few scenic photographs of places I'd never seen and probably never would. To my left was a closed door, presumably the bathroom.

Roland stood when I stepped inside, his expression grave.

"Miss Fosch, have a seat." He indicated the straight cushioned chairs in front of his desk, and without a word, I sat, though I would rather have stood.

He sat next, fiddling with the paperwork in front of him as he considered me.

"You went to the PSS, claimed authority over something that was not true."

I said nothing. It wasn't like he was asking me; he was merely stating facts.

"There are, Miss Fosch, protocols and procedures to be taken before one of us can step foot in that place, or any other government facility." He paused, and again, I said nothing.

Sighing, he said, "Once the two weeks are over, you will be disciplined for that."

"What are you going to do?" I asked, though I felt nothing. No trepidation, no fear, no anxiety. Just a vague sense of curiosity.

Sensing my lack of proper interest, Roland laced his broad hands atop the glass and examined me with his dark eyes. There were calluses on his palms, a sign that told me he didn't just sit in this office holding meetings with important officials. "I am not sure yet. But I know I won't be pairing you with George, or Chris, or Asra. You need someone stricter, someone who won't hesitate to put you in your place." He was talking like I was coming back, as if he was sure I'd make it passed the next two weeks.

"Why not Diggy? He's strict enough for everyone."

Roland's eyes chilled, and for the first time since I'd met him, I saw the cold fury of a predator in him. He got up, turned his back on me and looked out his window. Gradually, his anger, a frigid draft that penetrated to the bone, subsided.

He was trying to compose himself, I realized. When he turned again, his eyes were still cold, his voice had taken in a softer tone. "The Hunters are taking some heat right now, Roxanne. What you do and say will affect this facility, and I ask of you not to be reckless."

"I'm sorry," I said, because I wasn't talking to a superior, though I didn't know if I could call him a friend. He was certainly friendly to me, or friendlier than anyone else in the base, aside from Vincent.

True, I might not be coming back in two weeks, but the Hunters were here to stay, no matter what happened to me.

Resigned, he perched on the edge of his desk–a less authoritative posture. "Why did you go there, of all places?"

I considered his question, wondering if he hadn't heard the story yet or wanted to hear it from me again. "Mwara came to see me a couple months ago. I was walking home when I spotted her, standing against the pedestrian traffic, waiting for me." I took a long breath, considering my words. "She wanted me to promise her if her mother sent her to the PSS when she hit puberty, that I'd go after her, like I did for Archer."

Roland leaned forward, hands clasped together. "Why would she come to you, of all people?" He wasn't questioning the credibility of my words like Archer. He was truly wondering why Mwara came to me, of all people.

I smiled humorlessly. "A kindred spirit. Someone who would sympathize with her ploy. I don't know. She was afraid of the entire clan. I offered to talk to Vincent, but she was afraid of him, too."

He sighed, an odd expression in his eyes. "Did you sense the child there?"

"In the PSS? No. But if they have her, they wouldn't keep her on level two."

Roland's expression turned thoughtful. "Let me ask you something. Do you really think they have her?"

"I don't know."

He shook his head. "Let me rephrase the question. If I guarantee you that Elizabeth is Mwara's mother, do you believe the Scientists have her?"

I shook my head.

"Then they don't have her."

"But what if she ran and someone found her, and then sold her to the PSS? They wouldn't think twice about conducting experiments without reporting the kid."

He considered it. "The possibility of someone lurking around for an opportunity to snatch the Longlan kid from here, of all places, is very unlikely." He raised a hand to cut off whatever I was about to say and went on, "In any case, I don't think the PSS would be conducting clandestine operations for a while yet. It's come to my knowledge they are well behaved. After what happened with Archer, their donors became–let's say, somewhat frugal with resources. I don't believe they would try anything, at least for a few years."

I nodded once, said nothing.

"Do you have any other leads?"

I shook my head, thought about something, and hesitated.

"What is it?"

"I … nothing," I replied with a frown.

"*Tell me.* Whatever you believe may be a lead, no matter how insignificant, never discard it. Every detail is important, a part of a puzzle. If a piece is missing, the picture will never be complete. Now, tell me what you're thinking."

"It's just something you said." I frowned, trying to gather my thoughts. "About people lurking around." At Roland's nod I went on, "Back when Mwara came to see me? The following week, remember, I was ambushed by Angelina Hawthorn, not far from the spot where Mwara had intercepted me. I didn't follow her into the alleyway because I'm naïve or gullible. I knew it was a trap." I looked at him, but found no anger with the revelation I hadn't told him everything. "She told me she had my friend and implied she'd kill her if I didn't follow."

I got up and started pacing, too wired to stay seated while I pieced that night together in a coherent string of events. "She told me that my friend looked so young and fragile, she was afraid my friend wouldn't last long. Maybe she'd been talking about Mwara all along."

Roland's brow furrowed, eyes thoughtful. He straightened and moved to stand by the window, stared at the street below.

"She gave me a lock of hair, one I thought belonged to my friend. Vicky, my friend, is blonde, and so was the lock of hair Angelina gave me. So is Mwara." I closed my eyes, trying to remember the hue of Mwara's hair. "Maybe Mwara's was a shade darker than Vicky's. I don't know."

"Do you still have the lock of hair?"

"No, I threw it away when I realized I'd been tricked and my friend was safe." I paced to the window and back, gathering my train of thought. "It fits," I murmured.

Roland turned to face me, his eyes tired. Had those lines been there when I first met him? "Did Vincent tell you about what happened with his case?"

I frowned. "No. I assumed his presence here meant it's been solved."

He nodded once. "In a way, the threat down south was contained. But the case didn't close. We believe there's a higher master involved, the strategist behind all the fledglings. Angelina Hawthorn was seen a few times in that general vicinity, talking with the master vampire responsible for the turnings. We kept tabs on her but were never able to get close enough."

"You think Angelina was behind the *entire* thing?" I asked, astonished.

"She still is. Vincent didn't catch her. Or the fledglings. They disappeared overnight without a trace. Vincent estimated there were around sixty to seventy newly turned vampires in that group. The master responsible for their turning was found dead a day later near a pier."

"Do you think...?" I shook my head. "I don't understand."

"We believe she got a whiff we were closing in and packed up shop. She probably relocated to another state. We're on the look-out for a sudden increase of missing-people reports to determine where she might start over."

"But the fledglings, what does she want with them?"

"It's possible she's trying to start another power base here in the U.S., but she hasn't registered with any council, so all her movements would be illegal. I can't think of any other reason, unless she's trying to build an army to overthrow the master vampires here."

"Is that possible?" I asked, unsure about his tone.

"In a decade or so, if she continues building an army, yes. But it's unlikely she'll go unchallenged for that long."

"Maybe she'll take them back to her country?"

"Anything's possible. Vincent has a theory. He believes she's going to march on Juan Silva, the master from Mexico. They're long-ago rivals and her location down in Miami could've been a planned strategy."

"But where do I fit in all this?"

Roland clasped his hands together. "I don't think you were part of the plan. Jacob Black was one of her firsts, her right hand."

I slumped against the window. I was back to ground zero.

"How did Mwara find you?"

"Don't know. I never asked." Oh, how I wished I could turn back time.

"How did she get here?"

"When I told her she was a long way from home, she said it was a fast track through the paths."

He nodded. "The leeway. Start from there, then."

"Sure," I said. "Can you spare any Hunter to help?"

Roland's eyes chilled again and he shook his head. "The Hunters have no jurisdiction over clan affairs, as long as they aren't breaking the law."

"So executing me after two weeks is a sanctioned practice?"

The frost in Roland's eyes evolved into heated fury. "Preternaturals have harsher rules and laws to abide by, Miss Fosch, and I can't change them to accommodate one member."

I stood. "Is there anything else?" I asked, unable to hide the bite from my voice.

Roland moved behind his desk, radiating anger. He picked up papers, shuffled them around. I was about to leave when he asked, "Are you sure about your abjuration ritual?"

"Yes, I am."

He only nodded. "Let me give you a piece of advice, Roxanne," He met my gaze again and the anger was almost under control, nothing more than left-over residue. "Stay away from Zantry Akinzo."

I blinked. That wasn't what I was expecting him to say. "*Why?*"

"He's been labeled a traitor, accused of murder. You were seen walking with him, that looks suspicious."

"Suspicious *how*?"

"Archer believes Akinzo helped dispose of Arianna, and was able to sense the residue of his energy over you the other day. To Archer, that's another mark against you."

"He helped me heal from the attack in the Low Lands."

"Yes, I know that, but why did he help?"

I shrugged. "Ask him. I met him at the charity ball."

"It's believed that Arianna was Archer's mate, though it was never confirmed. At the very least, the two used to be an item, before his daughter was killed. Then Arianna and Zantry disappeared, and Archer tore the worlds searching for them. Now Zantry's back and everyone's on edge, hoping she's coming back too, knowing if she was, she'd have come with him." Roland tapped a finger over the glass of his executive desk. "Speculation is that it took Zantry and Remo this long to be able to dispose of her permanently, and now that she's out of the picture, Zantry's back to help Remo take control of the worlds."

I held Roland's gaze for a moment. "Do *you* think Zantry did it?"

Roland laced his hands behind his back and half turned to look out the window again. This close to the ground, traffic could be heard loud and clear, but with the windows closed and the heat on, the sound was muffled to a tolerable level. "I believe something happened that Zantry isn't telling. I believe he's either Remo's accomplice and he did what he did, or something else happened, something big enough that he's willing to be labeled a traitor rather than confess the truth. Because I have zero proof either way, I'll reserve judgment."

* * *

I strolled into Central Park with an easy gate, following trails deep into the greenery until I could no longer see the buildings, though the honking of busy traffic could still be heard. To anyone, I was just a lonely woman with nothing to do but kill time, no cares in the world. I went deep enough to see signs of the illegal deals that went down at night–empty syringes, broken bottles, crushed beer cans. I passed a few homeless figures, but no one glanced twice at me. When I found an empty bench clear of debris, I sat, letting my head rest on open palms. No tears threatened to come, though my despair could have doubled a grown man.

Start in the leeway. Easy to say. But I couldn't travel the leeway on my own. And with no one to help, I wouldn't be checking there anytime soon.

Would Diggy be considered inside help? No, Roland already said he couldn't appoint a member to help... the Hunters had no jurisdiction, he said.

"Think, Roxanne, think" I murmured, rubbing my hands over my face. Where could I find the body of a child who'd been missing for more than two months? What if she'd been eaten, like Dr. Dean and Remo Drammen? I shuddered with the thought.

Someone sat beside me and, although the smell of citrusy spices told me who, I still lowered my hands and glanced sideways.

"Are you stalking me?"

Zantry flashed a brilliant smile. "I'd rather make you company than watch from afar."

I looked away, not in the mood to banter.

"I'm sorry about the child," he said after a moment.

"Yeah, so am I."

"Can I help?"

I turned to him, bewildered. "Why would you?"

Zantry's eyes glinted with amusement. "Do you always question a gift horse in the mouth?"

"Why not? Nothing is free nowadays. And everyone tells me not to trust you." The latter was nothing more than empty words, meant to hurt and send him away, but he took them well enough.

"How notorious of me."

I looked down at my lap, examined my empty hands. I had no desire to talk, but I knew I couldn't afford to tell him to go.

"I heard Vemourly is taking a lot of heat because of you," Zantry said, stretching his legs. He was wearing jeans and black boots, both expensive brands.

I frowned, not sure if I'd understood him correctly. "Heat? For what? Because I got hurt in the caves?"

Zantry scrutinized my face before looking away and zipping up his suede jacket, clearly contemplating his next words. "He's been accused of the murder of the Longlan kid as well."

"What, why?"

"Because it's said you can't travel the paths on your own. And Vemourly has been taking you every day to the Low Lands under the guise of tutelage."

I stood and gaped down at him. "We were training!" But I shouldn't have been surprised. Logan had said as much to me yesterday. I just didn't think Diggy would be dragged into the mess with me. He wasn't even from the same clan. What's the point of an abjuration if the clan could just go and demand their holy due payment from other clans as well?

Zantry dismissed my outburst with a quick wave of a hand. "That's what he said. But you see, you two had the means, the opportunity." He ticked the items off on his fingers. "And motive."

My mouth opened and closed, open and closed. I said nothing. I should have seen this coming. And do what?

Zantry's shoulders twitched once. "There were some protests, of course, and Mackenzie had to step in, explain the sessions had been sanctioned. Then the entire guild was balancing precariously, until Vemourly assumed full responsibility for your deeds."

I sat, my legs going weak. "What did he do that for?"

The Hunters are taking some heat right now, Roxanne, Roland had said. Had he been talking about my confrontation with Dr. Maxwell, or something else altogether?

"He did it to defend the guild. But it's fact he was the one responsible for you for the past few months. If he isn't an accomplice, he overlooked your actions, or something to that effect, and we're back to square one."

"Where–where did you hear that from?"

"I have my ways."

Damn. Roland had been furious with the accusation, not me. Because of Mwara, he'd technically lost three members. And the entire base was under suspicion.

"They sent Vincent away." Even as I said it I waved a hand. "You probably know that already."

Zantry murmured a confirmation.

I looked up at the branches, the sky a white curtain above. "So does that mean if I fail, Diggy will pay too?"

Zantry said nothing. When I glanced at him, I found him watching me, those violet-blue eyes somber. "Yes," he said simply. "Along with Vagner, because he vouched for you."

I closed my eyes, regretting I didn't ignore Mwara on the street and kept walking home. Or maybe I should've accepted Vincent's offer to drive me.

Bitch was such a nice compliment to hindsight.

"Where is she?"

"I don't know."

"I thought you were omniscient or something?"

Zantry chuckled, the sound bitter. "No. I just got a few tricks up my sleeves."

I took a deep breath, gathered my fraying control, and asked, "So, Zantry, where do we start?"

He stood and extended a hand.

I took it, a warm static jolt coursing through me.

"We'll go a step at a time," he said, pulling me upright.

Chapter Twenty-Nine

I took Zantry home and showed him the notes Logan gave me. Halfway through, he asked a few questions, logical ones I should have made if only I'd gone over the papers myself, and the lack of answers had my hackles rising.

I left him to pour through the remaining notes and called Logan.

"Roxanne," he answered with a warm note.

"Hey. About Mwara," I began, too impatient for idle chitchat.

"Yes?"

"Where did you get the photos from?"

There was a thick pause that made my anger flicker with suspicion.

"It was mailed to us."

"When?"

"About three weeks ago."

Before I told him Mwara had come to see me. He already knew. *Ah, Roxy, you're such a fool.*

"Did you know those photos came from the bakery security cameras, where I met Mwara?"

"Yes, we figured that once you showed me where you two met."

"Oh?" I paused, "Were you able to go through their surveillance feed?"

Another thick pause. "No, the owner said the feed from December was no longer available."

"I see." The barrister had told me their feed deleted at 11:59 pm on the last day of every month, and started anew at 12:00 am on the first day of the new month. For those photos to have been printed, someone must have had them since December to ensure data wasn't lost.

"What are you thinking?" Logan asked in the silence that followed.

"That I'm being framed and you're either a fool or are deliberately turning a blind eye in the other direction."

I expected denial or something similar, but all he did was sigh. A long, resigned sound that had me gritting my teeth so hard, my jaw ached.

"Look, Roxanne, I know how this looks. I know you didn't do it. But I don't have anything to prove your innocence, I can't just stand and say all the evidence is bogus. Before you admitted to meeting with Mwara, I had everyone half convinced those photos were montaged, that someone was trying to frame you. But no one's listening to me anymore. The evidence is there and I have nothing to counteract it. Every argument I make on your favor is overruled by another piece of evidence. I know this means nothing to you, but I'm sorry the council won't see reason."

"I think they do. They just want me out of the way."

"It's not like that. You don't understand."

"Well, by all means, explain it to me then. Do they think this evidence is falling from the sky? Or maybe they think *I* mailed those photos myself?" I raised my eyebrows, aware he couldn't see my sarcastic expression.

Logan hissed. "I pointed out you were being framed and the culprit was whoever had sent the photos, but again, there was no proof. They say that there's the possibility someone saw the two of you and is trying to help the kid without getting involved in clan politics."

"If someone thought I'd done something to the kid and wanted to help her, they would have sent those photos in December, not three weeks ago."

"Not if they believed we'd be on to you in no time."

"Why save the photos if they were convinced you'd be on to me?"

"As a precaution, in case we didn't. And once this person had no choice, the photos were mailed so we'd know where to look."

I shut up, knowing Logan had a ready rebuttal to any question or excuse I made. Aware that his answers had come from the council when he'd posed those same questions to them. Beside me, Zantry put down the notes and watched, no doubt able to hear both sides of the conversation. Logan waited, and when I said nothing, he added, "The kidnapping of a scion from a prominent family can't go unpunished for months. We have the best trackers, excellent hunters, and yet no one can find any trace of a missing child."

"They'd rather execute someone innocent just so they wouldn't look like bumbling idiots? One day the truth will come out, Logan. What are they going to do then? Brush it off as an unfortunate event?"

"The point is if she ran and hid like you said she did, we'd have found her already."

"If she ran and hid, Logan, there wouldn't have been anyone trying to frame me."

Logan didn't reply, no doubt having nothing to say that wouldn't make the clan look worse than it already did.

Zantry made a gesture, mimed handing me something, pointed down at the photos. I tilted my head, not understanding, but got it when he repeated the gesture.

"Who mailed the photos?"

"We don't know," Logan replied.

My hand clenched the phone. "The *return* address?"

"There wasn't any. And I know what you're thinking, believe me, because so did I. I went over the envelope and checked, and then double-checked for a sign or trace. There was nothing to trace with the photos: no scent, no fibers, no prints. It was mailed from a post office in midtown Manhattan. I covered both angles myself." His tone was soothing, reassuring.

Zantry mimed opening an envelope and sniffing it. "I want to see this envelope."

"There's *nothing* there, Roxanne. Don't waste your time. Focus on another angle. I told you, I myself went to the post office. It's another dead end."

"Well, forgive me if I don't find that reassuring," I snapped. "I want to check the envelope *myself.*"

The pause was thick, tangible. "Alright. Where are you?"

"At home."

"I'll be there in an hour." He hung up and I glanced at Zantry.

"Someone is framing me," I said with a heavy heart. "Who hates me that much?"

There wasn't so much sympathy in Zantry's eyes as understanding. Somehow, it made me feel worse.

"I can go to the post office tonight, take a look around."

I nodded, but we both knew chances of him finding anything were slim to none. I wondered if Elizabeth would do this to her child to get at me. That was hard to believe, but it didn't leave me brimming with other options. "You better go before he gets here. I don't need someone else being blamed if I fail."

Zantry studied me with knowing eyes. "Are you worried about my well-being or about Logan seeing me with you?"

"What's the difference?"

A dark eyebrow shot up. "Avoiding the question?"

I shrugged. "I'm not sure. I don't want you to get any blame, but maybe I don't want Logan to see you here with me. I don't know if it's due to his warning about you, or..." I let the sentence die, not knowing how to finish that.

"Both, then." He leaned back on the counter, gazing around the apartment. "First, just to ease your mind, I can mask my imprint from the ether so all you sense is an ordinary person. This means unless Logan sees me with his eyes, his senses would never tell him otherwise. If I weren't masking my presence, it wouldn't matter whether he saw me or not; he'd know I was here."

"Are you masking now?"

"I am. The only times I wasn't was during the charity ball, and even then I only let a tiny part through to the ether. The other time was the other night in the Low Lands."

I recalled trying to sense his aura the night of the ball and sensing nothing but a faint, strange thrumming. Was that what he meant?

"Second," He went on, "I can see energy. I can sense emotions, see the way they change energy patterns, and I can read auras." His lips lifted into a small smile. "The energy pattern around you changed when you mentioned him. It churned when you talked to him. Passion is a complex and dangerous emotion. It's also versatile. You can hate someone with passion; you can love someone with passion. It can be a violent tempest; it can be a gentle breeze. It can level cities, it can calm raging hearts."

Ignoring his poetic description of my feelings, I latched onto his previous words like a drowning person. "I can see auras and sense emotions, too. But I don't see energy."

He was the first person I knew who'd openly admitted to it. It was as if he had nothing to hide from the world, like he'd tell everyone anything whether they wanted to listen or not. Yet, he refused to tell people he'd been a prisoner in the PSS this entire time to clear his name.

Zantry's eyebrows arched a fraction, his eyes puzzled. "How do you sense emotions?"

"That's not normal for a Dhiultadh?"

Zantry angled his head and searched my face. "Aren't you supposed to have two mentors? My understanding was they are both Dhiultadh."

"Diggy said it's called empathy."

"It is, but I haven't heard of a Dhiultadh with that trait before. How do you sense emotions?"

"I'm not sure if I understand what you mean. But I can sense people's emotions, providing they're strong enough. Sometimes–though not often–I sense something that I can't identify, and I figure it's probably something I haven't felt before, so I have no name or description for it. Is that how it is for you?"

"In a way. Emotions have something that disrupts the chaotic pattern of energy." He traced fingers through the air, presumably against whatever energy he could see. "They leave a mark, sometimes colorful, depending on the emotion and how strong it is, but more often than not, they just rearrange energy into different patterns. Negative emotions attract more energy, though genuine happiness is strong as well." He slipped his hands back into his pockets. "But you can't see energy?"

"No, I don't think so. Should I?"

"I've never seen or heard about a Dhiultadh who couldn't."

I frowned, trying to make sense of his explanation. "But if Dhiultadh can see energy, how come they can't see emotions? I mean, you just said emotions disrupt energy patterns, right? How come Dhiultadh can't see it then?"

Zantry's eyes gleamed. "There are levels of energy, some are complex, most are basic. The Dhiultadh can see the basic ones, the atoms and molecules, the normal currents in the ether. But complex energy can only be seen in the fifth dimension, and it's there where emotions act."

"Ether. Vincent said a member would help me see into the ether before my training was concluded."

Zantry's eyebrow shot up. "And if you *weren't* able to?"

I shrugged. "That's a possibility."

"You should explain, if the time comes, that even if you can't see the ether, your senses are attuned to higher dimensions. I bet Roland would love the idea of a member who can't see the fourth dimension, but is familiar with the fifth."

A headache began to build, and I rubbed my temple. "Is that how people know I have a shadow, even when Frizz is invisible to the eye?"

"Yes, though only his shadow can be seen in the fourth dimension."

"But when he stays home?"

"His shadow can't be seen, unless you encounter someone capable of seeing or sensing, dimensions higher than the fourth."

Ugh. I rubbed the other temple, feeling like I was being attacked by a heavy gong. Zantry smiled, waved a hand in dismissal. "The strangest part is you're a Dhiultadh and an empathic, which means you're up one dimension from the other Dhiultadh. Yet, you can't see energy."

"I don't see emotions. As I said, I can sense them, providing they're strong enough."

He nodded. "And if it's something you've felt before, you're able to identify it."

"Isn't that how it is for you?" Maybe I wasn't grasping all that nonsense about fourth and fifth dimensions and their baggage, but I also didn't think energies spelled out emotions in the ether.

"In a way, yes, but I must say there isn't an emotion out there I haven't felt before."

Does that mean you've been in love before? Who is she? Where is she?–He? The thoughts popped into my head unbidden. It was surprising how curious I was about this man.

"How does it feel, to live so long?" I asked, curious.

His expression turned somber, and he jingled loose change inside his pocket before answering. "Reassuring, when you know you'll have time in the future to do whatever. Lonely, when you watch your friends die or know they don't have the advantage of returning if they do. Overwhelming, to know you've seen and participated in things you know people will only read about in books." He glanced at me, his eyes sad, thoughtful. "Irritating, to know you have to stay on the sidelines, lest people recognize you in a decade or so and wonder how come."

"I guess that's something many preternaturals find annoying."

"Indeed."

"Do you have a mate?"

"So many questions." His lips twitched in a sardonic smile, but his gaze remained warm and friendly. "My kind, darling Roxanne, don't suffer those emotional trappings."

"I'm sorry," I said. "You said there wasn't an emotion out there you haven't felt before. I thought..."

"You don't need to be... romantically-inclined to feel love."

I grunted, not knowing what to say. He knew what love was, but he didn't suffer "emotional trappings". Was that a curse or a blessing?

"You think a mating bond comes with love?" he asked, curious.

I paused, considering the question. "It'd be easier for both if there's love, don't you think?"

"Hmm-mm. A mating bond is a sign of equality between two opposites. Unless the bond between the two is acknowledged, it doesn't fall into place."

As I mulled that over, a thought struck me. "So if there isn't love, they can both just move on without committing to each other?"

"Probably, but I've never heard about anyone walking away from a mate, love or no. For one, a mating bond is like connecting two halves. Of being compatible with someone else down to a molecular level. Even if there isn't love in the beginning, the sense of completion alone, the comfort of becoming whole... it's like realizing you've been traveling all your life and you've finally reached your destination." He shrugged a broad shoulder, waved a hand. "Those were the words of a friend, not mine."

I got it. His kind was incapable of having a mate because there was no one equal to his opposite. "Why not you and Arianna then?"

Zantry chuckled, shook his head. "Despite what some may think, coming from the same planet and being the same species doesn't make us equal to the other. In strength maybe, but Arianna and I are different on so many levels. Our friendship was always platonic. I never considered her in any romantic capacity and she never did me. She's just Arianna to me, a dear friend, I'm just Akinzo to her."

"How about children?" I asked, bold with my questions because I knew he was honest, open. It was refreshing, to ask a question and get the answer without having to barter for it. It was one of the reasons I enjoyed talking to him. Easy. It was so easy talking to him.

An unreadable expression crossed his face and he shook his head. "No. That's a pleasure I've never had."

"I'm sorry. I shouldn't have asked that." I placed my hand over his and squeezed. A pleasant shock passed from his hand to mine. I let go and rubbed my hands together. "Why do you keep doing that?"

An odd expression crossed his face. "What do you feel?"

I frowned down at my hands, rubbed them together again. "It's like, like being zapped by electricity." I looked up. "But it's kind of warm and pleasant, nothing intrusive or painful." A warm blush crept up my neck.

Zantry's expression didn't change. He tucked his hands back in his pockets and rocked back and forth on his heels. "So you can sense emotions, but don't see the patterns, and you can't see energy, but you can sense it. That's interesting."

Energy. Of course. How crazier could things get? Now he'd start talking about a sixth or seventh dimension. Another spike of pain lanced through my brain and I shoved away the thought.

"Ok, I never said I was normal," I muttered, rubbing my temple again.

"Maybe it's just left-over residue of when I tried to force your shift in the Low Lands," he offered, but there was doubt in his tone.

My hand dropped. "What? You tried to force me to shift?"

He chuckled at my stunned expression. "I tried, but I only succeeded in making Vemourly shift. It was right before I chased away the poison."

The memory had goosebumps erupting all over, and I rubbed my arms as exhaustion pulled on me. There was a knowing gleam in his eyes, telling me that he knew exactly how far my shift went. The moment became awkward, and he must have sensed it too.

"I should go." He strolled to the front door. "Logan will be here in a few minutes. I'll wait till he leaves and then come back to check the envelope."

Chapter Thirty

Logan didn't come in. He didn't ask to. Perhaps it was because I blocked the doorway, arms crossed. Or perhaps he was irritated I asked for the envelope and didn't take his words at face value. But why should I trust him? He would do whatever Archer told him, even if he didn't want to.

He'd brought the original photos too, just so I wouldn't ask for them later in a fit of paranoia and lose time on dead ends—his words, not mine. The envelope—a brown paper thing big enough to fit the prints—had no scent except for Archer's, Logan's and Elizabeth's. There was another, fainter scent Logan informed me belonged to a human who worked in the Sacramento post office. If there was another scent, neither I nor Zantry detected it.

Not surprisingly, Zantry didn't find anything suspicious in the post office either, but he promised to return during opening hours. He'd gone over the postal office's surveillance feed—I didn't ask how—and it seemed the post office had a similar system to the bakery. Their feed began on February first. By Coincidence—or not—the person who mailed the photos did it on January thirtieth.

Whoever mailed that envelope was either smart, or lucky.

Zantry didn't linger. Like Logan, he gave me the information at the door, letting the warmth from the apartment escape, and informed me he'd take a look at a few alleyways he had noted weren't mapped in Logan's notes. Tomorrow evening, we would start a backward trail from here to Sacramento to see if we could pick up any leftover impressions of Mwara in the ether.

With nothing else to do until tomorrow evening, I went to bed, where I tossed and turned all night long. Around dawn, I finally fell asleep, a restless sleep where I thought I was awake until I awoke to the aroma of coffee.

With a grunt, I pushed away the covers and padded barefoot to the bathroom. I took a hot shower, dried my hair and brushed my teeth before sneaking naked to the bedroom. While I dressed, I imagined Vicky's reaction to Zantry. If she had practically foamed at the mouth when she saw Diggy and Logan, she'd seizure if she saw Zantry, especially if he flashed her that killer smile of his.

The pang of jealousy that came was—unexpected, to say the very least. How could I be jealous?

Not wanting to debate on it, I stepped out of the bedroom wearing jeans and a knitted lapis-blue sweater Vicky had bought last week as a get-better gift. The color reminded me of Zantry's eyes, an improbable shade of blue that seemed almost violet.

The moment I spotted Frizz standing guard at the end of the corridor, I knew something was wrong. I say standing guard because he wasn't crouched, hands clasped together in front, but standing erect, his wings beating a soft buzz.

That's when I noted the soft humming of a song I'd never heard–by a voice that *wasn't* Vicky's. Heart pounding, I padded over to Frizz and peered into the kitchen.

And there she was, a six-foot-tall imperious warrior. My heart leaped and lodged in my throat when my brain realized why Lee had come.

She stood, a cup of coffee by her elbow as she fumbled with the stove. She was dressed like me, in jeans and a thick ash-gray sweater, voluminous red hair tied up in a high ponytail. Her aura blazed silver, shining like a star. She turned to me, forest green eyes glinting with something mischievous. "You are awake. Excellent. Come and help. Your little shadow won't come close."

I didn't move, frozen in place, Frizz beside me like a statue, save for the buzzing wings.

Lee's perfect ruby-red lips pouted, her expression growing sullen. "Don't tell me you're afraid too? Last time we met, you were grateful for my presence."

I snapped out of it, moving forward into the living room, keeping the half wall between us. It was no protection at all, but it gave me a modicum of false safety, separating me from the Seelie enforcer.

Lee's eyes gleamed with cold amusement, no doubt recognizing the feeble ploy. "I am not here to hurt you. I could have done that while you slept."

Her words HAD fear zinging through me. "How did you get in here?"

Lee rolled her eyes, the gesture so human, so normal, it crept me out. Did she come to earth often, observe human interactions? Trick a few innocent people into owing her? "Come now, we are linked. In addition," she gestured around with a spatula, "you have no wards to impede intruders. It's an open doorway."

I almost asked her how to ward the apartment, but swallowed the words in time. Her eyes twinkled, her expression knowing.

"Come on, show me how this works. My coffee is getting cold."

I ambled around the division and found... eggs. She was trying to light the stove to fry eggs–with the shells intact. Three whole eggs sat inside Frizz's bowl, waiting to be fried atop the stove. I burst out laughing. I couldn't help it. And if hysteria bubbled out with the laughter, I couldn't help that either.

"You dare mock me?" she asked, posture stiff, eyes no longer amused.

My laughter died as abruptly as it started. I shook my head, afraid to speak. Before she could do something about my insolence, I cracked the eggs into the bowl and placed a skillet on its place. Then I turned on the stove before grabbing salt from the cupboard.

"Ah, that's how. I admit, I almost lit it with blue fire." She gave me a puzzled frown and I offered to fry it for her.

She watched my every step, taking it all in. The butter when it sizzled and melted, the eggs being whisked with milk and salt, the mixture being poured into melted butter. When it began to solidify, she clapped and jumped twice. "Wonderful." She laughed, the sound musical.

When I reached for a plate in the cupboard, I realized just how much my hands shook.

She ate like a starving woman. As if this would be the last meal she would eat for a long time to come.

When she finished savoring the last bite, she smacked her lips in contentment, drank the last of the coffee, her eyes assessing me over the rim of the mug.

"Now, Daughter of Fosch," She began after placing the mug in front of her, "I am here to collect our bargain."

I swallowed, my untouched coffee on the island in front of me. My tongue seemed to be stuck to the roof of my dry mouth.

Lee studied me for a long time. Every second that passed with her eyes focused on me, my heart beat faster, my stomach churned harder.

"We have a bargain," she said. "I am here to collect." When again I didn't respond, her eyes darkened with anger. "Do you renege on your word as your cowardly sire did before you?"

She rose, and I hurried to do the same. She cocked her head, her green eyes glittering like two emeralds–cold and unfeeling.

Fear stabbed through my soul. "What do the bargain entails?" I asked.

"We have a bargain, aye or nay?"

I nodded, swallowed and replied, "Yes, we do."

"Excellent," she said, inclining her head in approval. "You will fulfill your original role, before Dhiultadh Fosch broke the rules and forfeited his existence."

I froze. Inwardly, I shook. My fear was painful, paralyzing in its intensity.

"Tonight you will come to the Sidhe land and meet with Oberon. I will come fetch you when the clock tolls twelve. Be ready." With that she disappeared, as if she'd never been. All that remained as proof of her visit was the empty plate and coffee mug.

Frizz pressed against my legs, and I glanced down, sensing his need to reassure. I scratched his head as if he were a cat, knowing how much he liked it. "Fulfill my original role?" His ears flattened and I scratched them, too.

A full circle.

"Maybe they'll kill me before Archer can." I picked him up and hugged him, soaking the comfort he offered.

Chapter Thirty-One

When Zantry arrived late in the afternoon, I was preparing chicken dumplings from a recipe I'd found on the Internet. He stepped inside, his hair must and wet from the cold drizzle, dressed all in black, those violet-blue eyes contrasting nicely. He smelled like hot spices, with an undertone of something citrusy. He carried an arrangement of colorful roses, some still budding, others in full bloom.

My God, he was so perfect. So beautiful.

His smile flashed, a hint of a dimple appearing on his left cheek.

I narrowed my eyes at the smug smile. Could he read minds?

He flicked a finger over my nose and stepped aside for me to close the door. "Your thoughts are written in your eyes, beautiful one." He bowed once, offering the gorgeous bouquet.

"Aren't you the smooth one?" I asked, accepting the flowers, my lips lifting with a genuine smile. I stepped aside for him to pass, wondering for the first time if he had a car.

Zantry paused by the fridge and I stepped around him, grabbing a glass pitcher from the cupboard and placing the bouquet inside. Should I fill it with water? Unable to help myself, I bent to sniff the perfume of the blossoms, a smile stretching my face from ear to ear. Realizing I looked like a fool, I checked on the dumplings, to give myself a few seconds to compose myself. I stirred once, fragrant steam rising with the motion.

"Hope you're hungry. I went wild here and made enough for a herd of elephants." I glanced back, a half smile playing around my lips.

He still stood where he'd paused. His unsettled expression had my smile dimming, my back straightening.

"What is it?"

"Leon. She was here."

My smile crumbled. I wasn't going to tell him. I was going to ask him to go alone to the Low Lands this time, make up an excuse to be home and alone by midnight. But now, here, seeing his wary expression, I wondered if it was the right choice. There was an easiness about our talks, an openness I only had with Vicky, an instinct of trust.

And there was so much about the Sidhe I didn't know; he could advise what to do and what to say. If there was a protocol I should follow not to offend anyone and find myself accused of a grave wrong.

"She was here earlier, yes."

Zantry stepped forward, his eyes searching mine. "Friend or foe?"

"I'm not sure. Not a friend, certainly, but I'm not sure about the foe. Yet."

"Do you want to tell me?" My choice. He wouldn't insist or push me to talk. And he'd be alright with either choice. I could see that from his open expression.

"Let's eat first. Are you hungry?"

Zantry sniffed once, glancing at the covered pan. "Like an elephant."

He set the table—or island—with plates, forks, knives, glasses and folded napkins. He removed a single red rose from the bouquet, placed it inside a tall glass, and placed it in the middle of the table/island.

I watched, half amused, half touched.

"Where do you put your candles?" he asked, opening a drawer.

Startled, I shook my head. "What for? I don't have any."

His astonishment was comical. And he wasn't faking it. "Why not?"

"I don't need them. I can see well in the dark." Now his surprise was genuine, and I couldn't help but fidget.

"You're the first woman I've met to actually say that and mean it. You aren't joking."

His bafflement was palpable, and I frowned, wondering what was wrong with my reply. Wasn't I supposed to have good night vision? Was that another anomaly?

A smile lightened his expression, widening and widening until he was laughing merrily.

"I don't see what's so funny," I muttered.

He shook his head. "Sweetheart, women use candles to dim the light, to emulate a romantic atmosphere, not to illuminate the dark."

"Oh?" I paused, considering, then chuckled and shook my head. Vicky would be so proud of him. "Missed those womanly lessons tucked up on the fourth floor, east wing. Room 418," I said that as a joke, but the moment Zantry's eyes went cold, I regretted it. "Sorry, didn't mean to kill the mood." I returned to the dumplings, turning off the stove, straightening the countertop and clearing up dirty dishes.

"You can turn off the lights. I bet your night vision is as good as mine, if not better," I said into the silence.

We ate with the lights on, the TV on low, Frizz in front of it with a plate of ground meat, watching reruns of *Dharma and Greg*.

"Do you think he understands it's not real?" I wondered.

"Why don't you try and explain to him?"

I glanced over, realized he was serious. "I already did," I confessed with a sheepish smile.

"Then he does know," Zantry replied, serious. "People don't give them much credit, but they're exceptionally intelligent creatures. They observe, they learn. And when they need, they exchange. Yours is a seasoned one. Older than a century, younger than two. You can see the awareness in his eyes. You chose well."

I glanced at Frizz, his ears pulled back, listening to us, his eyes fixed on Greg's mother. "He chose me."

"Oh? I'd like to hear that story."

I pushed my empty plate away and picked up the OJ. "How much do you know about me?" I leaned back and waited for him to finish chewing.

"Tell me. I'd like to hear it from you."

I stared at the wall across from me, contemplating my next words. "I was twelve when the PSS came knocking at my door. I was taken, kicking and screaming from a home I didn't know then was temporary, sent to the Scientists. I was normal, or as normal as teenagers can be at that age. I didn't have anything extra. I was smart, one of the firsts in my class, but I wasn't exceptional.

"I was taken to a military base in Elk Grove, an hour away from home that night, where I stayed for a few days before I was flown to Seattle, to the headquarters. I was met by Dr. Maxwell, a smiling, friendly shark. At first, I believed they were terrorists, but with time, I thought of drug cartels, slave rings, prostitution trades. Everything came to mind. Except what they really were. I refused to believe the truth, even when I saw it with my own two eyes."

I sipped the juice, not tasting it, my thoughts distant, back to the day I was thrown with the wolf. "I was thirteen when my talons first manifested. I killed my first wolf with them that same day. I was terrified. I saw my first aura the next day and thought I was hallucinating, that my shock made me see things. But everyone had them, and a few flashed white sometimes. Rarely were they green, and I could sense their animal forms, I could tell what they changed into. But those were rare, far between.

"When I was almost a month shy of twenty-one, I escaped." I offered a brittle smile before correcting myself. "Dr. Michael Dean helped me." At his narrowed look, I took a sip, glanced once at Frizz. "It turned out there was a contract with some clause about interrupted studies and penalties. Dr. Dean helped me go, and for every month I was away, there was a three-month penalty clause. Then Remo Drammen came along."

Zantry didn't seem surprised, so he must have known this part.

"He made a bargain with Dr. Dean, gave him Archer, and I was his. But when they rendezvoused in the Low Lands, I surprised Dr. Dean, pushed him against Remo, and they fell on top of Frizz and his band. They were gone in minutes, but I can still hear them at night," I murmured, the haunting nightmares as real as that night in the Low Lands.

Zantry took my hand and squeezed in silent comfort. A pleasant, warm hum played through the touch and I squeezed back, enjoying the sensation.

"I'm sorry about that," he said, "Why don't you tell me this story later? You can tell me about Leon."

"She's part of this story," I said, putting down the empty glass.

Immediately he picked up the carton, poured another glass.

"Thank you." I left my hand beneath his and picked up the full glass with the other. "Once they were both dead, I wandered the Low Lands in the dark, because I can't conjure light on my own. Eventually, Frizz and his band followed, but I didn't know why.

"I walked for hours, maybe days, afraid to stop, unable to keep going. And then finally, I could see again as far as the horizon."

At this Zantry frowned, as I knew he would. I hadn't told anyone about this. Logan and Elizabeth both knew I'd met Lee and that she'd granted me a boon for taking care of Dr. Dean, but nothing more.

"When I could no longer go on, I stopped to rest. And that's when Lee showed up, all smiles and friendly advice, telling me to ask Frizz for something, urging me to make a wish. Since he couldn't bring me back here, I gave him and each of his band a name, bid them farewell, then turned to Lee."

Understanding dawned in Zantry's eyes, but no recrimination.

"She granted me a boon for taking care of Dr. Dean, who she said had broken a rule by dragging me through the leeway without permission. She maneuvered me to believe she'd grant me information, had me curious about my father, about being the 'promised one'. So I asked about him."

"You made a bargain with her," Zantry concluded. "She came here today to collect."

I lowered my eyes and sipped my drink, letting my silence answer.

"Ah, Roxanne. What did she ask?"

I placed the glass down still half full, pulled my hand back from his. The hum lingered for a moment, and I closed my hand to preserve the warmth. "I'm to fulfill my original role. I'm not sure what that entails, though. I'm to meet with Oberon at midnight."

Chapter Thirty-Two

Zantry Akinzo explained the fine rules and art of meeting with a Sidhe royalty. I was glad I'd confided in him. If not, I'd have been killed within the first five minutes after arriving.

First of all, I was never to address royalty without being addressed first. Drink and food were good as long as I was under the Hospitality Code, and it was considered an insult to refuse to eat or drink then. If Queen Titania made a presence, I was not to kneel and bow, not even if everyone around me did so. To kneel meant I was acknowledging her as my queen, asserting myself under her sovereignty. Instead, I was to stand with my head lowered, until permitted to do otherwise. I was always to give my full attention, but was never to look her straight in the eyes. To do so was to challenge her.

I was never to lie, but clever evasion was not punishable. There were so many more other instructions, I was afraid I'd forget them when it was vital to remember.

So many rules, so little time. The acceptable, expected, unaccepted, frowned upon or punishable etiquette and protocol of court life.

Lee arrived at exactly twelve, not a second more. I know, I was counting down the seconds. The minute the clock turned twelve, there was a quick flash of light and there she stood, dressed in similar attire to this morning: tight low-riding jeans with high-heel leather boots that reached up to her knees and a close-fitting blouse that changed colors when she moved. Her hair was fastened in a high ponytail, golden threads twined between red locks, reaching past her lower back, even bound.

She wasted no time whisking us to the Sidhe land. She arrived, gave me a once over, and without touching or coming near, the world flashed and off we went.

I registered the sounds first. The stream of water tumbling on rocks. The soft music of the breeze among swaying trees. The sound of singing birds, a haunting melody sang in chorus, a choreographed symphony. The chattering of small animals. Then came the warmth. The sunlight touched my cheeks, brightening the land.

And what a land.

We stood at the edge of a clearing. Tall and lush ancient trees surrounded us, forming a warm cocoon. The vibrant green grass underneath our feet was soft, a carpet of soft dew. Birds of varying colors and sizes darted between branches, flew over our heads. They hopped from branch to branch, their multi-colored beaks long and sharp, their tails bushy like that of sheep. Small animals watched from beyond fat tree trunks, brown and white furry things similar to cats with droopy ears and long reptilian-like tails.

I turned to Lee with delight. "It's beautiful," I said with heartfelt sincerity.

Lee nodded in approval, as if my compliment was something I was obligated to give. Maybe it was and Zantry forgot to mention it. Without a word, she turned and made her way across the clearing, toward a thicket of trees on the other side, me following behind, looking everywhere, devouring the splendor with hungry eyes.

It was a lovely, peaceful land. Enchanted. The trees were tall, the smallest no less than fifty to sixty feet, the tallest double that, with round, old bark gnarled with age, some covered with so much moss and lichen, the bark seemed green at first glance. The leaves were larger than my torso, dark green and fragrant. It made for a magnificent canopy above, swaying in a slow dance with the soft breeze, to reveal glimpses of a vivid blue sky.

We stepped into the shadows and followed a narrow path. A carpet of old leaves, moss, and fir muffled our steps, made our footing slippery. The brown-and-white creatures ambled alongside, never getting too close. Not knowing if acknowledging them was harmless, I looked everywhere but at them, following Lee's lead. We moved for what seemed like hours, surrounded by trees on all sides, before we finally broke through.

A stream filled with wriggly things appeared as we left the woods, the same sound of rushing water I'd been hearing since stepping into the clearing. Ahead, against the horizon and setting sun, stood a splendid, enormous white castle, full of turrets and round-edged towers, arches, and sharp angles. The sight was so stunning, enchanted and majestic, it took my breath away. The setting sun, an explosion of dazzling colors, framed the castle, its tall arched windows gleaming, reflecting the land surrounding it.

I faltered, awestruck. It was as if I'd just stepped into another world, a fairy tale.

I chuckled, and Lee stopped, turning around to glare at me, her eyes colder than I'd ever seen. "You mock the Seelie palace?" she hissed.

Dangerous.

My amusement cut off so fast, I might have imagined it. "No–no. It's just I thought it was so beautiful, it's like being caught in a fairy tale."

Lee frowned, and I recalled reading somewhere that to call a Fee a fairy was to insult one. But Lee let it go. "I suppose that is a compliment I cannot see as such."

I nodded. "Yes, it is." Pathetically enough, it was.

With that disaster avoided, Lee turned and resumed walking. I followed, no longer seeing the land as something so beautiful as to be unreal, but as a place full of mines–ready to detonate the moment I stepped out of line.

The palace doors were open, a huge square entrance with darkwood double doors pushed to either side in invitation. No guards stood at attention, no one poked out a head to check who'd entered. Inside, the floor was made of thick marble, with green and gold and bright gleaming white veins running throughout. The scents of vanilla and lemon verbena hung fresh in the air.

The interior was as bright as the outside, the entryway wide and airy. To one side, unlit torches hung on the walls between intervals, to the other, tall, arched windows overlooked a cheerful, colorful garden. The ceiling was made of glass, letting in the sunlight and beauty of a vivid blue sky, with the occasional fat pink cloud.

Paintings hung between the torches, huge watercolors that depicted a land full of life and vibrancy, of two-headed animals that stared straight at me. I paused and blinked, almost sure the animals' second head just moved.

Then I hurried after Lee, about to round a corner and disappear. I caught up at the entrance to a huge room with a domed glass ceiling, an empty dais opposite where I emerged. Rich thick carpets covered the floor here and there, flowing tapestries covered the walls from top to bottom.

A table sat in the middle of the room, long and dark, with tall upholstered straight-back cushioned chairs surrounding it. It could seat at least thirty, with Natural lights above illuminating it like a precious museum piece. It was laden with succulent food and fresh fruits and desserts that made my mouth water. The aromas hit me, fragrant and spicy and sweet and yummy, enticing me in a way I'd never been before. With a strong effort of will that should have been nothing but a small, unconscious command of my brain, I looked away, focusing on Lee. I filled my thoughts with something else, anything that didn't include gorging on all that food.

Lee motioned to the right with a slender hand, and I followed, keeping my eyes averted.

That was when I noticed the others, sitting on huge, brightly colored stuffed cushions arranged in a semi-circle, facing us, their eyes watching. To their left was the empty dais, an elaborate throne of carved white marble.

On the cushions sat a man and two dark-haired women, their auras shining silver, just like Lee's.

I could sense their anticipation, their sense of triumph, a combination that caused dread to flood my stomach.

Lee stopped and bowed her head with deference.

"Dhiultadh Roxanne Fosch, my lord." She stepped aside, giving him a clearer view.

The man remained seated, looking up, but it didn't make him look any less. In fact, I was the weak one, the lowly subject, inferior.

He was lean of built, with dark musty-brown hair curling around the ears, a face full of edges and angles, eyes so brown they seemed black at first glance. He wore a green tunic tucked neatly inside brown trousers and leather boots. His coloring was ordinary, but the man was anything but. The gleam in those eyes alone would have given me pause. He studied me, his expression calm, nonchalant.

I stayed quiet, waiting to be addressed. He cocked his head, as if he couldn't quite understand what he saw. "I am pleased to make your acquaintance at last, Daughter of Dhiultadh Yoncey Fosch, the prize I was denied."

Jolting, I took an involuntary step back. Oberon. This was *Oberon.* I lowered my eyes, unsure if I was to answer. I'd expected to meet a man larger than life, a Viking, perhaps someone dressed in nothing but a loincloth and a spear.

Certainly not this, an ordinary-looking man seated atop cushions scattered on the floor.

He stood with a fluid, liquid motion, and I took another step back. He was shorter than me by a few inches, though not so much he had to look up. He moved around me, studying me, completing the 360-degree without a word.

When he stood in front of me again, he did the last thing I would have expected: he leaned forward and sniffed.

Had Zantry not warned me not to speak unless spoken to, had he not told me to show respect and fear without groveling, I'd have made a rude comment, if not outright snapped at him.

Oberon stepped back, motioning to a bright cushion. "You will sit."

I sat as he ordered, glancing at the two women across from me. I blinked once, twice. They were identical, with identical flat expressions, identical moles atop their lips.

Between us sat a big ornate platter brimming with fruits and cheeses and pastries, some of which I recognized, most I didn't. At the edge of the platter were vivid drawings, carvings of winged beasts and horned animals, some carrying weapons, others mounted by men.

"Would you share our feast?" Oberon asked beside me.

I reached for a fat grape, my mouth watering. Then I paused, hesitating, and glanced back at Oberon.

"Am I under your Hospitality Code?"

Oberon's brown eyes twinkled. He inclined his head once, the motion regal. "Roxanne Fosch, daughter of Dhiultadh Yoncey Fosch, the denied promised one, you are under this court's Code of Hospitality for as long as you remain a guest in this land. None from the court shall harm you as long as this code is held. Anyone who defies it shall be dealt with accordingly."

I was frozen to the spot. Hadn't this been one of Zantry's first instructions?

...Have Leon offer you the Hospitality Code the moment you arrive... He'd told me.

I glanced at the grape, unsure if I wanted it anymore. But hadn't Zantry also said it was an insult to refuse the offer of food when under the Hospitality Code?

Oberon sat with a hand propped atop a raised knee, watching me debate with myself.

I chose a fat grape as big as a baby's fist, and took a small bite. The pulp was juicy and sweet, tasting like no grape I'd ever tasted before. Before I knew it, I was licking my thumb and forefinger. I didn't reach for a second, and looked instead at the two silent women.

"Drozelle and Crozelle," Oberon introduced. Both Seelie lowered their heads a fraction.

With a nod, I lowered my eyes. No eye contact. It wasn't as easy a task as I'd imagined.

The cushion threads I was seated upon shifted and changed colors–from green to yellow, to blue, then white and purple. It was intriguing, and it was safer to stare down at it. And then I remembered Zantry's other instructions: give them your *full* attention.

God, I'd get killed on trivia.

The buzz of small wings broke the silence. I'd brought Frizz with me, but ordered him to stay unseen, and Frizz had always obeyed. At first, I couldn't find the source of the buzzing, but that was because I was looking for something Frizz's size. A small winged creature appeared in front of Oberon, screeching in an annoying high-pitched sound that set my teeth on edge.

A pixie, like the images I'd seen in the guidebook. It was about twelve-inches-tall, hovering a foot or so from Oberon's face. It spoke fast, the words running over each other in a garbled sentence, unrecognizable–at least to my ears. No one else seemed to have trouble understanding it.

Oberon nodded once to the twins and they stood, their motion as fluid as water, and followed after the sparkling dust the pixie left behind. They headed to the far wall, where a shadowed entrance was half-hidden beside a long tapestry of flowing caricatures. Once the three disappeared through, Oberon stood, his motion as fluid as that of the twins. "Follow me."

Standing, I glanced sideways at Lee. She inclined her head towards Oberon, and I trailed behind him, my heart drumming hard.

"We have been waiting for you for a long time, Roxanne Fosch," Oberon said, his words hitting something primordial within me.

What had I gotten myself into? Was leaving the Low Lands worth whatever waited for me around the corner?

Oberon moved alongside me, hands laced behind his back in a non-threatening gesture. Here, near the back of the room, the marble was pink-and-gold-veined, causing our footsteps to echo.

"You were supposed to be nurtured here, by our people, in *our* way."

Was I? I gave him a sideways glance, registering his almost friendly expression. What would it have been like, being raised here, away from Elizabeth and the PSS? Had my father known what his sacrifice would cost me? Would he have stepped back when the council decided to let the PSS take me? Would I have been happy here?

"Why? For what purpose?" I asked as we reached the doorway. From this close, it wasn't dark at all, as it had appeared from far away. It was lit by several torches, the flames a muted blue that turned white at the edges, the polished stone walls reflecting the light.

"Had Fosch not reneged on his word, things would have been different. For everyone."

Not what I meant, but I was afraid to repeat the question with an explanation and risk insulting him, so I said nothing.

Halfway through the hallway, Lee appeared out of thin air, and I jerked, startled and spooked. She gave me a cold, laser-sharp glance, motioned Oberon forward and murmured something. When she finished, Oberon glanced my way and nodded.

She turned and fell into step beside him, and I followed, noting that her heals were about four inches tall. Her boots looked like they belonged to some expensive brand, and I checked out her jeans, CK, and wondered where she did her shopping. Not the shirt, no human could replicate the shifting colors. Not yet anyway.

They paused by a torch and, silently, I waited for them to say something or start moving again. In those heels, Lee was almost a foot taller than Oberon, her demeanor more alert, meaner, and if I didn't know better, I'd have taken him for the weaker of the two.

"For millennia," Oberon said, his eyes a weird shade of brown and blue, "The Sidhe land have stood between your planet, the dimensional galaxy and whatever entities dwell there."

I started to nod, then remembered something. "Wait, I thought the Low Lands was the next closest thing to earth?"

Oberon inclined his head. "The land of the low creatures is a planet island, orbiting around the Sidhe land. I believe your people call it a satellite. A moon."

He went on, "Every leeway that leads to Earth travels through our land first," he explained.

A sinking feeling began at the bottom of my stomach, spreading out.

"Without the Sidhe here," Oberon shook his head once, opened both palms wide and finished with an earnest expression, "we are what the humans call a buffer between you and what lives out there. No one, nothing, passes through to earth and beyond without our knowledge."

I nodded again when he paused, my mind gone curiously blank. That bone-deep fear, however, grew with every heartbeat, as if the drumming fueled it somehow.

"If by happenstance the Sidhe land can no longer provide earth with a barrier, if we encounter demanding tasks to occupy us beyond our duties, your world would suffer as it never has before."

I swallowed, sensing a threat underlying those words, an impending sense of doom hanging in the air. "Why are you telling me this?"

"I am going to show you something, Roxanne Fosch, and you will pay *great* attention." He motioned with a hand, and the ground yawned opened; a staircase leading into darkness.

He stepped down first, his descent quiet, his shadow a darker impression against the black pit.

Despite not being forced, I didn't think I had any choice but to follow, so down I went, with Lee behind.

A few stairs down, the opening behind closed, sealing us in complete darkness. My steps faltered, and I had to brace a hand on the dry wall beside me. I kept moving, following the sound of Oberon's steps. Lee brushed by, and fear of being left behind had me moving faster, feeling my way on the uneven rock wall to my left.

Down and down we went, the dense rock wall shifting from dry and smooth to rough, damp and jagged. There was a certain muskiness in the air associated with closed, mildewed places.

Ahead, a pinprick of light appeared, and I made out silhouettes on the steps below. Still, we moved, down and down, until the air became stifling, my breathing gasping pants for oxygen. I stumbled when I found no more steps, and got caught on thick, sticky spider webs. I brushed my hands over my face and arms, my lungs constricting, and stumbled another step. And the sensation vanished. I gulped air like a drowning woman, realizing I just crossed a ward.

Shivering, I focused on the pinprick of light and made my way toward it, my hand bracing my progress on the rough-hewn rock wall. Footsteps sounded far ahead, and sometimes a silhouette would block the light from view, a sign that I wasn't alone in this dark place, and the knowledge kept me from outright panic.

When I bumped into something hard and warm, I shrieked with terror, jumped back, talons out. But a part of my brain that still clung to common sense had me lowering my talons before striking, and with a chill, Oberon, his profile obscured by the faint backlight.

I glanced around, at the uneven ground, the rough-cut walls. Everything was made of rock, grey and rough, with a few drawings carved on it–like–like hieroglyphs or strange runes or something with a more sinister meaning.

Oberon glanced sideways, and Drozelle or Crozelle came into view, looking nothing more than a shadow. She stepped forward, her hands holding an oblong rock of undecipherable color. Suddenly Iee was beside me, dressed in what seemed to be armor and chainmail, though it looked soft and flexible. When did she change? On her hip was an axe, the head glowing faintly, offering no outward illumination. The boots were replaced by sensible leather shoes.

I swallowed all the questions I wanted to ask and flinched when the rock beside me rumbled and moved aside, revealing a dark, yawning hole. A chill went down my spine, filling my veins with ice. My heart rattled and shook inside my chest like a caged beast wanting out. I took back a step, then another.

"We cannot keep the cell open for long." Crozelle–or Drozelle cautioned.

Cell? A dark cell in a cold, silent place. This was what hell must be like. I backed again, peeking into the darkness, but I couldn't make anything out. No walls, no ceiling, no ground. Just darkness. Then something moved. A black shape against the black. Crozelle–or Drozelle–opened both arms wide, one palm open toward the dark interior, the other clutching the oblong stone, thumb and pinkie pointing down at the ground. I couldn't see what she was doing, but I sensed the strange current coming off from her, and it must have been something powerful for the ground beneath us to rumble.

"What's she doing?" I asked no one in particular.

"Drozelle is Shielding his presence from the ether," Oberon said.

"What? Who?" I glanced at him, and upon seeing my confusion, light illuminated the small space. A keening came from the dark hole, a horrible sound that was painful to hear, even if it wasn't loud.

I shielded my eyes from the glare, and when I adjusted, I finally saw it.

A creature, about two feet tall, curled–no not a creature, but a person, a guy, curled into himself so thoroughly, no head or legs showed, just a broad, hunched back, the elbows sticking out as he tried to cover his head and eyes from the glare. The cell was about twelve by twelve, a square, empty hole with nothing, no bed, no pot, no bowls, no insects or rodents for company.

Oberon and Lee watched me, but I had no idea what they were expecting. Did I know that person?

I inched closer, and lee's warning stance stopped me. Something was wrong here. Very wrong. The guy in the cell shifted like a lizard, coming closer to the opening, his head lowered against the glare.

He wore filthy clothes, torn and stained, and the stench of unwashed body hit me, making me wrinkle my nose.

The light dimmed some, the earth tremored, and Drozelle shook. The keening sound came again, and I whimpered with sympathy. That's when that thing, for it was no man, hurtled for Drozelle with a ferocious velocity that belied any weakness. I stumbled back, falling on my ass, but no one else moved. Not even Drozelle, her arms still open to both sides.

The guy, just a boy in his late teens, had some scruff on his cheeks and a pale complexion that was either the result of illness or the lack of sunlight. He stood with his hands clawed in the air, less than a foot away from the dark-haired Seelie. The thing's aura, a solid, glowing black line that pulsated with power, looked like nothing I had ever seen, or felt, but his eyes, green that kept shifting to black as if he couldn't decide which color to keep, that was something I've seen before.

Alien, wrong. Something not of this world—my world.

Something glinted above his eyebrow, a piercing, I think, and my stomach clenched. His eyes shifted to green and stayed as if the darkness lost the battle, and he lowered his hands, shook his head, a crooked grin forming on his lips. If it weren't for the cold, malicious glint in his eyes, that boyish, crooked smile would have fooled me. There was a dark shape to the side of his chin, just under the corner of his lip, and I knew, I knew, it resembled a heart. Recognition slapped me on the face, had bile rising in my throat.

Fin, the boy on the photo from Vincent's office. Or at least, what remained of the boy. For what stood there, eyes as cold as an iceberg, hands clenched into tight fists, was not the boy with sharp green eyes that glinted with mischief.

I stood slowly, stepped back, my hand covering my mouth at the horror.

Then I took another step. Then another, and another. My heart beat so fast, so hard, I struggled to breathe. My hands shook, my legs were weak.

The rocks closed, revealing the carvings again, and Drozelle let her arms fall and shoulders droop as if standing upright was too much effort. Lee took a step toward the dark-haired Fee, hands grasping the handle of her axe.

Oberon gave me a long, assessing look before turning and making his way back. I didn't wait for an invitation, or for lee or the dark-haired Fee to give me any orders, but followed in his wake, trying to keep pace as best as possible in the dark, my shaking hand bracing against that rough stone wall, the carvings now taking a new meaning. Cells. They were cells.

I glanced back once, found Lee's lips drawn in a thin line, her eyes shadowed as she watched the now closed rock cell, the dark-haired

twin breathing hard. Neither followed us, as if they waited for something to happen.

Chapter Thirty-Three

We emerged through a hidden panel in a wall facing tall arched windows. Brightness assaulted me, but despite being blinding, it was a welcome respite. Outside, I could see the towering trees atop the sloping hill where I'd first glimpsed the Seelie Castle, and from our elevated angle, deduced we were on an upper level, perhaps even high on a tower.

Oberon turned left and, with unsteady legs, I scrambled to keep up. To the right were the tall windows, to the left a whitewashed wall decorated with large paintings, unlit torches, and small elaborately-carved niches.

We passed a painting of a hillside, full of verdant trees and strange animals grazing by a clear, glittering stream. Another was of a white deer, munching on the bark of a tree, the woods behind it cast in twilight. Another painting was of a child playing with a pixie atop tall swaying grass, surrounded by colorful flowers. There were many, all scenic, peaceful, so calming. My fear dissipated as if sucked away by the paintings. My shaking hands took longer, but the drawings were many and Oberon let me linger at every single one without a word. When we reached the far side, a pixie waited, bobbing up and down as if she floated in a swimming pool.

"Bennty will see you to your room. Rest, and I will send for you when it's time. If you need anything, she will provide it for you." He inclined his head at the pixie, turned and left.

I followed Bennty up a set of wide curving stairs and emerged in a bright hall similar to the one below. The only difference was here, instead of paintings, there were carved honey doors. In front of each door was a tall window, the woods far, far below.

Bennty paused by the second door and it opened, presumably with magic. The pixie hovered by the entrance and waited for me to step inside before following behind.

Like I'd expected, it was a luxuriously decorated bedroom, adorned with exotic reds, sharp browns, and intense blues. A huge canopied bed dominated the room, made of dark wood and sheer garnet-red drapes. A thick duvet with geometric patterns of blue, brown and red, covered the bed. On top were a dozen throw pillows in every color of the rainbow, along with a few colors I had no name for.

The floor was mahogany, polished to a glowing sheen, reflecting my silhouette like a mirror, with thick embroidered rugs covering a wide area around the bed. A carved dark wood bureau stood to one side and, through a half-closed door opposite the bed, I could see a sunken tub made of–gold? Or some yellow substance. Across from me the sheer ceiling-to-floor drapes danced from an unfelt breeze. It was there I walked to first, though I had no ultimate reason for the preference. On the other side of the drapes was a wide semi-round balcony and open air.

The sky was a deep blue with patches of pink and orange and yellow–the fused colors of a sunset, although I couldn't see any sun. I stepped onto the balcony, and the floor here was cold, made of an unusual dark rock with crisscrossing golden veins. I grasped the marble railing and looked down, and found... nothing. There was no ground below. A lonely cloud sailed nearby, moved by an unfelt current. My nails dug in until pain shot through my fingers.

I moved to the side of the balcony and peered up and down. There was nothing there. Nothing but the smooth stone of the castle, going as far up and down as the eyes could see. There were no windows, no balconies, no nothing. Nothing but smooth stone. It was like I was the only person standing in a world that was suddenly no longer.

Backing into the room, I discovered the pixie was gone, and so was the door that opened into the hall.

A prison then, I thought, sitting on the bed. I sank a few inches and splayed my hands on both sides, through the soft material of the cover. A comfortable prison, but a prison nonetheless.

"Frizz?"

He blinked into existence.

I lay down, patted the duvet in front of me, and Frizz snuggled in. Calmer, I scratched his head, his back. Maybe they'd keep me for a century or so and I wouldn't have to face the clan again. The thought was numbing. I wasn't sure if I should be angry I wouldn't have a chance to prove my innocence to the clan, or relieved I wouldn't face execution if I couldn't.

Zantry had promised he'd come for me, but how would I know he'd come if I was locked in this room? Maybe someday, if I got too tired, I could leap from the balcony and end it all. Would I hit a surface or fall forever?

Chapter Thirty-Four

The sound of buzzing wings woke me up.

"Go away, Frizz," I mumbled, shifting to the other side. The buzzing grew stronger, more insistent, followed by a whining pitch. I opened my eyes and sat up. Frizz would have gone away, not persisted. Awake and alert, I remembered I was in the enemy camp.

Bennty, the pixie, hovered near my head, expression anxious. She flew to the foot of the bed and returned, then hopped to the edge of the bed, motioning to the long dress draped at the edge, made of some undeterminable material.

"You want me to change into that?" I asked.

Bennty's head bobbed up and down.

"Why?"

She replied in a garbled, high-pitched voice and flew to the dress and back again, floating a few inches away, arms crossed, tiny foot tapping air.

"Alright. Let me wash and take care of necessities first."

The material of the dress was fleecy-soft and fit like a second skin. It was warm, silky, and I couldn't help but admire the way it felt against my body. Simple and sleeveless, the V-necked garment flowed to my ankles. It bore on the side of gold, but shifted to green and yellow and a pale shade of brown before rippling back to a dark shade of gold that brightened and shifted to yellow and green again. The sandals

Bennty passed me were made of the same material as the dress, the soles thicker to cushion the steps.

The moment I finished dressing Bennty started working on my hair, pulling it up and weaving a thin thread of gold through my wavy locks.

I searched for a mirror, curious to see how I looked, but there was none, not even a reflective surface. I tried to see my reflection on the polished floor, but it was hard to make out anything more than my silhouette.

Bennty urged me out the door that hadn't been there earlier, an insistent buzz herding me from behind. Every time I lagged, admiring a painting or a view beyond a window, the buzzing got louder and stronger, and the pixie would dash in front, only to hover before the doorway, motioning that I should follow, then return behind me.

Soon we entered the big room with the domed glass ceiling, and I stopped, unsure. It was no longer empty. There were others, dressed in court attire–shimmering, brilliant colors, reds, yellows, blues, whites. Like mine, some dresses shifted colors, but most didn't. The men were dressed in colorful formal suits, some in casual attire, pants and dress shirts, or strange skirts and vests.

Soft music played in the background, something with flutes and strings, mixed with the sound of laughter, tinkling glass. The typical sounds of a room full of happy people.

Of which I knew none. Their aura was that shiny silver, every one a beautiful star on his or her own.

I searched for Lee, Oberon, even Drozelle or Crozelle, found no familiar faces. Behind me, Bennty's buzz grew insistent, louder, but I didn't budge. Instead, I had this strong urge to turn and leave before anyone spotted me.

So I did, deciding I'd rather be in my prison with no one but Frizz. And almost plowed through Lee. "Oh. Umm, sorry."

Lee glanced at me, those green eyes as cold as ever, but no one could fault her beauty. She was dressed in a velvety burgundy dress with bell sleeves, the flowing skirt covered with sparkling sequins. Her hair was loose down her back, a cascade of fire with colorful stones looped around random locks like painted beads. Precious stones? She inclined her head toward the room, a silent command for me to follow.

Head lowered, I turned and trailed behind her like a wayward child going to confession after a day filled with sinful deeds. Those we passed stopped talking and glanced over, murmuring behind their hands. No one greeted Lee or met her eyes. No, everyone lowered their heads, eyes downcast until she passed. A sign of respect. A few even bowed or curtsied low.

We moved in a zigzag path toward the dais, the intricate throne empty, and with a spike in anxiety, I realized I was being brought to the apex of attention, the center stage of the courtroom.

When we reached the steps that led up to the throne we stopped. Lee turned to face the tall double-doors on the opposite side. As if on cue, they opened by an invisible force.

"All hail the queen!" Trumpets sounded, though I could see no trumpeter. Like magic, the crowd retreated to both sides of the room, leaving a wide aisle in the middle. There was no red carpet, no guards to call order to the room or to hold back the crowd, and I wondered if Queen Titania was too revered or too feared.

A moment later, a woman in a flowing dark purple gown holding a black staff glided into the room, radiating a beckoning light from within. For the first time in my life, I was able to see an aura from afar, and although hers was just like everyone else's, hers resonated with power and wisdom.

In unison, everyone in the room knelt and bowed their heads, including Lee. I started doing the same, recalled Zantry's instructions and stiffened. I lowered my head, eyes fixed on the ground, and it was like shining a huge spotlight on my head, or painting a red X on my back; I was so exposed. My stomach quivered with every heartbeat, my hands shook uncontrollably. I balled them into fists, realized I looked like I was ready to punch someone, and decided clasping them together looked less threatening.

Queen Titania's footsteps were silent, as if she glided on air instead of the floor. She exuded an air of authority, a wave of strength bathed in sunlight and fragrance, something that could turn lethal at a moment's notice. Lilies and night-blooming jasmine.

The hem of the purple gown appeared and I almost raised my head before I recalled Zantry's warning to wait for permission. After a moment, the hem disappeared from view, and I exhaled.

"Rise," commanded a melodious voice high from the left.

Everyone stood, the sound almost one, and Lee glanced at me before shifting to her queen.

I caught Titania's nod before Lee motioned me forward, up the steps. I paused on the last one, per Zantry's invaluable instruction: *never go up the steps of the throne unless invited, and never take the last one.* I fixed my gaze on Titania's nose, because I was to give my full attention but never look her in the eyes.

"Your highness," I said in a breathy voice I instantly hated.

Titania's eyes were a turquoise-green so deep, they reminded me of the ocean. Her skin was smooth and golden, the shape of her eyes like big almonds. Her lips were full and red, her chin oval. Her rich-honey hair was long and wavy, half loose, half twisted around a thick tiara made of sunlight and gold. She looked like she was in her mid-twenties, blazing with robust health and inner light.

Despite the radiance, however, there was a chilliness about her, a ruthlessness, an unfeeling emptiness like that of a cold-blooded shark.

Titania studied me, her expression portraying nothing. Oberon stepped beside me, took the last step, and moved to stand beside his queen, his posture relaxed, regal. On Queen Titania's other side stood Lee, and all three now scrutinized me, the stares unnerving. And I wasn't counting all the eyes drilling holes into my back. I was the sole focus of the entire Seelie court.

If I stayed this nervous, I'd either puke or hyperventilate, so I breathed through my mouth, exhaled through my nose, trying to keep a calm façade.

"This is the promised child, the one denied to us many cycles ago," Titania announced, addressing the crowd. Chills raced up and down my spine. I was brought to this gathering so everyone would witness what Lee saving me from the Low Lands cost me. "She is Dhiultadh Yoncey Fosch's daughter."

Murmurs rippled through a now-tense crowd. Did they know? Were they aware of the role I was to play?

Titania waited a few seconds to speak, drawing out the suspense. "She has come forth to offer compensation for a debt owed. All debts shall be paid, all justice shall be met."

The crowd roared with approval. Titania leaned back on her throne with a satisfied smirk.

Oh God. I should have run.

Anything that made this crowd cheer with so much enthusiasm wouldn't bode well for me. My heart squeezed with stabbing pain and I knew my poker face wasn't hiding my fear.

Lee strolled forward and looked down at me, eyes as cold as her queen's.

"Roxanne Fosch, daughter of Dhiultadh Yoncey Fosch, promised child." Her voice was loud and crisp. "I henceforth call for the payment of our bargain, beholden to the terms you set. Do you agree?"

I swallowed through the lump in my throat. "Yes," I croaked. "Yes," I repeated louder.

Lee scanned the crowd, making sure everyone heard my answer before addressing me next. "Roxanne Fosch, Daughter of Dhiultadh Yoncey Fosch, promised child, I call on you the broken bargain your father dishonored. You shall fulfill the role you were destined to fill all these many cycles ago."

The crowd went mad with cheers and shouts, and nausea churned in my stomach, making me dizzy. As my vision dimmed, I gritted my teeth and forced myself to breathe.

Lee stepped back to the side of the throne and Titania dismissed her subjects with a wave of a hand, before focusing her gaze on me.

Unable to help myself, I hugged my stomach, my hands clenched into tight fists. It was a vulnerable position, but who was I kidding? I was a kitten in a den of rabid wolves.

"She does not amount to much," Queen Titania observed in that rich, melodious voice.

"Nay, but she is the promised child," Oberon said.

"Perhaps it is because she was not raised in this court," Lee offered.

Titania drummed razor-sharp nails on the armrest of her throne as she regarded me. "Images are often misleading. But I do not sense strength in this one. We cannot afford to waste time."

"It is on purpose she lacks strength. Otherwise, she would not be ours today," Oberon said.

Titania glared at him. "Had not Fosch dishonored his word, she would have been ours to nurture. Do you think naught what will happen if you are wrong?"

Oberon bowed his head subserviently, but didn't back down. "Forgive me, my wisest queen, but she is the promised child, even if we do not sense strength. She is Fosch's scion and we do not sense him in her."

Titania's eyes returned to me, her expression frightening. She leaned forward and asked, "Do you know who you are, child?"

I opened my mouth, ready to give my name, but swallowed hard. I had a hunch—considering the context of their conversation—telling her my name would only anger her, insolence to be punished. "Your highness, I apologize, but I'm not sure if I understand what you mean... your highness." Titania cocked her head and leaned back on her throne, her nails tapping, the black staff still held in her other hand. "Has she seen it yet?"

"Aye, my queen. She recognized what it means, if not who it was as well."

"It lives?"

"Nay, my queen, we have disposed of the abomination."

Fin. Up until that moment, I'd pushed thoughts of him away, but now? I'd seen this corruption before I'd come to this land, before I'd joined the Hunters, even before I'd met Lee in the Low Lands. I'd seen it more than once. With the Edmond brothers—the bad boy team—back when they had ambushed me in that no-name motel. I'd witnessed the corruption in Dr. Dean's eyes and the eyes of Remo's guard back in the MGM Casino.

Titania read the trepidation in my eyes.

"Do you know what it is?" she demanded.

I shook my head, my eyes focused on her chin. "But I've seen it before, and I know who's responsible."

She was about to say something else when Oberon pressed a hand on her shoulder and motioned behind me. She glanced up, inclined her head once. A pixie flew straight to her, stopping beside her ears and motioning agitatedly. Something fleeting crossed Titania's expression, an emotion I couldn't read. She nodded to the pixie, motioned Lee toward me. "We will discuss this further in the morn."

Lee stepped forward and descended the stairs. "Come, child," she said, the words clipped, but there was an air of speculation about her, of excited expectancy.

I made my way down, lightheaded. What had I gotten myself into? Why did they have one of Remo's minions in their dungeons? Oberon's speech about the Sidhe being some kind of barrier between Earth and other dimensions sounded like a veiled threat. Why would Earth suffer if the Sidhe became preoccupied with other duties? He'd wanted me to recognize Fin, or what the corruption meant, had ordered me to pay attention. Was Fin some sort of threat as well, what the Sidhe would let rampage on earth if I didn't comply with the demands?

Or maybe it was nothing so sinister… They often demanded someone's firstborn to breed with them, to produce pure-blooded Seelie after a few generations before infertility kicked in. Was that it? Maybe they needed more warriors to prevent the corruption that had infested Fin from spreading to Earth and I was their breeding mare? Or maybe they had a bargain with Remo and I was their payment?

Lee paused at the bottom of the steps and I followed suit, stepping alongside her, my thoughts and stomach churning.

Then the double doors opened and my mind went blank as Zantry marched in, all smiles despite the two hulking guards escorting him.

He was dressed in a dark charcoal-gray suit, a black shirt underneath, no tie, and as handsome as ever.

He said he'd come for me.

Expression neutral, I watched him approach the throne. Some of the courtiers paused to view who'd entered, some murmured to their companions; all showed recognition. The murmuring slowly evolved into a crescendo, and a few of the Fee called to him, laughing with delight. Everyone present was glad to see him. A sideways glance showed Lee watching him with the barest hint of a smile lighting her cold expression.

Zantry ascended the throne steps without any invitation, and to my shock, he went up to Queen Titania herself, stopping right in front of the throne. To the delight of the Seelie courtiers, he made a show of bowing and kissing her hand.

"Your majesty, you look as lovely as always," he said with a charming smile.

"Zantry Akinzo, back from the dead."

"Never dead. But if you wish, majesty, if I ever go, I'll send my regards."

Titania's eyes gleamed with amusement and she said something I couldn't hear. Zantry replied and she laughed with delight, but I could no longer hear them, even if they were right there, no more than twenty feet away.

The conversation had turned private. Had the last part of my conversation with Queen Titania been private too?

Everyone resumed mingling, though some continued to gawk at Zantry and murmur.

Oberon joined the conversation. After a moment, I noticed Lee watching me.

"Will I know what fulfilling my role as the promised child entail soon?"

"Aye, in the morn."

Chapter Thirty-Five

The high table brimmed with fragrant, succulent food, some of which I recognized–roasted meat, stuffed duck, herbed fish, fruit tarts–and others I'd never seen before.

I was seated beside Lee, who in turn sat beside Zantry, who sat across from Oberon and to Titania's left, who sat, of course, at the head of the table. There were a few others seated on our table, Crozelle and Drozelle and another guy with pointed ears and sharp, animal-like teeth. Aside from these two strange features, he looked as normal as a human, if one overlooked the shining silver aura.

Flanking the royal table were two larger tables, laden with food and occupied by the Seelie nobility. All three tables carried the same food, as fancy and plentiful as the queen's.

Pixies hovered nearby, serving the royal table, filling our plates, our glasses. I ate as little as possible without seeming rude, because my stomach was churning like a lonely boat amidst a heavy storm. The minute I finished eating dessert, some pie filled with a sweet fruit I didn't recognize, I excused myself.

To my surprise, it was Oberon who escorted me to my room, not Bennty. We passed the same hall filled with paintings as before, now illuminated by the wall torches. Outside, darkness had fallen. The silhouettes of the trees could still be seen, reaching for the glittering stars in the sky. Again, the tranquil drawings on the wall soothed my nerves, even if the paintings were different than the ones from earlier.

Maybe this wasn't the same hallway? Or maybe it was and the paintings shifted and changed with the hour? It was an enchanted palace after all, wasn't it?

Passing a drawing of a huge gargoyle with enormous wings, I paused. This one looked massive, aggressive, monstrous. Two rows of needle-sharp teeth were bared at the artist, as if protesting against its image being drawn. The span of its wings was as huge as the gargoyle itself, and I wondered if Frizz's wings would ever grow like that.

Beside me, Oberon studied the drawing with me. "It *is* beautiful, is it not?"

I glanced sideways at him, wondering if he meant the masterpiece or the gargoyle itself, found his eyes fixed at the framed painting. I looked back at the drawing, studied it. The shell-shaped eyes glinted sharply with intelligence, the tips of the ears like spiky arrowheads. The wings spanned long to the sides, gleaming with whatever effect the artist could capture. He was bigger than Frizz, his built not like that of a thin child, but of a muscular man used to eating and frequent exercise.

"In a way, I guess it is."

"Blaxillium. Titania herself named him. Made him her familiar."

Surprised, I turned. "I had the impression that naming a shadow wasn't something common."

Oberon tilted his head, his brown eyes gleaming with a hidden secret. "A shadow like yours, nay, it is not common to name them. But Blax wasn't a common shadow. He was a familiar, a gargoyle, an old and powerful one."

Confused, I asked, "But I thought shadows and gargoyles were the same species?"

Oberon chuckled, amused at my naivety. "Not in a thousand years." He gestured at Blaxillium. "Gargoyles are called shadows when young. Once they round the millennium, they become something else, something more powerful and respectable."

"So you mean Frizz, when he reaches a thousand, he'll be like that?" I pointed a stiff finger, my tone waffling between awe and horror.

"If he matures with enough resources, perhaps."

"But what's the difference between the two? I mean, besides the obvious?"

"The difference is like water and fire," he said. "For one, only the strongest of the strong can hold a gargoyle familiar without the gargoyle's explicit consent. Blax, for one, raged against the bond for decades, and would have reverted the master-slave bond within minutes had Queen Titania not been the dominant of the pair." He studied the painting, his eyes conveying nothing of what he was thinking. "For a lesser being, I reckon the arrangement has to be mutual, lest the roles be reversed. It's an arrangement that has been progressively dwindling, one a lot of species have avoided throughout the years, even if the relationship is beneficial to both."

"But a young shadow, what can it do?" I pressed, wanting to know. Remo had said they were useful once you got one to owe you a favor, but so far I had no idea *how* useful.

"Mostly, it steals, kills, shadows. Parlor tricks. Make you believe something that isn't true. They are clever, and once they give loyalty, they are committed."

Alright, parlor tricks useful to an evil person, then. "And once they grow to be like that?" I gestured to the massive creature.

Oberon said, "They are powerful, dangerous creatures."

"Can they travel the leeway?" was what really circled my thoughts.

"Not unless they are bound to an entity from another plane. Shadows, even gargoyles, are creatures of the Low Lands, bound to it like a plant to soil."

I shifted, frowning at a disturbing thought. "Can they live away from the land?"

Oberon studied me for a long moment. "If they are cared for and are bound to a stronger entity, they can draw strength from their master and live a long time without needing to return. Likewise, the dominant can draw strength from the familiar in times of need."

I turned back to the painting, trying to diffuse Oberon's sharp eyes from me. "Is he in the castle? I mean Blax?"

I felt his pang of sorrow, quickly cut off as if it had escaped before he could contain it. His expression, however, conveyed nothing. Maybe I had imagined it? "Blax was a very old gargoyle. He was loyal and committed to what belonged to him. For that reason, He was one of the first to fall." He turned away from the drawing to look out one of the tall arched windows.

"I'm sorry about that," I said and meant it.

"All the older ones fell a few centuries before. Everyone who knows about the fall of the elders understands anyone who has a familiar from the dead-lands today will have a young shadow, no older than four centuries."

What would my aura look like if Frizz happened to grow old–and was still bonded to me? "Can a person break the bargain bond to a shadow?"

Oberon cocked his head and studied me, eyes all-knowing and astute in a way that made me nervous. "The bargain bond with a shadow can be broken, aye," he said, and I wasn't sure if it was relief or disappointment I felt.

"But yours, though unusual, falls under the familial bond, and those are absolute."

Shock, like a splash of frigid cold water, jolted my system. "What?" I squeaked. "How can that be?"

"I cannot say. It depends on the circumstance surrounding the event." Seeing the denial clear in my eyes, Oberon frowned. "Everything you do warrants a reaction, something that ripples back to you. Believe me; if he is your familiar today, it is because he has chosen to be, but also because you accepted it so."

I certainly did not. I'd tried to free him–and was still researching ways to break the bond.

Familiar. Like Blaxillium and Titania. I glanced back at the painting, trying to conceal my thoughts from Oberon's prying eyes, recalling how Lee had been so interested in the way I handled Frizz and his pack. Had she known all along? Did it matter? It changed nothing.

"Can this familiar bond be broken?" I asked.

"Not unless one of the two dies first." After a pause, Oberon added, "I can help you if you like."

I shifted, wary. "By killing one of us?"

He chuckled as if I'd said something funny. "That is an option, but at the moment, not in my best interest. Nay, both of you live. There is another way, free of pain, free of blood."

"And the price?" I asked skeptically, though still willing to listen.

"A small one."

A heavy silence followed his words as I thought about it. "There is a way?" I asked, and wanted to slap myself for even considering it.

"To break it clean? Nay, there is none. But we can exchange your familiar with something that suits you better."

Lips pursed, I slanted a glance at the giant gargoyle. "Like what?"

"One of our pixies, if you like. They are useful servants. And that does not please you, I see. Let's see. In your world, people use domestic pets as familiars. What about a cat?"

A cat would be nice, but I shook my head.

He tried again. "A canine?"

"No, I think I'll keep Frizz for now." I felt a pang of guilt, like I was betraying Frizz by considering switching him with something else. I sent him an apology through the bond, felt no answer back.

"Whenever you change your mind," Oberon offered.

"Sure," I said, but we both knew I wouldn't come to him. Not in the near future, and not unless I was desperate.

We moved on to the next drawings, pausing in front of each one. Most of them portrayed a peaceful and scenic night view. There was a dynamic painting of a two-headed animal, similar to the one by the entrance, but this time none of the heads were looking at me. Unlike the brown one downstairs, this one was pure white, and I had the urge to touch it to see if it felt as soft as the drawing suggested. On and on the paintings went and Oberon let me linger, patiently answering my questions. All had a story to tell and Oberon seemed obliged to explain.

I stopped before a painting of a small burbling creek and a distant mountain covered with verdant green blocking the dark horizon, and felt compelled to ask, "Who painted all these?"

"The Mandolia Mountain. It was a beautiful place once, full of pleasing sounds and bright colors. Full of life," he said with just enough regret to tell me this was no longer true.

A hint of unease stirred within, but I couldn't pinpoint the reason why.

"That particular one was done by Crozelle. But there are some done by Drozelle, some by Janise. Others by Leon."

"Oh?" was all that came to mind. The enforcer of the Seelie was an artist at heart?

We moved on, and at the end of the hall, I drew short. In front of the last arched window was a drawing of a night sky. I glanced once at Oberon, then backtracked to the drawings done at night. Now that I looked closely, I could see what had tugged at my conscience.

I paused in front of the one with the two-headed animal and pointed. "Those drawings..." I motioned to them, glancing at Oberon's bright eyes. They gleamed with an intensity that had my words faltering.

"Ay?" he prompted.

"Are they depictions of the Low Lands?" I wanted to slap myself. Of course they were.

Oberon glanced at the painting, studying the drawing for a long moment as if this was the first time he had seen it. "It is the Land of the low creatures, ay. Leon did this one. She is talented." He glanced at me, "you like them?"

"They are ... very vivid drawings."

Oberon clasped his fingers together and studied my face. "What do you know happened to the land of the low creatures?"

I hesitated. All night long I had ignored Zantry as if I had never met him before. To admit I knew what happened...

Instead of a lie, I turned to contemplate the drawing, trying to come up with a good enough reply. Zantry had warned me against lies, but he didn't say I had to answer every single question. Beside me, Oberon waited for a reply, then turned to look out the arched windows.

"Let me tell you a story, young child," he began, focused on the star-strewn sky visible through the nearby open window.

Chapter Thirty-Six

"There once was a nation, a planet full of beings without form, without definite shape. They were ruled by no one, by no law, by no deity that they can recall. They were beings with no feelings. Beings who existed. They could twist, bend, break." Oberon contemplated the night sky above the forest for a few seconds.

I glanced out the window, the night sky brilliant with stars, my heart beating faster than usual. I didn't speak, aware this information was being given without any payment asked.

"Then at a time, no one really knows when or how, one of the beings stole the life of another, realizing by doing so he became bigger. Stronger. He enjoyed the feeling of superiority and stole again and again. Others studied him, contemplated, did the same. And thus, greed was born in a world that had once simply existed.

"The beings who had been stolen from realized they became smaller and weaker, and so they gathered and went after the thieves. Other beings, against the greed, against the thieves, perhaps out of pity, donated some of their life-force to the smaller beings, so they could grow and become strong again.

"The now-stronger beings, filled with greed and the novelty of power, subjected the weaker ones to rules and dictates." Oberon paused and turned to me. "So was emotion born into a world with no rules, no laws, no religion. There was chaos then, and, with that, disorder. Many felt nothing, but many did and became restless. They still had no form, no shape, no name. They roamed their planet without any purpose, any goal. Their planet was vast, their numbers big, but because they were abstract beings, the size or shape of their planet didn't matter to most. But it did to some, and those set out to explore. One day, three such beings just disappeared out of thin air.

"They fell for a long time. They don't know for how long, for the concept of time was foreign to them. They appeared in a foreign land, one full of wonders, colors, moving things, of life. At first, they thought they had come upon the other side of their planet, but it didn't take long for them to realize they were no longer roaming the unnamed planes of their land.

"Reverently, they touched a tree, a roaming animal, a budding flower. The tree, the animal, the flower, withered and died. They touched another and another. Whatever they touched perished instantly. The grass beneath their phantom shape, the streams they crossed, the plants and trees and the animals. They didn't comprehend the total destruction they left behind simply because they didn't understand what they were doing.

"But they absorbed, they took. Reserved whatever life they brushed. Soon they began taking form, compacting the energy, giving solid shape for what they were. They realized that, and excitedly, they traveled faster, farther, brushing against everything, anything. In a matter of weeks the entire planet was dead, even the small insects under the soil. There remained nothing left to absorb.

"Guardians were sent to kill the intruders, and those too, fell into nothing but piles of dry bones. Paths were disturbed. Nearby planets wept for their lost kin. No one dared approach the three for fear they too would perish.

"So From afar, they were watched. Studied. Animals were sent as tributes, and quickly gone. Guardians were sent to fight, only to be met with the same fate. Birds, however, flew by unharmed, unless one of the three caught it. For you see, by now, the three were as solid as you and I and possessed no wings of their own."

Oberon turned from the windows and studied the drawings done at night, one by one, touching a few of the frames as he went.

"For years and years, nothing approached that land unless it could fly. Patrols were set out, a few from every planet, to watch the three and learn about them, their weakness, their strength. Some of the patrols were bolder than others, coming into view, letting them see and be seen. Soon every patrol did the same, and soon they were trying to communicate with the three.

Who are they? Where did they come from? They asked and asked. What did they want? Why did they kill everything?

At first, the three just watched them, never replying, never uttering a word to the others. The concept of speaking out loud, like that of time, was also foreign.

"Soon, they understood having things whither and dry by their touch was nothing normal. They may have been indifferent to emotions once, but fools they were not. They observed the patrols, listened to them argue and bicker among themselves. Soon they began to learn to form words, to voice them out loud.

'The patrols met and discussed the three, for no one wanted them in their lands, and all had agreed the three must die. They couldn't starve them out; it was one of the things they realized first about the three, having watched them go years and years without nourishment. They couldn't just injure them either; anything they threw at them was either absorbed, subdued or destroyed. Animals and gargoyles were their best food source, for they were full of life.

'Time passed and no strategy for the trio's demise was found. The three declared all they wanted was to find the way back to their planet, they would leave if they could find it. They expressed their sorrow about killing the planet, explained as best as they understood how the atrocity occurred.

"They were abstract of energy, sentient though unable to manifest. They believed because their planet had no form, neither did any of its inhabitants. It came to speculation the three acted as energy vacuums, that whatever source of energy came near would be absorbed. It made sense, but it did not negate the fact life did not exist around them.

"One day, one of the patrols, we will call him patrol number one, realized having the three for allies was equivalent to an assured victory against all his enemies, and so decided to approach the trio, to become friendly with one of them. It was this same patrol who realized the three could control their urge to absorb, who helped them hone the skill into perfection. He helped them to contain themselves, brought them animals so they could practice." Oberon's eyes hardened, his jaw clenched for a moment.

"This same patrol broke the first rule agreed upon and spoke about other planets, about the life and vitality that existed in each of them.

"Slowly, they learned control, they gave each other names." Oberon paused in front of the last drawing, and I glanced at it. The sky was dark, the vibrant planets orbiting it. Hints of a green forest showed at the edges below, a faraway peak appeared at the corner.

On the sky was a vague shape of wings, massive and mysterious. At the ground stood three, a woman with dark flowing hair and two men. All three had their backs turned, but I recognized Zantry, and presumed the woman to be Arianna, and by deduction, the third to be Remo, since he seemed different, muscular, taller, his hair a golden color instead of white.

"The woman called herself Arianna," Oberon said, studying the cascade of dark, shining hair on a trim build. In the drawing, she was almost as tall as Zantry.

"She was a beautiful one," Oberon continued, oblivious of my scrutiny. "Full of joy and curiosity, sympathy for the land and sorrow for what they destroyed." I blinked, surprised, and watched as the hands of the woman moved, palms raised in supplication. "She was ambitious, loving, strong-willed. Because she wanted to see more of the other lands, she learned control faster, better. She taught her companions the same, all while the patrol watched, patient.

"When he brought a creature from deep within the caves to the surface, Arianna didn't kill it. But her companion, Zantry, did. They weren't ready yet."

"The guest from the throne room," I said, because it was expected.

"Ay. The third, whom you already met, called himself Remo Drammen."

I traced a finger over Remo's figure, half expecting it to turn around. He was the tallest of the three.

"He looks different here," I murmured.

"Ay. Corruption will do that."

I let my hand drop and turned to Oberon. "Why do you tell me all this?" I asked, the answer something I couldn't fathom. Zantry told me the Sidhe were self-serving and I believed him. Although it seemed like this information was being freely given, I had this feeling Oberon was on a mission. If talking about how the trio came to be would further his purposes, then I should at least know what they were.

Except, the moment the question left my lips, he closed up and moved to the edge of the archway where a pixie waited. "Bennty will see you to your room. If you need anything, she will provide it."

Chapter Thirty-Seven

In the morning, Bennty woke me from a restless sleep where nebulous clouds of energy chased me across a dead land, trying to eat me alive. I bolted upright, sending the pixie spiraling across the room with a high-pitched shriek.

"Sorry," I mumbled.

We went through the same ritual as yesterday, with Bennty flitting back and forth between the foot of the bed and my face. This time I found a long skirt and a sleeveless blouse, the color shifting between peach and plum.

"Aren't you too bossy for such a tiny thing?" I muttered. Bennty let out a string of high pitched noise, her arms moving around, pointing at me and the clothes at the foot of the bed.

Like the dress from last night, the cloth was made of a material I'd never seen before, thin yet warm and would stay that way. I donned both under the watchful eyes of the pixie, and slipped on the bejeweled satin shoes she passed. When I was done, Bennty worked on my hair, twisting it into a simple bun.

The throne room was empty of milling courtiers, save for the queen, Lee, Oberon and, of course, their guest of honor, Zantry, sitting beside a smug-looking Lee. They were all seated on colorful thick cushions on an alcove beside the dais. Brightly-hued tapestries fluttered in a breeze I again couldn't feel, and the scent of lemon verbena was fresh in the air.

With the satin shoes on, my approach was silent, though my presence didn't go unnoticed. The moment I entered the room through a side door, escorted by Drozelle and Crozelle, everyone stopped talking and glanced at me.

My stomach, already jittery, flipped and flopped and fell with a gurgling moan.

Zantry's eyes met mine with interest, but no recognition. For a moment I feared he had forgotten all about me, that arriving in this land had a sudden bolt of amnesia going over him. And then I met Queen Titania's unforgiving eyes, just for a brief second, and I forgot all about him, my steps faltered, my legs almost buckling beneath my weight.

And we hadn't even started anything.

Determined to reach the group without needing to crawl, I focused my eyes at the opposite tapestry and thought about fun times with Vicky. Frizz's contentment washed over me, and I realized he was taking comfort from my thought too.

I came to a stop before the group and Queen Titania, and lowered my head while Crozelle and Drozelle knelt.

"Your highness," I said with a voice stronger than yesterday's.

Queen Titania tilted her chin up in acknowledgment before motioning to the low colored cushion arranged across from her. "Sit and we shall speak."

I sat, grateful my rubbery legs wouldn't have to support me through whatever came next.

A platter of food appeared in front of me, startling a squeak of terror from my lips.

"Break your fast," Queen Titania ordered.

I looked down at the array of exotic fruits, colored puffs, mini clouds and what seemed like a variety of cheese cubes. I chose a slice of apple, one of the few things on the platter I recognized. A few feet in front of me, Oberon spoke something to Titania that made her frown. Beside me and to the front, lee was murmuring something in Zantry's ears that made his lips twitch, his eyes glitter. Her hand rested high on his thigh, an improper, intimate gesture that had an unexpected pang of jealousy rattling in my chest.

I didn't like the way he was looking at her.

The way she was looking at him.

I liked even less my possessive thoughts.

Drozelle leaned close to my ear. "He is very handsome, is he not?"

I shrugged, tampering down on the jealousy as best as possible. Could she sense it?

"Back a time, there would be challenges among our finest courtiers for the privilege of his private company," she went on, and my eyes flew to Zantry, found him watching me with curiosity.

I looked down at the food, picked a random cube of yellow cheese. It was tangy and a little sour, with a bitter, faint taste at the end. I picked another one, this one lighter in color. When I sensed eyes on me, I expected it to be Zantry's, but it was Titania's, her cold, turquoise eyes hinting at an unpleasant stream of thought.

Whatever newfound appetite I'd found pooft away like smoke in the wind.

I leaned away from the platter, saying a polite "thank you" to her chin. The platter disappeared, and no sooner was it gone then an image full of shifting colors appeared in its place. It wasn't like a 3D image, but more like an open window. As if the projection had been a sign, Crozelle and Drozelle stood at the same time, bowed to their queen and exited the throne room without a sound. I barely paid any attention to their departure, riveted instead at the scene ahead.

The image zoomed in, and the colors took shape, forming a land so green, full of hills and trees, roaming animals, strange, colorful birds. Their sound was exotic, exquisite, joyful to hear. The scent of pine and verdant things filled the room, accompanied by an undertone of something moist. When the image shifted to an azure blue ocean, so clear you could see the creatures moving within the water, the humid scent of briny, salty air replaced the green, the sound of lapping waves soothing my nerves. The image kept shifting, showing the edge of an island, the peaks of tall, imperious mountains, the beauty of waterfalls and tree-covered hillsides, lush and green and yellow and flowers of every color I could imagine. The perfume of orange blossoms and roses permeated the room, a sweet, citrusy combination that blended perfectly. A village was shown next, and the Seelie folk roamed on the land, their ruckus laughter joyful, their words nothing I could understand. Some were merchants, their carts brimming with materials and other things I couldn't identify; some were dressed in long dresses, some in strange customs and headdresses. All wore vibrant colors, with not a single black to be seen. Animals, both familiar and strange, roamed freely among the Fee, some carried like babies around. It was a land of colors, of dashing animals, of life, of blooming energy. Strange structures that spiraled up like horns dotted the place, some with green intervals, others standing side by side. The structures, like everything else, were full of colors and glitters, with the occasional shadow of some large bird flying over.

"There is a place in my land no longer as beautiful, as vibrant as it should be." Queen Titania's voice lilted like background music to the image.

Zantry sat forward, his gaze focused on the projection.

"Show me," he demanded.

Queen Titania's eyes flared at the command, but the image fast-forwarded as if recorded by a fast-flying thing. It showed first the edges of a dark, dead patch of land, made more pronounced by the greenery bordering it. Darkness took over, showing acres and acres of death, tree and animal husks, parched, cracked soil … like in the Low Lands, this one more devastating for the beauty and tranquility I had just seen.

"Prior to this blasphemy, there were no unusual or abnormal frequencies near this land," Titania said in a subdued tone, as if she were afraid to call the attention of the darkness. "One moment green and life were abundant, the next death reigned upon my land." She waved a tight fist at the image, dispelling the illusion as easily as she'd conjured it.

"It's growing?" Zantry asked, eyebrows knitting.

"There is a shift in energy, sometimes dramatic, sometimes subtle, and the shadows expand. We have not yet detected for certain where it directs, but aye, it is growing."

Zantry leaned back, his eyes devoid of emotion. "What about patrol watch? Have you set any?"

Queen Titania's jaws clenched, but it was Lee who answered. "The animals that are unfortunate to cross into the zone are caught in some trance. If they stay long enough, they perish slowly."

He glanced at Lee, his focus sharp and intent. "I'll assume you've measured the frequency around this patch. Does it fluctuate?"

"It's not stable. During day time it's constant, but later it fractures, a dramatic increase at two opposite points, while it drops at another, seemingly at random. The instability turns chaotic, but it does not last for long."

"How frequent?"

"Too frequent," Queen Titania replied, her eyes tight with anger. "Every time the sun meets the horizon, an imbalance takes place deep in the earth, and energy begins to roil and drop, while above surface it fractures and rises before disappearing without a trace. It goes on until the sun breaks the horizon once more. By the time the sun is high above the castle, the patch has grown in size and the energy surrounding this deathtrap has lowered considerably. As the sun travels west, the energy keeps re-charging, only to fracture once more when the sun meets the horizon."

Zantry frowned at the far wall, his eyes distant.

"We believe in the middle of the patch is a vortex, a slither that opens during nightfall," Lee said.

"Can you show where the middle is?" Zantry asked Titania.

"Nay, it's too discordant for projections, but we calculate the midpoint by the circumference of the dead zone. We cannot get near enough to it to see what is there, and I cannot send my awareness that deep without feeling the discordance deep in my bones. Even from afar, I can feel it, like a sickness, a plague mutating and feeding from the land." Titania's posture was stiff, as if she abhorred admitting this weakness to anyone.

"Two of our best warriors, Madrigue and Ladrigue were dispatched to observe as much as they can withstand. They have yet to return to report." Oberon's words had Zantry looking up.

"Are they overdue?"

"Nay, not yet."

"It is different from when you first arrived," Titania said, the image of the dead land reappearing in front of us. Zantry leaned forward, his eyes scanning everything. "How so?"

"The energy is being drained from the environment without any obvious manifestation. Whatever it is Remo is doing, he is preventing the beings from taking form."

At this, Queen Titania glanced at me, and all the blood drained from my face. "An early patrol returned yesterday with one of Remo's agent in toe. He'd been captured while wandering along the patch of death, seemingly in a trance. When interrogated, Remo's pawn refused to answer any question."

Zantry frowned. "Where's the agent now?"

"Dead," Oberon replied, and Zantry returned his attention to the image. A well of dread filled my stomach and a quiver resonated through my being.

"When did this start?" Zantry asked.

"We are not sure. We first felt its presence when the death had eaten through three acres of the land, two moons past."

"How much do you estimate it's taken already?"

"Thus far, I believe over one thousand acres," Oberon replied.

The image disrupted, slower this time, as if it took effort to close the window. Zantry looked down at his hands, his expression troubled. Then he looked at me, his eyes conveying nothing of what he was thinking. "And she's here because?"

Every eye turned to look at me. The quiver turned into full blown-tremors. I took a deep breath that did nothing to help calm my nerves.

A sinking feeling overtook me, a sense I was about to be doomed forever, and I had to clasp my hands together to stop them from shaking.

Queen Titania met my eyes and held, hers full of unforgiving judgment. "It was agreed that the promised child would be nurtured in this court, a subject to my throne, to be educated as a warrior."

Whatever blood still circulated my brain left my head in a rush. On its wake an icy chill permeated my veins, leaving me lightheaded and unable to think.

Zantry cocked his head to the side, studying me with his cool expression. Gone was the friendly guy with the warm and fun smile I met in New York.

"What's so special about her?"

"She is the daughter of a powerful Dhiultadh, and granddaughter to Odra the Third."

"And a human," Zantry pointed out, baffled. "Her blood is diluted. What can she possibly do, even with thorough training? You have far more skilled subjects and fearsome warriors."

"Brutal force is not what we need," Queen Titania replied. "We tried this method before, and it did not work."

"So you think throwing a half-human to Remo will stop him?"

"We have gathered extensive knowledge about Remo's workings. With the proper guidance, we believe Fosch's daughter will become a worthy opponent and freeze, if not destroy, the portal permanently."

A silence so heavy it could demolish a building followed her words, broken only when Zantry snorted rudely. "Her?" he flicked a finger toward me. "What are you seeing that I'm not?"

"She is the granddaughter of Odra the Third, the daughter of Yoncey Fosch," Lee retorted.

"And a human," he repeated, his eyes moving from Lee to Queen Titania. "What aren't you saying?" he demanded. "I thought only an offspring who carried a combination of my blood and the blood of an energy manipulator could freeze the portal. And I know how that combination feels in an aura. I met Cara, and Roxanne's aura has nothing compared to it."

Cara, Logan's mate. Arianna's daughter.

Zantry shifted and leaned closer, and instinctively, I leaned back. His eyes scanned my face with an intensity that almost felt physical.

"Whose daughter is she?" Zantry asked, his voice carrying a tone I couldn't decipher. I choked on air, but no one paid me any attention. I didn't think I could get more nervous than I already was, but I was wrong. My stomach quivered with anxiety, and I had this urge to find the nearest bathroom.

"She is the offspring of Dhiultadh Yoncey Fosch and a mortal woman."

Zantry's eyes moved between Queen Titania and Oberon, trying to figure them out. "You know I know how this works, right?" When silence was all the answer he got, he demanded in a quiet tone, "What happened to Arianna?" And even I didn't miss the suspicion lacing his words.

"She disappeared around the time you did. Speculation was that you two ran off together."

Zantry waved a hand in the air. "She didn't come with me."

"You should ask her lover then, the leader of the Unseelie Dhiultadh Clan," Lee suggested.

He shook his head. "Until I came back, they thought she had been with me. Now they think I killed her." Zantry's lips twitched humorlessly, his eyes cold. He waited for a response, but none came. "What do you know?" He glared at Lee and Oberon, before shifting to Titania's dangerously flashing eyes.

The atmosphere in the room suddenly filled with crackling power, but Zantry didn't back down.

"Tell me, damn it. Where did she disappear to?"

Lee stiffened, her eyes narrowing at his tone. "Are you insinuating we have inside knowledge about Arianna's disappearance?"

"It's insinuating if I were dancing around the topic," he said tightly. "Since I returned, you are the only people not inquiring after her or accusing me of foul play. So forgive me if I'm blunt here and ask, did this court have a hand at Arianna's disappearance or not?"

"We did not," Titania replied, her voice frostier than an iceberg, "Arianna's disappearance is none of my or my court's doing, Zantry Akinzo."

"But you know what happened to her."

Queen Titania narrowed her eyes, and thunder rumbled nearby. "I do not like your insolence, Zantry Akinzo, nor am I obligated to tolerate it."

He inclined his head. "I apologize. I meant no disrespect. Do you have any knowledge of what happened to Arianna? Where she is?"

"Arianna is not the main concern at hand. Our world is dying, and Dhiultadh Yoncey Fosch's daughter will be primed to rid us from this intrusive foe," Lee replied, her eyes flashing with furious fire.

"We allowed you to witness this meeting because we value your opinion. If you have nothing useful to contribute you may leave." Titania's tone was icy, her eyes furious.

Zantry studied her for a moment, then shifted to look at Oberon and Lee's implacable expression.

His posture relaxed. "Tell me this, at least then. What do you suppose Arianna would make of this strategy to prime Fosch's daughter, a human hybrid, to defeat Remo?"

A moment passed before Oberon answered. "We wished for Arianna to be present when we prepared her." his brown eyes had a calculating gleam when he spoke, and his next words revealed why. "Perhaps you could aid in her preparation instead."

Zantry hesitated a second. "And do you believe she would have agreed that Fosch's daughter is the best candidate for this task?"

"Ay, Arianna believed this child would be the one to end Remo and undo the portal," Lee announced, her expression smug.

"How? Wait–Are you saying Arianna was in on this plan?"

When none of the Fee replied, Zantry turned to glare at me as if this was all my fault. He traced a hand in the air near my head before recoiling, realization sparking in his eyes.

"How old are you?" he demanded.

"What–Twenty-two. I'll be twenty-three in a few months."

Zantry turned his glare at Lee. "Arianna disappeared around the time I did, twenty-six and a half years ago. How could she be aware of Roxanne's existence? Where is she?"

"You have too many questions, Zantry Akinzo," Titania said, and another rumble of thunder sounded from nearby. "Curiosity does not become you."

As if just now realizing he was treading on thin ice, Zantry hesitated before speaking again. "I just want to know where she is. Come on, tell me. Is she here, in the Sidhe land?"

My heart clenched for him.

"Nay," Oberon replied. Even I didn't miss the certainty in his tone. He knew. They all did.

Zantry's jaw clenched, no doubt picking on the same nuances I did. "Alright. Tell me this: Did she believe that Roxanne could be taught to use and manipulate energy fluent enough to manage a portal?"

When no one answered, Zantry looked around sharply, one hand clenched into a tight fist. It was the only outward indication he was losing patience with this bunch. "You ask for my assistance, yet you refuse to answer some basic questions. Did Arianna believe Roxanne could be taught to manipulate energy enough to manage a portal or not?"

"Ay, she believed with the proper training this child would be the one to rid us from your other kin, as well as destroy the portal," Queen Titania replied.

"And so, I ask again, whose daughter is she?"

"We told you, Zantry Akinzo, and you know we do not lie. This scion is the daughter of Dhiultadh Yoncey Fosch and a mortal woman."

Zantry leaned back, his expression thoughtful. "You know there aren't many possible ways for a person, a preternatural, to manipulate energy at will. There are even fewer ways to become fluent enough to defeat Remo, much less manage a portal, so, please don't insult my intelligence."

I held my breath, waiting for a blow I knew must be coming at any time.

"You lose our time with your suspicions and insolence. Will you aid prime this child for the task at hand?" Queen Titania demanded, a thunderous boom following her question.

Zantry tilted his head to the side, looking at me with narrowed eyes. "Can you see energy?"

He knew I couldn't. I shook my head, my throat too dry for words.

"There's your answer," Zantry said with a grand gesture.

Queen Titania leaned forward, her eyes flashing with fire. "Ay or nay?"

"Tell me this first," he said, "Is Arianna coming back? Is she alive?"

Titania leaned back, her cold eyes assessing him. "Nay, she is not alive, and she is not coming back."

Zantry's face fell, his eyes stricken with grief and guilt. "You know that for a fact," he said, but he didn't wait for a response. He got up and stepped away, head lowered, back turned to us.

We all waited for him to come to terms with his grief, the knowledge his friend had died and wasn't coming back.

When he returned, his eyes gleamed with determination, and that determination was focused on me.

"I have one condition." He glanced at both Oberon and Queen Titania, waited for their nod of agreement before saying, "Once I assist prepare Roxanne as best as I'm capable, I want to know all you know happened to Arianna while I was gone."

Chapter Thirty-Eight

The feeling of doom clung to me like a second skin; no matter what happened next, no miracle would save me from a horrible end. Zantry warned the Seelie queen not to expect any quality results, though he'd assured her he'd do his best to teach me how to manipulate and bend energy at will, something he didn't believe possible.

When I arrived home, still reeling from my impending doom, I found Logan sitting on the sofa, feet propped on the coffee table. The moment my feet touched the hardwood floor, I sensed him, but it took a second for my brain to *understand the fact* he was there.

He held the *Guidebook of Preternaturals* in one hand, a cup of coffee in the other. Atop the table were other empty mugs, the dried, reminiscent drags of coffee stuck at the bottom. His clothes were rumpled, eyes tired, the skin underneath dark with fatigue, cheeks unshaven.

He'd been here for a while. Our eyes met and, despite the tired, disheveled appearance, his were sharp, shrewd. His feet dropped from the coffee table with a thud, but the mug and guidebook went down slowly. He took in my attire, the shifting colors, the elaborate hairstyle, then moved to Zantry standing beside me, dressed in Seelie finery as well. I could guess the thoughts rampaging in his head by the darkening of his eyes, the tightening of his lips.

For a brief second, I could also read the emotions in his eyes, before he reached a conclusion and they turned cold. I'm not sure if it was betrayal I read or disappointment–or perhaps disapproval. It had been so fleeting, I could barely discern it.

When his gaze met mine again, his eyes were empty. "I see you haven't taken my advice to heart. I didn't think you'd discard it so easily."

"Logan..." it's not what you think, I *wanted* to say, but the words remained stuck in my throat. Did I owe him an explanation?

"No words?" He took in Zantry's attire before shifting back and doing a slow perusal of my outfit. He stood then, and Zantry shifted. His stance was relaxed, but the aggression in the room amped a few degrees. Logan must have sensed it too, because his eyes narrowed and I could almost taste the refreshing coolness of his anger.

"Did he kidnap you, or force you in any capacity?" he asked.

I could tell he was ready to go for blood if I said yes. "No." I knew this reply was all he'd be willing to hear. He was giving me the benefit of the doubt, a chance to tell him that this wasn't what it looked like, but only on his terms. As far as he was concerned, I was either in cahoots with the enemy, or I'd been forced. Nothing I said would persuade him otherwise. And I was not telling him Zantry offered to help find Mwara. Call me paranoid, but I didn't think that would bode well with anyone. And I was not telling him about the Seelie Queen's plan for my future.

"Then my presence here isn't needed. In fact, I may be interrupting whatever remaining time you two may have left."

I stiffened, my anger surging. "What are you doing here, inside my locked apartment anyway?"

"I thought you'd gone missing, too. I called, and you didn't answer. And then you didn't come home either. Evidently, I had no reason to worry." His eyes moved between Zantry and me, took in the Seelie finery once more, as if he couldn't believe what he was seeing. His lips stretched into a sardonic smile, his eyes icy-cold. "Were you two lazing off in some exotic world?"

"You sound jealous," Zantry taunted, and Logan took a step toward him, hands clenched.

"Whoa!" I moved between them, not sure what I'd do if they came to blows.

Logan halted, his eyes meeting mine for a blink, his jaw tight. A muscle flexed on his jaw, then he pivoted and left without another word.

My shoulders sagged when the front door slammed with a final boom, and I wasn't sure if I was relieved or disappointed. With an unsteady hand, I rubbed the nape of my neck, trying to ease the tension lodged there. That was all I needed. Now they'd think I took off to enjoy sometime before I had to account for their missing scion.

Zantry exhaled slowly, relaxed the crackling energy from around him. "I'm sorry about that. If you want, I can go after him, tell him you asked me to take you to the Low Lands to search for clues."

"And got dressed like this for *what*?" I shook my head. "Forget it. He's drawn his conclusion and nothing I say is going to change his mind."

Zantry murmured something I didn't get and didn't care to know. I moved to the kitchen and picked up my phone. The battery was dead, so I busied myself plugging it to the charger. After a moment I turned it on and checked the time and date. My scowl darkened even more. All I had left were four days to bring back Mwara. Six days. I'd lost six days in the Seelie Castle.

Bracing my hands on the counter, I lowered my head and tried to clear my thoughts. Sometimes it felt as if the world conspired against me.

"Do you want me to leave?" Zantry asked from behind me.

I waved a hand toward the living room. "Make yourself at home. It doesn't matter anymore. I'm not finding her. In a few days, it will all be over."

"What about Titania?"

"I should sic her on the clan. It'd be fun." I jerked up a shoulder in an awkward shrug. I was too edgy to be smooth. "I guess she's not my problem." With a dry chuckle, I added, "I'm not sure which is worse, Titania's plans or the clan's ultimatum."

Zantry exhaled a big sigh and came closer. "Look, we'll figure this out, Roxanne. I'll help you."

"You shouldn't make promises you can't keep."

That's when it hit me, and it hit me hard. I was going to die, no matter how hard I tried, no matter how much help I got.

If not by the hands of the clan, then by whatever the Seelie had planned for me. Or if by some miraculous chance I got as far as Remo, he wouldn't let me live.

"What a mess," I murmured, my heart growing numb. An emptiness I hadn't felt for a long time made its presence known, and I welcomed the reprieve.

"Roxanne, please look at me."

When I turned and met his dark blue eyes, it was with a detachment I hadn't felt for a long time. Zantry's pupils contracted and sadness flashed in them before resolve took over.

"I never make promises I can't keep," he said fiercely. "I'll help you see this through. Whatever happens from now on, I'll be there for you." He looked so earnest, his words so sincere, I half believed him. Could he really do something? I searched his eyes, some of the iciness numbing my core starting to thaw. He meant what he was saying. Maybe it was his words, maybe it was the conviction in his voice, maybe it was something else I didn't want to examine, but I couldn't help my next move.

I stepped close, welcoming the static that jumped between us. I touched a hand to his shoulder, my eyes searching his for something I couldn't name. Zantry closed the distance between us, his arms going around my waist. I let my head drop on his shoulder and breathed in his scent. He leaned his cheek against the side of my head, and exhaled a long sigh. "From now on, Roxanne, you can count on me. I'll always be there." He smelled of lemon verbena and man, and before I knew it, my lips were brushing against his neck. Moving up to his jugular, behind his ear, then down again, to the edge of his shirt's collar, where I discovered a silver chain. He shuddered once, and I leaned back to look at him, our eyes inches apart. His were full of emotion–grief, hurt, longing, hunger.

I looped my arms around his neck, brushed my fingers through his hair. It was silky, the strands heavy. A shadowy stubble covered his cheeks, and I brushed the palm of my hand over it, enjoying the feel of stubble against my skin.

So beautiful.

His arms tightened around my waist, pulling our bodies closer, but instead of bringing his head down, all he did was wait for my next move, eyes hooded. So I pulled him closer.

The moment our lips touched electricity sparked between us, and a pleasant hum began to throb within my veins. I brushed my lips against his once, twice, then opened up and let him in.

Hmmm. So good, so… right. Like coming home after a cold and tiresome day to relax in front of a warm hearth. It was calm and soothing, and my heart ached for more.

His lips were soft and slow, but the moment our tongues touched, everything changed. My back hit the counter, our bodies touching in all the right places, and his lips became demanding. The calm, soothing mood suddenly changed to urgent and furious.

Kissing Zantry was like facing down a hurricane: I was certain I'd be swept away and lost forever.

We kissed like there was no tomorrow, no future, no later. His hand moved up my sides, brushed my neck, tangled in my hair, disrupting Bennty's bun before combing it down with his fingers.

Then his lips left mine and I opened my eyes to find his deep blue ones, full of turmoil, just a few inches away.

God, he was perfect.

His breath was hot on my face, and my lips tingled from our kiss. I thought he'd step back and apologize, instead, his head angled sideways, and his lips traced a path from my lips to my ear and back again before brushing against my lips. The kiss was slow now, made sweeter for the tender way he stroked my hair, the way his thumbs brushed my cheeks.

Then he did step back, and I knew he read the disappointment in my eyes as clearly as I could see the regret in his.

"We should save this for a time when we're not this emotional."

I nodded in agreement, aware a next time would never come. Instead of saying so, I said something that had been stuck in my head ever since Queen Titania announced it:

"Odra, my grandmother," I asked, my voice unfamiliar to my ears, "why is she so important?"

"Because she was a powerful earth witch."

Oh? "Does that make my father half-witch?"

"Yes. But the joining of Odra and Bran was deliberate. I wasn't around when it happened, but I understood it was an arrangement to benefit both the coven and the Unseelie Dhiultadh clan"

"And she could manipulate energy?"

"Yes. I heard she was great with runes and sigils, and fluent with the ones connected to earth. But I never met her. Arianna knew her though, spoke highly of her. They were competitive."

"How did she die?"

"It's said a rival coven killed her with some sort of poison spell. It was never proven, and the fact the rival clan swore their innocence with a blood oath kept the clan from seeking revenge."

I mulled his words over, trying to understand. "You said there weren't many ways for me to manipulate energy." I waited, and Zantry took a step back, tucked his hands into his pockets. "The strongest of the Fee can manipulate energy, but even they need something to concentrate the molecules and atoms, and for that, they use talismans–stones, staffs, crystals–though anything less than harmonical to nature is blasphemy. Their power comes from the elements, nature and life." I recalled back in the dungeon when Drozelle shielded the prisoner's presence from the ether. She'd held a dark rock in her hand, a talisman. And Queen Titania, she had a staff with her, a black one. Was it carved from a special rock?

"Queen Titania has control of all elements, as well as fire, ice, plants and animals. She is powerful, but when it comes to manipulating energy, she can't do it without several talismans."

I nodded and he went on, "All Sidhe can see into the ether and higher dimensions, even the lowly subjects. In comparison, all Dhiultadh, no matter how weak or strong, can see into the ether, or fourth dimension, but not any higher." I nodded again, and Zantry chuckled at whatever he read in my expression.

"Consider this, in terms of dimensions and energy manipulation," He pressed the tips of his fingers together and spread his palms apart, forming the tip of a triangle. "In the hierarchy of the preternatural, you have the Sidhe at the top, capable to manipulate energy tied to whatever element they can control. They can see the fourth and fifth dimension, no matter the cast or how strong they are.

Below come both Dhiultadh clans, and the strongest learn to master a handful of runes or sigils. Those who have lived a long time learn to construct wards, but often they are basic defensive works, nothing too complex or offensive. None of the Dhiultadh are fluent with energy manipulation, though they can read their patterns in the ether, no matter how weak or strong. They can't, however, see into the fifth dimension, not even the strongest of them."

I nodded. "Do they need talismans too?"

"Yes, they do."

"Who comes after the Dhiultadh?"

"The witches, the mages and any magic wielder. Those learn to manipulate energy tied to their elements without the help of talismans, but they can't power a working, or construct a ward without the help of a group effort. For example, an air mage can manipulate the atoms and molecules in the air currents and provoke a soft breeze to become a strong wind, but without a group effort, they wouldn't be able to construct even a small ward."

"But can they see into the fifth dimension?"

"Some can, others can't."

"And after the mages and witches?"

Zantry angled his head. "After them comes the preternatural community in general, and they're all at the bottom of the food chain, with most unable to even see the ether."

"So where do you fit in this pyramid?" I asked, curious.

Zantry gave me a wry smile and said, "Way at the top. I'm a being of energy, Roxanne, capable of bending and shaping energy at will." He waved a hand and said, "Of course, that's the food chain for energy manipulation only. Many of those preternaturals at the bottom of the food chain are as strong as a Dhiultadh." His eyes gleamed with humor and mischief as he added, "Unless you want me to count the preternaturals from distant planets; In that case we'd need to shuffle the hierarchy and start again. I'd say the elves would come toe to toe with the Sidhe at the top, but then we have the chimera and Volech."

I raised my palms and took a step back. "No, no. I get it," I hurried to say. Zantry chuckled and I continued, "But my father, he was different?" Because the impression I'd got from the conversation today was that being Fosch's daughter meant something.

Zantry sobered. "The combination of earth witch and Dhiultadh gave your father an extra edge. I think he could manipulate energy to his will, but no one really knew how fluent he was. That was something he kept to his inner circle, if not entirely to himself."

I mulled over his words for a moment, trying to figure where I fit in all this. "So, I'm a Dhiultadh," I began, "the daughter of Yoncey Fosch, granddaughter to Odra the third. But I can't see energy, which I gather means I'm low in that food chain you just explained."

"Hmmm. Maybe." Zantry hesitated before adding, "You can sense energy."

I angled my head, trying to decipher what was I heard in his tone. "Do you think the Sidhe know that?"

"They know something. They're banking a lot on you beating Remo's plans."

I swallowed, shook away the feeling of impending doom and asked the million-dollar question, "What could they possibly know?"

"I'm not sure. I know they're dancing around the truth, and they believe you are capable of doing what everyone else has failed. And if they say Arianna was in on the plan... God, I can't imagine what happened to her," he murmured, his words filled with sorrow, his grief a living beast with tiny pincers, pinching and pinching and pinching. I took an instinctive step back, unable to fathom how he could stand it.

"Hmmm. What does it take? I mean, to freeze the portal or defeat Remo?" I asked, trying to take his mind off his grief.

He exhaled, a big gush of air that seemed to empty him from inside and rubbed a hand over his face. The gesture was that of defeat, but at least the bite of the grief throttled down a few degrees. "There are a few theories for that, none we could prove without the real portal. Arianna and I once joined with the Sidhe and froze a few portals to some inhospitable planets. We varied on methods and strategies and concluded one of us and one of them would be enough to accomplish the feat." Zantry glanced at the closed window, and I wondered if he was remembering something or thinking about leaving. The drapes were closed, shutting the late-night traffic from view, but not the noise. "Then Arianna had another theory." He fell quiet, and I waited for him to continue. "It's hard for my kind to procreate. We thought it wasn't possible, but Arianna found a way. We never discussed the details," he smiled, a humorless movement of lips that didn't reach his eyes, "because I always figured when the time came, if the time ever came, and I decided I wanted a child of my own, I'd have enough time to ask her."

I took a step forward, but Zantry stepped back, not wanting to be comforted. "She thought if our powers combined could freeze the portal, there was a chance a child born with both genes would destroy the original portal, or at the very least, freeze it permanently. It didn't have to be a Dhiultadh, or one of the Sidhe Fee, just one of us and a strong preternatural capable to manipulate energy at some level. It was just a theory Arianna and I had, but we knew it'd work."

"Cara."

"Yes. Archer tried to keep Arianna's identity from the clan so word wouldn't reach Remo, but most everyone knew they were an item, and it wasn't hard to put one and one together. When Cara was old enough, Arianna and I started training her, and when she learned the basics, we tested our theory on real portals. She was still young and her powers were still developing, but we could tell she'd be able to do it on her own." He looked down at his empty hands before adding in a much quieter tone, "When I came back, I thought she'd be ready to fight, that all her abilities would be fully developed and honed to perfection."

And he'd come back to find both Cara and Arianna had died.

"But how does it work? Do you blast the portal until it freezes?" I asked, trying to understand.

"No, a portal is where a leeway ends. Imagine a train traveling from point A to point B. The leeway is the distance that connects both points, the portal a field of energy that keeps the leeway from spilling over the endpoint and scattering. To freeze a portal, you need to take the energy of that portal into you, until it no longer has enough to function properly."

I frowned at him, confused beyond belief. "But if it's as simple as that, why can't you..."

Zantry shook his head, smiling faintly. "If one of the trio tried it alone, we'd only merge with the leeway and redirect the portal into ourselves. It'd be a disaster. Imagine a portal supposed to open in the Sidhe land opening here, or at a restaurant, or wherever one of us happened to be at the time?"

"But Cara could do it on her own?"

"She could, yeah. We weren't sure if she'd be able to take in the entire portal, but we knew she could take enough to render it inactive for a time."

I thought of all I'd learned, still unable to make sense of everything.

"Why can't we just kill Remo? Because if Arianna died and isn't coming back," I gave him an apologetic look, "and the Sidhe know that, then this means there's also a way to kill Remo. Why not just kill him and then when we're not so pressed for time, deal with the portal?"

"I don't think the Sidhe know how to do that, else they'd already have mounted an attack against Remo. No, whatever happened to Arianna either can't be done again or Queen Titania doesn't know how."

"There must be a way," I murmured, thinking. "I mean, maybe there's something Arianna discovered while you were in the PSS, something that enables me, the daughter of a Dhiultadh and a human, to do what you previously believed wasn't possible, and because you weren't available, she told the Seelie queen?"

Zantry's brows furrowed, and he chewed on his lip as he thought about it. Then he shook his head and said, "She knows–knew how the Sidhe functioned. If she found something out, she'd have told someone else about it too, then told another someone to ensure the information wouldn't be misused or lost, and someone would have known to bring me the information the moment I returned."

"Maybe she thought you weren't coming back?" I offered, a headache brewing behind my eyes.

"I always come back," he said, his voice grim, his eyes distant.

"Well, maybe she told the Seelie court and someone else, and this someone else has yet to find out you're back."

"Maybe," he conceded after a moment. "Still, I can't see how you fit in. It takes a lot for a person, a preternatural, to freely manipulate the atoms and molecules in the ether, bend them to his will. To freeze the portal you'd need not only to learn the ins and outs of all the runes and sigils to use, but you'd need to be exact and fast, even for a small, weak portal. And I get what you mean, but I don't think that's it. If there was another way to freeze or destroy a portal and a Dhiultadh could do it, the Sidhe wouldn't sit back and wait for you to become available. They'd have found someone else to fit that slot, no matter what they'd need to do to see it done. No, it's you, and not the Dhiultadh in you."

We both fell quiet, lost to our thoughts. My mind resembled a chaotic pool of misshapen wants, needs, regrets and wishes. I regretted meeting Lee in the Low Lands. No, I wished I had been sharp enough to spend the boon she offered to ask for a way home instead of all that stupid information about my father and his delusional mate. I startled, recalling the tale, and glanced sideways at Zantry, his eyes focused at the far wall.

"Huh, Zantry, back when I was stuck in the Low Lands, Lee told me something..." I trailed off. Zantry whipped around, his eyes sharp.

"What did she say?"

I rubbed my hands together, unsure why I was nervous. "She said my father claimed my mother wasn't human when they met, and that he accused Oberon of tampering with her essence. She told me my father went as far as declare her as his mate."

At this, Zantry's eyes narrowed, "Did she say your father was wrong? Think carefully, I want to know her exact words, not what you interpreted them to mean."

I thought back to that time and shook my head. "I was half dead; I can't remember her exact words." I tried, but the more I forced myself, the foggier her words became. "The way I understood, she believed my father lost his mind."

Suspicion sparked in Zantry's eyes. "Lost his mind how?"

"I don't know. For claiming my mother as his mate. I need to think about it, see if I can remember her words."

"Did she deny your mother being his mate?"

I lowered my head and closed my eyes, thinking hard. "No, she said if there was a mating bond, she couldn't sense it."

Zantry was thoughtful for a moment before he said, "If the mating bond wasn't yet acknowledged, they wouldn't have been able to sense it."

"So she could've been his mate?"

"If she was, she wouldn't have been human."

"Lee said my father accused Oberon of tampering with my mother's essence. When I asked her if he did, she was insulted. She said no Sidhe possessed this capability."

Zantry slumped back against the counter. "That's true. If your mother didn't fit with the bargain, Oberon wouldn't have called it in."

He turned away, hands clenched over the counter, head lowered. The tension that had been emanating from him a moment ago turned flat, as if he'd unplugged his emotions.

To his back, I added, "She said Oberon denied sending my mother to my father, that their meeting was none of his doing either."

He raised a shoulder, let it drop, plowed a hand through his hair before turning to look at me. "That's probably all true. I can't see the Unseelie Dhiultadh not stepping in unless it's all true." But he came closer, studied me for a long time without saying a word, eyes unfocused.

After a long while, he waved a hand above my head once, took a step back.

"What is it?" I asked quietly.

He shook his head, frowned. "The energies that surround you, they're consistent to the energy patterns surrounding a human aura, but they're bound tighter, considerably thicker. I noticed it for the first time that day in the Low Lands when you were hurt. At first, I thought this was due to the poison, then I wondered if it was the residue of some working, but it hasn't worn any thinner or changed in any way." His eyes unfocused, "I can also sense the Dhiultadh in you, like this field of invisible heat, but your aura is completely human. I've never seen anything like it before." He opened his mouth to say more, shook his head again, reached a hand toward my face but didn't touch me. Static zinged between us, and there was a tug on my senses, a pull that turned prickly, growing stronger as the static between us grew.

I bit my lip and clenched my fist against the bite of his energy, forced myself to stay still as he continued prickling and tugging at my core. The smell of ozone grew thick and the metallic taste of blood coated my throat. I gasped, unable to stop myself when that prickling turned hot and burned something within. The static stopped at once. Zantry lowered his hand and stepped back. He looked troubled.

I rubbed my hands together and swallowed bile.

"What is it?" I asked, my voice unsteady.

Still frowning, he said, "I think there's something fused to your aura. It mimics the patterns, doubling it in an organized way. It could be a masking spell, but the patterns underneath are exactly the same as the one on top." His frown deepened and he came closer.

Dread made my hands shake, so I laced my fingers together. "Can you undo it?"

Zantry studied me—my aura—for a long moment before he shook his head. "I don't know. I just probed around the patterns and it caused you pain. Perhaps there's nothing wrong with it." But there was doubt in his voice as he continued to study my aura. "It's like the patterns flow inward instead of looping around, as if the chain tangled on something within. But instead of breaking the continuous rhythm as it should've, it formed a new one. I've never seen anything like this before. And I can't think of a purpose, or a person capable of meddling with an aura and not killing the individual in the long run."

"Maybe this is some new development? No one's ever commented on the patterns of my aura before," I offered.

"Because the patterns are visible in the fifth dimension. In the ether, your aura looks like an ordinary human aura, without a trace of the Dhiultadh within."

He paced the small length of the kitchen then, and I watched him, unable to formulate a cohesive thought. When he finally stopped, determination had replaced the frustration from a moment ago. "There's a lot I don't know to make any assumptions at this time. Whether there's something hinky in the pattern of your aura or not, it'll hold until we're not so pressed for time."

I nodded, rubbed my hands over the soft material of the skirt and gave him a valiant, somewhat wobbly smile, trying to ignore the dam about to break over my head. "Ok, where do we go next?"

Zantry's eyes darkened as he took a step closer, tucked a lock of hair behind my ear. "I have this strong urge to box you up and take you somewhere safe and far, far away," he said, his eyes intense and warm, "Away from here, away from all these power-hungry people, from the clan, from the Sidhe Fee. But the smart thing to do is to find Mwara first. Dead or alive, she's our first priority."

"Where could she be?" I whispered, a horrible dread growing inside my chest. "There are so many places to look, so many worlds she could have gone to, so many predators that could have found her first, and only four days left."

Zantry touched the tip of his index to my lips. "So we'll use our time wisely. You're not doing it alone. I will be with you all the way. I will do my best to see this through and help you come out the other end." His knuckles brushed over my cheek, "This, Roxanne, I promise you."

My throat constricted, but I swallowed through it. His eyes held a certain sadness that tugged at me, a touch of grief I knew stemmed from the fact he hadn't been there for his friend when she needed him the most.

I reached for him, touched a hand to his cheek. "I'm sorry about Arianna and all the things you missed because of Remo and the PSS."

His eyes softened, the violet a dark blue, and he caught my hand, pressed it against his cheek before bringing it to his mouth and brushing his lips against my palm. "Thank you."

Chapter Thirty-Nine

Zantry stayed the night. He slept in the spare bedroom where Vicky slept when she stayed over. It was comforting, to know I wasn't alone. To know I could count on someone to stand with me, to fight for me without expecting anything in return.

In the morning, he took me to the Low Lands. I had nothing of Mwara to give him a general sense of the child, so we searched for the energy of a Dhiultadh. He searched, I tagged along. I had no idea how this energy-tracing thing worked. I did feel out the place the way Zantry told me to, but for me, the place was as dead and sense-less as it had always been.

To Zantry, however, it was a bouquet of scents and imprints. Yet, although there was plenty for him to find, most he recognized as the lingering presence of people who'd come searching for her.

At one point, Zantry sensed the residual of fear and we tried to follow the "ethereal imprint", but we lost it before we could decipher anything. The problem with the Low Lands was even footprints were hard to find, considering the ground was nothing but cracked and packed earth.

We shifted back and forth, from alleyway to the Low Lands to alleyway, found nothing to follow, nothing to indicate where Mwara had skipped to, where she had dropped back.

When we returned home, an entire day had gone by. The next day, we resumed hopping leeways, jumping back and forth between planets. It came to a point where shifting with Zantry was like a twist on a waltz: predictable and pleasant.

Back and forth we went, the time difference sometimes playing in our favor, sometimes against. Twice more Zantry sensed the lingering presence of fear and, although we'd search widely from that point, going around in ever-widening circles, of a child we found nothing.

We even went to other planets, ones that weren't as close or parallel to the Low Lands or earth, but those with direct leeway paths, and easy enough for a child of eleven to follow. The waltz here was longer, two turns, perhaps a small dip, but it was still pleasant. We covered so much ground, I was afraid we'd return and discover my time was up, but all we lost on that second day was half a day.

We searched three planets, one intercepting with the Tristan Star, where animals were either monstrously disproportional or little furry things that made you want to pet them. A second planet with rainbow-colored vegetation that breathed and sighed whenever we passed by. And a third planet creepy for no other reason than the fact it was similar to Earth's topography, except for three low-hanging moons. They looked so close to the ground, I had a feeling if I jumped high enough, I'd be able to touch them.

Despite the discovery and the knowledge this was all waiting to be claimed and conquered, I found no joy in it, all my senses oppressed by the knowledge we were running out of time, and no traces of Mwara could be found.

We skipped enough leeways to emulate a path to Sacramento–it only took half an hour–and again, there was nothing to find but those lingering traces of fear that we weren't even sure belonged to the kid. We also skimmed the streets and alleyways of Manhattan with no result.

Now, all I had were two days. And that was it, I told myself while I prepared sandwiches. We arrived, starving and aching, and me in desperate need to use the john and have a long hot shower.

Zantry lounged on the sofa, one arm thrown around his face, the other drawing imaginary doodles on the floor with a tall finger. I hadn't rested or slept a wink for the past two days. Hell, I'd hardly eaten anything.

I prepared two turkey and cheese sandwiches, sighing every few minutes for no apparent reason, placed them in the toaster, then filled a bowl with ground meat for Frizz. Slumping against the counter, I watched him eat. "Do you know where Mwara is, Frizz?"

In the living room, Zantry lowered his arm and stared at the gargoyle with sharp interest.

Frizz's ears flicked back and he glanced at me, his shell-shaped dark eyes empty of any emotion, though I could sense his weariness. Maybe I should leave him home or send him to Vicky.

"No, master."

I sighed, not surprised. Frizz resumed eating, assuming conversation over.

Zantry stood and approached the gargoyle, a stalkerish air about him. His eyes held such sharp interest, even I watched him warily. Frizz's tail shifted left to right once, but aside from that and the flick of one ear, frizz didn't acknowledge him.

"Ask him if he knows who she is."

Startled, I glanced down at frizz. "Do you know who Mwara is, frizz?"

"Yes, master." He scooped the last of the meat from the bowl.

A jolt shocked me with his answer, but it seemed I wasn't on the same page as Zantry. "That's it. Let's go," he said.

I looked down at Frizz, feeling we were on the verge of something, yet unable to reach it. "What is it?"

"Come on, I'll explain on the way." He threw me my jacket. I grabbed my keys from the counter and followed, almost losing balance when Zantry skipped back to get both scolding sandwiches and a wad of napkins. "Can't leave the food behind," he explained with a sheepish smile.

As he pulled open the door, Diggy was raising his arm to ring the doorbell. His hand froze midair, his hazel eyes frosting at the sight of Zantry, before shifting to me, standing behind, one arm inside the jacket, the other still uncovered.

"Diggy," I said, shrugging on the jacket and zipping it up to my neck. "What are you doing here?"

His arm dropped, his hands dipped inside his jacket pocket. His lips formed a grim line as he looked from Zantry to me. "I figured I'd come and offer you some assistance, seeing your training was still ongoing and you have no tracking experience." His eyes shifted to Zantry, and before he could back off, Zantry cut in, "Good, let's go. Time is running out." He handed me one of the sandwiches before he moved around Diggy and bit into his, saying with a full mouth, "I'd offer you the other sandwich, Vemourly, but I'm too hungry to be polite."

Diggy raised an eyebrow at me. I shrugged, locked the front door and followed after Zantry. I didn't have time to argue about traitors or who I could or couldn't associate with. Seriously, I didn't even care. I took a huge bite of my sandwich—a hot piece of heaven, and didn't care what Diggy would say or think or report back to Roland.

Near the bakery where I met Mwara, we turned right into York, and Diggy fell into pace beside me.

I gave him a sideways glance. "Aren't you worried to be seen with Zantry the traitor?"

Diggy said nothing.

"Seriously," I insisted, "wouldn't this be worse than the Mwara situation?" Before he could reply, I added, "Wait, I thought Roland said you weren't allowed to help."

He shrugged. "Roland convinced everyone if I'm taking some of the heat, then it's only fair to let me help with the hunt."

"Oh. They waited awfully long, don't you think? Almost as if they didn't want us to find her." My expression was curious, but my tone gave the sarcasm away.

It took Diggy a moment to reply, "I've been searching for her for the past week." He glanced down at me and added, "I came by, but was informed you were missing too." He glanced next at Zantry, acting as if he couldn't hear us.

Ah, he must have found Logan. I studied his expression, trying to decipher his mood, but there wasn't any anger coming off of him or in his eyes. There wasn't even any heat there. On the contrary, he had on his preferred mask of calm aloofness.

"I take it you didn't find anything."

He grunted once and motioned at Zantry. "Where are you two going?"

"Not sure. Zantry thinks he's on to something." To Zantry, I said, "where are we going?"

He ducked into the alleyway we guessed Mwara used to shift to the Low Lands. "To the Low Lands. We'll have Frizz follow Mwara's sent from there, start skipping from wherever he loses her."

"Frizz?" Diggy asked, brow creasing.

"My shadow."

"Ah," Diggy's expression cleared, "I'll be damned."

I glanced at him, at his gleaming eyes, and a spark of hope lit inside me, began to spread.

* * *

But Frizz couldn't find her anywhere, and after a frustrating hour where we moved from point to point, shifting from alleyway to the Low Lands then to a foreign planet, back and forth, back and forth, Zantry finally called a halt to the merry chase in the middle of nowhere, Low Lands.

"Ask him if he can sense her presence now, here."

I turned around, saw nothing but a vast space, the ground dry and cracked, the odd blackened twig lying forgotten, still like that for centuries with no wind, animal or decaying fungus to displace it.

"Do you sense Mwara, Frizz?"

"No, master," he hissed, crouching beside me.

"How about we try at another point? Maybe Frizz can sense her somewhere else, if she's closer?" I offered, grabbing at straws. Time was slipping away, pushing me to the gauntlet.

It was Zantry who answered. "No, no. You see, these creatures are a part of this land. They sense things. Anything anywhere, everywhere. No matter where they are. That's how they know where to hunt. Ask him if he sensed her presence in the *recent* past."

"I already asked him that."

"No, you asked if he sensed her here. Present time. I want you to ask him if he ever sensed her presence here, in the *past*."

I tilted my head. Maybe he had a point. I relayed the question to Frizz.

Frizz's ears flicked back and forth a few times before he answered. "No, master."

I sighed, frustrated and confused. Did this mean Mwara never made it to the Low Lands?

Diggy sighed, shifted on his heels.

Zantry glared at Frizz, as if intimidation would make the gargoyle sense the child.

I sat on the ground beside my familiar and let my forehead rest against my raised knees. I was about to drift off when Diggy said, "His pack. The ones who helped him when you were in the cave. Have him go find them."

Zantry's head snapped up. "Yes, that's it," he said, snapping thumb and forefinger. "Have him go find them and ask them."

I groaned, rolling my head to the side and pressing my temple to my knee for a few seconds before standing on weary feet. "God, can't we just go home? I'd rather die rested."

"You're not going to die," Zantry snapped with a savagery that surprised me out of my haze. "Vemourly is right. Frizz might not know because he was with you when she came through here. But his pack was here. Now, have him go ask them. We don't have time to waste."

I glanced down at my loyal familiar, sensing his need to help. Bending, I picked him up and settled him on my hip like Vicky often did.

Zantry made a choking sound. Diggy huffed out a laugh.

I ignored both and focused on Frizz, his velvet-like wings buzzing madly with pleasure. I scratched his back and he closed his eyes, a contented feeling emanating from him.

When I scratched him behind the ears, the buzzing intensified. When he grow up, would the tiny wings grow also, allow him to fly for real? What would happen to him if I died? Would he return to this dead land, where he'd be forced to go without all the luxuries he'd come to know? I wondered if these past months with me had done him an injustice. Would he be able to acclimatize back to the life he'd once led? Who was I kidding, if I died, he would die with me.

"Frizz," I began with a rough voice, "can you summon the pack here, now?" The words had just left my lips when eleven shadows appeared, crouched in a semi-circle around us.

"Motherfucker!" Diggy jumped back and away.

"Son of a bitch." Zantry clapped.

Again, I ignored both and searched the faces of the eleven shadows. I found the one with a torn ear and focused on him, knowing he had taken Frizz's position as leader upon his absence. It wasn't something I'd known before, just something I recognized when my gaze landed on him, as if the knowledge had been offered, unbidden to my mind. They weren't bonded to me like Frizz, but they still owed me for the feeding, and they were here to pay.

"Taz," I said, and the gargoyle stepped forward.

Beside me, Diggy made a strangled sound. Zantry, however, had fallen quiet, expectant.

"Do you know who Mwara is?"

Ears flicking, Taz hissed with a harder-edged tone than Frizz's, "Yess" and made my skin crawl. How connected were we? At least he wasn't calling me master.

With a deep inhale, I asked, "Have you sensed Mwara in this land recently?"

"Yesss," he hissed.

I jolted, stunned at the unexpected answer.

Diggy murmured something undecipherable.

"Where?" Zantry asked, but the shadow ignored him.

"Where? Can you lead us to her?" I asked.

Taz unfolded his thin legs, gaining a foot of height, his wings buzzing with excitement. "Yesss. By the Mandolia Mountain."

I had an awful feeling when Taz uttered that name. The look in Zantry and Diggy's eyes didn't help either. "What?" I demanded. "You two *know* something."

But Diggy merely turned and vanished, and Zantry reached for me and shifted us after him.

Chapter Forty

It turned out, to my increasing alarm, the Mandolia Mountain was the same place I had hiked with Diggy not so long ago.

The moment Zantry flashed us to the foot of the hill, I hurried after Diggy and stepped in front of him. He stopped–it was either that or plow through me. "What? You owe me an honest answer, damn it."

Diggy glanced at Zantry, his eyes guarded, hooded. I could see the mistrust in them even with them shadowed.

"What were you doing here that day?" he asked, the frigid look returning to his eyes.

His words were like a shock of icy water, dumped over me all of a sudden. I stepped back, realizing both men were hiding something. I never questioned Zantry his presence that day when Frizz and the band brought me out of the cave. Never asked Diggy why he'd sent me in there, why he'd wanted to know what was inside.

Now I thought about it, I drew short, inhaled sharply, and turned to wait for Zantry's answer.

Mouth set in a grim line, he replied, "I sensed Remo Drammen on the other side of the valley and came to snoop on him, but by the time I got there I couldn't tell where he'd gone. So I set to scope the entire mountainside, found nothing and gave up. That day I walked you to base?" Zantry gave me a questioning look, and after my stiff nod, he glanced back at Diggy, "I decided to give it one last try, and instead of Remo, I found you standing by that rock, peering in. I stood back, waiting to see what you were doing, and that's when you came out, Roxanne." He addressed the last part to me. After searching my face, he turned back to Diggy, his eyes twin pools of cobalt fire, narrowed with menace. "What about *you*? Why did you send her in alone, then stood back and waited in safety?"

Diggy stiffened with the implication, drew himself high. "She wasn't supposed to engage. She was to scout out the place and return. I'd have broken the ward if I'd sensed any danger or if she stayed longer than a minute."

Zantry angled his head. "But you didn't answer my question, now did you? Why did you send her in there in the first place, Douglas Vemourly?"

Diggy glanced at me, his eyes icy. Anger radiated from him, but not guilt. Beside him, his hands fisted.

"Well?" Zantry prompted, and I narrowed my eyes at him, at his damning silence.

"Why did you send me in, Diggy?"

He took a step toward me, and I stepped back, keeping my distance from him. "The day of the panic attack, when I left you alone? I thought I sensed Mr. Drammen. I came to check it out, near the valley on the other side." He motioned a hand to the far right. "But there was nothing there but a lingering scent. So I went back to you, took you home. Ever since that day, after our training, I come back and check every hidey-hole, turn every rock large enough. But I found nothing of Mr. Drammen's. It was by chance that I found the warded entrance of the cavern, and it was only because I had been near enough to see the distortion, feel the soft hum."

I looked down at my hands, frowned at my bare fingers, empty palms. I was expendable. Everyone thought so. "You sent me in, even though there was a possibility I'd find Remo Drammen there."

"No. The ward isn't Mr. Drammen's. I'd have known it. I swear, there's no trace of him anywhere near that cave, or even on this side of the mountain. I wouldn't have sent you in otherwise."

I didn't say anything.

"Roxanne, look at me." Diggy waited for me to look up, face blank, empty of any emotion. "I'd never willingly endanger you. If you don't believe that, then believe when I say I wouldn't endanger you for the sole reason Roland would ostracize me, cast me away and announce me rogue."

I nodded. That was true. If anything, Roland would blame him for whatever happened to me on his watch. "Did he send you so we could search for Mwara together?"

"No." Diggy's lips twitched humorlessly. "There's strength in numbers, and despite all your faults, you're not stupid. Let's just say I have something to gain if we find this child in time."

I nodded, and Diggy turned to Zantry next. "Why are you helping? What's in it for you?"

"I have no ultimate reason for helping Roxanne. I am not a traitor, Vemourly. I'm not in league with Remo, never have been. I'd like nothing more than to see Remo gone," He glanced at me before adding, "You, Roxanne, of all people, shouldn't doubt my words."

I didn't doubt him. I never had. He'd suffered because of Remo, and being in league with him was a ridiculous accusation. For someone who knew the truth.

I nodded, and Diggy exploded. "What's this? You believe him, even after we told you he's suspected of killing Arianna, of joining hands with Mr. Drammen?"

I glanced at Zantry for help, but he said nothing, gave no indication if I should or shouldn't confide in Diggy. So I settled on a lame reply, laced with conviction. "Everyone's got secrets, especially around me. If Zantry has his, I at least know he's not in league with Remo, and Arianna's death is not his fault."

When Diggy began to protest, I cut him off, "I know that. I am sure of it, even if I don't know the circumstances surrounding her death. Do you understand what I'm saying, Diggy?" I asked when he opened his mouth to protest again. "I know Zantry Akinzo is not in league with Remo and that he had nothing to do with Arianna's death. Nothing."

"What did he tell you?"

"He told me nothing. I know because... because I know," I finished lamely. I couldn't tell Diggy about the PSS. I couldn't tell him about the Sidhe. The first wasn't my secret to tell, the latter would get me killed.

Diggy snapped his mouth shut and turned his eyes—now lit with an animal glow—on Zantry. "What happened to Arianna?"

"I don't know," Zantry said quietly. "When I came back last November, I was shocked to learn she had disappeared and that Cara was dead. I just found out a few days ago that she died and isn't coming back."

Maybe it was the sad tone of Zantry's voice or the raw grief in his eyes, but I think Diggy believed him. "Oh God," he said and covered his face with his palms. I realized Arianna had been a person a lot of people had cared about. And still hoped she'd come back. It made me wonder, no, it made me wish I had known her too.

"Where were you all this time?" Diggy asked through his hands.

"PSS HQ, room four hundred eleven. East Wing."

At this Diggy's hands dropped like two stones, eyes incredulous. He looked from Zantry to me, adding the numbers in his head. And by the way anger darkened his expression, no matter how he added them, two and two kept making four. "All this time? But how?"

"A spelled contraption Remo designed to keep me drained of energy," Zantry replied with a wry smile, but I knew the pain of all those years would never fade.

Into the silence that followed, I added, "They used the energy they took from him to power their concoctions, to give an edge to their elite guards by enhancing their senses and abilities and God knows what else."

Diggy's hands clenched hard. "Fuck, why didn't you say anything?" He shook his head. "The Hunters..."

"Wouldn't be able to do anything, seeing I'm a lone-wolf and am no longer in there."

"All the power they must have collected..."

"That they'll never admit to have."

Diggy clenched his teeth, but instead of pushing the topic he changed the subject. "Could Arianna be in there too?" My heart clenched at the hope in his eyes.

"No. I got from a valid source Arianna died a few years after I was taken. She's not coming back."

"How?" Diggy whispered.

"That's what I want to find out." Zantry placed a hand over Diggy's shoulder. "We have to go now, we're on the path with Zeta. We don't have much time left." Zantry turned, and I told Taz to lead the way.

Chapter Forty-One

When Taz paused in front of the warded entrance to the cave, I was sick to the stomach, even if somehow, I'd known we'd end up here. Instinct, or some bizarre ability to read my shadows?

I eyed the jagged slash on the face of the mountain, half-hidden behind all the boulders scattered around, my stomach knotting and unknotting with anxiety. Not again, oh God.

Then my thoughts ran in a different direction. If I'd barely made it out of there, which I wouldn't have if Frizz and the band hadn't come to my rescue, how could an eleven-year-old? Would I find something left of her inside? Had Mwara's bones been lying among all the others, while I was injured and bleeding? And if I couldn't find anything left to prove my innocence, would I be condemned, no matter what I told the clan?

Who would believe me? Not Logan, not after he'd seen me with Zantry. And no one would believe Diggy, since he'd assumed responsibility to my actions.

Had she been afraid? I hoped–for her sake–it had been quick, at the very least.

"I'll unravel the ward slowly so the maker won't sense it's gone," Zantry said.

"Do you recognize the signature?" Diggy asked.

"No, but it's an exceptional work."

"It can't be Mr. Drammen's. It doesn't feel like him," Diggy said, brow furrowed.

"No, he didn't do this one. Remo's ward would have been... more potent. And more dangerous. But,"

"What?" Diggy turned to face him.

Zantry rubbed a hand over the stubble on his cheek. "I can't think of one person capable of pulling this off."

Diggy frowned. "What about an earth witch?"

"A strong one, maybe. One willing to dip toes in murky waters, if you know what I mean."

Diggy grunted. "A few moved in this last decade or so. People steer clear of them. They give out the wrong vibes. We have some members keeping an eye out, but so far caught no questionable deed."

Zantry mulled over his words. "Maybe," he conceded, "But this doesn't feel like a group effort."

"What about you? Can *you* do it?"

Zantry's lips twitched, either with amusement or annoyance. "I can, yes. But I didn't do this one."

I frowned at them, standing there, legs braced apart, studying the darker shadow between the smooth boulders, debating the origin of the work as if they hadn't been accusing each other of treachery not long ago.

I turned to my loyal followers. Found the one I wanted. "Taz, did Mwara go inside?"

"Yess," it hissed, dashing any hope that we were wrong.

"Ok. Is she alive, inside now?"

Taz didn't answer, something I've come to learn meant he wasn't sure.

"He'd probably know once the ward is down," Zantry said.

God, was she still alive?

"Maybe you should stay behind," Diggy suggested, no doubt reading the horror in my eyes.

I stiffened. "Why?"

Diggy paused before saying, "Someone should go back and tell the Hunters what we found here. Bring reinforcements."

"Well then, that person can't be me, being that I don't know how to travel the leeway."

Zantry snorted, and Diggy's jaw clenched. If I didn't know any better, I'd think he wanted to spare me the horror, if that wasn't concern for my safety.

"We'll go in together," Zantry said. "We're both more dominant than the creatures of this land, they'll stay away from us."

"Then you warn the Hunters."

Zantry shook his head. "I don't think so. If I tell them we found Mwara trapped inside a warded cave, and I left you and Roxanne to guard the entrance and let's go, that everyone will follow my lead?" he asked in a reasonable tone. "They think I killed Arianna, Vemourly, they will never believe a word I tell them. If anything, they'll think this is a trap. And if you go, and Roxanne's time is up, you'll be held accountable for her absence." He pointed in the direction of the planets and added, "We're standing in Zeta's path, which means a minute here is an hour there, you know that. Her time is probably up. We can't risk going back now empty-handed."

"How did she get through the ward?" I wondered out loud.

Both men turned to look at me, but it was Diggy who replied. "Our young have an almost human-like aura because they haven't yet developed their alternative forms. When disguised, they can pass as ordinary humans, and not even the Sidhe can tell the difference."

Which meant the only thing keeping her in there wasn't the ward, but the inability to run. If she was still alive, I mean.

"He's right. We'll go in together," I said.

Diggy rubbed a palm over his cheek before exhaling. "Shit. You sure?"

I took a deep breath, gave him a cold smile that had made scientists cringe. "I'd rather die in there and have Archer and the clan believing I ran and hid, and keep them wondering for the rest of their miserable lives where I went to."

"That's my girl," Zantry said with a chuckle.

I turned to Taz next. "Is there another entrance into the cave?"

He stretched his thin legs, beat his wings. It took him a long while to answer. "Nooo."

"I'll unravel the ward bit by bit. If I do it right, there's a big chance whoever put it there won't know it's gone." Zantry moved closer to the gap in the mountain-face. Diggy stepped beside him, scanning the gap–the ward I couldn't see. It was strange, knowing someone standing right in front of you could see something you couldn't.

He pointed at the corner of the entrance, down low. "That one looks weaker."

Zantry slanted his head, examined it. He pointed to the top, way off the entrance. "That one, it's steady and solid, but it shouldn't be there. Zomos aren't right runes for strong wards. I think there's where I should start."

Diggy glanced to where he pointed. "Wouldn't the stray energy alert whoever put it there?"

"Probably, but I'm not letting the energy loose."

Diggy tensed at that, and I wondered what Zantry's words meant.

Still, Zantry didn't move. He scanned the ward a few minutes more, making me fidget and shift from foot to foot. I rubbed my palms together, blew on my fists. Had it gotten colder?

"That one." Diggy pointed at the middle. "I noticed it the last time but didn't recognize it. What is it?"

"Fragrac," Zantry replied, frowning.

Diggy angled his head to the side. "Never seen it before. Looks more like a cross between sifron and lax."

"That's because it's a combination of the two. It's used to contain, or kill if or when it's breached. It's mostly used for darker workings. I've never seen anyone use it outside of practice, and mostly on sketches for summonings." He fell quiet again, then stood straighter and said, "If by any chance the owner of the ward is in there, take Roxanne and search for the kid. I'll keep whoever it is busy until you find her."

"Zantry," I protested.

"The moment you find the kid or any valid proof of Roxanne's innocence, shift and leave. Don't wait for me."

"Zantry–"

"Fine," Diggy agreed.

"I'll tackle zomos. It's the one out of place and the least threatening." With that said, he raised his left hand, and I felt the energy he exuded, a soft humming like static. It reminded me of Remo, with an exception: Where Remo's energy bit and burned, Zantry's was warm and soothing.

His right hand stayed motionless beside him, his fingers relaxed.

The left hand gathered energy, the right released. I narrowed my eyes at him. Shouldn't he be using the right? I made a mental note to ask him about it later.

If there was a later.

He traced a symbol in the air, his hand twisting, lifting, dipping again. His motions were fluid and sharp, a maestro without his orchestra. Then he punctuated the air with his index, closed his fist. And pulled.

There was a small pressure in the air, but nothing else. That's when I realized Zantry was absorbing the energy of the ward. He worked like that for over half an hour, sketching symbols and punctuating and pulling, his right hand relaxed beside him.

Neither Diggy nor I spoke anything, and the small pressure lessened, until it disappeared. Zantry lowered his hand, rubbed the nape of his neck with the other. "Alright," he began, but his next word was interrupted by a small explosion. Everyone was flung back in the backlash, even frizz and the band.

I lay dazed for a moment, nauseous and scared shitless. I knew something had gone horribly wrong. Unraveling a ward bit by bit didn't cause small explosions. Zantry's face appeared above mine, his eyes searching. "You ok?"

"What was that?"

"Failsafe."

I sat and looked around. Frizz and the band were up, Diggy shaking his head. No one seemed to be hurt.

"Does this mean you rang the bell?" I asked lightly.

Zantry smiled, his eyes cold. "Yeah, let's hope there's nobody home."

Chapter Forty-Two

Diggy reached inside his denim pocket and withdrew a small cylindrical tube. He shook it once, pressed his thumb and slid it down, left, right. The tube lit, grew, formed a small sword, the blade polished black.

"If we find the ward's creator inside," Zantry said to him, "I'll keep him occupied while you search for evidence and get Roxanne out of here."

Zantry glanced down at me, extended a hand and helped me stand, but instead of taking a step back, he took one forward. He placed his palms on my cheeks, his thumbs brushing the corners of my lips. His eyes were confident and unafraid, and the frisson of energy from his circling fingers had my nerves settling. His lips touched mine once, a warm quiver of energy shooting from him to me. He pulled back a fraction, left his hands cupped around my cheeks, a tender, comforting touch.

"Keep your shadows around you," he murmured, "Give them the command to attack anything not friendly. If you and Vemourly are separated, have them bring you out at once. I'll find you."

I nodded, my mouth too dry to speak. He released my face and turned, and I grabbed his hand. "Be careful," I said, afraid for him.

"Always." He squeezed my hand. "I won't engage longer than I have to. The moment you guys find Mwara, or any evidence you can use and leave, I'll be right behind."

* * *

Like Zantry suspected, the moment the ward was down, Taz was able to determine Mwara was inside and alive.

My hope was overshadowed by dread, a sinking horror of what she must be going through.

Taz led the way, following Mwara's scent or energy, or whatever it was he sensed of her. The cavern was still the same, except now with the light I could see clearly. There wasn't any trace of my blood on the ground, and I wondered about that. The ceiling, as I'd figured was vaulted, the walls wide and smooth, unless you touched it. Then it turned pourousy, a land so dry, even the rocks felt the effect.

A downward slope led us to the three caves, where Taz hesitated a moment before following the narrow tunnel on the left. Behind him went Zantry, me, Frizz, Diggy, and the remaining shadows. A few yards later, we encountered another division in the cave and Taz took another left, this tunnel smaller, the walls closing in on us, and I had the urge to grip my throat and gasp for breath.

We turned right, left, meandered straight for a while, and took another left. On and on we tramped, until Taz stopped inside a small chamber, unsure. There was an opening leading to the other side, and beyond that sat a heavy darkness, the light unable to penetrate through.

The attack came without warning, without sound, without preamble. One second we were examining the darkness, the next chaos erupted.

The lights went first. Next, a mass of dark claws and fur fell on us. I wasn't sure where they came from, if they jumped us or if they fell from the ceiling, or closed from behind, but suddenly we were swarming with creatures, creatures that had featured more than a few times in my nightmares. They bit, scratched, hooked their long claws into flesh.

I kicked one, slashed at another trying to chew a path through my jacket to the flesh underneath, shrugged another off my shoulder.

Ahead, I could barely make out Zantry's dark silhouette, about half a dozen creatures attached to him. I opened my mouth to shout a useless warning when the creatures were expelled away, and I tasted the offensive bite of his energy for the first time. A creature jumped me out of nowhere, coming straight at my face, but frizz tackled it, ferociously ripping into flash with claws and teeth. I didn't know where Diggy was, the lighting was too dim, the room too small and the creatures too many, still coming by the dozens.

Shrieks, horrible and piercing came from the creatures, either dying or feeding, even off their fallen kin.

One grabbed my leg and before I could kick it, a dark blade flashed and cut it into half. Diggy struck another before it could land on my back and I sliced one before it could grab his thigh.

Frizz snarled when a creature dug claws into his wings and I struck it hard with my talons. I could barely see a foot in front of me. We need the light, I thought with a sinking heart. "They're sensitive to light," I shouted, but I didn't know if anyone heard me above the chaos.

"Lights, Akinzo, lights," Diggy yelled.

"Something is blocking it."

A creature grabbed on to my leg, claws digging in, another one to my arm, chewing cloth. Before I could pull either away, a third grabbed on to my other arm, its claws piercing skin where the previous creature had been chewing. Yet another one went for my other leg, its teeth cutting deep into my thigh. I gasped with pain, going down to my knees, dislodging the creature chewing at my leg. It adjusted, going for my hip next.

"Roxanne!" Zantry shouted, and a moment later the creatures attacking me were blown away. He helped me to my feet, his eyes glowing an electric blue. "Stay with me," he said and turned, giving me his back. He shouted something to Diggy, and after a moment, he too was pressing his back to my other side, both men cocooning me with their bodies.

Then he snapped something, his voice full of power, and with a ferocious snarl, frizz and the others backed off, as if some invisible force pushed them back against the three of us. When they were all circling us, Zantry raised his right arm high and circled it round and round, round and round. Static built, filling the small chamber, the smell of ozone almost masking the metallic smell of blood. The creatures scurried back, trying to escape whatever Zantry was conjuring. The pressure built until every hair on my body stood at attention.

With a shouted word, Zantry released the pressure, and a burst of blue fire circled us in all directions, eating anything without. The creatures dying shrieks and the stench of burning flesh filled the room, the sound reaching a painful crescendo. A long moment later the horrible noise died down, until nothing remained, not even the ringing fire.

Zantry's hand dropped and he turned to me. His eyes were a light blue, like the color of the sky on a bright summer day. They glowed like the eyes of a night predator. Diggy took out a penlight, the illumination dim, as dim as the light of one single candle.

Zantry scanned me from top to bottom, his mouth a firm, grim line. "How bad are you hurt?"

I flexed my muscles, stretched my legs. It hurt, but I shrugged it off. "I've been worse."

"Let me heal you." He reached for me.

"No." I stepped aside. "You should reserve your strength. You can heal me once we leave."

He inhaled and said, "Alright, but let me at least stop the bleeding."

"And check for poison," Diggy added.

I hadn't bitten any of the creatures but I wasn't stupid either. I had no way of knowing if their scratch and bites were venomous. I slashed the arm of my jacket, ripped it off and extended my wounded forearm.

He reached for my arm, studied the bite marks for a second before covering the wound with his palm. Like the last time, the process made my skin itch and burn like crazy, but he closed even the wounds on my legs and side. When he was done, I noted the glow of his eyes had dimmed.

"You think that was all of them?" Diggy asked, scanning the charred remains of the creatures. I was sad to see we lost two of the shadows, their bodies burned beyond recognition, save for the two lumps that marked small wings.

"Probably just the first line of defense," Zantry replied.

"Taz?" I asked, and he stepped forward, dark, viscous blood dripping off his face, his claws.

"Can you still lead us to Mwara?"

"Yes."

I motioned him ahead, and this time, Zantry and Diggy flanked me, frizz close to my heels, the remaining eight in a tight semi-circle behind us.

Chapter Forty-Three

The second line of defense came when we rounded a corner and entered another small chamber. A second patch of absolute darkness blocked the path ahead, but this time the light surrounding our group stayed steady, though Diggy held on to the penlight.

We paused, semi-prepared, and I sensed when Zantry sent his awareness ahead. I tried to do the same, aware of how wrong it was, its existence not just a mere absence of light, but the product of evil, an absolution of all things bright.

I could tell it was sentient, that it assessed us the same way we assessed it. Diggy clicked his penlight, and the thin stream seemed feeble, stopping at the edges, not penetrating for an inch.

"What is it?" I whispered, afraid to speak any louder.

"Dimensional pocket," Zantry replied, voice tight. His hands moved, fingers tracing something I couldn't see.

Diggy explained, "Like a room in limbo, a storage place in the vacuum between dimensions."

"A room?"

Beside me, Zantry cringed, stumbled back. I reached for him, but he pulled away, shaking his head, a finger rubbing his forehead as if the spot pained him.

"Talk to me," Diggy said, voice strained. He braced his legs, his sword at the ready. "Maybe we should skirt it and leave it be."

"It knows we're here." As if to confirm Zantry's statement, something moved in the darkness, a ripple that seemed to expand.

A piece of darkness detached itself, formed the shape of a man. Dressed in a ragged business suit, he moved forward, his eyes dark, his paces even and silent. He wasn't evil, exactly, but he was nothing good either. He was nothing I understood... nothing of this world.

He stepped into the light, not cringing, not even pausing to adjust. And kept coming.

Behind him came another man, then a woman, and a teenage boy. All carried the same dark look, moved the same way.

A primitive, cold feeling hollowed the pit of my stomach when I realized what they were. To whom they belonged.

"Zantry," I said. No doubt catching my terror, both men inched closer, but their eyes remained fixed on the threat ahead.

"Zantry." I stepped back, unable to form the words I should be speaking.

A sideways glanced showed that his lips were pressed into a hard line, his eyes tight. He either knew what I wanted to say, or he had an idea.

"What is it?" Diggy asked.

"Remo." I swallowed once and gripped my hands tight, "That's what he does to people."

"You're sure?" Diggy asked after a brief pause.

"Yes."

Diggy swore a vicious stream of curses, stuffed his penlight into his pocket and braced his weapon with both hands. Suspicion radiated from him in rancid waves. It took me a moment to understand the conclusion he'd drawn.

"Stop it," I hissed, somewhat nauseous. "We told you. Zantry isn't in cahoots with him."

The suspicion throttled back, coated with a heavy dose of uncertainty. The man with the tattered suit paused about twenty feet away, and the others moved to stand beside him.

I was expecting some speech, so I was caught off guard when they all attacked at once.

In synch they moved, each picking a target. The woman attacked Zantry, the man with the ragged suit Diggy, the teenage boy went for Taz, and another man came for me. I shouted at the pack to attack and kill, and kicked the man on the balls hard enough he should have been able to spit them out. Instead, he faltered a step and adjusted course as if his pain receptors were disconnected. I followed with a right jab, a left one, a kick to the kneecap. But if the guy felt anything, it didn't show or hamper his goal to reach me. He grabbed for me, his moves fast, agile. I jumped out of his reach, then kicked him hard on the abdomen. Hard enough to double him over, but he only stumbled back a few paces.

With a static hum, Zantry expelled the woman's attack with a burst of energy, sent another to an older guy I hadn't seen before. On the other side, Diggy was also fighting off two attackers. What I wouldn't give for a sword like that. Or for the ability to fight with energy like Zantry.

More of the dark human minions were coming from the dimensional pocket, filling in the place. The teenage boy was still up, deflecting two of the shadows with a kick and powerful backslap that sent one flying to the other side, the other bowling three shadows over. He reached and grabbed another shadow and pulled it close to his face.

I froze for a moment, and the man I was fighting grabbed my hair, pulled it so hard my eyes watered. I slashed with my talons and dodged the moment it let go. I glanced back at the teenager and found him... kissing? Sucking? At the mouth of my shadow, who was twitching non-stop.

The man moved in front of me, blocking my view, and I faked left, kicked his other kneecap, the impact opening the gashes on my injured leg, causing it to bleed anew.

I jumped back, my leg buckling with the impact. Blood sprayed my face, hot and metallic, and the man tumbled to the ground. First his upper body, then his legs. Behind him, Diggy lowered the dark sword, still polished, clean of any blood.

Zantry had five bodies at his feet. A quick headcount showed we'd lost another shadow, the one by the dead teenager.

Grimly, Diggy assessed the bodies. "Do you think this is Mr. Drammen's infamous lair?"

Zantry's eyes said he thought so, but he didn't say a word. We all knew to turn back now meant certain death for me, possibly Mwara, now that we knew where she was. Even if we went to the Hunters first and they assembled a team and came at once, they wouldn't find anything here, much less Remo. And the clan would never agree to give me more time, no matter what I told them.

In the end, it wasn't a choice.

"We should hurry," I said, shocking even myself. Both men looked at me with an you-shouldn't-be-here- expression.

I knew what they wanted to say even before they opened their mouths. "If you send me out, he'd come after me first. Then he'll use me against you." My tone was reasonable, but in truth, I was more scared to be left alone out there knowing Remo might come at any moment. Maybe he wasn't here. Maybe he had yet to find out his lair had been breached.

Diggy nodded, and I stood straighter, only to deflate when Zantry said, "If we find him, I'll distract him while you two find Mwara and get out of here."

Chapter Forty-Four

We moved forward, Taz leading the way, followed by Zantry and Frizz, just a few paces ahead. Diggy stayed close to me, his suspicion still there, though less pronounced. Both Zantry and I could sense it, but neither of us tried to ease his mind. For one, there wasn't any time, and trust was born from action, not words.

After we passed through a maze of caves and connected chambers with no additional ambush, we emerged into a familiar cavern, its walls pockmarked with small holes where I knew lay the remains of many humans and animals alike.

Lit like this, I could tell my first assessment had been right. It was a tall, enormous cavern. But it wasn't the memory of my recent near-death experience that caused my heart to jump and lodge in my throat. No, that accident was done and over, and I'd survived, despite the odds. What waited ahead was yet to come and I could still die a horrible death. Ahead, a hundred yards away, an army of darkness waited, with the clawed creatures hiding behind them, safe in the shadows.

So many. We couldn't fight them all.

God, we'd never be able to defeat them.

"Maybe we should... hmm-mm, any suggestions?" I asked.

"Fight or retreat?" Diggy offered.

I shot him an incredulous look. Was he insane? There were countless minions ahead, at least three, four hundred. And only three of us.

"I got them," Zantry said, stepping forward. "I haven't done this a while, so stay back, and get ready to engage." Pressure built, and the pungent smell of ozone permeated the air.

Beside me, Diggy shrugged his shoulders, popped his neck. Zantry kept going, the pressure in the air increasing until my ears needed popping. I yawned without taking my eyes off the army, afraid to blink and miss their first move. There were dark corners and shadows the light didn't reach, and in them there were movements. The ceiling too was dark, but I supposed it was because it was high.

Zantry stopped halfway between us and the dark minions, and the moment he paused, they moved. Fast and with an organized advance that denied their mindless status. Even from where we stood, I could tell this bunch was different than the one that attacked us before.

Diggy swore, and I took an instinctive step back.

These minions weren't just faster, they were preternaturally faster. Behind them the clawed creatures waited, emitting that child-like cry as they moved back and forth in the security of darkness, their silhouettes resembling medium-sized dogs.

"Get ready," Diggy said, his stance poised to attack, sword ready. "He won't be able to hold them all on his own."

I reached inside a hole and searched for a long bone. In this light, I couldn't mistake it for anything else. It could be the bone of an animal, but I didn't think so. This was a human bone, yellowed and scratched. The femur, I guess.

The minions were almost upon Zantry when he braced his legs apart, his shoulders tense. His hair danced with an unseen breeze, his jacket fluttering along. He raised his right arm, fingers splayed, palm facing up. A second passed. The minions were almost upon him. Two seconds passed. He turned his palm down, brought it together with his left hand in a clap. There was the sound of booming thunder, accompanied by a piercing flash of light and the sound of a savage roar. The minions blew back, propelled by an invisible force. I stood, some fifty yards away, frozen, speechless. Light spread as the things were shoved back, revealing more of the cavern with their passage. It was an enormous cavern, bigger than I'd imagined, with a dark hole the size of a small football field interrupting it before continuing on the other side.

I was almost sure, a few hundred years ago, that hole in the ground used to be a deep lake. A lot of minions fell into the hole, some with crooked necks, some shoved so hard, they were almost halfway through the gap before they started falling. Even some clawed creatures fell in, some blown by Zantry's kinetic shove, others while trying to back away from the light.

But some minions held on to the edge of the hole, and a handful from the sidelines escaped the brunt of the force. Those rushed at Zantry, even as others pulled themselves up from the edge.

An older man in tattered clothing reached him first. Instead of fighting him off, Zantry grabbed the man's arm, twisted and pulled his head close to his mouth. The way the teenage boy had done to the shadow.

He sucked him dry of whatever life still animated the body.

I took in a sharp breath. Beside me, Diggy stood motionless. I didn't think he was breathing.

When Zantry let go of the body, the old man resembled a shriveled corpse, as if dead for a long while. He lowered his head for a moment, and the cavern around us gave a static buzz, the sting sharper than before.

Some minions had frozen, watching him, but the moment Zantry let the dried carcass drop, they attacked. He didn't move, didn't twitch, didn't draw energy from the air. And then he did, when the minions were less than ten feet away. Fast enough that I couldn't follow, He drew something in the air, his fingers leaving a light impression of a symbol, like the infinity symbol with a horizontal slash cutting through. Then he moved his hand back, mimed lashing at the few dozen minions closing in. Diggy inhaled sharply, and a second later I discovered why. The minions fell, some with heads cut off, others without their upper bodies. Smoke curled off the cauterized parts, white wisps I knew would smell like cooked meat.

"Fuck me," Diggy murmured.

He's so powerful, my inner voice said, unsure of what to feel.

If he was this powerful, even as he claimed himself weak, how powerful would he become?

As if to undermine my thoughts, Zantry swayed and fell to one knee, head bowed. Without thinking, we ran to him, Diggy ahead.

I tried counting heads as I ran, but the minions still standing were fast and didn't keep to a line. At fourteen I got confused and tried again, then decided they couldn't be less than twenty, over twenty-five. At least none were climbing out of the hole. Only two were women. All seemed to have been around their late twenties, early thirties when they turned into this mindless thing. Some were dressed in nothing more than tattered rags, as if they'd been wearing them for a long time. Others were dirty and rumpled, their clothing still intact.

Shit, but they were fast. I paused by Zantry while Diggy waded through the minions, cutting and slashing as he went. I helped Zantry to stand, eyes focused on the fight. Diggy cut the head of one, stabbed another through the heart, kicked a third back and brought the sword on the neck of the one he stabbed. A tall guy with broad shoulders and a dark coat advanced on Diggy's left, and Diggy parried and slashed. I'm not sure if that move had been a trap or just a lucky draw, but the moment Diggy's sword came down on the tall guy's neck, the minion to his right grabbed his sword hand and twisted, even as momentum brought the dark blade free on the other side. The crunch of Diggy's wristbone reached me even as his sword clattered and retracted into a small tube. Still holding Diggy's wrist, the minion pulled Diggy closer and reached for his head—was that a pair of fangs?—But a huge black paw swatted at the minion's face. A huge black paw attached to Diggy's wrist. The moment the minion let go, that hand shifted into another feline paw, claws extended. Diggy inhaled sharply when the bones realigned, the motion clearly painful. Not losing any time, he swatted the one closest to him, once, twice, four times, favoring his left paw, even as he blocked the others with his body.

Zantry swayed on his feet, his eyes back to dark blue. He took a step back, and I let go as he turned to face the minions. Diggy held them back but barely.

Zantry shrugged his shoulders and rushed to help, both of Diggy's paws dripping with blood and gore. A group of minions immediately went for Zantry, and despite his weakened state, he kept them back. I directed half the shadows to go help.

For a moment I hesitated, unable to decide what to do. Should I go find Mwara on my own, now the minions were busy? Should I move forward and fight with them? A shadow gave a resounding hiss as a minion grabbed him by the wings. Zantry shifted to help, but three minions blocked his path. Diggy favored his left leg, and a dark bruise bloomed on his right cheek, his eyes almost swollen shut. A woman crept on that side, but Zantry blocked her, and two minions he'd been fighting rushed me, and there was no more choice to make.

They moved preternaturally fast, and I stepped back, caught the one on the left with the bone, slashed at the second with my talons. I jumped away, knowing I'd be as good as dead if they caught me. Frizz and another from the pack latched on to the leg of the man closest, and the rest followed, jumping on his arms and back. I gave Frizz permission to feed and focused on the one trying to grab my head. His ear was pierced; his jeans clean save for a few stains. A new addition? When he reached for me again, I batted his arm away with the bone. There was a loud snap, but that didn't deter him. He kept coming, and I kicked, slashed, and batted his advances away. The sounds of fighting and frantic feeding filled the spacious room, topped by the shrieks of the creatures in the darkest parts of the cavern. The minion kept me on the defensive, pushing me back, and I needed to do something before there was no more room for me to maneuver. When the minion rushed with a punch that would have put stars in my eyes, I sidestepped, caught the punch on the shoulder, my arm going numb at once. I kicked his leg, punched him on his side and jumped away. On my peripheral, I saw Zantry fighting off two minions while Diggy kept two more occupied, one whose face had been filleted by Diggy's massive paws, the other with an arm dangling uselessly on his side. All around them, bodies lay strewn on the ground.

They were relentless, not noticing they were actually getting hurt.

The guy in front of me reached for my arm, and I twisted away, batting him on the shoulder with the bone. He caught the edge of my coat and pulled, and I lost my balance and went down hard. I rolled away just as a booted foot came down on my stomach, missing me by a fraction. I jumped up, faked right and went left, behind the guy, banging the bone hard on his head and slashing his neck with my talons, then kicking behind the knee. He went down, tried to swipe my leg from under me. I rolled, stood, and kicked the still down guy on the head. He was fast, grabbing the leg of my pants and yanking hard. I fell butt down beside him and rolled away, and was grabbed by the hair this time. Heart in my throat, I wrenched myself away, leaving a big chunk of hair behind. When I turned to face the minion again, the clump of hair was white and brittle. A chill went down my spine, making my blood run cold.

The guy threw the clump away and rushed me, his dark eyes emotionless. I kicked and batted his advances away, barely staying out of reach. Then Zantry was there, and he grabbed the guy from behind, twisted his head and drew him near.

This close, I could feel the rush of energy from the minion to him. When the guy fell, Zantry's eyes were lighter, a dim glow radiating from them.

"You okay?" I asked.

"It's energy from my homeland. It gives me strength."

But you hate yourself for doing this, I thought, sensing his Remorse. I wanted to reach out, to say everything would be fine, but knew he wouldn't welcome the support.

"Thank you. For everything." I knew he could sense the sincerity in my words. I didn't wait for a reply, aware he needed the moment to come to terms with himself. I turned to the shadows, sad to see only five were still standing, the rest either dead or too weak to stand. I headed to Diggy, sitting on the ground, one leg extended, his pants ripped. He was injured, his hands still massive paws.

I wanted to urge him to shift, but said nothing. He knew better than I if shifting would help him heal.

"You ok?"

Instead of answering, he nodded to the other side of the hole.

I followed his gaze and sucked in a sharp breath. A bunch of minions stood there, nothing but the deep gap separating us. As we watched, one of the minions turned and headed toward an entrance on the rock wall, and a few followed. I didn't want to be here to see if that entrance connected with any of the ones on this side.

"Do you still know where Mwara is, Taz?" I asked the shadow with a new level of urgency.

Taz, crouched nearby, stretched its thin legs, his wings buzzing gently. "Yes."

I glanced at Diggy, and with effort, he stood. "Can you walk?" in response, he shifted into a big black panther, his hazel eyes glowing with that predatorily light. He shook his fur, and I had this urge to stroke his pelt and see if it was as soft as it looked, but I liked my hand attached to my body, so instead I told Taz to lead the way.

* * *

There were six exits–or entrances–on this side of the hole, but Taz couldn't decide which one Mwara had taken. He paused in front of one, shifted to another, then paused before a third.

Three caves. Three of us. Five shadows.

I glanced down at Taz and he flicked its ears, sensing my attention. "Which one is it?"

He didn't answer.

"We'll separate?" I suggested.

"No," Zantry said at the same time Diggy began growling. At first, I thought he was voicing his agreement with Zantry, but he was facing the direction we'd come.

I whirled, and there, some minions we just killed were getting up.

"Oh, shit."

Zantry narrowed his eyes. "The head," he said, and after a moment, I realized only the ones left with their heads attached were getting up.

Diggy surged forward, his powerful legs eating the distance in no time. He jumped high and caught a minion by the neck, bringing him to the ground. He shook his head left to right, jaw working until the minion's head rolled off.

Three more rose and yet more stirred. The teenage boy who'd killed a shadow ambled out of a tunnel, coming to join the others. A piercing shriek rang from high in the cavern wall, but no creatures leaped into the light.

I sent the pack ahead and rushed after Zantry. I wasn't at full speed–my adrenaline rush was spent, and my leg throbbed where a creature bit me.

He was way ahead when there was a thunderous boom, a furious shriek, and something huge fell from above. It covered Zantry top to bottom, a monstrosity with long sharp-tipped wings that closed around him. The beast lowered its head and roared, an ugly sound filled with anger.

Choking fear paralyzed me for a second before urging me to move faster than I ever did.

It was right there in front of me, yet I sensed nothing of it. No presence, no emotion, no heat waves.

With a roar of his own, Zantry expelled the beast from his back. He dropped to one knee, his head low. The creature crouched a few feet away, then shot into the darkness like a torpedo, wings bracketing its body. From a few feet away, Diggy transformed from panther to a red-tailed hawk and shot after the creature. Only for a minion to yank him back by his tail. He screeched and fell, a panther before he hit the ground and pounced, swiping the minion with a huge paw.

I hurried toward Zantry, scanning the darkness above.

"Get back," he warned, his breathing harsh.

I froze, heart squeezing with fear at the rivulets of blood running down his back.

Diggy's ferocious snarl had me whipping around, in time to see the last minion take hold of him and lower his head. Heart thumping, I rushed toward them, aware I was too far, aware I'd be too late.

I screamed, a savage sound of battle, but the thing didn't look up, didn't stop sucking Diggy's life. I jerked my hand into talons and, with an open jab, sliced the thing's neck so deeply, I almost detached the head. With a scream of grief and outrage, I kicked the semi-detached head again until it was free of the torso. Then I kicked one more time, sending it far into the hole. I turned, breathing hard, heart pounding, and crouched beside Diggy. With a shaking, bloodied hand, I reached for his neck. There was only one thought in my head: *this can't be it, this can't be it. Please don't let it be it.*

A deafening boom broke the silence, followed by another furious shriek. The beast came arrowing down on Zantry, and he braced, ready to take it on. I caught my breath, and at the last second, Zantry sidestepped, and the beast veered off, its massive wings a darker shadow against the dark ceiling. It came again and again, and I realized too late it was driving him toward the hole.

I shouted a warning, and that was Zantry's undoing. In the days to come, I'd wonder if my actions had been the turning point in the events that followed. He glanced at me, just a brief flicker of the eyes, and the beast struck him square on, pushing him far into the hole.

He fell, his shout of outrage cutting off abruptly. And the lights went out.

Chapter Forty-Five

I stood slowly, conscious of the fact I was alone, that my friends were no longer fighting beside me. I wasn't even sure how many shadows were left. I could only sense Frizz, his familiar presence like a shadowy cocoon surrounding me.

The sound of approaching footsteps had my heart shaking with fear, and without thinking, I moved back, aware there was a hole the size of Idaho somewhere behind me.

"Frizz," I whispered. He pressed against my leg, tried to reassure. "Lights. I need to see." My eyes scanned the darkness left and right. Bit by bit, I made out silhouettes, dim shadows that turned to figures as the light brightened.

The moment I was able to see what approached, I almost went down to my knees and begged. As it was, I almost told Frizz to let the lights go. But the clawed creatures threw up their hairy arms and backed away, shrieking as they went, hurrying back to the dark holes they came from. They bumped and slashed at the minions closing in. They may have been humans once, but they moved like a pack of feral animals with the scent of prey in the air, and that prey was me. I knew then whatever the outcome tonight, I would suffer before it was over.

I kept backing up, trying to widen the distance the minions kept closing. Frizz and whatever remained of the pack—only three more—followed me, until we reached the lip of the hole, and one glance was all I needed to know Zantry hadn't made it. He'd appear again, someday, but not tonight, not to help me fight my way out. The hole was deep and dark, a bottomless pit that I could sense was vast and... corrupt.

Was he still falling?

"Get us home, frizz!" I hissed.

Frizz buzzed his wings, said nothing. Through whatever this bond between us, I sensed his defeat, his sense of impotence at the inability to shift us out.

Outside of this planet, he could only go where I went. "Can you flash us out of the cave," I asked in desperation.

"No, master," He hissed, and I recalled the way he had to carry me out of here the last time. He could shift by himself, but he couldn't drag me with him.

The minions were so close now, I could see the swirl of darkness in their eyes, the vacancy of any humanity whatsoever.

Frizz stretched his legs; gained a foot of height before crouching again, a reaction I knew–felt–stemmed from his agitation, the certainty of our impending doom. His wings kept the furious buzz, though his hands stayed loose at his sides. He would fight with me, for me, and the moment I fell, he would fall with me. I should let the other three go, but I was too selfish, too afraid to lose this layer of protection, no matter how feeble.

I swallowed and took another tiny step back, a quarter of my left foot hovering into the abyss. I sucked in a breath of encouragement. All I needed was to take one small step back and it'd be over. Loose rocks tumbled down into the hole, the sound growing fainter and fainter, until I could no longer hear it. Ahead, one of the minions got into range, its aura completely black, polished the way Fin's aura had been. They were different, and I knew, like Fin, before becoming Remo's minions they hadn't been human either.

Five feet, I told myself. Five feet and I'll jump.

Another black aura flickered into existence, then another and another. The first one paused, less than ten feet away, the second one beside it. Then the third and fourth. There were at least twenty more still coming, though I could only make out their silhouettes. Behind them, the clawed creatures waited for the light to drop.

Ahead, the four minions stood, waiting. The fact they were waiting for something caused my anxiety and fear to spike ten folds, and I knew whatever happened, this was it.

Fight to the death, my inner voice told me. Never give up.

Never give up. I never did before. I would fight, even if the odds were against me. My talons appeared, and, sensing my resolution, Frizz and the remaining three shadows stretched and stood, ready to fight with me, despite their injuries and fatigue. I braced to lunge and a thundering boom had me jerking, and I grabbed on to Frizz to keep my balance. Without warning the winged beast dropped to the ground, a void blank where it stood, as if there was nothing occupying that spot. It was right behind the two minions directly ahead of me, its wings stretching far to each side, massive, black velvet things of hideous fur.

I was afraid to look away and miss an attack. But I shouldn't have worried. One moment there was nothing there, the next I felt it, a punch of potent power that licked and burned my skin, then dulled to a throbbing presence. A cold, nervous sweat broke around my temples, my upper lip.

The two dark minions stepped aside, and the beast stepped forward, pausing just a few feet away from me.

It was a tall beast, about eight feet of height. Yellowish eyes glared at me from a head similar to that of a bear, though rounder, the muzzle smaller.

I lowered my eyes, dreading–and knowing–what I'd find.

Instead of claws, five talons protruded from each of its six paws, huge, massive things that could kill with a careless swat.

Talons.

Like mine.

My heart stopped beating, and I tried to swallow the spit that had magically turned to dust.

Dhiultadh.

A rejected.

One of my kind, no less.

I would die at the hands of a Dhiultadh after all. How ironic life was. Or death.

And then my worst nightmare came true.

Chapter Forty-Six

I sensed him long before I saw him. Before he entered the huge cavern through a side tunnel.

The power of his energy, or his signature vibe, attacked my senses and brought forth the most primitive of fears, blocking reason and any common sense I still possessed.

His approach was silent, and it would have gone unnoticed had I not been able to sense him. It was the opposite effect I'd gotten from the rejected; I couldn't hear him, but I could definitely sense him. It was ridiculous, to be able to move like a phantom, yet have all that power to announce his presence like beating drums.

The second Remo Drammen cleared the minions in the back, the rejected shot into the air with a powerful flap of wings, the echoing sound of thunder and a small cloud of dust all that remained in its wake. It dove down into the whole, wings folding for maximum speed. Going after Zantry. A small frisson of hope washed over me, drowned with horror at what Remo would do to him.

Remo Drammen cleared through the four human minions and Zantry dropped from my mind like a pebble into the sea.

He looked the same way he had the last time I saw him. He had an albino complexion, a white, thick Maine of hair, big ears for his smallish round face. His eyes were small, black orbs I couldn't meet and hold for more than two seconds without involuntarily glancing away. Plastic, white round glasses framed them.

For a guy that barely reached five feet of height, he packed a strong presence.

Today he was dressed in a pale beige suit, a white collared shirt, sans a vest.

My eyes met his and skidded aside.

His energy lapped at my senses, a prickling sensation that turned more insistent the closer he got. Remo Drammen, unlike Zantry, had no aura. I wasn't sure if that was because he didn't have one ounce of humanity, or if it was simply the byproduct of too much corruption.

When he was about six or seven feet away, He paused, his head cocking aside, studying me, as if I were some animal he couldn't fathom. Silently, I waited for the blow to come, and tried to guess how, and in what form it'd be. If I fell, would the rejected catch me before I died?

If I couldn't fight and ordered Frizz to kill me, would he agree?

Beside me, Frizz's ears flattened and he crouched low, his wings quiet. I guess that meant no.

"You have so much to give, so much to help," Remo mused, startling me with that nasal tone I had mocked once.

Give? Help? My eyes moved to his army of dark minions, now a cluster of women and men waiting behind the four closest. I laced my fingers together in front of me, trying to quell the shaking. I needed to sit and take off the weight from my rubbery legs.

"So much capacity," he murmured, his eyes roaming over me.

Bile rose to my throat, but I swallowed it. "To become one of that?" I asked in a shaky voice, motioning to the army behind him with a hand that shook just as much.

I hated myself for all my weaknesses. He was powerful, yes, but he could still die. Not for long and not easily, but it was possible. I'd done it once. Survived to fight another day.

He waved a tiny hand. "No. To waste something like you for the mindless is not what I have in mind for you." Far in the back of the cavern, a creature cried, a long, child-like wail. It reminded me even if I got rid of Remo, the rejected and his minions, I still had to get through the blind, poisonous creatures. But maybe I didn't need to get rid, or through, anyone. Maybe all I needed was to outsmart Remo. Think.

"If you think I'm so valuable, why did you let your creatures almost eat me the first time?" Because if Frizz hadn't come when he did, I would have never made it out of here alive.

"Ah, poppet, an error in judgment," Remo said without an ounce of remorse. "Please accept my sincere apologies. Had I known you'd come calling, I'd have never left that day. At the very least, I'd have left my slaves suitable instructions for a proper welcome."

The rejected reappeared to my left, and my mind blanked at the sight of the limp body clutched in its set of extra arms. It dropped Zantry with a dull thump a few yards away and came to land beside Remo, wings closing around itself. The moment it stood still, it shifted, the wings, extra paws, fur, everything was sucked into the body as if it was a painless, natural transition. It was a woman who appeared after the shift, and she was not a bit concerned to reveal her traitorous identity.

Because she knew I wouldn't be leaving this cave alive.

She was, of course, no one I ever met. Her hair was a rich honey color that reached down to her backside. She was tall, almost my height, dressed in a brown ankle-length dress with one shoulder bare, no shoes but a thin cord around her right ankle. Her face was round, her eyes black. The recognition in them told me she already knew who I was.

There was something familiar about her... Unease settled in my stomach. "Who are you?" I asked, bile rising to my throat.

An emotion I couldn't read flashed in her eyes before her expression cleared and she straightened. "No one of your concern," she replied in a clear voice that had me closing my eyes. I knew that voice.

"M-Mwara?" I choked. Her voice was deeper, more mature, but still clear, still mellifluous. And now I had an image to compare, I could see it. My hand flew to my mouth. I took a step toward her, my hand clenching when a dangerous glint entered her eyes.

"Oh, Mwara. What happened to you?"

To my left, Zantry stirred. Hope sparked; he wasn't dead. Unfortunately, Remo also noticed.

He turned to watch him, waited while Zantry struggled to his feet and took in the scene. It wasn't a nice view. I, Frizz and the shadows faced Mwara, with Remo just a few steps to the side, an army of minions waiting for Remo's command. He scanned everything around us with one long sweep before returning his gaze to Remo.

"Remo," he said in way of greeting, before raising a hand and attacking with a blast of energy that made Remo skid a few feet back. I had to give it to Remo, he was fast. After a fraction of a second, Remo met the blast with a blast of his own. It was obvious Zantry was at a disadvantage, because Remo's blast gained on him, pushing Zantry back. He had been drained, deprived of his energy for over twenty-six years, while Remo built his strength. And whatever strength Zantry had gathered after leaving the PSS, he'd expended fighting Remo's creatures and minions. Yet, the power each exuded was overwhelming.

The energy was so strong; a supernova began to form where the two blasts met. The scent of scorched ozone filled the air. The hairs on my body stood at attention. An insistent whining sound grew in volume, and sparks flew everywhere. Wind stirred tiny rocks, blew them at my face. The light where the two blasts met was blinding, growing by the second, and for a moment I couldn't tell where Zantry's energy ended and Remo's began. Then the light moved closer to Zantry, and my breath caught.

Zantry shifted first, widened his stance, and I understood then he wouldn't be able to hold on for much longer. I had to do something. Without thinking twice, I took a step forward, and Mwara shifted, ready to prevent me from interrupting.

I couldn't watch Zantry die. I lunged forward, pirouetting around Mwara in a move Diggy had taught me, barely dodging her outstretched talons. I tackled Remo from the side, a gasp of pain escaping my lips when an unexpected burning zap of energy coursed through me. Both Zantry's and Remo's blast went wild. Remo roared, an inhuman sound that made my insides shrivel with terror.

An invisible force punched me, flung me away, the smell of burnt hair strong. Before I could finish falling, I was caught by Mwara and spun around, her talons at my throat. Zantry froze mid-lunge, his eyes focused at my neck.

Frizz jumped on Mwara's leg, digging claws and teeth, and with a pained shout and an extra arm, she hooked talons on his wings and flung him to the side like a small insect. He fell a few feet away with a heavy thump and didn't get up. The remaining three members of Frizz's band made to attack "No!" I shouted, and with a growl, Mwara dug her talons on my neck, breaking skin and slicing deep enough for blood to flow freely.

Zantry snarled at Mwara, his eyes glowing an electric blue. I swallowed against the pain and fear, the talons cutting deeper. I closed my eyes, trying not to take deep breaths or swallow and do anything that would kill me. That's why I missed what happened next. One moment Zantry was ready to attack, the next he was stumbling back. I assumed Remo hit him with some blast of energy.

But then Remo did something with his fingers, and a pulse of light appeared like a bracelet on Zantry's left wrist and he fell to one knee as if the thin light weighed the world. Slowly, teeth gritted, he struggled to his feet. I could tell just standing cost him. Remo watched him struggle, then plucked something out of thin air, something that pulsed light blue. Though Zantry dodged, he wasn't fast enough. It attached to his other wrist, and a soft blue light moved from one thin bracelet to the next. He fell to his knees with a heavy thump and a gasp, and my heart squeezed inside my chest. I knew what that light was. I had seen it before, when Zantry had been attached to all those machines back in the PSS.

A dark, shadowy movement to the far right caught my attention, but I didn't dare move–I liked my smiles white and above my neck.

Nearby to the left, Frizz was breathing, the rise and fall of his chest fast and erratic. He was badly hurt. I tried to reach out to Taz, but I couldn't sense him like I could sense Frizz.

Zantry's eyes met mine, and I read the pain, the agony in his eyes before he masked them, tried to stand again. First one knee, then the other. Remo watched the effort, waited until he was upright before plucking another thing from thin air, this one catching Zantry around the neck, like a choker made of blue light.

At this Mwara let me go, either confident I couldn't help, or foolishly believing that I wouldn't try again.

I pressed a hand to my neck, trying to staunch the bleeding, and whirled at Remo, but didn't approach.

"Let him go," I snarled, my blood boiling with the need to do harm. Remo didn't even glance at me.

Instead, he paced toward Zantry, and I took a step forward, but Mwara, talons bared, blocked my path, her eyes cold.

"What are you doing?" I snapped at her.

I caught another movement on my peripheral, but no one noticed.

"You look so pitiful, Zan. Did you know the humans begged me to bring you back, paid me a small fortune. The Russian mafia offered me a hundred vessels in exchange for your body."

My boiling blood froze in my veins.

"I will let them know," Remo continued, "you are the reason for her death. For his..." Remo glanced up in time to catch Diggy's lunge, fangs bared in a ferocious snarl.

Remo raised a hand, and I lunged, trying to sidestep Mwara. But she saw it coming, grabbed me by the arms and pulled them high on my back, her hold firm.

Diggy fell atop Remo, his bared fangs going straight for his neck, and for a moment I thought he'd rip his throat out, but instead, he roared and fell sideways.

I couldn't tell what was wrong until he licked his front paw and I noticed the thin chord of blue light contrasting against his midnight fur.

Remo stood, dusted himself off and chuckled, a sound that grated against my nerves. It was so easy. We were so easy. We were no match for him.

"I have grand plans for you, Son of Tammos," Remo said to Diggy before nodding to Mwara, who let me go and shot up into the air.

Zantry said something to Remo, his voice whispery thin.

Remo cocked his head aside. "What is it, Zantry?"

"I said. Let, her go."

"Why would I do that?"

Zantry gasped out a word, and I took a step forward, paused when Remo's energy grabbed me by the throat. Blood gushed faster through the slashes on my neck, and I thrashed, trying to pull back, the energy tightening. The moment I stopped struggling, the energy chokehold around my neck eased.

"What do you have that I want?" Remo asked.

"I. will. Go willingly."

Remo Drammen fell silent, his dark eyes studying his fallen kin before shifting to study me. He sniffed in my direction, his energy spreading all over me, caressing and burning. I took a step back, my knees buckling. Mwara reappeared behind Remo, shifted to her human form and stepped to my side, guarding me. Remo's energy retreated from around me, and he turned to face Zantry. There was a dark, glowing sphere in Mwara's hand, something like shadows shifting inside.

"I don't need your cooperation, Zan. It's too late for that now." Remo glanced at me and Diggy before returning his focus back to him. "I have you, I have the son of Tammos, and I have her." With that said, Remo motioned a finger in the air, and the buzzing energy concentrated. He drew an imaginary circle, cut it with a vertical line top to bottom, bottom to top and fisted his hand. The hairs at my nape stood erect, as if electrified. Zantry bowed his back, a tortured scream escaping his lips as an iridescent cage formed around him.

"Stop it!" I screamed at Remo, dashing toward Zantry. An invisible force grabbed me by the throat and hurled me back. I gasped for air, blood flowing like a fountain down my neck.

The iridescent cage faded–though I could still sense it. Zantry slumped, unconscious, his chest rising and falling with shallow breaths. Remo turned next to Diggy. Before I could think to advance,

Mwara grabbed me again, her hold like iron shackles around my wrists.

"Please, stop," I choked.

He traced the same symbol as before, the circle, the lines, then closed his hand again, and the sound that escaped through Diggy's panther form was a roar of torture that cut off abruptly when he too, passed out.

With that done, Remo turned to me. Mwara let me go and bowed her head with deference, offered him the glowing sphere.

Without any evident probing from Remo, a group of minions broke rank and moved toward Zantry's prone figure, surrounding him in a tight circle.

I took a step forward and Mwara snarled a warning, the sound ugly, full of menace.

My eyes narrowed at her, anger bubbling to the surface. What happened to that sweet child? I didn't like when some of that anger was aimed at myself. I had let her go, not once considering the dangers in her path.

"What have you done to her?" I whispered to Remo.

He ignored me, but Mwara snarled again. Maybe if I could reason with her, maybe there was still hope.

"You don't need to do this anymore," I said, taking a step toward her, my eyes pleading with her icy black ones. "I came here looking for you. We all came looking for you. I want to take you home." I raised my hand, let it drop when her nostrils flared in warning. "Your family's devastated. They have been searching for you, leaving not a rock unturned."

Some fleeting emotion flashed in her eyes before she banked it, her expression going hard. "I have no family left."

"That's not true. You have a mother and a father, a clan who loves you. Your mother's been worried sick, searching for you everywhere. Your father–"

"Left me here for years," she finished.

I shook my head, tried not to wince when the gash on my neck twinged. "No, they haven't. It's been but a few months back on Earth. Everyone's been looking everywhere for you."

Another fleeting emotion before she hardened her expression into a mask. "This is my place. My master has shown me what my family would never dream of giving me," she said with conviction. With reverence.

Devotion and love shone in her eyes, and I couldn't help but glance at Remo, narrow my eyes when that rage inside me surfaced with vengeance. "How could you do this? She was just a child."

Remo glanced at Mwara. "I only gave her everything. I made her the most powerful Dhiultadh to exist."

"No, you forced her to become a monster," I gritted.

"I was not forced to do anything," Mwara cut me off, straightened her shoulders, head held high as she announced proudly, "I am his familiar."

I drew a blank at her words before horror slapped my face, shocking me into terror. "No, you can't be. You were just a child," I said. My God, how can I undo this?

"There is nothing you can do," she said, her chin rising in defiance. I'd said that out loud.

"Look at you and your band of losers." She sneered, "I could crush you all with the power I have. One blow is all I'll need." She fisted a hand in front of her, her eyes flashing yellow. Rabid. She was rabid.

"I don't believe–No, I refuse to believe it. You didn't become a cruel monster just because he wants you to be. Think about your mother–"

"She is the reason I am here today."

I shook my head, held back my wince. "Because you misunderstood her. They came looking for you, Mwara. She came searching for you. They tore the city apart searching in every gap. They even came here with their best trackers."

"I know. I ran. I ran all the way to the top of the mountain." Again that sneer, that sense of superiority. "Their best trackers didn't even sense me. I found this cave, and hid inside. They never came again."

They couldn't sense you because there was no imprint in the ether. I glanced at Remo, knew he was the reason for that.

"I was scared, I was attacked. My mother should have known I was in danger. But she never came." She glanced at Remo, and the soft look in her eyes sickened me. "Then he appeared, and he took care of me. He healed me, taught me how to protect myself, how to create wards, to fight. He made me strong. He gives me power when I need it, he lets me draw from the bond without limit. He gave me the wings I wouldn't grow before my first century. He taught me how to fly. He kept me safe, something my own family couldn't do."

How could I refute that?

"You warded the cave's entrance," I said instead, understanding now why neither Zantry nor Diggy recognized the person behind the working. The proud glint in her eyes told me I was right.

Shit. She was proud to be here.

I tried to reach the child I met back on that cold evening. "Your father, he was desperate." When Mwara's eyes softened, I pressed on. "Vincent was devastated. Even Archer felt your loss." Wrong thing to say.

Her eyes chilled. "Archer just doesn't want us to win. He doesn't care about me. Look what he did to you."

She said "us" as if Remo's cause was her own.

I glanced at him, watching the exchange, his expression emotionless. My heart pounded so loud, I could hear it in my ears. "Let her go. Please, she's just a child. Don't do this to her."

"She doesn't want to leave. She likes what I can give her. And soon so will you. So will the son of Tammos. Perhaps even Zantry." he waved a tiny hand around. At me, at Zantry. At Diggy. At Mwara.

"But you don't need her!"

Remo didn't reply, didn't acknowledge my outburst.

"You can sever the bond." But even as I said it, I wondered if it was true.

"To sever the bond I'll have to kill her. Do you wish her dead?"

"No!"

Remo glanced down at the sphere, studied it for a moment. "In a few years, poppet, I will bend you into submission and make you my slave. And I will absorb all his energy and double my strength. Then I will make the son of Tammos one of my most powerful vessels. He is a powerful Dhiultadh. He can hold so much." His eyes gleamed for an instance, a vast universe within.

A cold so deep sipped through my bones, hollowed my insides. He would become indestructible. No one would be able to stop him. Not even with all the aid from the Sidhe.

"I am going to start with the son of Tammos. This sphere contains one being, a creature like me and Zantry. I want you to watch this." He brought the glowing sphere near to Diggy, near the light bracelet. A molt of glowing darkness jumped from the sphere to the bracelet, and Diggy whined.

"Wait. Wait. I can give you more." Without thinking about what I was doing, I took a step forward, hands clenched into fists. Remo glanced back at me, kept the sphere near the bracelet, and another molt jumped from it.

"I," I swallowed the bile that rose and tried again. "I'll exchange with her. I'll become your familiar. Willingly."

It was Mwara's turn to protest. "No!" She launched at me, hit an invisible wall and fell, whirled at Remo. "No! I'm your familiar. I'm loyal. She won't be," She begged. "She's tricking you. She's lying."

The vehemence in her voice frightened me. What had he done to her? Remo ignored her and stood, his dark eyes focused on me. The sphere was now far enough from the bracelet no molts jumped off it.

"Silence," he said to Mwara, and her protests abruptly cut off. She fell to her knees and sobbed quiet, silent tears.

"You will exchange with my familiar, take her place willingly?" he asked.

A sudden image of Titania hunting me throughout the worlds flashed in my mind. The thought was oddly comforting as I nodded, "with the condition you let Zantry, Diggy–the son of Tammos, and Mwara go."

His head cocked to the side again. "I'd give you three boons in exchange for one. And I already have you."

"A slave is hardly like a familiar. And, I come with my own familiar."

"Once a slave accepts his place, I can make him into a familiar."

"You know I would never accept that slot, not in a thousand years." I raised my chin in defiance, letting him see the truth in my eyes. The PSS couldn't break me with all the experiments they had run. They wouldn't have broken me even if I had never left. In a hundred years from now, I'd have still been looking for a way out of there.

Remo's depthless eyes scrutinized my resolve for any holes. "You would become my familiar, willingly, in exchange for their freedom?"

I'd be trapped inside this cave, never to see the brilliance of the sun again. I almost buckled then and there.

But if I didn't do this Remo would have all of us to do with as he pleased. Even if I escaped now, the clan would kill me for Mwara, who would never agree to come with me. And Zantry and Diggy.... I couldn't even think what Remo would do to them. This way, at least, I'd be the only one left behind. And alive to fight another day.

I strengthened my resolve and swallowed the lump of fear.

"Yes. On the condition I stay on earth when you don't need me."

"Hmmm," he said thoughtfully, taking a step toward me. I forced myself to stay still as he closed the small distance between us. "Say it," he demanded.

I tried to swallow, but there was nothing but dust in my mouth. "I," my voice cracked, "I will become your familiar, willingly, on the condition you let Zantry, Mwara and Diggy–the son of Tammos–leave... and they will owe you nothing. And you let me live on earth and only call upon me when you need me."

Remo's eyes gleamed with an intensity I had never seen before. With a hand flicker toward Mwara, her silent sobs ceased, and she slumped, dead or unconscious.

I stepped toward her, but his next word stopped me cold.

"Done."

No! I whirled, wanted to scream, would have if his energy hadn't slammed at me, taken my breath away, suffocated me, filled my lungs, my eyes, my ears, my heartbeats. My being. Clutching my head, I fell down to my knees, choking, sobbing. Dark spots appeared in my vision. I clutched my throat, clawing for air, but I forgot how to breathe.

"Do not fight it," Remo instructed, and when I tried, some of the pain eased.

"Accept the bond."

God, I didn't want to. But it was either I did or he took us all. Against all that was holy to me, I allowed his energy to course through me. When it stopped, I was raw, feeling used–corrupted in a way I'd never been before.

A sweet rush of air, void of Remo's dark energy, filled my lungs. I gulped large breaths, choking in its abundance.

For a while, I did nothing but enjoy the ability to breathe. My vision cleared again, and I braced my hands on the ground, breathed for a few moments more, head bowed low.

The first thing I saw when I raised my head was Mwara's limp body. I thought Remo had killed her and tricked me, but then I caught the steady rise and fall of her chest. I sagged, defeated, every muscle in my body aching as if I'd gone for a cycle in a meat grinder.

I looked around, found Remo gone, along with his mindless army. A few of Frizz's band members lay amidst bodies, very much dead. Everyone had fallen, except for the three left in Frizz's pack, crouched beside his stirring body.

Aside from them, there was no one left alive but Mwara, Diggy, and a livid Zantry. His eyes blazed with fury, and I looked away, unsure of what to feel. Guilt? Shame? Remorse? Should I be proud I'd spared Mwara? My eyes met Diggy's–now human and naked, but he glanced away, confirming that he too, knew what I'd done.

Would they try to kill me? My heart squeezed inside my chest. Was *I* the enemy now?

Frizz sat with effort, then slowly stood and approached me, his movements sluggish. He crouched beside me, his wings limp and torn in places. I met his expressionless shell-shaped eyes and felt a sooth-ing wave of comfort emanating from him. Trying to comfort me after what I'd done, what I'd become. My stomach gave a violent churn, and I leaned to the side, away from him and Mwara, and emptied the contents of my stomach until only dry, wrecking heaves remained.

Zantry's boots appeared in front of my eyes, narrowly avoiding the puddle I made. He crouched, his blazing eyes mere inches away. He reached for me, and when I flinched away, his hand balled, knuckles white. He dropped his hand and stood, turning away.

"I'll go and straighten things out, buy you some time," Diggy said, not looking at me.

I nodded once, and he disappeared.

Zantry crouched again, the fury in his eyes banked into crackling ambers. He placed a lock of my hair behind my ear, then gathered me close. Before I knew it, he flashed us away.

Chapter Forty-Seven

We arrived in my living room with Zantry still holding me, Mwara still unconscious. Frizz disappeared the moment we touched ground, to do whatever he did when he was in a higher dimension. He'd heal faster, so I didn't ask him to stay, even if I wanted his soothing presence more than ever.

Zantry stood, his motion agitated. There was strain around his eyes. He was hurt too, but I couldn't see anything beyond his tattered clothes, ripped where Mwara's talons had dug. There was blood, but nothing fresh, nothing still bleeding, not that I could tell.

When his eyes met mine again, the fury was back in full force, burning hot. Maybe if he killed me now he'd spare me the horror that waited for me ahead.

I wasn't sure if I'd put up a convincing fight, or if I'd protest.

He paced back and forth, clearly trying to work off some steam, then whirled to face me, finger pointed like a spear at my face. "You are the most stupid person I have ever met," he snapped, coming to crouch in front of me. "Do you have any idea what position you have put yourself in? No?" he bit off every word, his anger so tangible it was like hot air on my skin. He stood in agitation, paced as far as the opposite wall before spinning on his heels to glare at me. "You've played right into everyone else's game." His finger speared me with every word he bit off. "This is exactly the position the Sidhe wanted you in. The Hunters will lap up your downfall like cream in a sweet pie! They'll want to know everything Remo teaches you, his every move. The rejected will accuse you of treason and try to execute the thorn on their side. And Remo, Remo ... you've fucking played right into his fucking game!" he punched the wall, leaned his head in the hole that appeared.

Belatedly, it dawned on me his fury wasn't for what I'd become, but at the precarious situation I put myself in. Or that's what I hoped.

"You said once someone was trying to set you up. You asked who hated you enough to do this." He turned his head to look at me, the fury like a scorching touch. "Remo doesn't hate you. But he wants you enough to risk throwing you down the cliff to see if you'd bounce back. Maybe he hadn't set out to make Mwara his familiar, but he'd been watching you. He saw an opportunity and he cashed on the possibility you'd catch the blame. Perhaps he even thought if you couldn't come up on the winning end against the clan, you weren't worth his time."

He straightened and turned his back on me. With a muffled curse he raked his hand through his hair, glanced down at me and exhaled some of the anger away–to be replaced by fatigue and frustration. "I should have taken you away from everyone when I had the chance. I should have taken you away." He pounded the wall twice more, and though it didn't leave any holes, it still left two impressions. "I should have taken you away."

Stunned, I blinked up at him. "I put myself in this position, not you," I said in a raspy voice.

"Damn right you did," he said tightly. "Because I was too stupid to strike her." He pointed at Mwara's prone body. He had known who she was. She got the best of him because he hadn't wanted to hurt her. Oh, God.

"Should have killed her and taken her body to the clan," he muttered.

"I'm not sorry," I said, tasting the truth in my words. Terrified, yes, but not sorry. Back stiffening, the fury that had begun to dim suddenly blazed hot again in Zantry's eyes. "You should be. You will be." He chuffed, the sound dying even as it was born, his hot violet eyes like a punch. "That's what Arianna would have said. So noble, so stupid.

What you did back there, the stronger of the Dhiultadh wouldn't have. No one burns their skin to save someone else's these days. Bravery, my dear, is a sentiment long forgotten, even by the heroes."

I raised my chin, even if all I wanted was to curl in and sleep the nightmare away. "I'm not sorry," I repeated with a stronger tone.

Zantry studied me, then sagged against the divider, his anger gone, evaporated in thin air. "I can see you aren't. And fuck if that doesn't make me relieved." He shoved a hand through his hair, then came to crouch beside me. "Let's hope a week with Remo won't change who you are."

It was his words that finally broke me. Seeing what Mwara had become was not only sad but horrifying. Hearing someone say the same could happen to me made the possibility that much stronger. I didn't want to be like Mwara. I didn't want to believe in Remo. I didn't want to change. I got up with a last burst of reserve. With both arms around myself, I murmured I wanted to clean up and headed to the bathroom, where I let the first tears silently fall.

Chapter Forty-Eight

The stone circle turned out to be ruins of a medieval stadium on the Rahzar moon, a small planet parallel to the Sidhe world and the Tristan star. It was a land of vicious beasts, giant carnivorous birds, a place where people stopped trying to civilize long ago. It was to this land that Verenastra first took refuge when she fled the wrath of her mother and her lover, the leader of the Unseelie Court, Madoc.

It was in the ruins of this land the Sidhe met with the Dhiultadh, here they solved disputes and dealt justice, here the Seelie and Unseelie Dhiultadh met to resolve claims and complaints. A neutral planet, a place claimed by no one but the feral beings native to this land.

It was here as well my father had met his end.

I arrived late to the stone circle, though with the instability of time surrounding the other worlds, I couldn't tell how late. Beneath my feet the grass was brittle, the color of hay. As if it was autumn in this land instead of spring. On my right stood two impressive snow-capped mountains, to my left, the land sloped downward. There were no signs of inhabitants, no obvious signs of life except down ahead, in the middle of the circle, inside the last crumbling stone ring. From where I stood at the edge of the larger ring, it was easy to spot Archer, standing tall and rigid in the middle of the gathering, facing off with a dark-haired man. I had yet to be noticed, and took the opportunity to study the crowd, recognizing a few faces.

Logan, Elisabeth, Boris, even Xandra.

Logan stood behind Archer and to his right, while Elizabeth and five others flanked Archer's left. Behind the group stood another cluster of people, about a dozen in all. Across from Archer was a similar formation, with the man–the dark-haired leader–facing Archer to the front, Boris and Xandra to the man's right, four others to the left, and another cluster of people behind them.

Between both groups knelt Vincent and Diggy, their heads bowed in submission.

Either no one believed Diggy, or more time had passed than I'd guessed because clearly, this was no friendly gathering. Still, my progress was slow, as I had to maneuver around holes almost hidden by the tall weeds growing from the cracks in the stones.

The man facing Archer said something that made him stiffen, his legs brace apart. Was he getting ready to fight, or was this just for show? Archer pointed a finger at Diggy, and Xandra took a step forward, fists clenched. Boris pulled her back beside him, kept his hand around her wrist.

The man facing Archer shook his head, waved a hand at Archer, pointed down at Vincent, at the six gathered to his left. This man was shorter than Archer by a few inches, but lacked none of the predatory and leadership presence.

A stray wind brought the sound of Archer's voice, though I couldn't make the words out. Logan stepped forward, and across from him, so did Boris. Xandra wiped at her cheeks, but stayed put.

This was an execution trial–of Vincent and Diggy. Innocent bystanders, primed to pay for the likely event of my failure.

Didn't they listen to Diggy? Did they give him a chance to explain? Or was my absence enough to condemn my friends to death?

Or, maybe if Diggy had told them anything, this entire gathering would be tearing down the Low Lands, searching for me and Mwara. And Remo.

Diggy would have known that.

No, Diggy must have not told them anything.

I hurried my steps, knowing this gathering was nearing the end.

Chapter Forty-Nine

Elizabeth spotted me first, already halfway through the circle. I was amazed no one had sensed me before. Surely, a group of people so renowned for their fighting skills should have *better* senses.

She cried out in outrage, pointing toward me, and everyone turned to look. Even Diggy and Vincent dared to raise their heads.

Elizabeth broke rank and rushed toward me. Logan grabbed for her, pulling her back by her arm and handing her to a blond man I recognized from pictures. I had a momentary ping of surprise at the way he handled her, before I remembered he ranked higher. He was second only to Archer. And he was also the enforcer of the clan. Which one was he supposed to execute? Vincent? Or Diggy, his own friend?

Archer and the other clan leader marched toward me, closing the gap. Some other members followed suit, staying to the left or right of their respective leaders. Elizabeth and the man I recognized from the pictures–Ruben–also came forward, remaining on Archer's left. Even Diggy and Vincent rose, their expressions calm masks I'd come to recognize, but neither moved forward.

My skin prickled with warning, but my steps didn't falter.

Behind the group, far in the sky, I spotted the first native creature to this land. It brought to mind prehistoric dinosaurs, the serrated beak long and sharp, wings spanning eight to ten feet on each side. It cried–a lengthy shriek that echoed inside the circle. Only one person from Diggy's line glanced up, a tall freckle-faced guy with icy-blue eyes.

I was close enough now to hear some words, recognize the hostility in their gazes. The combined negative emotions made my queasy stomach churn with anxiety, and so I concentrated at an empty spot between Archer and the other leader, ignoring the sweat that pooled down my lower back. My leg still twinged from my injuries, covered with thick bandages to keep the native predators from smelling the blood. I'd refused to let Zantry heal me, knowing he'd almost drained himself dry in the caves.

I stopped a few feet away from Archer and let Mwara drop–not so gently–off my shoulders. The skirt of her long dress rose up to her mid-thighs, but no one hurried to cover her up. No one even glanced at her twice.

Elizabeth broke the hold Ruben had on her, or perhaps he let her go. With a raised fist, Archer stopped whatever insult she was about to throw at me. She stopped beside Archer, her eyes blazing with hatred, jaws and fists clenched. How could I have loved this woman once?

Someone muttered something about insolence, and after a brief hesitation, I bowed my head to Archer. "Sir."

"What's this?" Archer demanded. "Vemourly informed us you were bringing Ruben's daughter, that you found her."

Surprised, I looked at Mwara, the young woman she had become, the feminine curves the dress accentuated. She was still unconscious from the shock of the severed bond, her long hair conveniently covering her profile.

"...Because the notion was so ridiculous, so farfetched, he didn't see me. He saw someone, helpless and dying, and moved on." Zantry had once said, trying to explain why Logan hadn't recognized him that night in the PSS. Because they were expecting me to bring a child of eleven, no one expected this young woman to be her. In their defense, I myself hadn't recognized Mwara at first, but the resemblance was there, if one cared to look.

I glanced at Vincent, wondered about the task Archer gave him. What were the chances the Fin he was sent to find was the same one in the Seelie dungeon? I glanced at Diggy, found his empty eyes watching me, and then looked away, jaws clenching. He told them I'd found Mwara, and yet, he was being held accountable anyway.

My resolve hardened, and I met Archer's angry eyes head-on.

"You told me to bring proof of my innocence," I said in a clear voice, loud enough to carry over the entire circle.

Archer inclined his head. "So I did."

"This," I waved a hand down to indicate Mwara's prone body, "is the child I was sent to find."

"Liar!" Elizabeth cried out. A few murmurs broke from those in the crowd, growing in pitch until the murmurs turned deafening.

From the other line, no one said a thing. I swept a glance over them, found all eyes on me. A few had clenched fists, others had fire in their eyes. Despite the obvious indignation and anger of having to attend this fiasco, no one from Diggy's clan voiced a complaint. I glanced at Logan, at his empty eyes, moved on to Ruben, read the fear in them. He knew. Would he step forward and confirm my claim or would he stay quiet and let them judge me? I found that I didn't much care. I could leave now and sooner or later they would realize the prone figure on the floor was their beloved scion. There was little in the world worse than being Remo's familiar. Facing this group was not one of them.

"Silence!" Archer snapped, and the crowd behind him fell quiet.

"Explain yourself, Daughter of Fosch," he said tightly.

I glanced down at Mwara, studied her for a second. Then I glanced at Elizabeth, at the hatred blazing in her eyes. When I glanced at Archer, I could tell he was already sure of my demise. I could see my death in his eyes. He hadn't wanted me to make it. He didn't want to see the truth. Because I was a human hybrid?

Because of their prejudice against me, their daughter had paid. Vincent would have paid. And by association, Diggy would have paid.

Archer bared his teeth at me, not liking my silence, "Speak now, scion."

"I already told you. This is the child I was sent to bring for you."

Archer's face contorted. I was showing him disrespect in front of his clan. In front of his rival clan.

"I don't see how this could be. You left to fetch a child of eleven, or proof of your innocence. So far you have done nothing but proven yourself to be disrespectful and spiteful. The only reason you have been thus far tolerated is because of Fosch–"

"This is Mwara Longlan," I interrupted through gritted teeth. "Your denial won't change the fact, no matter how much you wished it did." I hadn't anticipated I'd need to convince them of Mwara's identity. I had expected shouts, gasps and a lot of crying and regret. I admit I hadn't expected any apologies, or for anyone to confess how much they had wronged me. But I hadn't expected to be questioned either.

Logan took a step forward, stopping beside Elizabeth, his stance vibrating with warning, his eyes cold. Unfeeling.

Ready to carry out whatever sentence Archer passed on.

I looked around the clearing, found every eye on me. There was speculation, anger, incredulity, pity. I could tell some believed what I was saying, I could tell some understood Archer would rather not believe.

Archer looked down at Mwara for a second, back up at me. Did he see, or was denial blinding him to the truth? His eyes were livid, and I wondered if he regretted making this meeting so public. "Do you mock me, Daughter of Fosch? This is no child of ours." He took a step forward, and I noticed so did Logan, the enforcer and executioner of the clan.

Would he hesitate if Archer ordered him to kill me? The emptiness in his eyes told me he wouldn't. His devotion to Archer hurt more than it should have.

I swallowed once, glancing down at Mwara to cover the motion. Her aura was no longer that silvery blue all the Unseelie Dhiultadh possessed, but glowed black as if polished, a side effect from dealing with Remo Drammen's energy. Something Zantry told would happen to mine if I siphoned enough of Remo's energy.

With calmness I didn't feel, I met Elizabeth's eyes, read the dread she couldn't hide so well. Beside her, Ruben covered his mouth with his hand, rubbed his face once. His eyes, black that shifted to yellow, met mine, and I could tell he believed. They knew.

I glanced next at Diggy, and he dipped his head once in approval.

I said to Archer, "This is the child I found with Remo Drammen, deep inside a cavern in the Low Lands, a place where time goes by much faster." My words dropped like a bomb in their middle, and several people took back a step as if burned.

Unable to hold herself any longer, Elizabeth threw herself on her knees with a loud cry, brushing the hair off Mwara's face with a trembling hand. Several people gasped, even Archer took a step back in denial.

Elizabeth's hands shook as she brushed her daughter's hair, sobbing uncontrollably. Ruben knelt beside them, straightening his daughter's dress, covering her bare legs, his hands unsteady. He reached out and touched a knuckle over her cheek, tracing the path of a dry tear, then recoiled as if bitten by a venomous snake and scrambled upright. He turned his back to the group and moved away, but not before I caught the anguish in his dark eyes. Elizabeth's hand paused mid-stroke, then recoiled as well. Mwara chose that moment to wake. She groaned, sat, still swaying a little. She blinked a few times, her tear-streaked face going from Elizabeth, to Ruben's back, to Archer, then coming to rest on me. Hate took over confusion in a blink. "You thief!" she exclaimed. "How dare you take my place?"

As if that was all the confirmation she needed, Elizabeth stood with an agile jump and whirled on me. "What did you do to my daughter?" Logan motioned her to stand down and grabbed her roughly by the wrist when she took a step toward me. Elizabeth shrugged him off, but stayed put, her eyes never leaving mine. I could tell not being able to throttle me for what happened to her daughter cost her.

"What happened?" Logan asked. "Are you alright?" he added, his eyes focused at the long puckered slash on my throat. My wellbeing was secondary.

I glanced at him, but it was Elizabeth I addressed. "Be grateful she's well and alive. Her presence here, today, cost me dearly."

"You reek of Drammen's corruption," the other leader, Diggy's leader, observed. Really, they could sense that on me but not on Mwara? I raised my eyebrows at him in a nonchalant gesture, but my heart kicked off in a gallop.

"Tammos. This is no fight of ours," Boris said, reaching a hand and placing it over his leader's shoulder.

Tammos. Son of Tammos, Remo Drammen called Diggy. I glanced at him, his eyes focused on his leader, on his father.

Vincent, standing beside Diggy, glanced at him once, saw no surprise in there and looked sharply at me, apparently sensing the same thing, but said nothing.

It was Mwara who answered. "She is his familiar!" she shrieked.

There was just a fraction of a second of shock before everyone prepared to attack me at her words. They would have if Zantry hadn't thrown an invisible field of energy around me. Elizabeth, the first one to attack, bounced off of it and fell butt down beside her daughter, her face contorting. The others also lunged, but paused at the edge of the field, their faces angry, filled with hatred. Everyone spoke at once. Even Xandra was angry.

Zantry appeared beside me, not saying a word. The shouts quieted to angry words, then murmurs when they realized who was protecting me.

"You dare invade this private meeting?" Archer spoke, his face red with rage.

"From where I stood, this private meeting was an attack on mine. Therefore, not an invasion."

There was a heavy pause as his words were processed. "Are you claiming this traitor as one of yours?" the other leader spoke up. Diggy stepped forward, placed a hand over his father's shoulder, and shook his head once.

"Yes, indeed." Zantry dipped his hands in his trouser's pocket. "As I remember correctly, Gerome, her reward for bringing back this child was to be abjured from this clan, correct?"

"No," Logan said. "She was to think about it."

"There's nothing to think about," I replied. I'd seen the horror in his eyes when Mwara announced my familiar status. It was to him I glanced first. "This clan has brought me nothing but pain and suffering. I told you abjuration would be a reward, not a punishment before, and I meant it."

"A traitor!" someone shouted from behind Logan. "Get rid of the cursed!"

Some of the rejected murmured their agreement. Some took a step forward, but when neither leader moved to strike, they quieted down.

Archer took a step forward, pausing inches away from the energy field and studied me with cold, pitiless eyes.

I raised my chin at him. The crowd went deathly quiet, not a murmur of sound to be heard. They all wanted to hear what I said to their leader. "You make the decisions you see fit, uncaring for the consequences or who will suffer because of it. If I am Remo's familiar today, it is because it was either me or her," I pointed a finger down at Mwara, making several people gasp. "It is my right to sever any ties to this clan, and you have already agreed to it. I brought her back, now I want out."

Someone chuckled from the other line, enjoying the show. Archer's face remained impassive, his eyes flashing with hot rage. Beside him, Logan's face hardened, but he didn't speak again.

"Very well, Roxanne Fosch, Daughter of Yoncey Fosch, Familiar to Remo Drammen"–this part was said with disgust, "I, Gerome Archer, leader of the first Dhiultadh Clan, Son of Bran, fourth ruler of The Rejected, bearer of the Sword of Tisha, here forth sever all of your ties with this clan, to protect or judge, to nourish or defend, to claim or kin, of you or any of you, from today and forth on." With a long talon, he cut a line on his palm, letting the blood bind the oath. "You are no longer honored to be a Dhiultadh from this line. I announce you rogue, in front of everyone as witness."

A murmur went up in the crowd from both sides, some name-calling thrown in between undecipherable words.

"She's game!" someone shouted, but I couldn't tell from which line.

"Very well," Zantry called above the insults, "Roxanne Fosch is now of mine, and any who shall harm her will deal with me. If anything of foul comes upon her," Zantry looked around at both crowds, "you will bear my wrath like no other." a light veil fell over me, the touch feathery light, as if spun from gossamer. I glanced sideways at Zantry, but he hadn't moved, hadn't taken his hands off his pockets.

"Traitors, both of them," a woman called from our right, from the other line of rejected. I searched, found Diggy's eyes on me, clear of expressions, standing beside Xandra and Boris. The woman who spoke took a step forward, not afraid to show herself.

"Maybe you'll just kill her like you did your other woman kin." Another woman sneered from behind Archer.

Zantry inclined his head and said, "That will be my problem, Bebbette, not yours." He searched the crowd twice, his stance relaxed, hands still deep in his pockets. "Anyone else have anything to say?"

"Have you joined your kin, after all?" Logan spat.

"I never did, no. But I'm not afraid to face him." with that jab he flashed us out of there, without having to touch me.

We arrived at my living room, and I sagged on the floor, drained beyond belief, too exhausted to even move to the couch. I hadn't slept or eaten for so long, I lost track of time. Three days? Four? I lay down on the carpet and closed my eyes. Zantry lay down and stretched beside me.

"I'm so tired," I murmured.

"I know," he said, tracing a finger over my cheek. "Sleep, Roxanne, I'll be here when you wake." He brushed his lips over my cheek once, and I snuggled closer. I could sense his urge to protect me, and despite everything, I knew that as long as he lived, he'd do anything to keep me safe.

Chapter Fifty

I stood in front of the blue-and-yellow townhouse, unsure if I should knock or turn and return home. Zantry stood a few feet away, leaning on a light pole, waiting for me to decide what I wanted, not pressuring either way.

I glanced at him, his hair tied back in a stubby tail, his handsome face bearing a hint of stubble, hands tucked in the pockets of his black jeans. There was a bond between us, formed almost two weeks ago in the stone circle, a connection that grew with every passing day. I was so aware of his presence, it was as if he was part of me–in a comforting, soothing way.

Zantry tilted his head. The front door opened and Matilda appeared in the doorway, dressed in black loose fitted trousers and a brown button-down shirt, her salt-and-pepper hair pulled back in a tight bun. She glanced from me to Zantry, posture stiff. There was an air of animosity around her that hadn't been present the night of the charity ball.

"Hmm-mm. Hi," I said, uncertain. "You once said you had something to tell me. You gave me a note with your number and this address."

Matilda pointed her chin at Zantry. "You alone, not him."

Zantry straightened, his brow furrowed. "I didn't know we had a problem, Mattie."

"We do. You're not welcome in my home," she spat with so much venom, I retreated a step.

Maybe coming here hadn't been a good idea. "Ok," I said, taking a step toward Zantry. "We'll leave now."

"No," Matilda barked. "You and I need to talk. He needs to go."

I sensed Zantry's surprise, his confusion and hurt. He had no idea what Matilda's problem was.

I shook my head. "Look, I don't know what your problem is, but if Zantry isn't welcome, then neither am I." I moved to stand beside him. He glanced from me to Matilda, brow creased with confusion.

"It's ok," he said, "Go on, see what she has to tell you. I'll meet you later." He squeezed my hand, took back a step.

I opened my mouth to protest, but the reassuring look in his eyes had me closing them again. I turned to Matilda, still standing at the door, blocking the way.

"Ok," I said, unsure.

Matilda stepped aside for me to pass, and with a last look at Zantry's retreating back, I stepped inside, into an average-sized living room.

I glanced around, taking in the oil paintings, the gleaming crystal figurines, the embroidered framed mirror anyone coming in or going out had to pass. There was a thick, fancy-looking rug between two sofas the color of bleached sand facing each other. To my left sheer curtains blocked a view of the street, to my right, wooden stairs lead to the second level.

"Would you like to sit?" Matilda asked politely.

I sat at the edge of the sofa and met her eyes. "Here I am," I spread my hands to the sides. "Let's hear what you have to tell me."

Matilda came closer, her dark eyes scrutinizing me. "There's something different about you. What happened to you?"

I gave her a thin smile. "You first."

She sat across from me, clasped her hands together and said, "Ok. I suppose it's only fair I go first." She nodded, frowned, fell quiet for a few seconds. "Ok, I'll be blunt because I don't know any other way to go about this." She waited for a beat and asked, "What do you know about your parents?"

Surprised, I sat back, taken aback by her question. "You said once I looked like my father. Why don't you tell me what you know?"

She nodded again with a frown, and I sensed her anxiety, a soft, scratching sensation. "I didn't know him," she began, and was interrupted when the elder man she'd been with during the charity ball entered through a side door. Unlike Matilda, he still wore all those beads around his neck, though the formal suit had been replaced by sweatpants and a white t-shirt. He gave me a polite smile, the crinkles around his eyes deepening, placed a small box on the low table between us and with a nod, disappeared through the same door.

"I didn't know your father," Matilda said again, not reaching for the box. "But I knew your mother. We were, in fact, close friends."

My mother. That elusive part of my past that didn't make sense.

I leaned forward, a sudden knot of emotions balling inside my stomach. "Who was she?" I asked, unable to contain the excited vibrations from my voice.

Instead of replying, Matilda stood. "Come with me." She motioned and started up the stairs. I followed, surprised at how nervous I was. "What was her name?" I asked. "Where was she from? Did she have any siblings?" The possibility of relatives gave me a delicious thrill, and I realized how much I wanted it to be true.

Matilda paused at the landing. There were two doors up here, opposite each other, with a closet-size space in between where I could just make out a washing machine and drier, side by side.

She met my eyes, hers dark and serious, mine excited, maybe a little anxious. "Know what you'll discover today, only a selected few are aware of." She waited for my nod before continuing, "Its powerful knowledge that can, in the hands of the wrong person, be harmful not only to you, but many, many others."

The ball of excitement turned into dread. I'd known somewhere deep inside my mother's anonymity didn't happen by chance. "Who was she?" I asked again, uneasy.

She placed a heavy hand on my shoulder and squeezed, her dark eyes worried, earnest. "You have many enemies, Roxanne, some you're aware of, others who dress in the disguise of a friend. I don't know who they all are, but I'd advise you not to trust anyone who smiles and tells you what you want to hear."

I stiffened, catching the meaning underneath her words. "I trust Zantry with my life."

Matilda nodded. "So did your mother once."

The ball of nerves in my stomach took a led like quality and made my legs weak. "Did he…" I clutched my hands together. "Did he kill her?" And even as the words left my mouth, I was ashamed of myself for saying it.

"No, but he's the reason she's dead today."

"How? Why?" My nerves rattled "Wait, I was told she died giving birth to me."

Instead of replying, Matilda turned and opened the first door to our right. "When your mother came to visit, this was the room she stayed in."

Heart pounding, I stepped in after Matilda, taking in the simplicity of the room. A single bed sat on the corner beside a closed window, a honey-colored nightstand beside it. There was an armoire to my left, a bathroom across the bed. I moved into the room, circled around. It was clean, with an air of abandonment, as if it hadn't been used in years.

Either no one had been here after my mother, or… or I was projecting. The room was simple, clean and sparsely furnished, and it didn't mean no one had slept here in years.

I glanced at Matilda, still standing by the door.

She pointed her chin at the nightstand. "She left something here for you."

My heart beat a frantic beat, and with an anxious knot, I looked down at the nightstand, the honey polish of the wood. But I didn't reach for it.

"Who was she?" I asked again.

"I'll answer your questions once you've seen what she left for you. I'll be downstairs once you're done." She didn't wait for my next question, but turned and closed the door. I listened for the sound of a lock, felt for any kind of magic. But all I heard was Matilda's light footsteps down the stairs, all I felt was the growing lump in my stomach, in my throat.

I moved to the bed, sat down and stared at the drawers.

Zantry nudged at the bond, no doubt sensing my turmoil. I nudged back, wishing he was here with me.

"...He's the reason she's dead today..."

Slowly, hands shaking, I reached for the first drawer.

My eyes zeroed on the envelope at once, at the words handwritten in a sprawling scroll.

"To the child of mine," it said in thick black marker.

I picked it up and rummaged through the other paraphernalia inside, procrastinating. Beaded bracelets and necklaces lay inside, and with a frown I wondered if those belonged to her. Was she a charmer as well? There was also a tube of chapstick, a small deodorant bottle—empty—a notebook, and a stubby pencil. I found a shirt's button, put it atop the nightstand. The second drawer was empty, save for a small lock of black hair, carefully braided together and tied on each end with an elastic rubber. I placed it beside the button, closed the drawer and stared down at the envelope.

"To the child of mine,"

The seal was never broken, I noted, flipping the envelope. I sniffed the paper, roses, faint but unmistakable. Was that how she smelled?

I looked around at the sparse room again, took a deep encouraging breath, ripped the edge of the envelope, and started reading.

To the child of my womb,

If you're reading this it means I succeeded with the first steps in my plan, and that things are moving accordingly.

Before I go any further, I want you to know the decision to bring you into this world wasn't made lightly, and that your father, whoever he may be, had no part in this plan.

Understand, my child, that when my kind loves, we love unconditionally. I could not live through losing another child, through the war I know will come if I don't take matters into my own hands.

I mean that figuratively, as I would survive against all odds, be the last one standing.

I would not hold it against you if you hate me for what I've done. I would not hold it against you if you called me a coward.

For the position I put you through, you'd be right on both counts.

The Sidhe will teach you all you need to know. They have been briefed, they have agreed to help. Matilda can be a friend, you can trust her if you want. She will guide you in times of need. I didn't do right by her, I didn't do right by the people who loved me the most.

But I no longer have it in me to continue this fight alone. This is my last stand–and as the last one left to prevent Remo from winning, I'm giving it my all.

I know this is unfair of me, believe this if nothing else, I do know.

My apologies will mean nothing, my regrets are all my own.

I don't know if I should wish you success–for the sake of everyone else, or if I should wish you failure–for your own.

But I know, and I admit I'm relieved, that I won't be there to know either way.

My deepest regrets,

Arianna Lenard.

I let my hand drop and stared blankly at the wall. For a long time, all I could think, all I could see were those two words at the bottom of the letter: Arianna Lenard. Arianna Lenard. Arianna Lenard.

God, Arianna Lenard.

My mother.

I wasn't sure how long I sat there, my heart numb, my thoughts blank, when a commotion downstairs broke me out of it.

"Where is she?" Came Zantry's angry voice.

"Back off," Matilda warned. Stomach lurching, I stood and hurried downstairs, only to find Zantry at the door, both Matilda and the elder man blocking his path, their hands raised, some beady string clutched in each of their hands.

The color of Zantry's eyes was light blue, and with another stomach lurch, I jumped off the last three steps. He looked up, eyes worried, scanned me from head to toe.

"If you don't leave now," the man began.

But Zantry didn't pay him any attention. "You alright?" he asked me, not caring two pissed off charmers blocked his path. I had this feeling he'd trample right over them to get to me, realized the feeling came from him.

"Stay back," Matilda said to me, and if it wasn't for the roiling knot inside my stomach, I'd have laughed.

"It's ok," I said. "I'm alright," I told him, placing a hand above my stomach and pressing down, unable to help myself. There was this thing in my belly, a stretching of muscles I couldn't explain.

Zantry's eyes tightened, either in anger or worry, I couldn't tell from the nausea that suddenly overtook me. He took a step forward, and both Matilda and the man tried to block his path.

"If you don't move," Zantry growled in warning, "I'm going through you."

Again that stretching came, and suddenly I knew, deep inside and from a part of me I hadn't known existed, that I was being summoned.

It was nothing spiritual or psychic, but more like a physical tug, a stretching of muscles I couldn't control. I went cold all over, my lips forming a silent oh. My eyes met Zantry's, and I knew he understood what was happening.

"Move!" he thundered at Matilda, and she must've had some sense of self-preservation because she stepped aside.

He was beside me in a blink, and I reached for his hand, needing the connection, my terror overwhelming.

"What's going on?" Matilda demanded, realizing too late something was happening to me.

The tug came again, this time more insistent, and my legs collapsed from under me. Zantry picked me before I hit the ground and carried me to the sofa, laid me down and knelt beside me.

"Talk to me." His voice echoed from far away.

Matilda said something, the sound distorted. Zantry's lips moved, but I couldn't tell if he was talking to me or her.

The tug came again, and I was a fish, hook and line tugging me, and I looked at Zantry one more time, at the anguish in his beautiful eyes before I was hurtling away into the dark, mouth open in a silent scream.

Chapter Fifty-One

I fell and fell for seconds that seemed forever, then jarred when my feet touched hard ground. I stumbled with the impact, fell to one knee. The familiar sting of the needle-sharp rock went unnoticed, taking a backseat for the jolt of paralyzing terror filling me. It was that familiar fear every time I came near this man, that cold terror riding with the blood traveling through my veins, filling my body with its potent venom. It made me forget reason, and the terror was now combined with the certainty I was his to command, his to be called upon whenever, wherever, no matter what.

I stayed on one knee, eyes as big as saucers–a reaction he no doubt was used to. His energy battered at my senses, my heart pounded in a painful rhythm.

Remo's head cocked to the side, his hands went behind his back. His eyes studied me contemplatively, his nostrils flaring. Taking me for what I was worth, studying me in a sense that went beyond physical.

"She doesn't look like much. I don't understand why she's so important," a familiar voice to my left said, and with a jolt, Angelina Hawthorn came into view.

"Looks are often deceiving, ma fleur. She is much more than meets the eye," Remo replied, still studying me.

Angelina's presence here.... explained much, changed nothing. My mind whirled a million miles, fitting all the missing puzzle pieces. I was right after all. That lock of hair had been Mwara's. And Roland's suspicions had been on target too. The minions we fought when we came for Mwara hadn't been humans warped by Remo. No, they were the fledglings that disappeared from Vincent's case. Hadn't I noticed fangs when we were fighting the minions?

Vincent's case had closed that same night I left to scope the caves for Diggy. The only reason Remo hadn't been here that day was because he had been down south, seeing to the fledgling's transportation.

All that crossed in my mind in the blink of an eye. Vincent's case was bigger than they'd imagined. Angelina was gathering an army, yes, but not to invade Juan Silva, the vampire master of Mexico. No, the army was for Remo Drammen.

I closed my eyes, the puzzle image clear–and all along all the pieces had been right there. Didn't Angelina speak about business associates? Paranoid me believed a Hunter member had hired her after me. Stupid, Roxanne.

Remo took a step forward and my eyes popped wide open. Did he know whose daughter I was?

It was then I recalled his words to me the first time we met, back in his penthouse: "...You remind me of someone... Pity she died..."

He knew.

"I want to see your wings. Shift now, familiar."

My eyes widened, and I had to swallow the maniacal laughter bubbling in my throat.

I had no alternative form, much less wings.

Nothing bound me to his command, so not to anger him, I shifted my hands, letting my sharp talons appear, the pinkish and brownish scales going as far as my wrists.

Remo glanced at my hands–my talons–his expression conveying no emotion. His energy didn't shift, didn't tell me anything. I couldn't tell if my inability to shift bothered him at all.

In contrast, Angelina's amusement and disdain were palpable.

"Shift, familiar," he commanded again, and this time the compulsion to obey was there. Unbidden, patches of brownish fur appeared above my wrists, going halfway to my elbows, but no further. I swallowed hard, looked down at myself, at my legs, noticing the places the sharp rocks had cut me below the cuffs of my Capris. There was blood on my skin, but there was no fur, no extra pair of legs.

There was no time for relief.

Remo took a step forward, and fear had me by the throat, squeezing so hard I couldn't breathe. I was having a heart attack. Or a panic attack. Or just an attack.

When Remo reached for me, I flinched away. He paused, looked once at me, then reached again. I forced myself to stay still, aware he'd command me not to move if I flinched away again. So, against all that was holy to me, I let him take my hand with both of his small ones, his touch like something slimy and scaly against my skin. The contents of my stomach churned violently. I swallowed bile twice and focused on his nose.

"Shift, familiar, and let me see your wings!" he commanded, and a foul torrent of energy hit me like a fret train. If he hadn't been holding on to me, I think I would have been blown away. His energy enveloped every fiber of my being, pressured my senses, my body, suffocated my soul. I was aware when something inside of me gave, the moment his energy took over my body, all my senses, tore at my core. Angry wasps stung me, fed from my flesh with tiny, sharp teeth. I screamed and swallowed more of his energy, the pain overwhelming. My vision dimmed, millions of spots appearing in front of me, blinding me. There was acid on my skin, seeping into my muscles, my bones. I screamed again, or I think I did, my back bowing with the pain. Remo's energy was relentless, coursing over me, tearing me from inside out. It entered through my pours, clustered in my muscles, attacking every single nerve ending, every major organ. My ears popped, my lungs hurt, my lips stretched wide and thin, and my jaws unhinged with the potency of my screams.

I don't remember when Remo let go, or when his energy left me. Its echo stayed for a long time. All I could tell was I was on all fours, head bowed, the weight of the entire galaxy on my back, gasping for air. I could hear Remo breathing beside me, the steady beat of his heart.

Pain put everything into sharp focus. I could make out the tiny grains on the floor by Remo's feet; could make every fiber of his baby blue suit, the pours on his small face. We were eye level, even down on all fours. I shifted, and wasn't expecting all the weight that followed my command. I stumbled sideways, falling over something warm and furry. A glance down had me freezing.

My skin was no longer bare.

My body ... no longer human.

I was sitting on the soft fur of a huge wing, tipped at the ends with sharp talons, like the ones on my hands. I had four of them.

Oh my God. Oh, my God. Oh. My. God.

Something built in my chest, growing and growing and growing, until I could no longer hold it.

Panic.

Despair.

I roared, the sound monstrous, like a roar of an angry lion magnified by a bullhorn.

When I finally stood on my feet—or paws—without tumbling sideways with the extra weight, I topped Remo by twice his size. Despite being horribly unbalanced, I lunged for him, unable to see reason.

Before I reached his throat with my extra pair of talons, his head with another pair, ready to yank it out and lob it at Angelina's shocked face, I froze. I struggled, wings outstretched, talons poised.

I roared again—all I seemed to possess control of. My body was incapable of moving forward, even an inch.

Remo looked me up and down, examining me, then moved around me, examining my wings, the powerful muscles of my back. When he stood before me again, black eyes gleaming with an unnatural light, anticipation and triumph wafted off of him in waves.

"We will start with basic sigils and runes," he said, his voice carrying a strange tone.

And that's when I realized how right Zantry had been.

Want to know more?

Follow me on Facebook:

https://www.facebook.com/JinaBazzarOfficial/

And be up to date on new releases, sales promotions, freebies, read excerpts and much more!

Dear reader,

We hope you enjoyed reading *Heir of Doom*. Please take a moment to leave a review, even if it's a short one. Your opinion is important to us.

Discover more books by Jina S. Bazzar at
https://www.nextchapter.pub/authors/jina-s-bazzar

Want to know when one of our books is free or discounted? Join the newsletter at http://eepurl.com/bqqB3H

Best regards,
Jina S. Bazzar and the Next Chapter Team

Who am I?

A wanderer in this vast world, I'm just another body with a passion for the written word. There is no boundary I can't cross, no limit I can't push; my mind is my passport, my thoughts my mode of transportation. I've traveled to many planets, seen plenty of civilizations, old and new, both in this galaxy and others.

On this earth, my name is Jina S. Bazzar. I'm a freelance writer, a blogger, a mother, a baker, a chocolate fiend, a coffee enthusiast, and sometimes a poet—but those are only informal titles. I have many traits, some contradictory, others complimentary, depending on the circumstance. If I were to ever describe myself, I'd say I'm a pragmatic idealist, a sarcastic cynic, a curious adventurer, a joker, and upon occasion, a cautious realist.

Like most writers out there, my love of books began at a young age, with comic books and alphabet poetry two of my favorite and earliest memories. Growing up, I wasn't an awkward kid, and I didn't prefer books to people. Unlike most writers, I never aspired to author a book, never enjoyed writing essays, and although I had intended to one day become a surgeon, my first attempt at creative writing happened during my senior year in high school, a pastime project that wasted plenty of A4 papers and the ink of multi-colored pens. The story had an Indiana Jones theme with a touch of humor, and I was nowhere near finished when patience ran out and those few thousand words were tucked in some dusty drawer and forgotten, taking a backseat to finals and SATs.

Soon after graduation I developed a chronic disease that caused gradual vision loss. Dreams of med school was put on hold for 'a later' time, and eventually, during my twenties, I became blind and med school was no longer an option. Reading also became just a fond memory, and writing not even that.

That is, until I started working for a non-profit organization for women with disabilities and became acquainted with screen readers.

After I quit my job, I picked up reading with vengeance, but soon realized it was no longer enough, and so I started writing, this time with an aim to pursue a career. *Heir of Ashes* is my debut novel, a creation born from my love of anything fairy, of action-packed stories and a touch of romance. Besides fiction, I've written dozens of articles for *Conscious Talk* magazine, on topics of health, food, poetry and the writer's life.

When I'm not writing or networking on social media, you can find me in the kitchen, listening to loud music while baking (often mis-shapen) goodies, or cooking favorite dishes and adding new touches to them. Upon occasion, I enjoy traveling, and with a real passport, I've been to the U.S., Dubai, Jordan and Sweden, and hope one day to travel around the world. Currently, I live in the Middle-East.

On my blog at www.authorsinspirations.wordpress.com I talk about all those hobbies and passions, as well as funny mishaps and contemplative musings about children and sometimes about disabilities. I also enjoy connecting with people from all walks of life, all around the world.

I speak Portuguese, English and Arabic fluently, as well as passable Spanish, and lately I'm contemplating learning Italian or Greek.

I was born and raised in a quiet, small town in Rio de Janeiro, Brazil, where I've had a happy and fulfilling childhood. I literally played in the middle of the street, climbed tall trees and hiked worn trails, biked to the top of mountains to have picnics, swam in small lakes with murky water, surrounded by wild flowers. I've played pranks on cranky neighbors, cried over lost pets and climbed electric poles when no one was watching. My inspiration comes from most anything, a discussion, a friend, an animal or plant, events, memories, music, etc–in other words, from life itself.

Heir of Doom
ISBN: 978-4-86745-543-2

Published by
Next Chapter
1-60-20 Minami-Otsuka
170-0005 Toshima-Ku, Tokyo
+818035793528
1st May 2021

Lightning Source UK Ltd.
Milton Keynes UK
UKHW012121120521
383626UK00001B/66